THE GREATWOOD PORTAL

DORIAN HART

THE GREATWOOD PORTAL

© 2019 Dorian Hart

Cover art by **Gareth Hinds**
http://www.garethhinds.com

Formatting by **Polgarus Studio**
http://www.polgarusstudio.com

This is a work of fiction. Any similarity between the characters and situations within its pages and places or persons, living or dead, is unintentional and coincidental.

Comments and inquiries should be sent via e-mail to
Dorian.hart@comcast.net

ISBN-13: 978-0-578-52704-8 (Jester Hat Books - paperback)

For Anthony Ridgway

"A word is worth a thousand pictures."

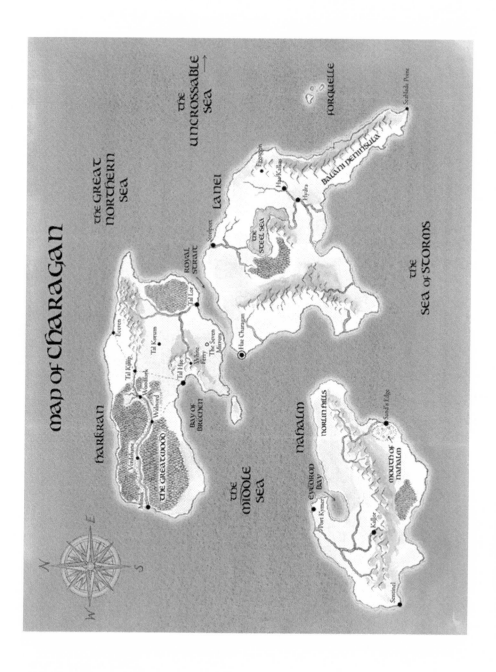

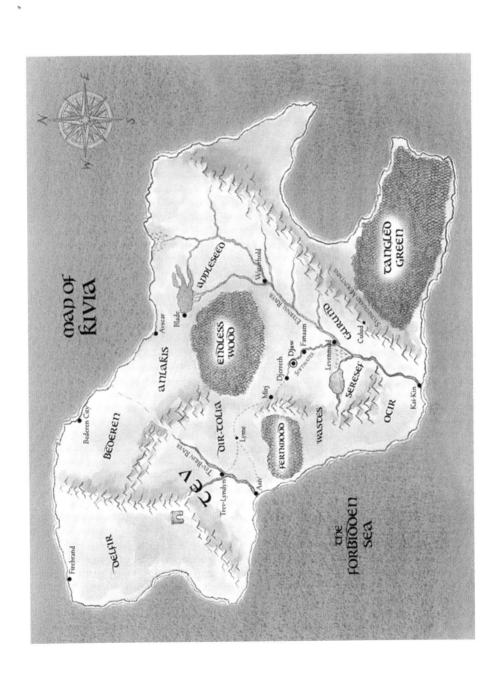

CHAPTER ONE

Ivellios Forrester's shoulder blades pressed against something smooth and hard as glass. A stone ceiling glowed a dim blue-gray—not with the flickering light of torches or lamps, but a cold, steady, unnatural glow. He sat up and looked around, discovering that the blue light shone upward out of the slab on which he lay. And it *was* glass, a translucent glowing rectangle the size of a large bed, that either floated in the air or (more likely) sat upon a pedestal directly beneath. The room, a stone square not more than a dozen feet on a side, showed a troubling lack of doors. Ivellios's sword still pressed at his hip, and his pack rested beside him.

He moved to swing his legs over the side and dismount the glass slab, but his feet met resistance. A bit of feeling around confirmed that he was trapped in a small box whose sides and roof were invisible, cold, and unyielding.

"Hey!" he shouted into the blue shadows. "Hey!"

No answer came. Did his voice even carry beyond his cage? He pounded a few times against the unseen walls and ceiling, both with his fist and the hilt of his sword, but gained only a bruise on his hand.

"Gods damn it," he muttered.

The glow from the glass slab made it hard to see the details of his prison, but maybe he could spot a clue as to where he was or how he might escape. Ivellios shaded his eyes with his hands and squinted at the ceiling. Words and pictures were drawn there, difficult to see clearly. He fumbled for his light-rod, wrapped in a scrap of cloth so it wouldn't shine awkwardly from his pocket all the time. Its white light drowned out the hazy blue from the slab as he held it high, right up against the invisible top of his cage.

"Oh, crap." A large black circle, covering over half the ceiling and positioned directly above the glass platform, was drawn upon, or perhaps set into, the stone blocks. Dark lines stretched across it, and inside its boundary were spirals of cramped lettering and odd geometric figures.

Hells and damnation! Ivellios knew the Black Circle bastards were going to try to kidnap him. He had counted on being protected within the walls of the Greenhouse, had hoped Abernathy and the other bigshot wizards would devise a way to keep him safe. But no, here he was, an insect caught in a jar, yanked into this sinister trap straight out of Aravia's *teleport*.

Despite the plain reality that magic had saved his life many times over since he joined Abernathy's band, he never entirely trusted it. A moment ago, Ivellios had stood in a forest with the rest of Horn's Company, the forest where Aravia's cadre of divine cats had their secret meetings. She had made the gestures, spoken the strange words to teleport them back to the Greenhouse so they could turn the Crosser's Maze over to the archmagi—though how one could give away something embedded in one's own head, he had no idea.

This time, something had definitely gone wrong.

Ivellios recalled the vision shown to him by Solomea in the Crosser's Maze.

The Silverswords have divined that the prime instrument of Naradawk's escape will be a direct descendant of Naloric's chief arcanist, Moirel Stoneshaper. Having tracked down and executed all other such descendants, the only two remaining are Ivos Forrester and his son, Ivellios Forrester.

So Ivellios was going to be "the prime instrument of Naradawk's escape"? The gods only knew what that would entail, but he greatly doubted he'd enjoy it. Maybe it involved keeping him in this enchanted cage, but with luck the Black Circle cultists would need to get him out of here to perform some sort of unspeakable ritual upon him. That would be his best chance to escape. Ivellios lay back down on the slab, kept his hand on the hilt of his sword, and closed his eyes.

Time passed; it felt like hours. Once, he dozed off, then came awake with a flash of fear, uncertain as to how long he'd been sleeping. The hand around his sword grip didn't feel stiff or cramped, so it hadn't been long. Only when he began to wonder if he'd ever be let free did lines of light draw themselves on one wall, describing a doorway. A section of stone pushed inward, and Ivellios quickly returned his head to the glass, feigning sleep.

Soft footsteps. A small exhalation.

"It's true. You're alive." A woman's voice, whispering. Then, louder, "Can you hear me?"

Ivellios didn't move. Let her think he was asleep or unconscious, increase the odds she'd lower her guard, make a mistake.

"I think you can," the woman said, her words soft and hurried. "My name is Essik. They will be coming for you soon. Do not fight them; they would prefer you alive, but they can still work their rites upon your corpse if they have to. I will seek a means of your escape, but I cannot do it openly. Be patient, bide your time, and I will figure something out. All I ask is that you not give me away."

A pause. "Be strong, Ivellios."

Ivellios warred within himself. Should he betray his wakefulness and talk to this woman, learn her identity, and discover why she wanted to help him? Should he trust her at all? If he was in a Black Circle headquarters, she could be a ruse, someone meant to quell any thoughts of escaping on his own. Conversely, she might be his only means of getting out of here, and that was worth a hefty gamble.

Before he could make up his mind, additional footsteps sounded in the doorway.

"Better late than never," said a man's voice. "Essik, please inform the council that the Pivot is in our custody."

"Of course."

Ivellios listened to her depart but kept his eyes closed, his body still.

"Sit up and face me," said the man, sounding impatient.

Ivellios did not oblige.

"Fine."

Pain spiked, a knife-strike in his head. He cried out despite his best efforts.

"Good. Now you're awake. Sit up and face me, Ivellios."

His gut told him to resist, to be as uncooperative as possible. If they were going to use him, let them do the work. But he might learn more if he pretended to cooperate, and fighting them could make it more difficult for Essik to find ways to help him. Ivellios opened his eyes and sat up.

"We have some busy days ahead of us." The man's features were obscured by the blue light of the platform, but Ivellios could make out his loose black shirt and black trousers. "They don't have to be unpleasant for you if you can see fit to be obliging."

"Maybe we can meet each other halfway," said Ivellios. "What's your name?"

"Naul." The man crouched down so that Ivellios could see only his head and shoulders over the edge of the glass slab. From his arm motions and a light scratching sound, Naul seemed to be drawing something on the floor.

"Why did you call me the Pivot?" Ivellios asked.

"Because that's what you are." Naul didn't look up from his drawing as he spoke. "The worlds of Spira and Volpos are going to overlap, in a manner of speaking, and you will be the axle around which they both spin." He stood, a piece of dark chalk in his fingers. "Now, Ivellios, I'm going to paralyze your torso and limbs so that I can disarm you safely, and then ask you some questions to which I expect truthful answers. Unless you'd like me to cut your pack straps, please take it off now and leave it by your feet."

Ivellios stared at his captor, fought down an urge to unleash a string of profanities, and shrugged out of his pack. Naul, seemingly satisfied, chanted softly and moved his hands through a series of odd patterns. Ivellios's limbs became rigid, unresponsive to his wishes. He resisted an instinctual upwelling of panic; if the Black Circle wanted to kill him, they could have teleported him into a fire or something similarly deadly.

Having rendered Ivellios helpless, Naul changed the rotation of his wrists and fingers, while his unintelligible words became clipped, staccato. After a few seconds of this, the blue light emanating from the glass bed faded to a shadowy indigo, then black. This left the room without any light at all; Essik had closed the door on her way out.

Hands fumbled at his belt, and Ivellios heard more than felt his sword being drawn from its sheath, his pack being lifted away. Despite his resolution not to fight, Ivellios couldn't help but test his paralysis. It was futile. His head might as well have rested atop a scarecrow.

"One last thing," said Naul. Ivellios heard him take a step back, then more chanting. This went on for over a minute, during which time Ivellios became increasingly nervous. Was Naul casting a spell upon him? For what purpose? He was already helpless.

An odd thing happened in his mind, swift and sudden, something he couldn't easily describe because he'd never experienced anything like it. If he had to explain it, he'd have said a cloud of whirling knives had sprung up inside his head, leaving his own thoughts untouched but threatening anything that might encroach upon them.

The chanting ceased abruptly. The doorway opened again, its rectangle of light blocked briefly by Naul leaving the room without further comment. Several minutes passed, during which Ivellios continued to struggle fruitlessly against his enchanted torpor. Had Naul been trying to read his mind? Dranko's tales of Black Circle priests contained multiple instances of the bastards trying to do just that.

But something—he had no idea what—had protected him. Perhaps whatever made him the Pivot also defended his mind from attack. That seemed like something the Black Circle would have foreseen, but Ivellios was hardly an expert in how one sort of magic would interact with another.

After a short time the doorway opened again. Naul was flanked by two women, both wearing the same outfit of black shirt and pants. One was tall and thin, the other short, but with the only light coming faintly from beyond the cell door, Ivellios could make out no more detail. His muscles were starting to cramp, paralyzed as he was in an awkward sitting position.

"How are you blocking our magic?" asked the shorter woman without preamble.

"I don't know," Ivellios said truthfully. "And could you release me from your freezing spell? My legs hurt."

"Not yet." The short woman frowned down at him.

"I think you're lying," the taller woman said.

"Which is ironic," said Naul, "because we have no way of knowing."

"I'm not lying," Ivellios insisted.

The short woman continued to stare, as if trying to bore holes into his skull with her gaze alone. "He must be wearing an enchanted object that shields him."

Naul gestured to the floor. "Quia, you can use my circle." The tall woman took a diagonal step forward, glanced down, and began to cast. Whatever magic she invoked took only seconds, after which Ivellios felt a slight warm tingle at his wrist and his right ear.

"By the Circle!" Quia swayed as though a gust of wind had struck her. "His bracelet and his earcuff are two of the most potent magics I've ever felt."

"We know about the bracelet," said Naul. "That's no surprise. But what is the earcuff? A ward against psychomancy?"

"No." Quia frowned. "It translates, I think. Both written and spoken words."

"Then what is keeping us from reading his mind?" asked the shorter woman.

"I don't know."

Naul tilted his chin sideways, cricking his neck. "Does it matter? We don't need to know his thoughts to use him in the merging ritual, do we?"

"No," said Quia. "But it would make things easier. More certain."

"Take the earcuff." The short woman sounded bored, business-like. "Leave the bracelet. Check him thoroughly for hidden weapons, then let him move on his own. Bring him to the laboratory."

The two women departed.

Without wasting time on chatter, Naul unfastened and removed Ivellios's earcuff, then patted down his legs and body. Ivellios still couldn't feel anything below his neck, but glancing down he saw Naul fumble at his belt to remove his utility knife.

"I'm going to release you," said Naul. "If you attempt to run, or hurt me or anyone else here, you will be caught, paralyzed again, and tied up for the remainder of your stay. And possibly tortured. So."

Naul slashed the air with his hand and muttered a few words, upon which Ivellios's whole body prickled and stung like a sleeping foot coming awake. He stretched his cramped body, shook life into his limbs, and decided not to check, for the moment, whether Naul was bluffing.

"Follow me, please." Naul stepped back into the doorway. "Stay close. Don't touch anything."

Ivellios had no idea what he'd see beyond his cell. Perhaps a row of similar chambers, like a jail block waiting for those unfortunate enough to be abducted by the Black Circle cultists. What he saw instead was much more troubling. He emerged blinking into a large round chamber, a light-gray stone cylinder, windowless, lit by unwavering fist-sized globes—certainly enchanted—set into the walls. His little prison room was a freestanding stone cube in the exact middle of this larger space, and surrounding it was a circle of black stone bricks set into the floor. It reminded him at once of the much larger version he had seen during the last of his "gut-churners" while traversing a range of Kivian mountains.

A second circle was set opposite in the ceiling, the two like mirrored reflections, sea and sky. Both were crisscrossed with painted black lines and ornamented with numbers, equations, and mysterious diagrams. Ivellios was baffled by the particulars, but it was abundantly clear that a complex and painstaking ritual had been prepared for the sole purpose of imprisoning him. That only a single door opened onto the cylinder reinforced his suspicion.

Naul walked briskly, so Ivellios had to hurry to keep pace. The exit led to a long stone hallway with imposing wooden doors on either side. Each of these doors—all closed—displayed an indecipherable painted glyph. From behind one came a faint, tuneless chant; beyond a second something pounded rhythmically, like a hammer against rock.

At the last door on the left, before the hallway opened onto an ascending stairwell, Naul stopped and knocked. "I have the Pivot," he called. "He's been disarmed and divested of enchanted objects except for his bracelet, but his mind is shielded. We don't yet know how."

"Send him in," came the reply—a man's voice, low and oily.

Naul pushed the door open and motioned for Ivellios to enter. His sword-for-hire instincts warned him against stepping through, and he paused despite Naul's earlier warnings. Was this his last chance to try a fighting escape? Naul wasn't armed, and Ivellios could probably overpower him and make a dash up the stairs.

No. Too much risk. Furthermore, if Essik was truly conspiring to spring him from this cultists' hive, it would be useful for him to learn as much as possible in the meantime.

He stepped into the laboratory. Enchanted light-globes on the walls showed Ivellios a room crowded with objects, saved from hopeless clutter by a strict imposition of order. Sheaves of parchment were stacked high, either on small tables or the room's single large desk, but each was perfectly collected, without even a corner out of place. Dozens of books of uniform height and color filled their shelves like soldiers at attention. Upon a long narrow table against the left-hand wall stood a half dozen gleaming copper armillary spheres, set out in a perfect line and connected by taut lengths of white string.

The entirety of the wall opposite was a giant schoolhouse slate, covered top to bottom with neatly chalked strings of numbers and symbols. A man in a black shirt and trousers stood before the slate, his back to the door, a length of chalk in his hand. As Ivellios watched, the man wiped away one of the numbers with a cloth, then reached up to turn a melon-sized globe that hung from the ceiling by a wire.

"Ivellios, sit." The man didn't turn around. The room contained only two chairs, and one was behind the desk. Ivellios chose to stand.

The man wrote a new number to replace the one he had erased. The harsh squeal of chalk buzzed in Ivellios's teeth.

"What do you think?" asked the man, still with his back to Ivellios. "Have I now accounted properly for inter-body jolt? The third derivative of position is absolutely critical. If we get it wrong, I lose half the army, and you probably wind up shredded into two separated spatial frames. Neither of us wants that, I'm certain."

Ivellios had a rudimentary knowledge of arithmetic from helping with his parents' carpentry business. "I think you forgot to carry the two."

The man gave a close-lipped chuckle. "By the Circle, you sound just like Dranko."

He turned, showing a face thick with scars, a puckered crosshatching of ragged stripes far worse than Dranko's map of cuts.

Ivellios had never met the man, but he could guess his name. "Mokad."

Mokad gave a little bow. "I suppose this is when I sarcastically tell you I'm at your service, Ivellios Forrester. But we both know it's the other way around."

Ivellios crossed his arms and stared.

"What is shielding your mind?" asked Mokad.

"Like I told your friends, I don't know."

Mokad gazed back at him with heavy-lidded eyes. "I believe you. I assume that Naul told you why you're here?"

"Not really." Ivellios flicked his eyes to the row of armillary spheres.

Mokad let out a long sigh. "Ivellios, I can see you're asking yourself a number of questions that you are unqualified to answer, so let me help." He gestured to the armillary spheres, the motion pulling his shirt up his arm enough to show a wrist thick with scarring. "First, this room. You could smash everything in it, break my instruments, erase my slate, and burn my notes down to ashes. None of that would matter. I have an eidetic memory. Do you know what that means?"

Ivellios gave Mokad a sardonic half-grin, thankful for once for Aravia's habit of using oversized words. "It means you remember everything."

Mokad raised his eyebrows, which bunched the scars on his forehead. "Yes. That's right. It means I could restore this room to order in a day. We have extras of all the physical pieces, and the rest is in here." He tapped his temple. "The lost time would be irksome, but the way we would make up for it would be specifically uncomfortable for *you*."

Ivellios frowned. Sabotage had been at the forefront of his thoughts. But maybe—

"Furthermore," said Mokad, "harming or killing yourself would be equally fruitless. A bother, certainly, but our rituals can be made to work on your body if necessary. You would accomplish nothing besides deny yourself a place of prominence after our inevitable success."

Ivellios forced himself not to ask what Mokad meant by a "place of prominence," which was obviously what the bastard wanted him to do.

Mokad reached up and cradled the hanging globe between his thumb and two fingers. "I look forward to working with you, Ivellios. Truly. Not only will we restore the ruling power over Charagan to its proper place, but we'll learn more about arcane dimensional theory than has ever been understood by mortals." A gentle turn of Mokad's wrist made the globe spin. He regarded it thoughtfully.

Ivellios glanced around the room as subtly as he could while Mokad's attention was diverted. Three strides to his left, a large glass bottle with a thick translucent base rested on a small table. And some of the armillary spheres looked hefty enough. Mokad might be a wily son of a bitch, but Ivellios was younger and quicker.

"Were those traditional armillaries," said Mokad, still looking at his globe, "the spike indicating the equinoctial colure might be considered dangerous in the hand of an assailant. But mine have no spikes, and you'd never get close enough to club me with one." He turned to look at Ivellios and whispered a quick syllable. Ivellios's arms went dead, numb.

"Of all the things you might damage, sabotage, shatter, or disrupt, I and my fellow adherents are the least likely." Mokad let go of the globe and smiled. Everything about him was greasy—his voice, his hair, even his teeth. "Put aside any thoughts of that sort, Ivellios. Instead, let us talk about how you might assist us in our grand endeavor and have your revenge on the Silverswords who murdered your father."

CHAPTER TWO

ranko had lost track of how many times Aravia had teleported him. Four? Maybe five? Not that he wanted to downplay the staggering experience of being regularly whisked by magic across hundreds or thousands of miles, but in terms of physical sensation her *teleports* were whisperless eye-blinks. One second *here,* the next second *there.* A moment of reorientation and on you went with your strange new life as an archmage's lackey.

Not this time.

He had stood in that forest, the one in Kivia where Aravia had finished checking in with her Cat Council, or whatever the heck it was called. She had spoken magic words, waved her hands around—and then he had been pushed through a cheese grater face first. Dranko had felt time passing, excruciatingly, as though he were being pressed slowly through a wooden wall with only a few holes and splintery cracks in it, his body extruded through the gaps and reforming on the far side. The feeling was every bit as unpleasant as being shot with a crossbow, nearly dying from too much channeling, and some of his more memorable hangovers.

Then, *thump!* As if someone had grown impatient with his slow oozing progress, Dranko was shoved all the way through, and the Greenhouse front door loomed in front of him. He promptly fell down; maybe his legs hadn't finished reforming.

"Ooooh, my stomach." Ernie lay on the ground beside him, clutching his midsection. "Aravia, what happened?"

"Mrow." Pewter gave a plaintive cry, but Aravia didn't answer.

Tor stood patting himself down as though making sure all his body parts had made the trip. "Aravia, you did it!"

Dranko let his head loll to one side—easier than standing up—and saw Aravia lying beside him, eyes closed. Pewter sat on her collarbone, alternatingly licking her face and mewling.

Dranko heaved himself to a sitting position and squinted into the late-afternoon sun. Ugh, his stomach! Was this how Kibi felt every time Aravia teleported them? Or how Grey Wo…how Ivellios felt when Naradawk tried to pull him into his prison world?

"Hey Ivellios, I think we finally understand why you look like you're going to puke whenever…" He turned his torso one way, then the other. Everyone else was present, even the Sharshun Lapis, sprawled on her back, lips slightly parted, eyes open but unseeing. But Ivellios was not among them.

Ernie propped himself up against the jamb of the Greenhouse door. "Where's Ivellios?"

"Not here, looks like," said Kibi.

Tor looked worriedly down at Aravia. "I'll bet Aravia knows, but her *teleport* across the ocean must have sapped all of her—" He scrunched up his brows. "—arcane potential. Kibi, can you help me get her inside?"

Ernie took a step away from the door and fished in a pocket for his key, but the door opened on its own. Eddings stood in the threshold, translucent handkerchief still wrapped around his eye sockets and a wide smile on his face.

"I thought I heard your voices outside. You've come back! I'm so pleased. Give me a few moments, and I'll conjure up dinner from the Icebox." He looked down at Lapis's awkward form. "Oh dear. That's one of those Sharshun, isn't it. Is she all right?"

"That's a tough one to answer," said Dranko, "but we should get her inside either way. I'll carry her."

One by one they entered the Greenhouse, until Certain Step stopped at the threshold.

"I can't go in. Some enchantment forbids me."

"Right," said Dranko. "Certain Step, please allow me to welcome you to our lovely home. Won't you come in?"

* * *

An hour later Horn's Company lounged in the living room, nervous and disoriented but well-fed at least. Dranko had dumped Lapis on Mrs. Horn's old bed, figuring that when Aravia woke up she'd know what to do with her. Aravia herself was laid out on the small sofa, Pewter curled up on her stomach. Her chest rose and fell, and they all thought it best to let her sleep and recover. Eddings had prepared the same meal as on their first night in the Greenhouse: yellowbeans, roast chicken, and wine.

Ernie had been up to the secret room with the crystal ball, but Mister Golem had delivered his monotone message that Abernathy wasn't available. Dranko had to laugh; all those weeks of travel, all those perils and attacks and getting sucked into a city in a bottle, and now that they had Abernathy's doohickey, he wasn't around to take possession.

According to Eddings, Abernathy had last visited two evenings previous, with a detailed explanation of how long he expected the archmagi could hold out against Naradawk's ever-more-forceful battering at his prison door. Sister Previa had been by yesterday morning before dawn to hear Eddings' report (already delivered to Morningstar), and again this morning, though Eddings had nothing new to pass on.

"What should we do about Ivellios?" asked Ernie.

Dranko felt a bit sozzled, having downed almost a full glass of wine before his first bite of food. He pointed at Aravia. "Wait for her to wake up and ask her what happened? I'll bet he accidentally let go and got left behind in the forest. I hope the god-cats don't eat him."

Morningstar sighed but did so with a smile that was mildly amused rather than exasperated. "When this happened to Kibi, he wasn't too far away and found his way back to us. It wouldn't surprise me to see him walk through the door before we go to bed."

Pewter stirred, pawed at Aravia's chin, and let out an unusually loud meow.

"What's the matter?" Dranko asked. "Is she all right?"

Pewter shook his head. Dranko rolled up his sleeves, wished he had stayed a bit more sober, and moved to Aravia's couch. He checked her pulse first, which was racing as though she were in mid-sprint. Her breathing was similarly frenetic. "Huh. That's not good." He gently lifted one of her eyelids. "Whoa! That's...I don't know what that means. Look at this."

The others crowded around. Aravia's eye was a black void: no iris, no pupil, no white, but tiny stars twinkled in the darkened socket.

"That happened to her before," said Tor. "Right after she got the Crosser's Maze from Solomea."

"So she's in the maze?" Dranko still didn't understand it. "But the maze is in her head! How does that work?"

"Same way Solomea did it, I reckon," said Kibi. "Pewter, should we try to snap her out of it? Shake her shoulders or somethin'?"

Pewter made a motion that looked as much like a shrug as a cat could manage. Dranko let Aravia's eye close, and for a few seconds they all stood over her, baffled and worried.

Both of her eyes snapped open, and she sucked in a loud, deep breath, like she'd just surfaced from being held too long under water. The star-fields in her sockets faded, revealing her usual green irises.

"Aravia!" Tor reached down and took her hand.

"Ivellios." Aravia's voice crackled as though from long disuse. "I think the Black Circle has him." Tor helped her to a sitting position, Pewter scrambling to stay on her lap. "When I…There was…" She shook her head and rubbed her temples. "Teleporting us across the sea was unexpectedly difficult. Without the added power of the Crosser's Maze, I doubt I would have succeeded." Aravia blinked several times as if shaking off a blow to the head. "During the process, I felt as though Ivellios had been diverted. Rerouted. As though some enchantment had been in place that redirected him to a different destination."

"What makes you think the Black Circle did it?" asked Ernie.

"I—" Aravia's voice broke into an incoherent whisper. Eddings brought her a glass of water, which she downed in one swig.

"Thank you, Eddings. Ernie, don't you remember? When Solomea showed us Ivellios's true memory of what happened to his parents? One of the Sharshun said they'd capture Ivellios once he had 'already crossed the boundary, and his mind had opened in a place that is all places.' The boundary might mean the Uncrossable Sea, or it might mean the metaphysical border between Volpos and Spira, but either way he's crossed it now. And the 'place that is all places' is certainly the Crosser's Maze. Neither of those criteria had been met until I brought us out of the maze."

"Could you tell where he was taken?" asked Morningstar.

"No. I was extremely distracted. The Crosser's Maze is confusing, even for me, and I was struggling to focus enough power to teleport us such a long distance."

Certain Step stood a little ways off from the group, the glass of wine in his hand largely unconsumed. "You have the Crosser's Maze now," he said. "Do you know how to use it to prevent…oh, what is his name?"

"Naradawk," said Morningstar. "To prevent Naradawk from escaping from Volpos?"

"Yes," said Step. "Naradawk." He peered at the living room window. "Are we truly on the far side of the Forbidden Sea?"

Dranko clapped him on the back. "You sure are. You're in the city of Tal Hae, on the Duchy of Harkran, in the Kingdom of Charagan. Djaw is several thousand miles that way." He pointed generally eastward. "According to Aravia and Tor, who actually understand that stuff."

"I'd be willing to give Abernathy the maze," said Aravia, "if he ever comes by to take it. But according to Morningstar we have only three weeks to stop Naradawk. I think in the meantime I should start to learn its ways myself. Because right now, no, I don't know how to use it."

Kibi wiped some wine from his beard with his sleeve. "But we still oughta get Ivellios back, right? Those Silversword people Solomea showed us, they said the Black Circle was gonna use Ivellios to help Naradawk escape. What if havin' him prisoner lets 'em do that even though we got the Crosser's Maze?"

"Of course we should get him back," said Morningstar. "But where do we start? The Black Circle could be holding him anywhere. He might even be back in Kivia."

Dranko sat up so suddenly he sloshed his drink onto the carpet. "Praska! My friend who found out about Mokad's operation to dig up the blood gargoyle. She broke into Mokad's room and read all sorts of notes. Maybe she remembers something about their plans to capture Grey Wo—damn it. To capture Ivellios. First thing tomorrow, I'll head over to the church of Delioch; she's probably gone back there since Mokad and his crew abandoned ship. I'd go tonight, but..." He held up his now-empty wineglass by way of explanation.

"We should all get some sleep," said Ernie. "It's been a long day. Er, days. I guess we don't really know how much time passed in Calabash and the Crosser's Maze, but the last time I remember sleeping was after Mrs. Horn visited us in the Greenhouse."

Eddings, hovering nearby, stiffened.

"Right." Dranko stood and stretched. "Eddings, we'll tell you all about it tomorrow, but among the stranger things that happened on our trip was that Mrs. Horn was allowed to leave heaven to pay us a quick visit, and she did it in a fake magicked-up version of the Greenhouse."

"I see," said Eddings, his calm demeanor quickly reasserting itself. "I suppose that's no more improbable than intelligent gemstones burning out my eyes to deliver prophecy while leaving my vision intact."

Dranko slapped Eddings on the back. "That's the kind of attitude that makes you the perfect butler." He lifted his empty wine glass. "Here's to Horn's Company, and our successful quest for the Crosser's Maze against impossible odds."

Tor raised his as well. "And to Ivellios's quick return."

* * *

Dranko stuffed a forkful of scrambled eggs into his mouth—ordinary yellow chicken eggs, thank Delioch, and not those oversized purple things he'd eaten in Djaw. "Step, I want you to come with me," he said while chewing. "I'll show you that most priests of Delioch take their religion seriously. As soon as we're done eating breakfast."

"If you wish it," said Step. "It is said a man ought never turn down the opportunity for new experience, lest he die beneath a heap of dust. I will be the first man of Djaw to visit the temple of a foreign god."

"Well, yeah, about that," said Dranko. "It might not be, uh, prudent, for you to mention that you're a whaddyacallit, a Sunwarden of Kemma. As far as anyone knows here, the only gods are the Travelers and Pikon. If word gets out that there's a whole other family of gods out there, it could lead to—I don't know exactly, but unrest for sure, and the priests themselves might get put out."

"I am not yet a Sunwarden. And you want me to lie?" Step sounded skeptical.

"No, no! Well, maybe a little. Just a lie of omission, really. What was your primary duty as a wannabe Sunwarden?"

Certain Step looked down at his plate. "I was still trying to find my true calling within the church. I was a bell-ringer, I worked in the library, catalogued our medical supplies, learned to cut stained glass, and of course I studied extensively as a healer."

Dranko chased his eggs with a mouthful of water, hoping it would dispel his mild hangover. "Perfect. I'll say you're an old friend who's studying the medical arts, and I told you I'd show you around the place, let you talk shop with some of the healers. Channeling isn't a common skill; most of what the church of Delioch does is straight mundane medicine."

"I suppose that would be acceptable," Step said tentatively. "And I can't see that I have any other business right now. Other than needing to be with you when you encounter the 'last of five,' I'm uncertain how best to be of use."

"Fantastic," said Dranko. He looked around the table, where the others ate mostly in silence. Aravia had a dazed, faraway look in her eyes (though they were their usual green and not creepy star-fields) while Tor next to her looked as worried as he ever did. Poor kid. You finally tell a girl you're in love with her, and she says she loves you back, but then she has to put you aside for a while as she figures out how to use the world's most complicated magical gadget to prevent catastrophe. Tough break.

Morningstar was also quiet, but in a contemplative sort of way.

"Did you meet with the dream team again last night?" Dranko asked her. "And could you pass the water pitcher?"

Morningstar slid the wooden pitcher over. "No, because they were all awake. Thanks to the time shift between Charagan and Kivia I've been able to meet with my sisters while we were all asleep together. But last night while I slept, Previa and the others were awake. I'm going to give them an hour or two, and then meet them this morning once they've gone to bed.

"But you'll be awake," said Ernie. "Won't you?"

"While training my sisters, I've taught myself to drop into the dreamscape whenever I wish," said Morningstar. "I don't need to be sleeping."

"Great," said Dranko. "And Aravia, I imagine you'll want to start puzzling out the Crosser's Maze as soon as possible?"

"Hm?" Aravia turned to him in slow motion.

"The Crosser's Maze," said Dranko. "Figured it out yet?"

After a beat, Aravia smiled. "No, not yet. It's still a trifle overwhelming. But I'm confident."

Dranko poured himself another cup of water. "How about the rest of you? Ernie? Kibi? Tor? Any big plans?"

"Someone ought to be awake in case Abernathy tries to get in touch," said Ernie. "And to try the crystal ball every so often. Aravia, we all know you're a wonderful wizard, but I'd feel better if Abernathy at least knew we had it."

"I was thinkin' a' takin' a walk back to the Seven Mirrors," said Kibi quietly.

"Oh?" said Morningstar. "Why is that?"

Kibi fidgeted nervously with a spoon. "Well, last night, I had a funny dream. Things comin' too often for my comfort, but there you are. Dreamed about the Eyes a' Moirel, and the Mirrors too. They told me again to be ready 'when time is right and world is wrong,' though I still got no idea what it means. I checked on the Eyes in the basement, but they ain't gotten out or nothin' while we've been away, and they didn't say nothin' when I picked 'em up. So I just got a feelin' maybe the Mirrors have somethin' to tell me."

"You shouldn't go alone," said Morningstar. "Mokad is still out there, and the Sharshun."

Tor hadn't taken his eyes off of Aravia for more than a few seconds at a time during the whole of breakfast. He looked at her now as he spoke. "Ernie, why don't you go with Kibi? I'll stay here with Aravia in case…in case, uh, something happens while she's learning to use the maze. She'll need someone to snap her out of it if something goes wrong. And I'll be here in case Abernathy shows up."

Dranko pushed his chair back from the table, stood, and tilted his neck until it popped. "Then we'll see you all back here later. With luck, Praska will remember seeing a Black Circle plan to kidnap Grey Wolf with a clear address included."

"Ivellios," said Morningstar.

"Damn. Right. Ivellios."

"What if Praska doesn't know anything?" asked Ernie.

Dranko didn't have a ready answer, and neither, it seemed, did anyone else. "I don't know, Ernie," he said to break the silence. "In that case Ivellios will have to rescue himself."

* * *

Dranko filled his lungs with the salty, fish-smelling autumn air of Tal Hae. "Gods, I didn't realize how much I'd miss this place until I spent a couple of months away from it." And it was more than that. Their traversal of Kivia, followed by however long they were in the thrall of Calabash, not to mention their bizarre journey inside the Crosser's Maze, had left Dranko feeling unanchored from reality. Now that his native cobbles passed beneath his feet, it struck him hard.

"See that guardsman there?" he asked Certain Step. "The short one with the beard? I almost got caught by that bugger a few years ago. Fortunately my cloak had a big hood and he never got a good look at my face. And there used to be a nasty lady with a fruit cart where that tailor's shop is. Gods, I lost track of how many apples I nicked from that wrinkled old bag."

Step looked at him with ill-disguised disapproval. "You were a criminal? I thought you were a priest!"

"I *am* a priest. Well, was a priest. No, I still am. Obviously. You saw me heal that fellow in Culud, right? That was one hundred percent divinely channeled energy from Delioch himself."

Step turned sidewise to avoid a woman carrying a basket of linens. "Why would a priest be stealing fruit and fleeing from the watch?"

"Hard times, my friend, hard times. The church and I had a falling out when I was younger, so I spent a few formative years on the streets, picking pockets and drinking more than was good for me."

"You still drink more than is good for you," said Step.

"I'm practically a teetotaler compared to the old days. Anyway, about the church, the truth is I haven't been back there in a few years. They, uh, might not believe I'm a channeler."

"I will vouch for you," said Step. "I have seen your healing with my own eyes."

Dranko pointed his chin to the left. "Let's take this alleyway, it's faster. Not as fast as the rooftops, but I've discovered the guard frowns upon city-folk scaling the walls. It's nice of you to offer your testimony, but if you start making outlandish claims about me, they'll wonder more who you are exactly. And like I said, telling them you're a cleric of a foreign sun goddess from beyond the Uncrossable Sea will not make them more likely to believe anything else you say."

The Pious Quarter was not a quarter. Tal Hae didn't have quarters in the traditional sense, but nicknaming neighborhoods "quarters" was a tradition left over from a forgotten past. The centerpiece of the quarter was a huge public park, a lovely ten-acre swath of trees, gravel paths, man-made ponds, and flower-dotted lawns. "Gods' Green," the people of Tal Hae called it, for spread around its perimeter stood the church buildings of most of the traveling gods, as well as a Blessed Farm of Pikon, god of farmers and the harvest. You could always tell that one by the smell of dung. Why Pikon's worshippers thought it a good idea to build a little walled farm inside a city, Dranko couldn't guess.

"That's the main temple to Corilayna, goddess of luck." Dranko pointed to a long, low building fashioned of green-tinted stone. Above the doorway was Corilayna's symbol: a six-sided die balanced on (and likewise hanging from) one corner. "I spent most of my life cursing her. My life until recently was crap. Obviously my fortunes have improved since Abernathy hired me, so maybe I should drop some coins in her box."

"So she is Charagan's counterpart to Laramon," said Step, scowling. "We do not curse him, even when our luck is poor. It is said that a man who leaves his life wholly to chance treads upon Laramon's toes. The priests of Laramon tell us their god favors those who actively bend the odds to their own desires."

Dranko chuckled. "I like your god's style. I guess it's a good thing there's an ocean separating Corilayna and Laramon, then. Otherwise what would happen if I flipped a coin, and Corilayna wanted it to come out heads while Laramon wished for tails?"

"What they wish is immaterial to us," said Step, sounding peevish. "The Law of Interference prevents the gods from meddling in our coin flips."

Tell that to Morningstar. "Yeah, I suppose. Though it's said Corilayna causes some people to be born as what they call 'luckbenders,' who enhance the fortunes of those around them. What's funny, though, is that the luckbenders themselves don't know who they are. Almost there. You can tell the Church of Delioch from the tall iron fence around the grounds. They don't want to be overrun with sick and injured people demanding to be healed."

"The church of Kemma faces the same dilemma," said Step. "It is a hotly debated matter of philosophy, as our resources will always be eclipsed by the public's needs."

As was typical, two people stood guard at the main gate to the compound, a man and woman both wearing white robes with the stylized healing hand of Delioch emblazoned on the fronts. Dranko didn't recognize either of them, and (fortunately) they didn't seem to recognize him either.

He strode up boldly to the gate. "Greetings, my friends! May Delioch smile upon your souls."

The man smiled and nodded. The woman narrowed her eyes and wrinkled her nose; Dranko resisted an urge to jokingly sniff his armpit.

"How may we help you gentlemen?" asked the woman.

"I'm a former acolyte of the church," said Dranko. "I practically grew up inside those walls. I'm here to visit sister Praska Tellenhien. Is she in?"

The woman quirked an eyebrow. "You know Praska?"

"We were good friends years ago. She's probably been expecting me to show up sometime."

The two guards exchanged a glance.

"What?" asked Dranko. "Is there something wrong? Is Praska well?"

"She's fine," said the man. "But—"

"There's been some unusual activity in the church this last half a year," said the woman. "But I'm sure Praska will tell you about it. I'll let her know you're here. What is your name?"

"I'm Dranko and this is…Certep, another old friend. He's been studying lay medicine on his own, and I told him I'd see if I could get one of our better healers to chat with him."

The woman bowed, went through the gate, and walked across a lawn to a distant building.

"Dranko." The man looked thoughtful for a second, and then his eyes widened. "Dranko Blackhope? The kid who burned down the—"

"Yes, yes, that was me. I'm a different person now, rest assured." *I'm more careful with fire, for one thing.*

The watchman appeared to try hard to maintain a straight face. "Some of the older priests still tell stories about you. Is it true you once glued the head chaplain's hat to his head? They say it tore off a quarter of his scalp when they finally removed it, and the blood was so profuse you can still see the stain on the rug in his bedchamber."

"It seemed like a good idea at the time," Dranko deadpanned.

Step tugged on his sleeve, leading him a few steps away. "You caused one of your betters to tear his scalp with glue?" His whisper was harsh. "And you committed arson?"

"He wasn't my better," said Dranko, keeping his voice low. "He was a complete git who called me 'monster boy' and made fun of how many scars I earned."

Dranko was spared having to explain the outhouse fire by the sound of his name being called. "Dranko!" Praska's voice, a bit breathless, carried across the lawn as she ran to the gate. "You're back!" She pushed past the guards and gave him a fierce hug. Her red hair was longer than when Dranko had seen her briefly a couple of months ago, but her freckled smile was just as wide.

She released him and sized him up. "I was hoping you'd come visit. We have a lot of catching up to do." She flicked a glance at the guard. "Elgin here hasn't been giving you a hard time, has he?"

"No, no, he's been unfailingly polite. He tells me I'm something of a legend around here."

"Don't get a big head," said Praska. "And I'd say you're more of a cautionary tale than a legend. Who's your friend?"

Certain Step had stayed a respectful step back. "This is Certep, though we call him 'Step' for short. He's a friend I met on my recent travels. I'd love to tell you all about it, somewhere private if possible. Also I have some questions, related to what happened last time we met."

Praska's smile faded. "Ah."

Step bowed. "A pleasure to meet you, Miss Praska."

A grin returned to Praska's face. "He's much too polite to be hanging around with *you,* Dranko. How about we take a walk through the garden? There shouldn't be anyone near our old climbing tree, and there's a bench we can sit on."

"Perfect," said Dranko. To the guard, looking on with some amusement, he said, "Don't believe everything you hear about me." He winked. "They always leave out the best bits."

* * *

The leaves were turning to red and gold in the church gardens, though most still clung to their branches. An early few patterned the grass, or lay draped atop the heads and arms of marbled Deliochan saints. Dranko didn't often feel nostalgia for his time as a ward of the church, but when he did, he thought of this garden, these trees, his moments of escape from Mokad and the rest. Praska would join him when their schedules allowed, and they spent their best hours tree-climbing. Praska had always been more nimble, reaching high branches that Dranko couldn't, but he never harbored any resentment—not against his only true friend.

The stone bench and surrounding paths were empty, and the two of them sat, looking across the lawn at the small cathedral. Praska had left Step to talk shop with an old woman named Sister Temer. "Once she starts talking about how to dress wounds and stuff poultices, it's hard to get her to stop."

For a minute they just sat, listening to a nature-speckled quiet.

"You first," said Praska. "Mokad tried to kill you at Belle's shop almost two months ago. When I went to the Greenhouse later in the week, your old butler with the blindfold told me you had gone, and he couldn't guess when you'd be back. He wouldn't tell me where you went, either."

Dranko took a deep breath. "Right. First, all that stuff I told you last time was true. The archmage Abernathy hired me and some others to help him." He pitched his voice lower, even though no one but Praska seemed to be nearby. "The world is in danger, but almost no one knows it. We're trying to save it."

Praska's face couldn't settle on either serious or amused. "You're not winding me up?"

"Praska, I swear on Delioch's name that—"

"Yes, I remember, you swore last time too. It's just hard to take you seriously about this. I'm sure you understand why."

Dranko sighed. "Yeah, I do." He gazed into Praska's eyes and looked as serious as he could. "Praska, you were my only friend for many years. Please. I'm not kidding around. Everything I'm telling you, that I'm going to tell you, is true. Please, *please* believe me."

Praska smiled and held up both hands, palms toward him. "Fine, fine, I believe you! Tell me more."

Dranko glanced around again. Should he have gotten permission to tell Praska about what was going on? "I will, but first, promise you'll keep all this to yourself."

"Okay, I promise."

So Dranko told her everything: about Naradawk and the archmagi, about the Crosser's Maze and their long journey to find it; and about the Black Circle and all their machinations.

"The Black Circle thinks that one of my team, a man named Ivellios, is going to be instrumental in freeing Naradawk. And they've kidnapped him. It's possible that even if Aravia and Abernathy work out how to use the Crosser's Maze, the Black Circle will still be able to use Ivellios to free Naradawk."

Praska stared at him. "How? How will they use him?"

"We have no idea. Our concern right now is that we need to find him, but we don't know where he is. That's where maybe you can help."

"Me?"

"You broke into Mokad's room and got a good look at his papers. We're hoping you remember something that might help us find Ivellios. Ideally something like the location of a secret lair. Maybe a map with a big 'X' and a note about 'HERE'S WHERE WE'RE TAKING IVELLIOS.'"

"Dranko, that was half a year ago."

"I know. But you're our only lead."

Praska said nothing for a moment, scuffing a leaf with her foot. Looking down, she spoke quietly, haltingly. "Mokad had me thrown in the Closet for a week after he caught me snooping the first time. That was pretty awful. By the time I came back after running away, the priests all knew what Mokad and some of the other scarbearers had done. It's been a cause of great commotion around here. Mokad had stolen hundreds of gold crescents from the church coffers and extracted hundreds more in credit that the church has to pay back. The priests realized I was the only one who suspected anything, and they've treated me well since I returned. I'm well on my way to becoming a Sister of Delioch."

She brought her hands to her temples. "High Priest Tomnic is back. Some high-ranking priests, mostly scarbearers, had contrived the paperwork that transferred him to Hae Charagan in the first place. Those priests all vanished the same night as Mokad; the conspiracy had spread to…had…"

"Praska, are you all right?"

"Sorry, Dranko. Talking about this gives me a headache."

"It's important, Praska. Can you—"

"No, I mean a *serious* headache. This happens every time I talk about the Black Circle. The priests have asked me many times what I remember, what I saw. Each time, I feel like I'm going to pass out or throw up. Like now."

Dranko cursed silently to himself. Had the Black Circle bastards figured out a way to sabotage Praska's memory? If so, she was probably a dead end in their search for Ivellios. On the other hand, it implied she knew something the Black Circle wanted to keep a secret.

"I have nightmares," said Praska. She turned to look at him, her face grown shockingly pale, skin sweating, eyes watery. "I've dreamed about the Black Circle, about Mokad, almost every night since I hit him with that horseshoe. But in the morning I can't remember any details. I try, but—"

She threw herself away from him on the bench, bent over at the waist, and vomited on the gravel path. "Gods, Dranko, I'm sorry."

Dranko put his hand on her back. "Stop talking about it. Stop thinking about it." He paused. "But all that about dreams gives me an idea. I want you to come back to the Greenhouse with me, if you feel up to it. I want you to meet a friend of mine."

CHAPTER THREE

Morningstar sat on the bed in her dark room, its thick black curtains blocking out the mid-morning sunshine. She had worked out the days with Eddings, counting out the time spent traveling across Kivia. As impossible as it seemed, it had been only two days since she and Previa had spoken, since she and her sisters had last trained for their looming battle with Aktallian Dreamborn. It felt so much longer. The cycles of Calabash blurred into a mist of fading memory, but due to the divergent rates of time's passage, those months in the City Vitreous had accounted for little more than a day on Spira. The time they had spent in the Crosser's Maze was even stranger to contemplate, a dream within a dream.

Morningstar still suffered the revolting full-body nausea of her oath to Shreen the Fair. Her promise to Dralla, Mother of Monsters, had shadowed her across Kivia, into Calabash, and through the winding iron halls of the Crosser's Maze. Even now, back on the proper side of the Uncrossable Sea and in the safe confines of the Greenhouse, her oath lay lodged in her mind like a jagged splinter.

Lapis's head and the Crosser's Maze. That was what Shreen had demanded. They had dumped Lapis on Mrs. Horn's old bed, her head still attached to her body, and the maze was inside Aravia's head somehow. The debt to Shreen wouldn't come due until Aravia's work was done, and that was weeks away. In the meantime, Morningstar had things to do.

Sitting cross-legged in her black Ellish robe, Morningstar closed her eyes and dropped into the dreamscape, choosing to appear in the starry glade where she and the others always met. It was unexpectedly difficult; typically she dreamed herself to the peaceful grassy clearing with no effort at all, but this time it felt as though she pushed through a barrier of stifling cloth. All of that time in Calabash and the Crosser's Maze, where the Tapestry had been inaccessible, must have set back her abilities.

She persevered, pushing through the obstruction, and dreamed herself into the glade. She expected that Previa and the others might be there already, waiting for her, perhaps engaged in the training exercises they had worked out. Morningstar had missed only a day, and Previa knew that the dangers she faced in Kivia might prevent her from joining the rest. Morningstar would share with her team the good news about the Crosser's Maze, but impress upon them the imperative of continuing the training to the very end.

The glade was dark. Always before there had been a bright moon shining above the trees surrounding the clearing and the bright pinprick lights of stars. Now there was no light at all. Even her darksight was foiled. She couldn't see the grass, the trees, or any sign of Previa and the others. But this was her glade, the one in which the avatar had trained her. Wasn't it?

A slow dread filled her. Darkness should be a comfort to a sister of Ell, but the hairs rose on Morningstar's arms, as though a predatory animal lurked in the sea of dark. She imagined the moon shining out again, a trivial thing she had learned to do with little effort. A pale round disc appeared above, but its light was slow to fill the glade. A corruption congealed around her thoughts, around the reality that ought to be hers to create. She hardened her concentration and the moon brightened more quickly, showing her that there was still grass beneath her feet, still trees standing guard around the edges.

A small dark object rested only a few feet away, lying on the grass. Morningstar's dread grew, threatening to become panic. She enforced her will with a surge of purpose, and the moon and stars shone brightly upon the ground.

In a circle of bloody turf lay the severed head of her sister Sable. Morningstar stared down in horrified disbelief. Sable's eyes were missing, her face stretched into a grotesque silent scream. Morningstar heard her own heartbeat, noticed the absence of her breath, felt the clench of shock in her gut.

She forced herself to take a breath, to think calmly. The ghastly object wasn't Sable's actual head; this was the dreamscape, and everything in it was a figment. It might have been placed here to scare or threaten while Sable herself was fine and healthy just a half hour's walk away. She stared at the gaping sockets and attempted to alter the dream so that the head was gone.

She failed. The head remained. She manifested a wooden cup, and that was not difficult. Likewise she removed a patch of grass and replaced it with a little pyramid of bricks. But the head would not be moved or transformed. It persisted despite her efforts, like the tip of a subterranean mountain jutting through the surface. How could this be?

The answer was obvious though she didn't want to think upon it. Aktallian. Somehow Aktallian had done this. He had found and penetrated this sanctum and left Sable's head as a warning. Or mockery.

Morningstar reached down and picked the head up from the grass. This she was able to do. The head felt solid, its black hair sticky with globs of congealed blood. It felt *real*. The neck had been sliced clean through, as though by a sharp blade.

And even as she held it in her own hands, she could not be rid of it.

Ell's Shadow, but what if Aktallian were marauding through the dreams of all her sisters, cutting off their heads? They'd be asleep right now, vulnerable. She had to warn them! Morningstar dropped Sable's head, willed her hammering heart to slow, and cast her awareness upward and outward, beyond the Tapestry, to the befogged edges of the dreamscape. There below her were the dreams of the people of Tal Hae, glinting like lonely candles seen through a violet mist. Not many still dreamed in the late morning, but a cluster of dreamers populated the temple of Ell, where most of the sisters would have gone to bed for the day.

She sought first for Sable but failed. The simplest explanation was that she was asleep but not dreaming, or perhaps she was awake despite it being mid-morning, but Morningstar feared a more terrible reason.

Previa dreamed, fitfully. Morningstar observed from outside as Previa struggled with the handle of a white door set into an infinitely long black wall. She pulled and twisted it, then threw her shoulder against the door, but it held fast. Confounded, she took a step back and stared at the door, willing it to change into several different shapes: round, trapezoidal, oval, irregular. But the wall changed to match the door, and each time Previa tried the handle, the door didn't budge.

Morningstar didn't bother with a natural-seeming entrance. She appeared standing next to Previa, then put out a hand to her friend's shoulder before she could fling herself against the door another time.

"Morningstar! Am I dreaming this?"

"I am truly here," Morningstar told her.

"You're alive!"

The dream shifted abruptly, and they stood in a glade, soft moonlight drifting down to the grass. But this was not *the* glade, but Previa's dream of one like it.

"I tried meeting you in the glade not long ago," said Previa, "but it wasn't there. Or, rather, I felt as though it existed but was blocked off. Were the others there?"

Morningstar considered gentle ways of breaking the news, but time was critical. "Previa, I need you to wake up and then awaken the others in the Tal Hae temple: Amber, Gyre, Belle, Scola, Jet…and Sable. Go to Sable first. But, Previa, I have to warn you. I think Aktallian may have killed her."

Previa looked horrified, as Morningstar expected, but then her mouth became a hard line and frustration filled her eyes. "Ell's shadow," she whispered. "I told her…told them all…"

"What? What did you tell them?"

"Yesterday, when you weren't at the glade, I reminded the others that you might be nearing the end of your quest for the Crosser's Maze. They know how dangerous your life is, and some of the sisters thought we should consider the possibility that you had been killed. Amber argued that since none of the rest of us had made any promises to an avatar regarding the Injunction, we were free to involve others. Only Sable and Gyre agreed with her; we reminded her of the promise we all made to you, in Ell's name, to maintain secrecy. But Sable was adamant that with you possibly…out of the picture, we should start searching for where Aktallian might be lurking in the Tapestry. I told them that would be unwise, that you were more than likely merely delayed, not dead. Amber, Gyre, and Belle said it would be worth the risk. I tried to assert my authority as the first of your recruits and forbade them from searching out Aktallian. They would not make me any promises."

"So you think Sable went looking for Aktallian." Morningstar shook her head. "I'm sorry to say she might have found him. Go. See if she lives. Regardless, wake the others. They are vulnerable to Aktallian in the Tapestry. Gather yourselves, secretly. I want to talk to all of you at once."

"Where? Can we meet in the glade?"

"No. Aktallian has corrupted it somehow. I can make us a new meeting place, but I don't know how long it will take. I will come to the temple myself as soon as I have spoken with Obsidia and Starbrook."

"But you can't—" Previa started to protest, but checked herself. "Never mind. I forgot you can walk through Tal Hae in daylight." She sounded appalled at the notion.

"I still have dispensation from the High Priestess Rhiavonne. You cannot come to me, but I can come to you. Have someone ready to meet me at the door in half an hour to let me in."

"Come to the laundry door in back," Previa suggested. "Most of the sisters will be asleep, but you're more likely to be seen coming in through the front door. The laundry door is the leftmost along the back wall. The right one leads to the kitchens. Avoid that one. One sister or another is visiting at all hours."

"If Sable is dead, there'll be no keeping it a secret," Morningstar said, mostly to herself. "But if the worst has come to pass, we'll need to think of a plan together. Now, go. Wake our sisters, and I will see you soon." She reached for Previa's hands and held them. "I'm sorry for what you might see."

Morningstar left Previa and once more rose into the dusky purple cloud above the Tapestry. At the speed of dreaming thought, she traveled across the length of Harkran to the coastal town of Minok, where Obsidia and Starbrook served. She had never traveled there in person, but found the Ellish temple by the cluster of people dreaming while the sun shone.

Obsidia was not dreaming, but Starbrook was. The old sister dreamed that she stood on a high ledge in a chain of mountains, watching a black comet in the shape of a fist drift lazily across a smeary gray sky. Morningstar appeared beside her; Starbrook startled slightly but didn't take her eyes from the comet.

"The Dreamseers have been seeing something like this for months now," Starbrook said quietly. "Do you know what it means?"

"I do not," said Morningstar. "And I have no time to dwell upon it."

Starbrook turned to face her. "Something is wrong."

Morningstar told her all of what she had shared with Previa. "When I leave, wake and visit Obsidia. Make sure she's alive and tell her what I've told you. I'll visit you again as soon as I've established a new sanctuary."

Starbrook nodded her understanding, glanced once more at the comet, and vanished from the dream. The ledge remained, a new patch of Tapestry. Morningstar lingered for a handful of heartbeats, watching the comet, troubled without knowing why. But she had troubles enough. She woke.

* * *

The lower floor of the Greenhouse was quiet. Aravia and Tor sat together on a sofa, holding hands and talking in hushed tones. The voices of Ernie and Eddings drifted from the kitchen over the sounds of clinking ceramic and the sawing of a bread knife. There was no sign of Dranko, Kibi, or Step. She slipped out the door into the sunshine, undaunted. She no longer asked for Ell's forgiveness on instinct. She did the Goddess's will.

Most of the Traveling Gods had their largest churches directly abutting the park at the center of the Pious Quarter, but the temple of Ell was set back a block, surrounded by other tall buildings that shielded it from the nearest street lamps. Morningstar spared only the briefest glance at the cathedral walls, patterned in inverted black triangles, before hurrying around to the back and in through the laundry door. What if Sister Corinne, or one of the other more hostile sisters, were there to catch the White Anathema sneaking into the church in broad daylight? Morningstar decided she didn't care.

The young woman Jet was there to greet her, far enough inside that light slipping through the open door wouldn't touch her.

"Morningstar! Come in, shut the door. Previa woke me a few minutes ago and told me to wait for you here. I couldn't get into the Tapestry, like there was a thick curtain around it I couldn't push through."

Had Previa sent Jet to spare her from what they might find in Sable's room? "Did Previa choose a meeting place?"

"Yes. She said as soon as you arrived, we should meet the others in the southern reading room down in the archives. Morningstar, what is this all about? What has happened?"

"I'll explain once we're all gathered together." She was loathe to say more until she knew what had, or had not, happened to Sable.

It was a short walk to the archives, up some stairs and down others. The windowless halls were dark as pitch, but Morningstar could see intricate wall carvings and patterned mosaics on the ceiling. Everything looked older and more solemn than in the plain corridors of her home temple in Port Kymer. *Or is this my home temple now? Or is my dark room in the Greenhouse now where my soul speaks truest to Ell?*

They walked quietly through the series of chambers holding the books and scrolls of the archives, meeting no one, until they reached a plain black door. Jet pushed it open. Her sisters waited, gathered close around a table in a round room not meant for so many.

All of their faces were ashen. Some were tear-streaked—and Sable was not among them.

"Sable is dead," said Previa, seeming to strain with the effort of keeping a level voice. "Beheaded in her sleep."

Jet gave a little gasp, her hand flying to her mouth.

What do my sisters need more right now, comfort or steel?

Morningstar guided Jet into the room and closed the door behind them.

"I'm sorry," she said, feeling their eyes upon her. "I know Sable was your friend and that some of you knew her for many years. Her soul is safe now, in the heaven of Hallowed Darkness."

Her sisters said nothing. Some shuffled their feet or looked down in silence.

"But I warned you!" She swept her gaze over her sisters. "I warned you to leave Aktallian alone. Previa warned you also. I'm sorry this is what it took to teach you I was serious."

"We didn't doubt you were serious." Amber put both her hands on the table, palms down. Anger burned in her eyes. "Sable took that risk because you convinced us how serious this all was. You tell us every day how dangerous your own quest is, and then, right after we learn we have less than three weeks before we need to fight Aktallian, you don't meet us for training."

"It was *one day*," said Morningstar. "I know some of you were itching to scout for Aktallian. You—"

She checked herself. Her sisters were angry and scared to varying degrees, and blowing anger back at them would not help matters.

"Perhaps it is my fault for not properly conveying how powerful Aktallian is. I thought I had, but…" It was difficult to find words of comfort. She wasn't certain there were any.

"Are Starbrook and Obsidia alive?" asked Previa.

Thank you. "Starbrook is well. Obsidia wasn't dreaming when I visited, but I imagine she is also unscathed. It appears only Sable was attacked, from which we can take some small comfort. It gives us hope that Aktallian doesn't realize Sable was part of a larger group. Unfortunately, he somehow tracked her back to our glade. That is why none of you could reach it tonight; Aktallian defiled it. It is no longer safe for us."

"Then what do we do now?" asked Jet in a trembling voice.

"Make no more missteps," said Morningstar. "You have all learned to walk in the Tapestry as part of our training, and in other times that would be safe, but there is a deadly spider in the web of empty dreams. I will make us a new place to train, and you must promise to go nowhere else while dreaming. Sable was a valuable member of our team, and a friend to all of us. We cannot afford any more losses. If you want your vengeance, continue to train. Continue to work. We *will* bring him down, I promise."

Gyre, Sable's closest friend in the group, wept openly. "How can you promise that?"

Goddess, how has it come to this? "Because I am the White Anathema. I am the white meteor of the Dreamseers. Ell holds us like a spear, risking the Injunction to hurl us at our enemy. You are the haft of the spear. I am the blade at its end."

CHAPTER FOUR

Tor, I don't know what's going to happen. I am well out of my element."
Aravia held his hands in her own, feeling his callouses, the warmth of his
palms. His left hand lacked its little finger, sliced off while he defended his
friends from the Sharshun. He had been gallantly unselfconscious about it since
the day it happened.

She gave his hands a squeeze. "But knowing you are here, guarding me, will be
a great relief."

Tor's usually ebullient face was a taut mask of concern. "When you went into
the maze before, your eyes went starry and you seemed half dead. I'll be here to
shake you out of it, but how will I know if you need rescuing?"

Aravia rubbed the side of his hand with her thumb. "I don't know. If
something about me changes or looks suddenly pained, jostle me until I wake. If
it turns out to be premature, we'll at least have learned something. I imagine the
process of learning to use the Crosser's Maze will involve a great deal of trial and
error."

I could look after you just as well. Pewter flicked his tail nervously.

*I know. But I want you with me in the maze. I will inevitably be distracted, and there might
be dangers lurking. You will be my senses if I am oblivious.*

Boss, we don't even know if it will work!

Aravia let one hand slip from Tor's and stroked her cat's gray fur. *If it doesn't,
you can stay here and keep Tor company.*

Tor glanced briefly down at Pewter before returning his gaze to Aravia. She
had discovered that staring into Tor's bright blue eyes could be perilously
distracting. His gaze was unexpectedly deep.

"How long will you be away?" he asked. "Will it be like Calabash, where it'll feel like weeks or months for you but only a few seconds for me? Or maybe the opposite?"

"That's one more thing I don't know," she said. "When I go in, we'll choose a duration ahead of time. Let's say an hour. You give me a good shake to bring me back, and then we can compare my own relative experience of time's passage to yours."

"What if shaking you doesn't work? Should I pinch you? Stick you with a pin?"

His face was so close to hers, she could smell his warm breath. An unexpected feeling came over her, almost mischievous. "If all else fails, try this." She leaned forward another few degrees, closed her eyes, and kissed him gently on the lips.

She suffered a momentary confusion regarding the relative experience of time's passage.

When she pulled back, Tor's face had flushed a deep pink. His eyes stayed closed a moment longer, and when he opened them, his face broke into a lovely grin.

"Maybe I could try that first," he said.

Ugh. You humans and your lips.

Pewter, hush.

"I should start," she said, feeling her heart beating faster than it ought. "The world depends on my ability to learn something extremely complex. I should start." She touched his chin. "One hour. Try not to become distracted."

Aravia cast her consciousness inward to the infinity it contained. More quickly than before, her mind accepted her immersion in the totality of time and space. She floated in a sea of charged aether while around her the ever-expanding cosmos spread itself out like an ocean.

Boss, help!

Pewter! She had held onto his mind as she entered the maze, but so great was its distraction that she had momentarily forgotten about him. He was not physically there, any more than she was, but sharing her vantage, he was panicking.

Pewter, you're fine. Your body is safe in the Greenhouse, but your mind is joined to mine. Relax.

If you say so. Pewter's voice in her head was the same as it ever was. *So this is the Crosser's Maze? It's…big. But what do we do?*

I have an idea. Or, rather, Solomea had one. He suggested we seek out a previous Keeper of the maze and ask for advice.

That sounds smart, said Pewter. *How do you find someone in this place?*

Aravia directed her focus to the interior of the Greenhouse, and as before, she sensed what was immediately close to her physical body. Tor was there, and Pewter. As she observed, Ernie came near and spoke to Tor. Aravia strained to hear—no, not hear, of course, but to *understand* the words. She could not. She wasn't entirely certain how she knew they were speaking.

If I am going to locate another Keeper in all of this vastness, she said to Pewter, *I will need a wider perspective.*

You don't think they're lurking in the Greenhouse?

Aravia imagined rising up and out of the house, high above the ground, so high that she would leave the surface of Spira behind altogether. As she imagined, so it became. There she hovered, looking down upon a great sphere, a stunning marble of blue and green and brown, flecked and smeared with white patches like swathes of paint.

Pewter again sounded frantic. *Whoa! What is that?*

That is Spira. And to think a majority of its citizens believe it to be flat.

It's a reasonable thing to think when you can't see the whole thing at once, said Pewter.

Aravia spun slowly in place, sensing something was behind her—and it was. A second enormous sphere, another world, drifted in space not far from where she hovered. Unlike Spira, this one was patched with orange and beige. Furthermore, it was translucent, more like a world's ghost than a solid place one could walk upon.

That would be Volpos, she said to Pewter. *Where Naradawk is bound. It's not truly so close to Spira, not in the sort of space one ordinarily deals with.* She stared at it a moment. *But in this frame of reference, it's moving closer.* She thought some more. *Perhaps that is how Naradawk intends to escape his cage. We know that Ivellios occasionally finds himself at a moment of overlap between Spira and Volpos. Naradawk could be maneuvering the two worlds such that, in a controlled moment of that overlap, he could move freely from one to the other, bypassing the portal in Verdshane entirely. That would explain why the Black Circle needs Ivellios in their power. They may need him to guide the worlds into proper alignment.*

I'll just assume everything you say is true, said Pewter, *because as smart as I am, I'm not really following.*

Aravia was dissatisfied with her thesis. *But Solomea said that Naradawk is specifically trying to tear open the portal and that the Crosser's Maze can be used to seal it up. So the portal must be integral to their plans, regardless of what's happening with Ivellios. There's far too much I don't know. I need to find King Vhadish XXIII.*

Who's that? asked Pewter.

Solomea said he was the greatest of the Keepers. That makes him an excellent candidate as a teacher, I think.

Pewter gestured mentally out into the endless swirling dark. *There's the universe. He must be out there somewhere. Should be like hunting a blind rat, right?*

Very funny. But Solomea wouldn't have suggested finding him if that were impossible. Perhaps, being a Keeper myself, I only need to concentrate upon him.

Don't let me stop you, said Pewter. *I won't go anywhere, I promise.*

While Aravia did feel an ineffable mental attunement with the maze, she couldn't imagine quite how one projected one's thoughts into it. Still, she gave it a try, sending her will into the expanse, thinking the name of Vhadish as clearly and as "loudly" as possible. She kept that up for what felt like a minute or two, then stopped and waited. Spira and Volpos loomed huge behind her, inching ever closer, but nothing else had changed.

Some time passed. Aravia sensed Pewter growing restless.

I know this is an artifact so powerful it contains all of time and space, but I'm bored, said the cat.

You could offer suggestions instead of complaints.

Hey, you're the genius wizard. I'm just a cat.

Aravia cupped her hands on either side of her mouth and shouted. "King Vhadish XXIII! I seek your counsel on a matter of grave importance to Spira!"

Boss, I'm not sure your voice carries as far as you think.

Beside her, a window opened in the void. It appeared as a rectangle of darker blackness, suspended or floating, a hole from space into space. But while she was surrounded by stars and near to the bright twin globes of Spira and Volpos, the region beyond the window was relatively empty. She turned to face the opening, such as it was. With time to focus, she saw shapes hovering on the far side, dim and distant, like derelict ships in a dead ocean.

Was it the thinking or the shouting that did the trick?

Aravia ignored Pewter' comment and slowly willed herself through the opening. On the far side her mind cleared, became sharper, though she was no closer to understanding what she saw.

Are we still in the Crosser's Maze? Pewter asked.

I think so. But something is different about this new part of it. I don't know what.

A little line of blue lights, like candle-flames lifted from their wicks, glowed up from nothing and dotted a trail away from the window, into the void. Aravia began to follow the path but checked herself.

What's wrong?

It is possible that I attracted Vhadish's attention, whether by my thinking or shouting, as you put it. It is also possible that something else has noticed me, and is attempting to lead me astray.

We haven't seen anything else alive in the maze, said Pewter. *It's pretty sparsely populated.*

True, said Aravia. *We know there are past Keepers still living here, but not how many, or if anything else has come to inhabit the place. But I don't see that we have a choice right now.*

She moved by thinking, a natural way of traversing the frictionless emptiness. How far she traveled she could not say, nor even if concepts like yards or miles had any meaning. Most of the unknowable shapes stayed fixed, the way the moon held its place in the sky no matter how far or fast one traveled on Spira. But one, ahead of her and off to her right, grew gradually larger, and it was toward that one that the trail of blue lights led.

Onward, flinging herself along the lit path, Aravia came to realize both her impossible speed and the immensity of the object that seemed her destination. A slowly rotating iron pyramid dozens of miles on a side floated in space, and she hurtled toward it like a falling meteor. The lights flashed past her until they blended into a single azure line. Only at the very end did the facing triangular wall rush up to meet her, and part of her brain expected she wouldn't be able to slow down quickly enough to avoid crashing into it.

Boss!

She stopped with a fortunate, though puzzling, lack of inertia and so was spared a deadly collision. The lights had led her to a silver triangle of metal set into the huge pyramid's exterior wall. She estimated it at six feet on a side, more or less. It felt smooth and cold. Was it a door? It lacked a handle, hinges, or other sign it was anything other than a plate. She pushed it to no avail.

"King Vhadish!" she called. "I am here!" She projected similar thoughts toward the silver triangle and detected a slight shuddering in the…air? She inhaled, exhaled, and all felt normal. Time passed with no sign of movement. The iron wall of the pyramid stretched away from her in all directions, but nothing stirred along its surface.

What do we do now? asked Pewter. *Knock?*

Aravia pounded her fist several times against the silver triangle, but the sound was muffled and no one came to acknowledge it. *Well then. I suppose I'll try what I was trained to do.*

Powerfully charged aether surrounded her, suffused her, wherever she went in the maze. She floated back a bit to give herself some space, and began a variant of *arcanokinesis,* one that gave up speed in exchange for power. The aether practically crackled between her fingers as she made the gestures and muttered the words. When the spell was complete, she released her power into the silver triangle.

The plate buckled, collapsing away from her with a hollow boom, a sound like a mallet striking a great gong. It tore free of the iron wall and spun away into the pyramid's interior. Some short time later came a quiet clang as it struck something distant.

"You've made your point, whoever you are." A man's voice, sounding mildly irritated, came from the far side of what was now a triangular hole in the pyramid's iron face. "Please come in, if you feel you can refrain from causing further damage."

Aravia drifted through the hole into a large space, an empty tetrahedron the size of a small cathedral. Pale, steady light, sourceless, illuminated iron walls that reminded her of Solomea's labyrinthine domain. A man floated nearby and drew nearer, wrapped in an ermine robe and wearing an ornate golden crown. His face was craggy but not ancient, peppered with a close-cropped beard that had gone mostly to gray. His voice carried boredom tinged with annoyance, but his eyes showed curiosity.

"You lack patience, clearly, and decorum, but your power is…unusual," he said. "Who are you, and why have you sought me out?"

His body was tilted slightly, as though his definition of "down" differed from hers by a few degrees. She adjusted her slant to match his. "My name is Aravia Telmir. I am the current Keeper of the Maze, and I came looking for you at the suggestion of another previous Keeper, Solomea Pirenne."

"Solomea. Pfft." The man blew out a scoffing breath. "And why would that imbecile have sent you to me?"

"I need to learn how to the use the Crosser's Maze to seal a rift between two Prison Pair worlds, and I have very little time."

The man regarded her in a way that made her feel like a specimen in a laboratory. "You are extremely young for a Keeper," he observed. "I can only assume you somehow convinced Solomea to give you the Maze, though I'm surprised he chanced across a moment of sanity long enough to do it. Perhaps you charmed him with your pretty face."

"Perhaps I impressed him with my intellect," said Aravia, feeling stung.

The man frowned at her. "Do you know who I am, Aravia Telmir?"

"I assume you are King Vhadish XXIII."

"That is correct." Vhadish gave his head a little shake. "Astonishing Solomea Pirenne with your mental acumen would hardly be a feat worth mentioning. Solomea was an idiot. Yes, his variably bounded pocket dimension was clever, but his inability to do modest calculations got him sucked into his own creation. If you wish to impress *me*, you could start by demonstrating your knowledge of formal address when one is speaking to a king."

Boss, this guy is way too full of himself. Couldn't we look for someone else?

Aravia carefully kept a straight face. "I understand, Your Majesty."

Vhadish smiled. "Good." He glanced at the hole where the silver plate had been, waved his hand lazily, and a new plate appeared, filling in the gap. "You're not the first person to come looking for me, Miss Telmir. Most of those who come as far as my Tetra are unable to get inside. It's a useful test to screen out those unworthy of my time. Of course, the few who do find their way in are invariably *also* unworthy of my time."

He gave Aravia a pointed look, which she did her best to ignore.

"Your Majesty, if you find guests so tiresome, why do you provide seekers a pathway in the first place?"

Vhadish nodded, as if that were a reasonable question. "First, because it does imply a certain wisdom for someone to want to find me, specifically. I want to reward such sensibility with at least the possibility of an interview. And second, because hope springs eternal. A part of me longs for discourse with something approaching an intellectual equal."

Did I say, "way too full of himself?" I don't think that's putting it strongly enough.

Pewter, hush.

"Do you get many visitors, Your Majesty?"

"No. I've been visited by a few other Keepers who maintain domiciles in the maze. Some stragglers who were caught or abandoned. One unusually lucky wizard worked out a way to translate himself here directly from a terrestrial world, but he was unremarkable in other regards and I sent him away. But one thing all of them had in common was that they gained ingress to the Tetra with *finesse*. Certainly some of them *tried* to batter their way in, but all of those failed. I would have said it was impossible." He steepled his fingers in front of his nose. "Until now."

Aravia gave Vhadish a small smile, but tried not to look too pleased. "I used a modified variant of *minor arcanokinesis*, slower, so as to build up the—"

"Yes, I know what you did." Vhadish had perfected the dismissive hand-wave. "But *minor arcanokinesis* is called minor for a reason. It should have taken you hours or days to build up the kinetic potential necessary. The last person who tried anything similar, a sad little Keeper named Pelgret, used *augmented arcanokinesis* and took even more time about it than you did. Do you want to know what happened to him? Not noticing I had placed *Aubry's abjurative shield* on the door, he failed to account for reflected energy and blew his own arm off. I don't know what became of him after that and don't much care."

Aravia looked over her shoulder at the reinstantiated door. Had it been shielded for her? *Minor arcanokinesis* should never have been able to penetrate an *abjurative shield.*

"I know what you're thinking, and yet it did," said Vhadish. "So you can understand my curiosity."

"It's the aether," said Aravia. "The aether here is far more potent than—"

"I know that. Please stop assuming I lack basic knowledge of how the world works. You are from Charagan on Spira, where the aether is not especially potent, so the stuff here in the Crosser's Maze feels to you like a raging forest fire compared to the little patch of warm sunlight you're used to. Miss Telmir, what aether do you think I used to build my Tetra and its defenses?"

Aravia thought back to what Solomea had told her. *You fit to the maze like a key to a lock,* he had said. "I must be particularly attuned to the Crosser's Maze," she told Vhadish. "I don't know why."

King Vhadish XXIII gave a great sigh. "You have intrigued me sufficiently, I suppose. Though on the subject of the aether, I advise you not to dip into the maze to power your magics on a material world. The magic here is meant for the maze's interior. Drawing upon it on Spira or elsewhere could damage your mind."

Aravia thought worriedly about having already used the maze to get Horn's Company across the Uncrossable Sea. But given how difficult that had been, the maze's potent aether might have been necessary.

"Thank you for that warning, Your Majesty."

"As for why you have sought me out," said Vhadish, "you want to seal the rift between Spira and Volpos—I assume that's the Prison Pair you're talking about—and you want me to teach you how. Fine. But first, what will—"

The air around them vibrated as it had done outside the Tetra. It sent a shiver down Aravia's back and made her temples throb. A faint metallic echo reverberated around the four-sided chamber. Vhadish peered at her, annoyed.

"Someone in Spira is shaking you, Keeper."

Tor! "Your Majesty, I humbly beg your leave. I must return to the real world, but I would be extremely grateful if you would allow me to return and continue this conversation."

"Yes, fine," said Vhadish. "Run along." He vanished.

And Aravia returned her mind to the Greenhouse, as simply as wishing that she had.

CHAPTER FIVE

Sometimes Kibi could see them, even with his eyes closed.

"See" was maybe not the best word to use, but it was better than any other. He considered how they appeared to him now, as he rolled up an extra shirt and stuffed it into his pack. The Eyes of Moirel, one purple and one green, were two stories below him and to his left, sealed in a sludge-filled pot that was locked in a trunk inside a closet. He sensed their direction, their color, their size, two sparkling stars that showed themselves to his mind, past his eyelids, through his skull. Eyes closed or open, it didn't matter.

As Kibi moved about his room, neatening and straightening so things would be nice when he returned, the Eyes kept watching him, waiting for him to...what?

"If you stupid things would just *talk* to me, you'd make my life a right bit easier," he grumbled. He cinched his pack, but loosely, since he'd be adding food and cooking gear before he and Ernie headed out.

Downstairs, Ernie was stacking bundles of dried fruit, bricks of hardtack, and jerky on a low table in the living room. Aravia lay sprawled out on a couch while Tor gently shook her shoulders.

"Everythin' all right?" Kibi asked.

"She's in the maze," Tor answered. "We agreed I should try to bring her out after an hour."

"Could be she's in the middle of somethin' important," said Kibi, though he didn't have the slightest clue what Aravia might be up to, specifically. "Give her a few minutes, I'd say, and then try again."

"I *am* trying again," said Tor. "A few minutes ago I couldn't bring her out, but her hour is up. I need to snap her out of it somehow." He looked at Aravia's face, blushed for some reason, and then gave her shoulders another light jostle.

"I'm ready when you are," said Ernie, tossing a filled-up water skin that Kibi fumbled slightly but caught before it hit the floor. "We should be able to reach the Seven Mirrors in a week if all goes well."

Kibi looked out the living room window; the sun shone down from a cloudless pale blue sky, giving him hope that the day would be on the warm side for autumn. "Least it's a nice day for a walk." The Eyes were no longer watching him, but the damn things would be back before long.

"We can take E.R.," said Ernie. "The mule's been growing fat out in the yard. It'll be good for him to get some exercise, and it'll be easier for each of us to have our own tent."

Kibi figured he could carry both tents and all his gear without much difficulty but didn't say anything. Ernie seemed happy at the thought of the mule tagging along. As usual, the boy didn't like to say the mule's full name, "Emergency Rations."

Aravia sat bolt upright on the sofa and sucked in a huge, gasping breath. "I found him!" Her eyes were ovals of a starry nighttime sky.

Kibi allowed Tor a few seconds to lean over her in concern, making sure she was all right, before asking, "Found who?"

"King Vhadish XXIII. A former Keeper. I anticipate he'll be willing to teach me how to use the maze."

"Fantastic!" said Tor. "I'll bet you'll be able to learn in no time."

She rubbed her eyes, and when she lowered her hands, it was as though she had kneaded normal color back into them. She looked at the pack slung over Kibi's shoulder. "Are you leaving for the Mirrors?"

Kibi nodded. "Figured there ain't no point in waitin'."

"It's a week to walk there and a week to walk back," said Aravia. "Abernathy may need us for something important while you're away."

"Guess that's possible," he said. "But I can't shake the idea the Mirrors need to talk to me. Or at least that I can learn somethin' from 'em."

"Then why don't you let me teleport you? If it's just the three of us, I can get you there and return here on my own without depleting my reserves too severely. I can come and retrieve you tomorrow morning. Will that give you enough time?"

Kibi didn't like the idea of getting teleported. It always made him feel woozy, and that last one, all the way from Kivia, had felt like being hurled through a brick wall.

Ernie looked out the window with a wistful look. "I suppose you're right," he said to Aravia. "Better we not stay separated longer than we have to. E.R. will just have to wait on that walk."

"Guess we won't need so much food," said Kibi.

Aravia asked for a few minutes to compose herself. Tor dashed to the kitchen and back to bring her a glass of water.

"Do you think you can learn in time?" asked Ernie. "How to use the maze, I mean?"

Aravia stood with her cup and walked to the window, looking out at the late morning sun rising over the buildings on the far side of the Street of Bakers. "My relative perception of time in the maze is approximately equal to time passing on Spira. I had hoped for an imbalanced ratio in my favor, so that I could have more time to learn." She turned back to where Kibi stood beside Ernie and Tor. "On the other hand, an imbalanced ratio in the other direction would have been disastrous. But to answer your question: I don't know. I don't know anything yet, but finding a skilled instructor was an important first step. I am hopeful."

"You'll figure it out," said Tor. "I know you will."

Aravia gave Tor an open and joyful smile, something Kibi hadn't often seen on her face. "I will endeavor to be worthy of your optimism," she said. "Kibi. Ernie. Are you ready to go? I can remember where I waited outside the ring of the Seven Mirrors well enough to teleport you there without great risk of mishap."

Kibi gulped reflexively. "Sure enough. Let's just get it over with, then." He and Ernie collected their packs and tents, then put their hands on Aravia's shoulders. She spoke the strange words that bounced straight off his memory, drew patterns in the air with dancing fingers, and—

dizzy darkness whirlwind queasy ear-pop

Reality returned, and there Kibi stood, his arm outstretched where he had gripped Aravia. Aravia herself had moved a few yards away, standing beside Ernie. Pewter was draped around her shoulders.

"There you are," said Ernie with relief. "You still seem to get lost when Aravia teleports us."

Kibi gave the sides of his head a vigorous rub. "'Least I didn't end up miles away and underground."

The Seven Mirrors loomed giant-like, maybe a hundred feet off. Once he had regained a bit of stability, Kibi quieted his mind and sought the bone-shaking rumble he remembered from his previous visit. He sensed it, but distantly, the rumor of an earthquake in a far-off land.

"No one is here," said Aravia.

"There's no reason for anyone to be visiting," said Ernie. "Flashing Day is a big deal, but that's only once a year, and the next one won't be until spring. None of the paths between villages comes anywhere near here."

Aravia turned to face the Mirrors. "Kibi, if the Mirrors will talk to you immediately, I can stay to teleport you home. But if it will take more than half an hour or so, I'm going to return to the Greenhouse and come to collect you tomorrow morning. I feel like every minute counts when it comes to the maze. How long do you expect this to take?"

Kibi laughed. "I ain't got no idea. Rocks are tricky things to predict. But I'll see if they have anything to say right off."

They walked across the flat, scrubby ground that surrounded the Mirrors. The standing stones cast stubby shadows as the sun rose towards its noon height. On Flashing Day the Mirrors lit up at noon, so that seemed auspicious. No Mirror was different from any other beyond the natural variations in their rough stone backs, so he strode up to the nearest one, took a deep breath, and set his hand against it.

Kibi hadn't had much cause to ride in carriages in his life, but he recalled one time taking one to a gathering of stonemasons in Hae Kalkas. Once in the city, the carriage had juddered along cobbled streets, shaking him in his seat, rattling his body.

Touching the Mirror was like that. Invisible energy vibrated out of it, passing through his fingertips and setting his arm to quivering in sympathy.

"Why do I keep seein' the Eyes of Moirel? Do they want somethin'?" he asked it. Kibi received no sense of intelligence from the obelisk, and it did not give him an answer.

"Anything?" asked Ernie.

"Not yet." Kibi closed his eyes. Aravia, Dranko, and Morningstar talked a lot about concentrating when they did their magic or practiced their divine arts. He focused his mind on the point of contact between palm and plinth.

"Last time I was here, you told me my time was long past but hadn't come yet. You told me to abide and return. Well, I've been abidin' for months, and now I've returned. You got any more riddles for me?"

Part of Kibi felt silly, standing there with his hand pressed to a huge rock, talking to it. Mostly, though, he felt like a child waiting patiently for an adult to turn its attention to him. The question was, how long would the Mirror make him wait? Another minute passed. He heard the small stirring sounds of Ernie and Aravia growing impatient. Pewter meowed.

"You ain't gonna make me wait till next Flashing Day I hope," Kibi muttered. That was the problem with talking to stone. No one could know how it measured time. Maybe for a Mirror, the time between its flashing was like a person drawing a breath between sentences. The thing might think itself hurrying even if from Kibi's point of view it was going to wait for months.

He had placed his left hand against the rough black stone, noting the similarities between its faceted texture and the patch of gnarled skin that stretched from his knuckles to the base of his thumb. It had certainly gotten larger since he had first noticed it, but slowly, and far from causing him any discomfort, it felt right. Inevitable.

The Mirror still vibrated, making Kibi's whole body feel like chattering teeth, but it offered no words, no puzzles, no wisdom. "I'm sorry," Kibi said at last. He took his hand from the stone. Stillness returned; the carriage had come to rest. "If this thing is gonna tell me somethin', it's not in any rush."

"Then good luck," said Aravia. "I would offer to stay, but I'll feel better exploring the Crosser's Maze in the safety of the Greenhouse. I see no point in making you have to guard my unconscious body for hours on end. And Tor will expect me back. I don't want him to worry."

Ernie grinned at her. "I'm sure he misses you already."

She cocked her head slightly, as though working out a puzzle, and smiled back. "I miss him too." She thought some more. "I love him, you know." Aravia spent a half minute casting, and vanished along with Pewter.

Kibi put his hands on his hips and looked up at the ring of standing stones. They put him in mind of a seer dream Morningstar had once told him about, a dream of a circle of seven giants, but he couldn't remember the details.

"I hope it's warm tonight," said Ernie. "It only just occurred to me that we didn't bring any firewood, and we're a long way from the nearest trees."

Kibi peered across the plain. Some dots on the northern horizon might be trees, but Ernie was right. "Just as well we'll only be here a night," he said. "And our bedrolls are warm enough, I'll reckon."

"Do you think it's safe if I touch one of the Mirrors?" Ernie asked. "When I came here with my parents, nobody would touch them. Said it was bad luck, that the stones would eat your soul. But you don't seem bothered."

Kibi shrugged. "I'd be lyin' if I said I knew for sure. The Mirrors haven't harmed me none, but it's clear I got some kind a' special rapport with 'em."

Ernie reached out a hand, pulled it back, reached again, then closed his eyes and pressed his hand to the Mirror. "It's cold," he said. "But I don't feel like it's sucking out my soul or anything."

Kibi chuckled. "Let me know if it decides to talk to you."

"I don't speak Mirror," said Ernie.

"But you got your earcuff on, so that wouldn't matter none."

"I suppose. But I—Holy Pikon's Pancakes! It talked!"

Kibi laughed again. "That's a funny one, Ernie."

"No, really!" Ernie's eyes were wide, and he stared at his hand. "I'm not joking."

"What did it say?"

"It said 'Carabend, not yet.'"

"Who's Carabend?"

Ernie turned to face him while keeping his hand on the Mirror. "Me! I'm Carabend! That's my middle name. Ernest Carabend Roundhill. Carabend has been a family name in White Ferry for generations."

Kibi tugged at his beard. "Keep listenin'! Is it sayin' anythin' else?"

Ernie took a step closer to the Mirror and cocked his head, as though he hoped to hear it whisper in his ear. Kibi held his breath. Ernie squinted, then frowned. "No. I think it's finished." He let his hand fall from the stone. "What does that mean, 'not yet?' Not yet what? Does it mean we should leave and come back some other time?"

"Not sure," Kibi admitted. "But either way, we oughta stay until tomorrow at least, since Aravia's comin' back for us."

"Its voice was so deep," said Ernie. "I'm not sure I was even hearing it with my ears. It felt more like a faraway landslide was speaking Chargish."

"Sounds about right," said Kibi. He looked thoughtfully into the center of the ring of stones. "I wonder. The different Eyes of Moirel don't all think the same things, we know that. Remember that argument they had about whether or not we should have let Aktallian summon up the giant turtle? Maybe it's the same way with the Mirrors. I'm gonna try each one of 'em, and I guess you should too since they've decided you're someone they'll talk to."

Not seeing any reason to pick one Mirror over another, Kibi went in a leftward circle. Each stone sent the same thrumming rattle from his hand, up his arm to the shoulder, and then through the rest of him. None of them spoke.

"How about some lunch?" Ernie suggested. "I brought a lump of butter for the bread and two apples for each of us. I also brought the leftover yellowbeans from the night we came back. It's a miracle Tor didn't finish them."

They moved to a spot well outside the circle of the Mirrors and ate their quiet meal on the grass. Kibi felt more and more foolish as he ate. "Looks like I wasted Aravia's time. I hope usin' up her magic on a couple a' *teleports* doesn't make it harder for her to learn how to use the Crosser's Maze."

Ernie spun his wrist, signaling he had something to say once he stopped chewing. "We still have a whole day, and they talked to me right off. We should keep trying every few minutes."

The boy had a point. If the Mirror hadn't uttered words to Ernie, Kibi would've assumed they could only talk during a Flashing Day. He took a swig of water from his skin and lay back, his bedroll under his head. The afternoon was as perfect an autumn day as one could wish for: warm, sunny, slight breeze, clear sky, a few birds wheeling and crying.

"Ernie, isn't White Ferry not too far from here? Is it close enough for us to visit while we're out here?"

"It's close, but not that close," said Ernie. "It took us about a day and a half back when we made the trip."

Kibi yawned and stared at a cloud that remind him of a keystone. "Shame. I'd a' liked to see that statue of you they dug up. Ever learn anythin' more about it?"

Ernie's face went red. "My mom sent more news with her last care package. They moved the whole thing out of Murgy's basement and set it up in the town square. It's twelve feet tall! The whole town likes it because they think I'm off in the big city, helping Abernathy save the world."

"Ain't that what you're doin'?"

"I guess. But they don't know any of the details. I think my parents are trying to make me sound much more heroic than I truly am. Mom, especially."

Kibi chuckled. Ernie's humility was a powerful thing. "I'll wager your parents are right fine people who know you better than you know yourself."

* * *

The afternoon stretched on to evening, the sun pulling itself down behind a late gathering of pearly clouds. Kibi and Ernie took turns trying Mirrors at random, without any success. An unaccustomed restlessness began to build in Kibi, his stoicism put to the test. Somewhere out there, on an entirely different world, Naradawk Skewn was three weeks away from invading Spira, and he couldn't do a damned thing about it. This was all he could think to try, and it wasn't working a lick.

"It's getting cool," said Ernie, rummaging in his pack. "And with no fire, it'll be a cold dinner. I packed seed cakes and figs, and we've got some jerky."

"We'll survive for one night," said Kibi.

Ernie handed him a cake. "When we get back, we should see if Aravia can work out a way to make her light-rods give off some heat."

"I reckon she's got better things to do with her time right now."

"True."

They ate, tried two more of the Mirrors to no avail, then set up their little tents just outside the circle. Dark came on, and the stars showed themselves, first in twos and threes, then by the dozen, until the whole sky was a blazing map of constellations. For a time they sat outside their tents, bedrolls wrapped around them, listening to a chorus of crickets off in the scrub.

"Strange to think we were in that bottle city two nights ago," said Ernie.

"Everythin' that's happened to us since we all got together has been strange," said Kibi, "but I'll grant you that business with Mazzery and Solomea is as strange as it—"

A bright orange flame the size of a cabbage flared in the center of the Mirrors, then vanished.

"Did you see that?" exclaimed Ernie.

"Sure did!"

They shucked their bedrolls and gained their feet. Ernie reached for his sword. The flame appeared a second time and lingered. It wasn't ordinary fire; that much was certain. For one thing it burned in midair, four feet off the ground. For another, it didn't flicker and dance the way campfire flames would. Its patterns moved too slowly, and it didn't give off any sparks or loose licks.

"It's like a blob of burning orange marmalade," said Ernie. "What do you think it is?"

"I ain't got no idea," said Kibi.

After ten seconds it winked out again, and in the immediate darkness that followed there came a sound like someone landing after a jump, accompanied by a soft grunt. The orange light had left Kibi blind in the dark, so he took his light-rod from his pocket and shone it into the middle of the Seven Mirrors.

A Sharshun stared back at him. The blue-skinned man wore loose black trousers and a close-fitting black shirt. His left hand, balled into a fist, trailed squirming strings of orange light. He stared back at Kibi with a look of obvious confusion.

While Kibi stood there, open-mouthed, the Sharshun's expression moved from surprise to realization to satisfaction. The blue-skinned man calmly drew a long, curved blade from his belt with his right hand and jogged forward. Kibi instinctively backed up, dropped his light-rod, and held out his hands. He remembered catching Vawlk's fist before it contacted his chin in the goblin arena; maybe he could do the same with the Sharshun's sword-arm. But that had been a stroke of luck more than anything else, and from what Kibi had seen, Sharshun were a right bit quicker than the goblin champion.

The Sharshun broke into a sprint and closed the remaining distance in seconds. Kibi readied himself, steadying his feet, feeling them dig into the dirt. The Sharshun's blade came down at his head, far too fast for him to stop—and was blocked by Ernie, parrying with Pyknite at the last moment. The blades met with a deafening clang inches from Kibi's nose. Kibi fell backward, heart thumping like mad, as Ernie positioned himself between him and the Sharshun. He scrambled for his light-rod and held it up so that Ernie could see his attacker.

Ernie set his feet and shoved his blade forward, pushing the Sharshun back two steps. "What are you doing here?" His voice didn't waver. Damn, but the boy had guts!

The Sharshun smiled and said nothing, but moved again to attack, swinging his blade downward in rapid angled strokes. To Kibi's untrained eye, Ernie fought desperately from the start, throwing his sword into the path of the Sharshun's viper-quick strikes. Other than starlight and the fleeting traces of orange from the Sharshun's fist, only Kibi's light-rod illuminated the battle, giving it a stuttering shadow-play look. It was possible the Sharshun could see in the dark, so making sure Ernie had plenty of light was Kibi's highest priority.

Ernie parried blow after blow and settled into something like a rhythm. Kibi was no warrior, but he had watched enough of Ivellios's practice sessions to understand the basics of what was happening. The Sharshun tried feints, sweeps, spins, and all manner of trickery, but Ernie dodged or deflected every attack, pushing the curved sword off to one side or the other, or deftly stepping out of reach. Kibi scooted this way and that, keeping Ernie between him and the Sharshun, and shining his light to Ernie's best advantage. The closest Mirror loomed behind them all like a watching goliath.

As Kibi maneuvered himself, he saw a method in Ernie's approach. The Sharshun was expending more energy in his attacks than Ernie was in defending against them. Come to think on it, Ivellios had suggested that sort of strategy when it became obvious how good Ernie was at blocking and parrying. It seemed to be working; the Sharshun was breathing harder than Ernie, and did Kibi imagine that his swordplay was slowing a bit? It couldn't be helping that the blue man kept his left hand in a clenched fist, orange light oozing out from between his fingers. Surely that was an Eye of Moirel in his hand, and holding onto it was as high a priority for him as battling Ernie. Kibi and Sagiro had both used Eyes as weapons, but the Sharshun seemed to lack the time or inclination to blast Ernie with his.

The Sharshun raised his weapon as for an overhead swing, but before it came down he stumbled to his left. Had he tripped? No, damn, it was a fancy maneuver that Ernie fell for. The blue man swept his right foot as he fell, knocking Ernie onto his back. The Sharshun straightened, lunged, and brought down his weapon for real this time, and Ernie couldn't quite roll out of the way. The blade caught the edge of his shoulder and blood sprayed out.

But Ernie kept rolling and pushed himself upward in mid-tumble, springing to his feet almost as if by magic. At least the wound wasn't to the boy's sword arm. Kibi was transfixed by the skill of the two of them and only belatedly realized he had stopped moving himself. The Sharshun turned to him, smiled again, and took a menacing step forward, but Ernie was back quickly, engaging him with a fury the blue man couldn't ignore.

In the light of Aravia's rod Kibi saw a startling anger in Ernie's face, as though the pain had touched off an inner transformation. Ernie stopped fighting defensively and pressed his attack, executing a variety of tricky-looking strikes that likely would have left even Tor astounded. The Sharshun avoided most of them, but Ernie kept advancing, shouting wordlessly. He opened a gash in the Sharshun's thigh and another along the side of his head above the ear. Ernie's foe backed ever closer to the center of the Mirrors where he had first appeared. Kibi followed at a distance, keeping his light on the combat.

Faster and faster came the thrusts, cuts, and parries. Ernie must have been growing tired too, but Kibi didn't see any sign of him flagging. Blood dripped from both of them, staining the ground inside the circle with dark spatters. For a moment their swords came together and slid against each other down to the hilts. Ernie cried out and kicked his opponent in the knee, causing the Sharshun to stumble and turn slightly sideways. Ernie yelled again and hacked with a furious strength—and Pyknite cut right through the Sharshun's sword arm below the elbow. The curved blade fell to the dirt, a blue hand still clutching its grip, and yet the Sharshun did not scream, or even look particularly disturbed by the loss of his weapon, let alone his arm and the blood coursing out of the stump. He took one more step back and held up his remaining hand, orange light still spilling out from his closed fingers.

Ernie held Pyknite out in front of him. "I said, what are you doing here?"

The Sharshun grinned at him despite his gruesome wound. "Setting things right."

"What does that mean?"

"It means that nothing you do will matter." The Sharshun turned his head slightly to look at his fist. "Return to the fortress!"

Only then did Kibi realize the Sharshun had gotten himself to the very center of the Seven Mirrors. The blobby orange light flared out from the Sharshun's remaining hand, and when it faded a second later, he was gone.

Ernie's arms flopped to his sides. Kibi rushed up to him. "Damn, Ernie, how bad are you hurt?"

The boy's chest heaved in and out like a forge bellows from the exertion. "Shoulder hurts. He cut me pretty badly. Nicked my ankle too, but I don't think it's as serious."

"Wait here." Kibi dashed to his pack and returned with water and bandages. He helped Ernie out of his blood-soaked shirt. The cut looked ugly, blood oozing steadily out of it. "I ain't no medic, but it don't look good," Kibi said. "I'm gonna wash it out and wrap it up, but Dranko or Step oughta give it a look when we get back. Can you hold this up with your other hand?"

He handed Ernie his light-rod and dressed his wound while the boy sat, grimacing. "We shoulda taken along some a' Dranko's medicines," said Kibi. "We got so used to all travelin' together, we should start thinkin' more carefully about what we might need when we split up."

"Ow!"

"Sorry. But if I don't make this tight, you'll lose more blood."

Kibi wrapped a bandage around Ernie's ankle too. "At least Morningstar had the sense to suggest you come with me—and for exactly this reason. If you hadn't been here to fight that bugger off, I'd be sliced into a dozen pieces by now."

Ernie's breath slowed a bit, but his whole body trembled every few seconds.

"I can't believe I beat him. He was so fast!"

"But not as fast as you!" Kibi resisted the urge to pat the boy on the back. "That was some incredible sword fightin'. As good as I've seen Tor fight, and he's a wonder himself."

"I've had good teachers," said Ernie, shivering again. "Old Bowlegs drilled me in the basics for years, and Ivellios and Tor have shown me all sorts of tricks and techn—" He shook his head. "What I mean to say is, thank you. I remember Mrs. Horn once telling me I ought to take compliments better." He grinned at Kibi. "I just took on a Sharshun and beat him!"

"Damn right you did." Kibi would have said more about Ernie's prowess, but a little spark of orange light caught his eye. He turned, half expecting to see more Sharshun appear, but what he saw was a faint tracery of orange playing along the shiny surface of the closest Mirror.

"You be all right a minute?" he asked Ernie.

"Go."

Kibi approached the Mirror and pressed his hand to it. The earthquake vibrations coming from it were stronger than before; he felt a need to push hard so that his hand wouldn't be jolted away from the surface.

Kibilhathur. All moments approach.

"Anything?" called Ernie.

"Shush a minute, yes!"

Soon you will need to take refuge. All of you.

"What? Where? Why?"

The wizard's house will serve. The infinite tower will protect our child. He has already gone into it and failed of his purpose.

"What does that mean? Why will we need refuge?"

When the time is right and the world is wrong, only those in refuge will be spared.

"Spared from what? And why was that Sharshun fellah here?"

A final calibration. Like you, they need only three.

The frantic lines of orange light were fading from the Mirror's face.

Kibi tried to hold on to that word, "calibration." He didn't know it, but Aravia might. "Spared from what?" he asked.

The unmaking of the world.

"Can't we stop it before it happens?"

There is no such thing as destiny, Kibilhathur. Circles, patterns, probabilities, yes. But circles can be broken and redrawn.

The last orange zig-zags vanished from the Mirror, and the vibrations coming out of it grew less. Kibi took his hand from the stone and rubbed his temples with his thumb and middle finger.

"Guess a straight answer was too much to ask for."

CHAPTER SIX

Ysabel Horn floated in the strangest place. Far below her, on a flat brown expanse, thousands of soldiers massed around a glowing blue ring, hundreds of feet high, standing on its side. That she could be here at all, hovering high above like an eagle riding the wind, was strange enough, surely.

But stranger yet, a woman had come to join her. Ysabel hadn't seen her approach, so maybe she had just popped in out of nowhere. She had never seen someone with skin so dark or a smile so wide. Her long green dress billowed around her like a cloud of spring leaves.

Nineteen days, the woman had said, until the two worlds would overlap, though Ysabel didn't understand the rest. She spent a few seconds laughing quietly at how much a fish out of water she was.

"My name is Ysabel Horn," she said with a small curtsy, made awkward by the fact that she was floating in the air. "I don't believe we've met."

The woman laughed, placed a hand to her belly, and bowed deeply. "A pleasure to make your acquaintance, Ysabel Horn. I am Kayrimpa-Tem-Sonolaf, Keeper of the Maze, though my time of keepership is now centuries past. That is a long name for one from Khar-gan, so I would be pleased for you to name me Kay."

"That's funny," said Ysabel. "I met a man recently named Solomea Pirenne, and he said *he* was the Keeper of the Maze."

"Solomea spoke the truth," said Kay. "He was. But that was long after my own dissolution."

Ysabel thought of her husband William, waiting for her on the Endless Shore of Brechen. "Solomea visited me in the afterlife and brought me to see my friends who were still alive. They were *in* the Crosser's Maze. I assumed he'd bring me back afterward, but he seems to have forgotten all about me. I found myself floating around in this…" She waved vaguely about herself.

"Solomea passed the Crosser's Maze to a successor and chose to end his own existence," said Kay, looking solemn for the first time.

Ysabel still recalled most of what her friends had told her during their brief visit. They had been trying to find the Crosser's Maze but had been drawn into it instead, and were trying to convince Solomea to give it to them instead of…oh, that wicked woman whose name she couldn't recall. "Kay, do you know who Solomea gave the maze to?"

Kay nodded, her grin returning. "Yes! A woman named Aravia Telmir now contains the Crosser's Maze. I see that pleases you. Do you know her?"

Ysabel felt a great relief. "I do. I mean, I did, when I was alive."

"We are now both inside of Aravia's mind, in a manner of speaking," said Kay. "She is back in the physical world. I hope she proves a worthy Keeper."

"I'm sure she will," said Ysabel. "Sharp as a glass edge, that one." She looked at Kay, who had turned her attention back to the armies massing below. "Kay, with Solomea gone, could you guide me back to heaven?"

Kay clucked her tongue. "Solomea never met a boundary he didn't want to test. The Crosser's Maze can do many things, but some are less wise than others and stretch its nature in ways I believe its creator did not intend. You are a dead soul, Ysabel Horn, a spirit floating free in the maze, a dandelion seed in a maelstrom. To my knowledge, you are the first. I know many things and was considered great among the Keepers of the Maze, but never has a dead mortal been set loose inside. Can I guide you to heaven? I do not know."

"But will you try?"

Kay sighed. "Of course I will try, Ysabel. And when I try something, I usually succeed."

Ysabel nearly asked Kay to start right then, but she found her gaze again drawn down to the insect-mass of soldiers swarming around the tall blue hoop. "I wonder. Is there some way I could help my friends while I'm here? How exactly does the Crosser's Maze work?"

Kay laughed again, a rich, deep laugh that almost made Ysabel believe she could see it rippling in the air. "How does the Crosser's Maze work? Oh, child of the lesser realm, what a wonderful question! And I would tell you, if only we had as many centuries before us as stretch out behind me, and you would allow me to spend most of that time learning what I still do not know. I was a Keeper for fifty years, and what was most obvious to me on my last mortal day was that for all of my brilliance and all of my wisdom, I knew of the maze what the ant knows of the whole of Kai Kin."

"Yes. Well. I see I asked the wrong question. How about this, Miss Sonolaf. While you owned the Crosser's Maze for fifty years, did you learn enough to help me help my friends down on Spira?"

Kay set a forefinger to the side of her nose. "Perhaps, perhaps. You are a ghost, a dead thing, a strip of soul adrift in the universe, so who can say what you might do?"

"But you talked about your last day alive," said Ysabel. "Aren't you a dead thing too, then?"

"Oh, no. Like so many Keepers, I used the maze to cheat death. I am not ready for the heaven of Laramon just yet, for he is capricious, and who knows what would befall me? No, child, I retreated to the maze, made my fastness, and spend my decades exploring, learning, drifting. My body is long eaten by worms and maggots, but my mind is very much alive. And lucky for you! Here I was, eager to see how two worlds in a Prison Pair might be made concentric, and there you were, a little fish out of her fishbowl."

"You live here?"

"Yes, in a fashion. The Crosser's Maze has two parts, alike and unlike. An Inside and an Outside, you might say. We are Outside, in the endless universe, the reflection of everything, the source of the maze's power. I, and all other Keepers who sought the maze's refuge, live Inside, a smaller place, an inland sea, you might say, in which float the mansions of the great minds who once were Keepers."

This Kay lady certainly liked the sound of her own voice, but then Ysabel always did have a weakness for asking questions. She pointed to the blue-green-white sphere set moonlike in the sky. "That world up there. That's Spira, right?"

"Yes."

"If I got close enough to it, like I am here, could I see my friends? Talk to them? Make a difference? They're doing something very important, you know. They told me all about it. There's a bad person named Narrydawk who they're trying to keep from invading. I guess that's his army down there. If I can help them, I should try."

Kay regarded her gravely. "You are a good woman, Ysabel Horn. Yes, you can see your friends, if you know where to look. I do not think they will see you, though. Not even I could make them see me, for the Crosser's Maze shows us a mirror, and you cannot talk to a reflection." She narrowed her eyes and studied

Ysabel's face. "But then, you are dead, and who knows what limitations that might impose or remove? If you want to observe the lives of those on Spira, I can show you how."

Ysabel thought of William, waiting. She thought of heaven, waiting. And she thought of her friends, known only that one short week, but who struggled on. Horn's Company.

"Yes, please. Show me how."

CHAPTER SEVEN

Two days had passed since Ivellios's capture—at least that's what it felt like. He'd slept twice. Both times the cultists had returned him to the glass slab onto which he'd been teleported the first time. It wasn't a comfortable place to sleep, but he'd endured worse. The lack of sunlight bothered him more. It was like being in the goblin tunnels of Kivia, with no sunrises or sunsets to mark the passage of time.

For the hours he was awake, most of what Ivellios had experienced was boredom. Naul had led him to one of the rooms they had passed on his first visit to Mokad's laboratory, a mostly empty stone cube with two overlapping circles drawn on the floor. The walls and ceiling were covered in equations and diagrams, some drawn directly onto the stone, others written on clean parchments fixed in place with glue.

Ivellios had spent hours yesterday standing in that room while an assortment of Black Circle adherents had come in and out, casting small spells, asking him to take two steps this way or three steps that way or to spin in place. The taller woman he had met that first day, Quia, was there most of the time, directing the activities of the others. Naul was present as well. There had been no sign of Mokad. Or of Essik.

He was in there now, several hours into his second day as a test subject, eating a corn muffin while standing on the spot where the two circles on the floor overlapped. His captors brought him breakfast and dinner in his cell, but for a midday meal he was expected to eat "on the job," as it were.

"Ivellios, please step fully into the annulet on your left and turn to face the large triangle on the wall opposite." An annulet, he had learned, was the specific shape of the ubiquitous black ring that featured in all of the Black Circle's rituals.

He took a slow bite of his muffin, not bothering to keep crumbs from falling on the floor.

Many times in the past two days he had considered withholding his cooperation. But what would have been the point? They could paralyze him and continue on. Or they could kill him and use his corpse. As long as he stayed alive and alert, he had told himself, he could gather information and keep open the possibility of escape.

But it grated against his nature to obey these people so meekly, like a dog afraid of being beaten. Maybe Essik was going to rescue him, and maybe she wasn't, but in the meantime he decided to test some boundaries.

"Did you hear me?" Naul glanced up from a scroll, looking annoyed. "Step into the annulet on your left and face the triangle."

Ivellios stuffed the remaining piece of muffin into his mouth, held up a hand by way of apology, and chewed with exaggerated deliberation. When he had swallowed the last of it, he smiled. "Sorry, could you say that one more time?"

Naul rolled his eyes. "I asked you to—"

"Ivellios!" Quia interrupted her fellow. "I'm certain Mokad has already spelled out the consequences if you fail to cooperate. Do as you're told, or you will suffer those consequences."

Ivellios made a show of considering her warning. Every second he delayed could make a difference down the line. "Now that you mention it," he said, "Mokad was a bit vague about the details. Could you review them for me, just so I can be sure?"

"We don't have time for stupid games," said Naul.

"No," said Quia. "We don't." She pointed at Ivellios, whispered something under her breath, and flexed her middle finger. Sharp, hot pain erupted deep in the bones of his legs, making him cry out and crumple to the floor. But even as he lay on the cold stone, gasping for breath and fighting back tears, he managed to choke out a bit more defiance. "How…can I step into your…circle…if I can't…stand up?" Gods, but he expected to see smoke pouring off his legs. He had suffered a campfire burn once, a careless accident of his youth, and this felt as though he had inadvertently stretched his legs into a bonfire.

After a few more agonizing seconds, Naul said, "I think that's enough for now."

Quia gestured, muttered, and the pain departed as quickly as it had arrived. An involuntary gasp of relief escaped Ivellios's lips.

"Allow me to refresh your memory," said Naul. "If you don't cooperate, we will incentivize you with torture. If that doesn't work, we will immobilize you and manipulate your body through magic. The latter is likely to be quite uncomfortable for you, with minimum effect on our preparations."

"But not no effect," said Ivellios, sitting up. "Enduring some discomfort in order to slow down your mumbo jumbo even a little seems like it could be a good tradeoff."

"Suit yourself," said Quia. She raised a hand and pointed at him. "Would you like to make that trade immediately? That pain you felt just now could be your permanent loving companion. You need only give the word." She smiled with pressed lips. "Or you can stand in the left annulet and face the triangle on the wall."

Cursing beneath his breath, Ivellios stood and walked to where he was bidden, then pointed his feet at the triangle. Well, nearly so. Maybe a little error here, a few inches there, might cause trouble later on.

Quia, standing in a circle chalked on the floor, cast a short spell that made Ivellios's scalp prickle. Many of the Black Circle rituals had odd effects on his body. One had made all his hair stand on end; another had made his eyes water. The cultists had assured him with earnest sincerity that none of this was in any way harmful.

The door opened, revealing Mokad holding a notebook and quill. He nodded at Ivellios, consulted his notebook, and looked thoughtfully at the wall with the triangle. "Erase the numerator of the Swarle Equation," he ordered. "Replace it with four b raised to the power of five, minus q. That will account for the induced acceleration of Volpos's approach."

The cultist did as instructed, and at a nod from Mokad, Quia cast another spell. This time various numbers and circles glowed slightly, and the air in the room became warm and humid over the course of seconds.

"Excellent," said Mokad. "Well done, everyone. Ivellios, I think we are past the preliminaries. Your cooperation has been most appreciated. You must be thirsty, and I have a well-stocked cabinet upstairs. Come with me."

Ivellios expected that Naul or Quia would report his earlier misbehavior, but neither said a word. It was troubling, of course, to see Mokad in so jovial a mood, but Ivellios wouldn't mind a drink. He followed his captor out into the hallway and down toward the end of the hall. This would be his first opportunity to see something of the story above; with luck he would catch a glimpse out a window, or spot something that might lead to his escape.

Two black-clad cultists passed them going the other way—and one of them was Essik. She caught his eye briefly as they passed and gave a little nod, which he took to mean she was still working on some plan to help him.

"With the Circle's blessing, we could be only a week out from the confluence," Mokad said over his shoulder as they climbed the steps. "Things are coming along nicely." The stairs took a sharp bend to the left and opened, disappointingly, onto another bare stone hallway. In both directions it stretched away for twenty yards before ending at closed doors, and like the hall and rooms below, it was lit with magical globes mounted on the walls. Mokad turned left and led Ivellios all the way to the door, which he opened.

Inside was a library, or at least a room lined with bookshelves. Two large padded chairs flanked a fireplace on the far wall, most of the stone floor was covered with an ornately patterned carpet, and on the left wall stood a small and delicate-looking wooden desk. As with Mokad's lab below, everything was immaculate and ordered. The books were so evenly arranged they might have been painted onto the shelves. The carpet showed no bumps or tears, and the logs in the fireplace were perfectly stacked. A variety of fireplace pokers and a pair of tongs leaned inside a rectangular metal rack at the edge of the hearth.

The remaining feature of the room was a tall wooden cabinet. Mokad whispered some words, snapped his fingers, and the fireplace blazed to life. "Please, sit. Would you care for a glass of peach brandy? Or red wine? It's of an excellent vintage, pressed from the grapes of western Nahalm. Or if you desire something stronger, I have a variety of flavored spirits that might tempt you."

Ivellios paused at his chair and looked around the room. "The brandy would be fine, thanks."

Mokad removed a fancy bottle from the cabinet, decanted two glasses of red-orange liquor, and brought them over to the fireplace. He handed one to Ivellios, sat in the rightmost armchair, and took a long sip. Could drink be Mokad's weakness? Could he get this scarred bastard drunk enough that he couldn't stop Ivellios from making a run for it?

"Sit. Drink." Mokad raised his glass. "And then tell me, are there any burning questions you've been pondering about our operation here?"

Ivellios sat. The brandy was, alas, more fruity than potent, but it did have a nice finish.

"Yeah, I have a question," he said. "Why would you bother telling me anything at all? I'm your prisoner, your test subject. We're not friends. What am I doing here in your fancy library drinking brandy?"

Mokad smiled, and it *looked* sincere, though Ivellios doubted that it was. "You are our prisoner only out of an abundance of caution. In a perfect world, I'd call you our colleague, a partner in a grand endeavor."

Do you regularly have your colleagues tortured? Ivellios managed, barely, not to say that out loud.

"As a partner," Mokad continued, "I feel you have a right to know as much as you want. Both of us will benefit from mutual trust."

Ivellios deeply suspected an ulterior motive, but it wouldn't hurt to get some answers. "Fine. Tell me about the Silverswords. Tell me about the people you say killed my father."

Mokad took another sip. "The Silverswords are a cadre of violent zealots. Their mandate is to thwart the Black Circle at every turn and at any cost—even if the cost is the lives of innocent people. They have plagued us for centuries, leaving a swath of corpses in their wake, but I'm happy to say they have not spoiled our plans."

Gods, but Mokad's greasy voice was even more disturbing when he was happy.

"As I told you the day you arrived," Mokad continued, "one of those casualties was your father, Ivos. The Silverswords discovered that someone of your bloodline would be important to us one day—which is true—and sought to wipe it out. They succeeded in killing your father, but we stopped them before they could kill you as well."

With a start, Ivellios realized that Mokad assumed all of this was new to him. He had no way of knowing that Solomea had shown Ivellios exactly what had happened. It would be an interesting test of Mokad's honesty to see if his account matched.

"Did the Silverswords know exactly why I would be important?" he asked.

Mokad whispered to the fire; the logs shifted, and the flames blazed brighter. "I cannot be entirely certain. Presumably they know we intend to release Emperor Naradawk from his exile."

Ivellios swirled his glass. "Since we're being honest, Abernathy is under the impression that if Naradawk gets loose, he's simply going to lay waste to everything and enslave everyone. That doesn't sound very appealing."

"Abernathy," Mokad said with a snort. "The Spire thinks they know everything, which is pathetic given the nature of the Black Circle. Naradawk is the rightful sovereign of Charagan, son of King Naloric the Just. Naloric's dukes rebelled, fought an extremely prolonged war, and banished Naloric to Volpos, a prison world from which the only escape is back to Spira."

That was something Ivellios had never quite grasped. "Are you saying that if Volpos wasn't a prison world, Naradawk could escape to some *other* world?"

Mokad took a small sip of brandy and licked his lips, reminding Ivellios of a snake. "Of course. There are many other worlds, infinitely many in fact, but only the most formidable arcanists can move between them. No one alive on Spira has that ability. But Naradawk could, in other circumstances."

"And Naloric?" Ivellios asked.

"I'm sure he could have as well, but as I said, the nature of Volpos made that immaterial. Naloric did escape his prison, of course, but soon afterward the wizards of the Spire killed him. Naradawk may punish those who unlawfully rose up against and then afterward murdered his father, but the apocalyptic rhetoric of Abernathy and his ilk is absurd. Naradawk only wishes to rule."

Ivellios thought back to what Abernathy had told them all those months ago. "What happened to Naloric the Just? What did he do that caused the dukes to rise up in the first place?" This time he kept Abernathy's story—that Naloric had literally turned into a monster—to himself.

Mokad looked at Ivellios over the rim of his brandy glass. "King Naloric found enlightenment. He received a blessing from the Black Circle, and was granted knowledge unparalleled. Knowledge of the dukes. Knowledge of the people. Knowledge of Charagan's potential. The dukes chose to rebel when they realized King Naloric knew all of their darkest secrets, their hidden vices, their whispered plots. They would not abide a ruler who could see into their most private hearts, so they chose to overthrow him."

Ivellios peered at Mokad's scar-pocked face, searching for any of the usual signs that a person was lying. He found none. Were the Spire and the Silverswords desperate to keep Naradawk out not because he would conquer and enslave, but because he could betray their secrets? Had it been for that that his parents had died?

"I'm guessing Abernathy told you a different version of this story." Mokad drained the remainder of his glass, mostly empty, in a single go. "I told your friend Dranko at our last meeting, and I'll tell you the same thing. *History's pen is held by the victor's hand.* You get to hear Abernathy's version of events because the Spire won the war. But the truth is somewhat different. May I top you up?"

Ivellios looked down at his glass, still half full. "No, thanks."

"Suit yourself." Mokad returned to the cabinet and refilled his own glass.

"What about the Sharshun?" Ivellios asked. "Who are they? *What* are they?"

"Favored servants of the emperor," Mokad answered brusquely. His face pinched into a sneer—an unexpected loss of composure given Mokad's air of self-assurance. The scarred man returned to his chair but didn't sit. He peered down at Ivellios. "Have you encountered them?"

"A couple of times," Ivellios answered. "We got the impression they also worshipped the Black Circle." Noticing that Mokad's face still registered distaste, he added, "So are you buddies? Are there any Sharshun here with you?"

Mokad sighed and sat, carefully, not spilling his glass though it was refilled to the brim. "No. The Sharshun may venerate the Circle as we do, but they have their own agenda. They have shown little interest in our work here."

"To hear Dranko tell it, you and Lapis were in touch at least."

"Yes." Mokad's voice went flat again. "She agreed to lead the team excavating the blood gargoyle. In return, I provided her with all the funding necessary, and then some. But it wasn't a relationship I enjoyed. The Sharshun have their own theories about how to free Naradawk, theories in which I have little faith."

"Do you know what became of Lapis after she got the gargoyle out?" Ivellios tried keeping his voice as coolly neutral as he could, but Mokad gave him a small, knowing smile.

"No, I don't. But you do."

Ivellios didn't actually know, but if all had gone according to plan, Lapis was back in the Greenhouse in a catatonic state, awaiting the day they'd return her head, attached or not, to Shreen the Fair in Djaw.

"Yeah, you got me." Ivellios waited for Mokad to ask for more details, but the man just sipped his drink and spell-fiddled with the fire again.

After an uncomfortable half minute of silence, Ivellios raised the subject Mokad had first suggested. "What are all those circles and lines and equations for? And why exactly do you need me to make it work? What's special about me?"

"Excellent questions," said Mokad.

There came a polite knock at the door. "Excuse me," said Mokad, standing. Quia stood in the hall outside, and the two had a brief whispered discussion that Ivellios tried but failed to overhear. But looking over, he saw not only that Mokad had turned his back, but also that Quia had taken a step to the side, and no longer had line of sight to the room.

Praying there would be no telltale clank, Ivellios leaned forward and drew the smallest and seemingly least-used fireplace poker from the rack while Mokad's back was turned. As quietly as he could, he stood, stuffed the poker down the left leg of his pants, and retightened the drawstring so that it mostly held the metal rod in place. When he sat down, the end of the poker made a small bulge at the knee. He covered this with his hands and waited, his heart thundering.

After a minute Quia departed, her footsteps receding down the hall.

"Nothing wrong, I hope?" asked Ivellios.

Mokad smiled at him as he sat again. "Quite the opposite. Now, you asked about why you are so special, so necessary. I'll tell you. You, Ivellios, are the last living descendant of Moirel Stoneshaper."

So that at least matched the details of Solomea's vision. "Who was Moirel Stoneshaper?"

"Don't be coy." Mokad arched an eyebrow. "Moirel crafted the Seven Mirrors and the Eyes of Moirel, as well you know."

"Yes, but who was she? Why was she important?"

"Ah. Moirel was Emperor Naloric's personal arcanist. She constructed the Mirrors at his command."

"Why?"

Mokad's smile grew just a tad forced. "We believe they are a powerful teleportation circle. Different combinations of Eyes will take you to different places."

"You believe? You mean you don't know? I thought the Black Circle knew everything."

"Very droll, Ivellios. No, we do not know *everything*, and the magic of the Eyes and Mirrors is unusually resistant to our divinations."

"But Moirel was one of you," said Ivellios. "Why would she have made things that would resist your own magic?"

Mokad shrugged. "Perhaps it was an unfortunate necessity, given the nature of the things."

Ivellios considered all of this. Mokad was certainly in a talkative mood. Could be the brandy, or maybe he simply enjoyed gloating. It was even possible that Mokad had been earnest with that nonsense about mutual trust. Whatever the reason, Mokad wouldn't be spilling all of this unless he was certain Ivellios would not or could not escape.

"That still doesn't tell me why I'm important. So, I'm Moirel's great-great-whatever-grandson. So what?"

Mokad set his drink down on a small table by his chair and leaned slightly forward. "The first and only time Moirel used the Seven Mirrors, something went wrong. The Mirrors needed more arcane power to activate. They couldn't draw that power directly from Spira without shattering, so they reached out beyond the confines of our world. They found Volpos, bound it to Spira, and drew on its power to function. That was the moment Spira and Volpos became intertwined, with Moirel at their center. The magic that connects the two worlds was infused into your bloodline. Now the last of it resides in you."

Ivellios considered that for a moment, then laughed out loud.

"Why is that funny?" asked Mokad, narrowing his eyes.

Ivellios grinned. "If I understand you, the only reason there was a world to which Naloric could be banished was because his own wizard screwed something up and connected it to Spira. In a way, your emperor built his own prison! I can't imagine how embarrassing that must be for you all-knowing Black Circle types. It's like when kids are playing bladder ball and one accidentally kicks it into his own goal."

Mokad did not laugh along. "I think I've answered enough of your questions for now. You will be returned to your cell for a few hours, and tonight we will continue the calibration. You may find the next stage to be more physically taxing than what you've endured so far. Get as much rest as you can."

CHAPTER EIGHT

This was Aravia's fifth visit to King Vhadish XXIII, and each time his notion of "up" within his pyramid was different than the time before. She suspected he did this on purpose. She swiveled her body around in multiple dimensions until she stood right side up on a tiled floor.

Vhadish had taken to decorating this interior pyramidal space as a throne room, its ceiling supported by fluted blue-gray columns, its walls adorned with abstract frescoes, and its floor tiled with alternating diamonds of silver and white. The king himself wore the same ermine robes as when she first met him. Perhaps he never took them off.

"Welcome back, my young pupil." He rose from the throne—a gaudy chair of wrought silver with multicolored gems like clusters of children's sweets decorating the outsides of the armrests.

"Your Majesty." Aravia bowed. He liked it when she bowed.

"We should resume your lessons," said Vhadish. "With my wisdom guiding you, perhaps you will continue to progress."

I think he takes lessons in being a pompous ass, said Pewter.

With some effort, Aravia kept her expression neutral. "Your Majesty, have you given more thought as to how I can practice focusing the maze's power without living people to draw upon?"

That was her greatest worry. Aravia was satisfied with her improvement in other avenues—mastering the maze's supercharged aether, understanding the theory of how cosmic fabric could be deconstructed and rebuilt, and drawing power out of the maze's great expanse. Her fast progress had astounded Vhadish, so much so that His Majesty's rudeness had changed in tenor entirely, from his initial sneering arrogance to a sort of benevolent patronization.

But one matter troubled her more than any other. In order to seal the portal between Volpos and Spira, Aravia would have to focus the raw energies of the Crosser's Maze through the arcane potential of willing people, just as Solomea had warned her. Here in the maze, only a handful of former Keepers still dwelt; not enough for meaningful practice, even if she and Vhadish were to find them and convince them to cooperate.

"I have," said Vhadish, arms out expansively to accentuate his magnanimity. "Since your previous lesson, I have crafted for you an array of simulacra in lieu of living beings. They will provide almost ninety-five percent authenticity for your purposes. No lesser man could have achieved such a feat. Come. Let us move to the Outer Maze."

Vhadish's Tetra, along with the lasting abodes of other former Keepers, occupied a relatively small space within the Crosser's Maze. He called it the Inner Maze, a zone of relative quiet and stability that the maze's original creator had provided for that specific purpose. To draw upon the maze's full energy required one to float in the Outer Maze, wherein stretched the full infinity of creation.

Vhadish waved a hand and produced a hanging black rectangle, a window onto the Outer Maze. "After you, Aravia."

They moved through it. Drifting on the far side, bobbing slightly in the emptiness of space as though caught in a gentle current, were hundreds of gleaming prisms standing on their ends.

"I thought it fitting," said Vhadish, "since the prism metaphor is the cleanest when considering what you are doing. Prisms are more often used to diffract white light into its constituent wavelengths, but they can also be used for the opposite effect. Just as a prism can collect light from throughout the spectrum and emit a pure white beam, so will the volunteers through whom you will focus the energies of the Crosser's Maze."

Aravia's study of optics under Master Serpicore had been brief, but she did at least understand the rudiments of prisms and how they worked.

"Use the techniques I taught you on your previous two visits," said Vhadish. "These prisms are fragile, brittle. Like the people through whom you will focus power in Verdshane, their arcane potential is minimal. If you use them without finesse, you will destroy them, just as you would snuff out the life of a living being." Vhadish pointed at nothing, and there was something, a large green oval some distance from the nearest prisms. "That will serve as your target. Pretend it is the portal you wish to seal, a weakness in the fabric of reality that separates Spira and Volpos. Do you understand, Aravia? Or do my explanations outdistance your young mind?"

"I understand, Your Majesty."

His Majesty is a pretentious blowhard, said Pewter.

I can't disagree, Aravia said, *but he also knows things I need to learn.*

Aravia closed her eyes and cast her awareness out into the depths of the Crosser's Maze, reaching for its power. This was easy for her, like reaching into the ocean hoping to scoop out a handful of water. She knew that her intellect impressed King Vhadish, but it was this collection of energy that truly awed him.

"You have mastered in an hour what should have taken you a year," he had said, the first time she had drawn power out from the maze. "You are something the maze has never seen before." Vhadish had redoubled his criticisms soon after, doubtless aware of his unseemly effusiveness.

Now for the hard part. To focus and transmit the collected power through willing beings, she needed to harness the overcharged aether of the maze. Vhadish had shown her how, had taught her ways of thinking, methods of mental organization, and these she applied carefully, slowly. Too much too soon would burn out the "lives" of her lenses. Too little would be insufficient; the energy would be lessened, not enhanced, by its passage through a person's arcane potential.

Trickiest of all, she would need to perform that focusing hundreds of times, maybe thousands, all at once, and then divert the augmented beams to a single point: the portal between the worlds.

"Imagine an archer," Vhadish said. "Imagine he needs to fire an arrow against an angled metal plate and strike a distant target. Too much draw on the bow, and the arrow will puncture the metal, destroying the plate. Too little, and the arrow will fall to the ground well short of its mark.

"Now imagine a thousand such archers, facing a thousand different plates at different angles, all firing at once with the same purpose. All the arrows must strike the target at the same time.

"The plates are living beings. The target is the portal. And you, Aravia, are the entire regiment of archers."

She sensed Pewter watching, sensing, staying quiet so that she could concentrate. She'd have preferred hard mathematical rules about the flows of energy, about the balance of forces, but now her success depended more on finesse, on feel. Ironic, she thought, given how she had spent her recent life trying *not* to feel. That, inevitably, sent her thoughts to Tor, whom she loved. Whom she loved! How strange that felt, and how wonderful. Tor had faith in her. He was sitting by her side right now, guarding her—unless he had slipped out to grab something to eat. That would be just like him.

Focus. She had to focus. Literally and figuratively.

She gathered up the maze's energy and combed it into strands, a loom in reverse, one thick sheet coming in, hundreds of threads spinning away, lancing through the prisms and angling toward the target. It would be impossible to focus on each thread individually; she had to enter a mental realm that was almost spiritual, to allow her intellect to work its miracles on a subconscious level.

The energy flowed. She directed it, carefully, so carefully, out into the lenses, and once it had been focused, purified, she bent its myriad paths toward the green oval. Countless tiny systems of equilibrium, tilting, surging, ebbing, all held steady enough under her control. The bottomless energy of the Crosser's Maze was in thrall to her will; it thrummed through her body, coursed away from her, and poured itself into the target. She felt in complete control. She felt like a goddess.

One of the lenses began to overheat, in a manner of speaking. The energy was too great for it. Aravia eased up on that particular thread, but in doing so she devoted too much focus to it. Several more lenses glowed brightly, and one of them erupted, popping into a cloud of dust like a shattered glass ornament.

Leave it be. She had to maintain her concentration.

But Aravia's delicate equipoise had been disrupted, and she was losing her strands. Her instinct was to exert an iron-willed control over each one, but there were too many even for her prodigious intellect. The state of arcane serenity had left her. By the time she understood the hopelessness of the situation and disengaged from the deep power of the maze, dozens of lenses had cracked, exploded, or vaporized.

Don't worry about it, Boss. You'll get the hang of it.

Beside her, King Vhadish gave her a sympathetic look, but Aravia saw a trace of disappointment in his eyes.

"That was very good." Vhadish reached out and patted her shoulder. "That you have come so far in so short a time is nothing short of astonishing."

"But will I be ready in only a few days, Your Majesty?"

"Your skills are adequate," said Vhadish, "as is your ability to learn. So there is some hope. Keep practicing; train your mind."

Aravia stared out into the starry void. "Your Majesty, I have been thinking upon the nature of the Crosser's Maze, and how it provides energy that can affect and change the physical world. Solomea said it was 'a matter of matter,' that huge amounts of energy were necessary to create even small changes in matter. But surely I am not drawing the sum total of all the universe's energy when I follow your instructions. How, then, can I hope to focus enough energy to seal away Volpos?"

Vhadish cocked his head and looked at her appraisingly. "An astute question, young pupil, and a timely one." He chuckled to himself. "Solomea, as I would expect, did not fully understand how the Crosser's Maze works." He gestured to the distant stars. "What is out there isn't just the entirety of the spatial universe, but the temporal one as well. The maze contains all times as well as all places. When you draw power, you funnel from the past, present, and future. Most of creation is emptiness, but even the tiniest pulses of energy become prodigious when you consider how long they have existed, and will exist."

Aravia frowned. Solomea had said similar things, and she had sensed that dimension of the maze when she had first entered it.

"Solomea also implied that one could use the maze to see the future and that he had done so himself."

Vhadish shook his head. "Solomea was a madman. Observing future events using the maze is a purely theoretical possibility but impossible in practice due to paradox. Suppose you, as Keeper, saw that five minutes in the future you were going to hold up your right hand. Five minutes later, being contrary, you decide to raise your left hand instead. The universe will not abide such a discrepancy."

"Could I see into the past, then?"

"Yes, but even for you that would take weeks or months of practice and training. Perhaps when you have solved your current difficulties with Naradawk Skewn, you can return and I will continue mentoring you."

"That would be most kind." Aravia decided this was not the time to mention her promise to turn over the Crosser's Maze to Shreen the Fair.

"There is speculation," said Vhadish, "that the maze, existing as it does in all times simultaneously, was created in the far future. I think that's ridiculous, but it's a theory impossible to disprove."

"If that were true," said Aravia, "how could it have been moved back in time so that we could possess it now?"

Vhadish shrugged. "Who knows? It is hard to imagine what limitations there might be for a being capable of creating the Crosser's Maze in the first place." He graced Aravia with a condescending smile. "Best to put the theoretical out of your mind. As someone with such limited experience, you will have a difficult enough road ahead." He waved a hand and a new array of prisms appeared around her. "Let's try this again, shall we?"

CHAPTER NINE

Exhausted and satisfied, Morningstar sat upon the dirt. High stone walls, capped with iron rods tipped with sharp black triangles, surrounded a large outdoor enclosure. Rising behind and above the wall to her left was the outer wall of the main church building of Port Kymer, its dark stone façade windowless. The true, physical building also had no windows, and the façade was all she required.

Other than her spare dormitory room, the sparring yard behind the Ellish temple in Port Kymer had seen more of Morningstar's waking hours than any other place she could remember. She had trained there long and hard, learning battle techniques, gaining speed and strength, and venting the frustration and sadness of being an outcast. She knew every divot in the ground, every scrape upon the walls where combatants had strayed too close. Her sweat, and occasionally her blood, had stained the dirt of the sparring ground.

Nonetheless, it had taken her two full days and nights to recreate it and solidify its place in the Tapestry. She could bring her sisters here, and they would be safe—or as safe as she could contrive without knowing the extent of Aktallian's knowledge and abilities.

She ought to start now, visit Previa, visit all of her sisters, and begin rebuilding their resolve after the horror of Sable's murder. Aktallian's strike into her most sacred place had shaken apart her hopes that they might easily best him when the time came. Every minute spent training her sisters, physically and mentally, could mean the difference between success and failure, between life and death.

But she had another task, one that Dranko had convinced her was just as important. She left the sparring yard and floated free, out of the Tapestry, into the purple cloud that surrounded it. The church of Delioch was not far, a quick waft across the Gods' Green. Yesterday, during one of her brief spans of wakefulness in the Greenhouse, Dranko had introduced Morningstar to his friend Praska. They had established enough of a rapport, Morningstar hoped, and both she and Dranko had explained to Praska what to expect tonight. Praska, for her part, was eager to accept. Something had been done to her, something that rose up in her mind and fogged it whenever certain topics were raised. With luck and encouragement, Praska could dream of events that had been barred from her waking mind.

Many were dreaming within the buildings of the church of Delioch, but Praska was not one of them. Morningstar waited, wishing for a patience she did not at the moment possess. Her sisters needed her. Previa would be wondering at the delay and giving assurance to the others without having any herself. Morningstar quieted her mind and sought her inner peace, her calm equanimity that had bridged so many moments of self-doubt throughout her life.

Instead, she found Shreen the Fair.

Her promise to that foul creature still held her, still saturated her. When her time was occupied with other worries, she could almost forget her oath, but when what she needed most was peace, the corruption of Dralla encroached most strongly. It was a slick of oil across the surface of calm water, a rotten tooth, a lump of night soil on a clean curb. Only by returning the Crosser's Maze to Shreen (and Lapis's head besides) would Morningstar be free of it. Until then, Shreen's filthy mockery would stain her soul like a sickly light wrecking a pure darkness.

Unable to find serenity, Morningstar occupied the passing minutes imagining new tests and challenges for her sisters, until she noticed that Praska had begun to dream. She came close to observe; Praska dreamed of a religious ceremony, a joyous rite of passage with herself as the focus. Morningstar couldn't be certain, but it seemed as though she were being elevated in rank from novice to something greater. She knelt at the center of a brightly lit nave draped with golden banners showing the healing hand design of Delioch. The pews were thronged with people, most in religious raiment but a few in ordinary street clothes. Dranko sat in the center of the front-most pew, a wide tusky smile on his scarred face.

Morningstar inserted herself in the dream next to Dranko, and when Praska turned in their direction, Morningstar raised a hand and waved. Praska peered at her in apparent confusion, perhaps drawn to her black robe among the predominantly white and gold garb of the onlookers. The congregation faded away as she stared, and soon the chapel was empty save for Praska, Morningstar, and Dranko.

"Congrats," said Dranko. "Praska, you've gotten what you've always wanted."

"But the ceremony isn't over," said Praska, distantly, and still looking at Morningstar. "There's something more I'm supposed to do."

"Praska," said Morningstar. "Do you remember our meeting yesterday? How I told you I would meet you in a dream, but our discussion would be real?"

The chapel vanished entirely, replaced by the Greenhouse living room. Dranko and Praska sat beside one another on a couch, while Eddings stood nearby with a tray of sweets.

"I remember," said Praska. Her expression changed from happiness to trepidation.

"Good. Praska, you told me that thinking about the Black Circle brings you discomfort. Try thinking about them now. Think about Mokad."

Praska nodded and narrowed her eyes. Dranko and Eddings vanished from the dream, leaving Praska alone on the couch while Morningstar stood next to her. The living room darkened. Shadows threw themselves on the walls without anything to cast them: wavering black circles, some as small as saucers, others as big around as millwheels. Dark writing appeared floating in the air. Sequences of numbers and odd symbols drifted like submerged strips of ribbon.

Praska cried out as if in pain and brought her hands to her head. The room brightened again, the circles and numbers vanished, and Eddings and Dranko reappeared. Eddings presented Praska with a platter of small cakes. She took one and ate it. "I'm sorry, Morningstar. I tried. I really did."

Morningstar gave her a sympathetic smile. "You need not apologize. I thought something like that could happen."

"You did?" asked Dranko—or, rather, Praska's dream of him. "That wasn't very nice." He waved at Eddings. "Bring me a beer, would you? Oh, and before you go." He also took a cake from the butler's tray.

"It would have been the easier way," Morningstar said with a sigh. "I have another idea, but I fear you may find it more difficult."

Praska flinched, but Dranko put a hand on her shoulder. "You know how important this is. If we don't find Ivellios, our whole world could be screwed. You can be a hero, Praska. Make Delioch proud."

The Dranko of Praska's dream was slightly younger and less scarred than the one Morningstar knew. His voice was less gruff, and his tusks slightly longer. But Morningstar approved of him.

"Right," said Praska. She faced Morningstar with eyes full of resolve. "What do you want me to do?"

"You told me that you often have dreams about Mokad and the Black Circle but cannot remember the details afterward."

"That's right."

"You may find it possible to remember those dreams now," said Morningstar, "since you're in a dream already. Can you try?"

Praska nodded uncertainly. She cast a final glance at Dranko, who gave her a reassuring smile, and then she closed her eyes.

The Greenhouse faded, again taking Dranko and Eddings with it. At first nothing took its place, but a stone room slowly formed around them, as though Praska were swimming up to consciousness out of dark waters.

Praska was no longer on the couch—there was no couch—but lay on her back upon a stone slab like an altar in the center of the room. She wore a baggy black smock that revealed only her bare hands and feet.

A circle of black stone bricks was set into the floor, slightly larger around than the length of the altar and centered beneath it. The walls were covered in scrawled equations like the ones that had recently manifested in Praska's dream of the Greenhouse. In each corner of the room, black-robed figures stood whispering and flicking their fingers in the air. All four wore black circle pendants.

Morningstar willed herself to fade into the shadows, though a piece of her wanted to give Praska some comfort. It was more important that the girl relive this dream precisely as she recalled it. Praska's body appeared paralyzed though her head turned from side to side, taking in the room with wide, terrified eyes.

Mokad stood over her, appearing in the dream as if he had teleported into place.

"What is all this, you greasy bastard?" Praska spat.

"Tut, tut," said Mokad. "That sort of attitude could earn you another stint in the Closet."

Praska's body twitched slightly, as though she were struggling within constricting bonds.

Mokad lowered his face until it was inches from Praska's. "You cannot escape this, poor girl. I can't have you talking about anything you might have seen or overheard. Best you lie back and relax. This kind of work is not over quickly."

Praska twitched again, her head thrashing from side to side. Mokad watched with a cruel smile on his face. "Go ahead. Flail about if you wish. It will only make the pain worse."

"If the point of this is to shut me up, why don't you just kill me?"

Mokad chuckled. "That's not the *entire* point. There's also your friend Dranko to consider."

"Dranko?" Praska's voice became tremulous, less belligerent. "What does this have to do with him?"

"I want him to suffer," said Mokad pleasantly. "All those years posing as a Scarbearer, cutting my own flesh to establish my legitimacy, were unpleasant enough. That I had to endure Dranko's constant childish idiocy, his stupid pranks and willful disobedience, made it near a living hell. No matter how much I cut him, his antics never ceased. You were there, Praska. You know what I'm talking about. You *encouraged* him. So. Someday, when he understands exactly what I've done here, it will crush his spirit. I want to imagine how betrayed he will feel. I want him to know it was all his fault, in the end."

"Betrayed by what?" Now Praska sounded confused.

The cadence of the whispers changed, becoming more regular, more urgent.

"I'm sorry we don't have more time to talk," said Mokad. "And I wish I could say this wasn't going to hurt, but that would be a terrible lie." He put his hand to Praska's forehead and pressed downward, pinning it to the stone despite her struggles. Mokad spoke a word, and the circle on the floor glowed a putrescent purple. Praska's feet quivered, and she screamed as though her soul had been set aflame. Her face reddened, tears ran from her eyes, all the muscles in her face strained and stretched. Morningstar stood, stoic, watching, fully cognizant that she could free Praska from this twice-dreamed torment. She needed to know if Mokad admitted anything more during the dream, something that might provide a clue about Ivellios's whereabouts. And even if he didn't, Morningstar could use this pain, turn it to her advantage.

The screams poured from Praska's throat until Mokad released his hand, at which moment he vanished, the room vanished, the Black Circle adherents vanished. The Greenhouse living room returned, with Praska seated on the couch, breathing as heavily as if she had sprinted a mile to arrive there.

"What—" she gasped. "Mokad! What did he do to me?"

"Praska, look at me." Morningstar took Praska's chin in her hand and turned her head until their eyes met. "That was the worst pain Mokad could inflict on you, but look at yourself now, unharmed. This is a dream, and in this dream Mokad no longer has power over you."

Praska blinked away a tear.

"I want you to remember," Morningstar continued. "That day when you broke into Mokad's room and read his notes about the Mouth of Nahalm. Picture that room, that morning. Your eyes see more than your conscious mind remembers."

"But—"

"Do it! Mokad has tried to block you from that moment, but you are stronger. Nothing his magic can do will be worse than what he has already done, worse than what you endured and came through unscathed. There is nothing he has done that you cannot overcome, not here, not in my domain. I will help you."

Praska closed her eyes tightly. A few seconds passed, quiet but as tense as a bowstring. Once more the Greenhouse darkened, and unseen circles threw their shadows onto the walls.

"Your memory is there," Morningstar said evenly. "Mokad has not removed it. He has only put something in the way, an aversion. We can push that aversion aside."

More tears dripped from the corners of Praska's eyes. The circles grew more numerous, sliding around the walls like predators waiting to spring inwards. Strands of writing twisted through the air like eels.

This was not the Tapestry, not yet. Morningstar could try to change the nature of Praska's dream, but she did not know the girl well enough to be confident it would work. Beyond that, it was necessary that Praska recall the scene exactly as it was. Morningstar might muddle the details, which would defeat the entire purpose.

"You can remember!" she exhorted. "Mokad's spells might be real in the waking world, but here they are only as you dream them. You can dream past them! You are stronger here than he is!"

Praska's fingers dug into the padding of the couch, tearing holes in the fabric. She let out a low growl that rose slowly to a shriek, even as the circles and writing multiplied and sped, swirling around the Greenhouse living room like a flat tornado of shadow.

Then those shadows tore free, fleeing to the edges of the room and vanishing into the seams. Morningstar found herself standing not in the Greenhouse, but in a large wood-paneled office, and Praska stood as well, peering at a long piece of parchment in her hand. She mouthed silently as she read, then put the parchment down on a wide desk and picked up another. Dozens of papers lay spread out upon the desk, and on a round table next to it. Morningstar kept still and quiet, not wanting to disturb the memory.

Praska picked up a third sheet and began to read, but jerked her head toward the door at a noise from whatever lay behind it. She dropped the paper and moved quietly to press herself to the wall by the doorjamb. It opened, revealing Mokad, red-faced, furious. He strode to the desk, allowing Praska to slip out the door. The moment she was gone, Mokad disappeared. The room rippled with a shimmering vibrancy but remained, a real, solid place.

Morningstar graced the office with a wry smile. All of this was happening inside of Praska's present dream—a dream in which she was reliving the memory of fleeing Mokad and the church, going into hiding out in Tal Hae. But now that Praska had left this room behind, it had become part of the Tapestry. It was a place from a dream, but one in which the dreamer had recalled details that were real. Somewhere beyond it she sensed that Praska was waking up, but that no longer mattered. She had contrived that Praska should dream of what Morningstar wanted to see.

Morningstar walked to the desk and examined the papers. The one Praska had dropped was a ledger sheet for expenses related to a mining operation: salaries of workers, the deliveries of food and water, the cost of materials including the specifics of the desert-crossing kits.

She read every sheet that Praska had laid eyes upon, and thus were able to be read. Some were blurry or illegible, not because of Mokad's penmanship (which was neat and precise) but because even Praska's subconscious memory hadn't been imprinted with the details. But others were clear enough, and Morningstar perused them closely.

Most of them were more ledgers, scrupulously kept. Morningstar set them aside, looking instead for letters, plans, anything with the words "Grey Wolf" or "Ivellios." Nothing. A few mentioned the Black Circle, but not in any context that gave her new information. Nowhere did she see mention of Naradawk, Volpos, or anything about a ritual that would allow the banished emperor to escape.

Deflated, she let a handful of papers fall back to the desk. All of this effort, the torment she had encouraged Praska to endure, had been for nothing. She was on the verge of waking up, but something nagged at her. She reached again for the ledgers and gave them a more thorough look.

Among the more frequently listed items on the tallies were barrels of ink and shipments of something called "lava-glass." The former had been sent from various cities around Charagan, while the lava-glass was shipped from Sentinel at the far western edge of Nahalm. These deliveries had been made to a single warehouse in Minok, a coastal city on Harkran only three days down the Greatwood Road from Verdshane.

Morningstar scanned the ledgers once more. Other supplies had also been sent to Minok: lumber, digging tools, black paint, lenses, slate, chalk, two dozen armillaries, and a custom set of bronze hand-bells. Added up, it told a story of some large Black Circle endeavor in the city. If the cultists planned to use Ivellios as part of a ceremony to release Naradawk from his prison, it seemed logical that the two events were related.

Satisfied, Morningstar set the papers down and dropped out of the Tapestry, returning her consciousness to her waking mind in the Greenhouse. She stood, stretched, and looked out the window at a heap of moonlit clouds.

"Thank you, Praska," she whispered.

CHAPTER TEN

Ernie lay in bed, fidgeting, flopping about, entirely failing to sleep.

It had been two days since Aravia had teleported him and Kibi back to the Greenhouse. She had been uncharacteristically impatient, spoke some brief arcane mumbo jumbo about the "inter-weavings of space" or something similar, and retreated to her room the moment they returned. Tor had accompanied her, looking worried.

Ernie had been at his wits' end since, knowing that the end of the world was barreling toward him and being helpless to stop it. Sparring with Tor might have helped burn off some of his nervous energy, but Certain Step warned that he'd likely pull out the stitches in his shoulder.

Kibi had been down to check on the Eyes of Moirel in the basement, had taken them out of their cauldron, talked at them, waved them around, rolled them across the floor, anything to get them to speak. Ernie even brought his stuffed bear, Bumbly, and set him down next to the Eyes in case they needed a body to inhabit in order to impart their weird wisdom. Nothing worked. Nothing they did sparked the Eyes to life.

Kibi had also wanted to talk to Aravia about what the Seven Mirrors had said to him, but she was either exploring the Crosser's Maze or sleeping every hour of the day. The only part Ernie had understood was that if things went wrong and Naradawk invaded, they could take shelter in the Greenhouse—that bit about taking refuge in the wizard's house. But the rest had made no sense.

Everything had made sense, of a sort, when they had been questing across Kivia for the Crosser's Maze. They had a clear goal, all of them together. Now, while Aravia and Morningstar had something to focus upon, Ernie had nothing to do but wait.

While mentally composing a letter to his parents, and despairing of how he might explain Calabash and the Crosser's Maze in simple words, Ernie was jolted into a near panic by a loud trilling sound coming from nearby. The crystal ball! Abernathy was calling!

He burst into the hallway at the same time as the others, most with spiky bed hair and wearing nightclothes. Tor emerged from Aravia's room wearing his normal daytime attire, though Aravia was not with him. He blushed when he caught Ernie staring at him. "She's in the maze. I'm just there in case something goes wrong."

Ernie decided it would be kinder not to ask what might go wrong.

Certain Step stumbled out into the hall, a puzzled look on his face. "What is that terrible sound?"

Some of the others exchanged looks.

"Step," said Dranko, putting his arm around the Kivian. "It's nothing for you to worry about. Also, it's something we're not allowed to show you, so go back to sleep. The noise will stop in a minute or so."

Step blinked, nodded in sleepy confusion, and returned to his bedroom.

Inside the secret room with the crystal ball, it was less crowded than usual without Ivellios and Aravia. Ernie hoped to see Abernathy's face and to hear some good news, but what they all saw instead was the faceted metallic visage of Mister Golem.

"I am instructed to tell you that there shall be a meeting at noon, in the Greenhouse. The attendees will include whichever of the archmagi can be spared, as well as several powerful political and religious figures, including his majesty King Crunard IV. Please make the Greenhouse as presentable as possible, have a meal prepared for twenty, and see that all of you are present."

The sphere fogged, and the face vanished, leaving them, for a second or two, collectively speechless.

"The king?" Tor's mouth hung open. "Coming here?"

Ernie's head spun. "Twenty people!"

"Excellent," said Dranko. "Finally I'll be able to complain about Tal Hae's crappy roads to someone in a position to do something about it."

"Something must have changed," said Morningstar. "Perhaps the archmagi have found a way to extend the time they can keep Naradawk at bay."

"Better hope it ain't the opposite," said Kibi.

The blood drained from Ernie's face. "You mean Naradawk might have just escaped?"

Kibi gave a nervous laugh. "That ain't exactly what I meant. If it were that bad, I doubt they'd be waitin' until lunchtime and askin' us to cook and tidy. But maybe we don't have as much time as we thought."

"No point in wondering now," said Dranko, stifling a yawn. "We'll find out tomorrow."

Back in his room, Ernie found himself even farther from sleep. The King of Charagan was coming to the Greenhouse? And powerful religious figures? Did that mean local prelates? Perhaps some of the Travelers' high priests and priestesses resided in Tal Hae, or had traveled from other cities. Was he going to meet the High Priest of Pikon?

Ernie imagined telling his parents that he had met King Crunard and the leader of the Pikonish religion. They'd tell all of White Ferry. They'd probably have a parade for him the next time he found the time to visit home.

Home. But was White Ferry still his home, or was the Greenhouse and Tal Hae? The question had a calming effect on his mind as he turned it over. Either way, he was still a baker. Twenty people would need more food than the Icebox could provide. But bread for that many? Rolls? Biscuits? He might not be able to explore magical artifacts in his head, or train dreaming priestesses to do battle, but by the gods he could bake an oven-full of perfect manchets.

Ernie glanced out the window into the black night, made his decision, and threw off his blankets. Sleep was not going to get any easier, and he'd always been an early riser. As his father always said, the loaves never bake themselves.

* * *

"Maybe the wizards are going to tell us the world's ending ahead of schedule," said Dranko, coming down the stairs carrying a chair, "but they're going to do it in the best-smelling house in Tal Hae."

Ernie tried not to feel proud, but he couldn't help himself. The mouth-watering aroma of fresh loaves filled the Greenhouse, and all of his friends had commented on it. He brought a tray of sliced sourdough from the kitchen and set it beside a wheel of ripe yellow cheese on the living room table.

"No eating until the guests arrive," he told no one in particular.

At Tor's suggestion, they had used the Icebox for a roasted and sugar-glazed turkey stuffed with spiced breadcrumbs, a huge double-layered frosted cake decorated with sugar-crowns, and as many pears soaked in red wine as would come out of the magic box in one go.

"King Crunard never visited our castle," Tor said, "but he did send dignitaries, and we often received nobles from the large islands. Those were all my father's favorites to have served at fancy dinners. They should be good enough for whoever shows up today."

It wasn't long after that the first guest arrived: Ozella, clomping down the stairs from the secret room. Ernie only then remembered Ozella's rejection of his bread at their last meeting, and quickly thought about the items on the menu via-a-vis the old wizard's teeth.

"I hope she likes wine-soaked pears," he muttered.

"Don't tell me I'm first!" Ozella looked around the living room in disapproval, as Tor and Kibi finished hauling more chairs down from the upper floor. "It's nearly noon already!"

She seemed about to say more but was interrupted by a knock on the door. Eddings was standing at the ready; he opened the door and bowed low.

"Please, enter," he said formally. "All three of you."

In stepped a broad-shouldered woman, middle-aged, with short black hair and commanding eyes. She was followed by two tall men in boiled leather armor reinforced with metal strips. Both had swords at their sides, and they looked around with open suspicion.

Eddings nodded politely. "Please, if you would be so kind as to leave your weapons in the foyer."

The guards stared back at Eddings, but the woman gave them a slight nod, and they unstrapped their sword belts.

"Who are you then?" Ozella asked loudly when the woman stepped into the living room.

The woman tilted her head slightly and smiled. "I am Duchess Terla of Nahalm. To whom do I have the honor of speaking?"

Ozella bobbed her head up and down, setting her goiter to wagging. "Ozella Westbrook, archmage. Sit down, Duchess, and relax a bit. As soon as everyone's here, we'll begin, but no one else seems to have decided the fate of the kingdom was worth showing up on time for."

Ernie stared at this exchange with his mouth open and saw from the corner of his eye that most of the others in Horn's Company were doing similarly. The duchess peered doubtfully at Ozella. She did not sit.

Another knock sounded at the door, and this time Eddings invited in a tall, angular woman in a sweeping red gown. Her long brown hair was loose and not well brushed. Around her neck hung a small ruby cube on a silver chain. It took a second for Ernie to realize it was a gaming die.

"High Priestess Irichan of Corilayna," Eddings called into the house.

"May fortune favor us today and every day," Irichan said solemnly.

"We're gonna need it, missy," said Ozella with a chuckle.

After that the pace of the guests' arrival quickened, several showing up at once. It didn't take long for Ernie to become numb to the presence of so many powerful and important people. Duke Nigel of Harkran, old and bony, came in chatting animatedly with Roaq, the rotund but high-spirited High Priest of Pikon whose long robe showed the wheat-sheaf symbol of his church. Soon after came a towering man in what must have been ceremonial armor. He had glossy black hair and a drooping black moustache. Eddings announced him as Dalesandro, and his breastplate showed a red gauntlet over a heraldic shield: the sigil of the Stormknights of Werthis.

"Who's in charge here?" Dalesandro demanded. "I'm delaying my journey to Verdshane for this. We should begin."

Ozella sighed and removed her feet from the ottoman. She was the only one in the room sitting down. "I am, and yes, we should. But we're waiting on some stragglers."

Those "stragglers" turned out to include high-ranking priests of Delioch and Brechen, two women and a man dressed in what Tor whispered were high-ranking military uniforms, and, to Ernie's knee-knocking astonishment...

"His Royal Majesty, King Crunard IV of Charagan." Eddings, to his credit, did not sound as overawed as Ernie felt. Two more guards, their weapons and demeanor similar to those who attended Duchess Terla, marched into the living room. Behind them strode a man who seemed in his sixties, with thinning gray hair and a heavy face creased with wrinkles. He was dressed expensively—a scarlet cloth surcoat over a silken shirt, embroidered breeches, a fancy blue oval-shaped felt hat— but without a robe, crown, or other adornments Ernie had always figured a king would flaunt. His Majesty swept a commanding gaze around the room, a frown tugging down the corners of his mouth.

Duchess Terla's guards dropped to their knees, but King Crunard waved them impatiently back to their feet. "No need for that. Since I'm not officially here and had to be smuggled in a merchant's carriage after an unannounced teleportation from the capital, I don't see any reason to stand on ceremony. Now, which of you are the wizards?"

"I am," said Ozella, who looked as impressed with the king as she might have with a street-sweeper. "But we're still waiting on Abernathy."

"Can we not start without him?" asked the king. "If things are as dire as your brief missives make them out to be?"

Ozella shook her head. "Best we don't, since he knows the most. Also this is his house. Not surprised he's late, though. Brilliant fellow, Abernathy, but hardly what you'd call punctual."

Ernie's mouth opened and words came out, much to his surprise. "Your Majesty, and, uh, other honored guests, we could all sit down to lunch while we wait. We've prepared what I hope is a suitable meal for people of your, uh, rank and stature."

King Crunard IV, His Royal Majesty, the most powerful man in Charagan, turned to regard Ernie with penetrating brown eyes. "And who might you be, boy?"

Could be the turtle's nose. "Ernest Roundhill, Your Majesty." Ernie was amazed at the steadiness of his own voice. "I am a member of Horn's Company, hired by Abernathy some months ago to assist him in his work."

"Hmm." The king seemed to find that troubling. He gestured to where Tor, Dranko, Morningstar, and Kibi stood bunched together near the fireplace. "And are those people also members of this company?"

"Yes, Your Majesty. There is also Aravia, a wizard, and Ivellios, a swordsman, but he…" Ernie trailed off, realizing he was on even less sure footing than before. He looked at Ozella, who shrugged at him.

"He what?" asked the king.

"He's gone missing," said Ernie. Was he supposed to keep secrets from the king? He couldn't imagine why, but he also didn't feel it was his place to share Aravia's guesses. Where was she, anyway?

The king glanced at the Duchess Terla, then turned to Ozella. "Abernathy hired a mercenary company? I know you wizards enjoy a certain latitude, but if you needed people…" He gestured to the various members of the company. "We could have hired him experienced men and women, skilled in whatever Abernathy needed."

"They aren't mercenaries." Abernathy spoke from the foyer, having arrived at the bottom of the stairs. "And it is because of them that we have a chance of seeing the far side of our current crisis with your kingdom intact. I'll thank Your Majesty not to impugn their abilities."

King Crunard crossed his arms and looked at Abernathy with an expression that told everyone present he was unused to rebukes, however mild.

"Abernathy," said Duke Nigel, "we have been putting a great deal of faith in your prediction of an impending invasion. This meeting required an inordinate amount of logistical maneuvering, not to mention—"

"Not to mention there already *is* an invasion," Dalesandro interrupted. "I shouldn't have to remind anyone here that we are barely holding our own against an incursion of foreigners on the Balani. Charagan lacks the naval forces to take the small beaches near the tip of the peninsula, and the enemy never seems to lack for reinforcements. Our Stormknights have held the front, but if we're talking about committing more troops, I'd advise we send them to where we're actually engaged with enemy soldiers."

"Exactly," said King Crunard. "Abernathy, I have already dispatched five hundred soldiers to Verdshane from Minok and Tal Killip, in addition to several hundred support personnel, despite an apparent lack of enemy for them to fight. And what reports we have received indicate a severe morale problem wherein our people feel an unnatural reluctance to approach the area you say is where the enemy is most likely to appear."

"Ah, that." Abernathy looked thoughtful. "I suppose there's no point in maintaining an *aversion* zone, as long as it's made very clear to everyone not to approach the stasis field. We'll shut it down."

The woman in the fancy soldier's uniform, General Anapark, cleared her throat in overly conspicuous fashion. "On the topic of spells, I understand that you archmagi are exceptionally powerful. Can you come to Verdshane yourselves and improve our tactical position by means of your wizardry? Or simply blast the enemy with fire and lightning when they arrive?"

"No," said Ozella.

The woman blinked, obviously taken aback. "Why not?"

"Because we're busy!" Ozella snapped. "We've reached the point where if any of the five of us leave our towers, the spells we maintain to keep Naradawk out will fail, and your invasion will start today."

High Priest Roaq gave Ozella a puzzled look. "But you're not in your tower now."

"I've enchanted the Greenhouse to serve as a sort of honorary tower, so that we could have meetings like this," said Abernathy. "But it was a great bother that I cannot repeat." He looked slowly around the living room. "I trust Aravia is not here because she is studying the Crosser's Maze?"

"That's right," said Tor. "That's about all she does these days, other than eat and sleep."

"Good, good," said Abernathy. "Please make sure to share with her everything that is said today."

"I think Ernest is correct," Ozella said abruptly, and Ernie experienced a moment of confused panic. "We should eat. I'm hungry and haven't had many decent meals these past few decades. We can keep talking over lunch." Without waiting to see if anyone agreed, she lurched forward out of her chair and tottered into the dining room.

Ernie nearly followed on her heels, eager to make sure the table was set properly, but realized that perhaps he ought to let the king of Charagan go first. Thank goodness that Eddings was already there, straightening utensils and pouring wine.

There were chairs enough for everyone, though the table was undersized for such a large gathering. As such, most of Horn's Company gathered along one wall, plates balanced on laps, leaving the table to the luminaries. The guards who arrived with the king and the duchess stood behind their charges, seemingly willing to forgo the feast without complaint. Ernie privately vowed to sneak them bread if the opportunity arose.

King Crunard nodded approvingly at the banquet and seated himself at the head of the table. The duchess of Nahalm and duke of Harkran took places to either side of their sovereign, and the rest filled in the chairs. For a few short minutes the dining room filled with sounds of clanking dishware, requests to pass platters, and quiet exclamations of surprise at the quality of the food. Ernie found it disconcerting to see the most important people in the kingdom acting so informally, talking and eating and interacting no differently than when Ernie's parents invited the Thorn family over for dinner.

He leaned to his left and whispered to Tor. "Why is everyone so calm? All these nobles and priests and generals must have been told *something* about Naradawk."

"Maybe it's just that they have faith in the archmagi," Tor whispered back. "Or the gods. Or both."

Ernie shook his head. More likely it was simply that people, however powerful, couldn't fully appreciate a danger without evidence or proof.

Duke Nigel set down his fork and cleared his throat. "Abernathy. Ozella. I think the time has come for you to tell us—"

A loud, thumping knock came from the foyer. Eddings smoothly exited the dining room. Ernie heard the sound of the door and some quiet discussion.

"That would be Rosset Finch," said King Crunard, a fleeting twinge of worry passing across his royal countenance. "He told me he might be joining us."

"Who is Rosset Finch?" asked the duchess.

Footsteps approached, and a tall figure stepped into the dining room. Ernie bit back a gasp of surprise; he knew this man! He was much older than the one time Ernie had seen him before, but his face had the same shape, the same angles, even the same short beard, though now it was graying in patches. His tabard displayed two crossed blades across the front, and over his broad shoulders was draped a bright silver cloak.

Ernie was not the only one to recognize the man; his friends stared with open mouths. Dranko stood and pointed.

"Hey, it's the guy who killed Grey Wolf's dad! What in the hells is he doing here?"

All heads swiveled to look at Dranko, whose eyes blazed with an anger Ernie had seldom seen.

Rosset turned gracefully to the king and gave a formal bow. "Your Majesty." Then he faced Dranko and gave a thin smile that wrinkled his face. "I am here for the only reason I go anywhere: to see that the Black Circle's designs are thwarted."

"Even if it means killing innocent people?" Dranko challenged.

Rosset inclined his head. "Of course. We take no joy when that is necessary, but many more innocents die when we fail to act."

This statement was met with silence around the room. Dranko still looked angry but said nothing more. Ozella's perpetual look of impish impatience hardened to a narrow-eyed stare.

"Sit down, Mr. Finch," she said, her voice flinty, matching her expression. "Have some lunch. We're just about to get to the point." She gestured to the remaining empty chair, between High Priestess Irichan and the Stormknight Dalesandro.

Rosset did not sit. He walked slowly to the chair at the head where King Crunard sat, glowering.

"Your Majesty," said Rosset, his voice smooth. "I'm sure I need not remind you of the Silversword Pact. We are most certainly here to discuss the machinations of the Black Circle, and therefore I humbly request to be given directorship at this gathering."

King Crunard's fist tightened around his fork, and the wrinkles of his face reshaped themselves slightly into an expression of displeasure, but he did not speak right away.

"My understanding," said Duchess Terla, "is that we are going to hear more detail about an impending invasion in the Greatwood. Why do you think the Black Circle is involved?"

Rosset acknowledged her with a brief nod. "Your Grace, I do not *think* the Black Circle is involved. I know it for a fact. I have gleaned auguries from our fragments of the Watcher's Kiss; it is the will of Uthol Inga that I am here."

Stormknight Dalesandro leapt to his feet, legs banging the table and setting the wine glasses swaying. "You worship the accursed Watcher? And you dare show your face? Who are you, to come in to this meeting and ask for directorship? You ought to be thrown in prison! And what is the Silversword Pact?"

"Sit down, Dalesandro." King Crunard let his fork clatter and waved wearily at the Stormknight. "Prosecute your religious feud later. But for the benefit of everyone here: Rosset is one of the few remaining members of an ancient order called the Silverswords, whose mandate—whose *royally bestowed* mandate—is to root out and destroy any living practitioners of the Black Circle religion, along with whatever designs they are engaged in. The Silversword Pact gives them unusual authority in matters where the Black Circle is concerned."

"Authority even over you, Your Majesty?" Roaq was aghast. "You are the king of Charagan!"

Ernie could hardly believe what he was hearing. The man who had stood among the murderers of Ivellios's father, and who would have killed Ivellios, was being given precedence over the king?

Rosset smiled in what Ernie took to be triumph. "Yes. And His Majesty has already agreed that this is a matter where I can rightfully invoke the Silversword Pact."

Stormknight Dalesandro did not sit down. His face reddened beneath his moustache, and he deliberately addressed the king, not the Silversword. "Your Majesty, this meeting is meant to address an imminent attack, with a strong implication that our Stormknights will be committed further to Charagan's defense. But we will not, under any conditions, place our men and women at the disposal of an accursed Utholite! I don't care what sort of agreement he made with the crown. The Church of Werthis will not compromise in this."

Rosset Finch ignored the outburst, except for flashing a tiny, mocking smile. "Abernathy, Ozella, I understand that you are under some significant time pressure. How long have we to discuss the difficulties facing Charagan at the moment?"

Abernathy glanced down at the ruby pendant that hung from his neck, the one Ernie knew could return the archmagi to their towers in an instant. But it was Ozella who answered.

"We don't know, exactly. The portal between Spira and Volpos is being maintained by the three remaining archmagi—Fylnia, Grawly, and Salk—along with Caranch, a fellow wizard and longtime associate. I believe they can hold things down for a few hours, but Caranch has told us this will be the last time he can lend his aid, without which it will be much more perilous for any of the five of us to leave off our work to attend dinner parties."

"A few hours should suffice," said Rosset. "Now, Ozella, or Abernathy, whichever of you wants to talk: Please explain the nature of the threat, as completely and specifically as you can."

"You mean like we were going to do anyway before you showed up late?" Ozella shook her head. "Fine. Abernathy, would you like to do the honors?"

Abernathy blinked a few times before shooting a final dark look at Rosset Finch. As Ernie looked around the room, no one appeared pleased to see Finch: not the archmagi, not the priests (especially Dalesandro), not the nobles, not King Crunard IV, and not the others in Horn's Company, all of whom had witnessed this man's compatriot strike down Ivellios's father in cold blood.

"Some hundreds of years ago," Abernathy began, "King Naloric the Just was transformed by means unknown into a creature now remembered as Naloric the Monstrous. Thereafter, Naloric committed such atrocities upon the kingdom that the dukes and duchesses rose up and—"

"Yes, I'm sure we're all familiar with the background," said Rosset. "Perhaps you should skip to the difficulties of the present day."

"You asked for completeness and specificity," said Abernathy, in an acid tone Ernie had not heard before from the old man. "But, as you wish. Naradawk Skewn, son of Naloric, is currently trapped on a world called Volpos. There is only one possible point of egress for him: a portal between Spira and Volpos at the one place where the fabric between the worlds is weakest. On Spira, that place is in the Greatwood, outside the village of Verdshane. We archmagi have been keeping that portal shut for centuries and have set a stasis field around it so that if something does cross over, it will be trapped.

"The difficulty of the present day, as you call it, is that Naradawk is breaking through, and the stasis field is failing. Already he has slipped a swarm of skellari through from Volpos, as well as a powerful lieutenant named Aktallian. Aktallian is responsible for conjuring the Ventifact Colossus that wiped out Sand's Edge and completing the ritual that allows the Delfirians to invade the Balani. Now he is harassing our dreams during our short periods of rest, which makes maintaining our wards more difficult."

Rosset steepled his fingers in front of his face. "And how long will it be before your wards fail entirely and Naradawk breaks free?"

"Ah. We don't know exactly, but as things stand now, perhaps a week. Ten or eleven days if Morningstar can defeat Aktallian."

A murmur of concerned voices rippled around the dining room.

Morningstar gasped. "A week! But only days ago you said it was closer to three weeks!"

"We did," said Ozella. "And that was our best guess. But something has shifted in the enemy's designs, and things have sped up a little. One of the primary reasons for us calling this meeting was specifically to tell you that. If your Ellish dreamers are going to do something about Aktallian, you'll have to do it sooner than we anticipated."

Rosset looked curiously at Morningstar. "What is your name, Ellish sister?"

"Morningstar of Ell."

"Morningstar, please enlighten me. How did you come to be involved in the archmagi's efforts? And what exactly is your part in it?"

Morningstar looked over at Abernathy, who nodded at her.

"There's nothing secret about what you're doing," said the old wizard. "Remember that we're all on the same side here."

Nonetheless, Morningstar kept her answer brief. She gave an account of Abernathy's original summons, followed by an explanation of how Aktallian lurked somewhere in the fabric of dreams, causing his mischief to the archmagi. She told Rosset about her gathering of sisters whom she trained to fight him, though without any mention of her avatar or elevated status in the eyes of Ell.

"At Abernathy's request," she finished, "we have been waiting as long as possible before assaulting Aktallian, so as to hone our abilities as much as possible."

Rosset stared at her for a long moment after she had finished, while the other guests fidgeted. "Thank you, Morningstar of Ell," he said at last. "Abernathy, if I understand things rightly, Morningstar here can buy you three or four days at most. That will give us more time to move troops to Verdshane, but as we all know, Naradawk will not likely be troubled by an army of any size."

"It still matters," said Abernathy, a bit testily. "As part of maintaining our wards upon the portal, we have made it arcanistically inverse. That means that once it begins to fail in earnest, it will hedge out the most powerful arcane entities the longest."

"In other words," said Ozella, "if Naradawk has an army of his own, which seems likely, he will be able to send ordinary soldiers through before he can escape himself."

"And do you know how many troops Naradawk has at his command?" asked Rosset.

Ozella shrugged. "Nope. Could be five, could be fifty thousand. Best prepare for the worst, I'd say."

"And how much longer will it take Naradawk to escape, once the portal is opened to his lowliest foot soldiers?"

"Can't be sure," said Ozella. "I'd be surprised if it was more than a day or two."

Rosset frowned at her. "Then I still do not see that it matters much. In a week, perhaps a few days more, Naradawk Skewn will push his forces into Spira, and we will have no recourse but to fight a pointless battle for 'a day or two' until Naradawk arrives himself."

"Of course we have recourse!" Everyone turned to look at Tor, speaking for the first time since the Silversword's arrival. His hands were balled into fists. "Aravia will figure out how to use the Crosser's Maze and stop Naradawk for good!"

Rosset swiveled his head to stare at Tor, the same cool, unnerving look he had given Morningstar. "I see there are several people here who are not nobles, or clergymen, or high ranking members of the kingdom's military. I assume these are the others of Abernathy's summonees?"

"That's right," Abernathy said quietly.

The Silversword swept his gaze around the room, lingering on each member of Horn's Company. When it was Ernie's turn, he felt his cheeks flush for no good reason. "There is obviously some history of this group which I am missing," said Rosset. "I wish to hear it. All of it. Who is Aravia? Where is she?"

"Learning how to use the Crosser's Maze, as Tor intimated," said Abernathy. "A pursuit I suggest we allow her to continue since its use is our best hope to prevent Naradawk's escape."

"I'm sure she can spare some time for a gathering of such profound import," said Rosset, smiling. "Obviously the Crosser's Maze is something about which I should be informed. Please, will someone fetch her?"

"I don't think that—" Abernathy began, but Rosset banged his hand down on the table, causing a chorus of clinks among the plates and silverware. It seemed to shock everyone else in the room; the man had been so calm. "Fetch. Her. I will want the entire history of Abernathy's mysterious team, and will want to question each of its members. The Black Circle is bound up with these people, I can feel it. Since by your own admission time is precious, I suggest Aravia present herself to this council as soon as possible."

"I'll get her," said Tor. "Sometimes it takes a few minutes for her to notice I'm shaking her." The sound of his hurried footsteps filled an uncomfortable silence. Rosset adopted a thoughtful expression and turned to Dranko.

"Who is Grey Wolf?" he asked. "And why do you believe I killed his father?"

Dranko gave Rosset a big tusky grin. "Technically it wasn't you, it was your boss, but you were holding his old man steady, so I'd say you share some responsibility. I believe you Silverswords killed his father because I saw you do it. And you know who Grey Wolf is, though you're more familiar with his real name, Ivellios Forrester. He's been with us since the beginning."

"That is a lie." Rosset turned his icy gaze on Dranko. "Ivellios and Ivos Forrester are dead. I watched them die."

Ernie glanced around the room. The entire assemblage was captivated.

"I know what you saw," said Dranko. "You saw Orleah hack their heads off, and then you were attacked by Sharshun. You and the other Silverswords valiantly fought them off, and you were the only survivor, though you took a bolt in the leg and another in the shoulder. How am I doing? Pretty close?"

The color drained from Rosset's face. "How—?"

Dranko's grin widened. Gods, but he loved winding people up. "But here's the kicker. That's not actually what happened. The Sharshun attacked after you had killed Ivos but *before* you could kill his son. They killed the rest of your Silverswords but left you alive, then changed your memory so that you believed Ivellios was dead. You're an expert in the Black Circle, so I'm sure you know that's something they can do."

Rosset visibly struggled to regain his composure, which took him a few seconds. "That is an extraordinary claim. I assume you can provide some proof that Ivellios still lives? And how did you witness this?"

Dranko scratched his nose and appeared to ponder. "That's a tough question to answer. We saw it in a place called the Crosser's Maze. An old fellow named Solomea showed us."

"And where is Ivellios now?"

"Aravia thinks he's been kidnapped by the Black Circle. Otherwise we'd make introductions, and you could disbelieve his existence to his face. But maybe

Abernathy could convince you?"

Rosset's head snapped to look at Abernathy, who sighed.

"When I summoned my team," he said, "one of those was Ivellios Forrester. He was a man in his late thirties or early forties, rugged, black hair with some gray. He preferred to be called Grey Wolf."

"And that is the same Ivellios I remember watching die?" Rosset challenged.

"I couldn't be sure," said Abernathy, "but I am certain Dranko here is not lying about what he saw."

"You don't properly understand what the Black Circle is capable of," said Rosset, his voice losing its edge of uncertainty. He straightened his shirt and smiled grimly. "They could make you see what they wanted you to see. The man who showed you this vision could be one of them. I find it more likely that your collective memories have been tampered with than those of a Silversword."

Footsteps once more echoed on the stairs. Aravia walked slowly into the dining room, her hair mussed, dark circles like bruises beneath her eyes. Did Ernie imagine it, or were her eyes themselves darker than normal? From talking with Tor, Ernie knew Aravia hadn't gotten much honest sleep in the past three days. Tor was at her elbow, shadowing Aravia as though she might topple at any moment, and he'd have to catch her.

"This is Aravia?" asked Rosset.

Aravia looked dreamily at the Silversword. "I am. Tor told me you needed to speak with me." Slowly she looked around the table, taking in the unusual collection of guests. "Are we having a dinner party? This hardly seems the time."

"Aravia," said Rosset, "I understand you are studying a device called the Crosser's Maze that you believe can prevent Naradawk Skewn's invasion. Is that true?"

Aravia looked over at Abernathy before answering; the old wizard gave a slight nod.

"Yes," Aravia said. "Or, I was. But then you demanded that Tor interrupt me." Her gaze sharpened as she looked back at him. "I know you," she said, her voice strengthening. "You are one of Orleah Farthing's Silverswords who killed Ivellios's father. The one whom the Sharshun spared. The one whose memory they were going to rewrite."

This time Rosset looked more nettled than shocked. He pursed his lips, then spoke to Abernathy. "Why, exactly, did you summon these people?" He gestured broadly to Horn's Company.

Abernathy shifted in his chair, straightening himself. "As you know, we archmagi cannot spare any time outside of our towers, this house excepted. I realized I needed a team that could investigate and deal with various threats that beset Charagan. These are the people I summoned."

"And why, exactly, did you summon *these* people in particular?"

Ernie had wondered the same thing since the beginning; they all had. Abernathy had never given them a clear answer. Would he give one to Rosset Finch?

"I cast a spell, and the spell chose them." He held up a hand to forestall Rosset's next question. "I cannot speak about the specifics of the spell. I'm sorry."

Rosset gave a lopsided smile. "And your spell just happened to summon, among others, Ivellios Forrester, the last living descendant of Moirel Stoneshaper, the man destined to bring about Naradawk's escape?"

"That is correct," said Abernathy.

Rosset took a deep breath and licked his lips. "You seven, stand along the wall together please, so I can observe you all at once."

Step moved to join the others, but Aravia stayed where she was. "This delay is foolish," she said. "I ought to return to my studies."

"Aravia," said King Crunard, "I am your sovereign, and I must command you to indulge Rosset in this matter."

From the king's vexed tone, Ernie guessed that His Majesty agreed with Aravia's opinion. Aravia sighed and strode to the wall.

"Now," said Rosset, flexing his fingers in a way Ernie found unsettling, "I want you to start at the beginning, when Abernathy summoned you. Broad strokes are fine; I'll ask you for details when I want them."

"Before you start," said Ozella loudly, "we need to take care of a few details. If and when Salk and the others need us back, it will be without warning, and as this will be the last time we can speak before Naradawk either invades or doesn't, I want to make certain we get the important items out of the way."

She produced a necklace from the folds of her voluminous clothing, a slender silver chain with a small green gem. "Morningstar, wear this. If it doesn't sound an alarm, wait no longer than one week from today before attacking Aktallian."

Morningstar walked to the old woman's chair and took the chain. "And what if it does sound an alarm?"

"Then you'll have about two hours," Ozella said with a chuckle. But she sobered up quickly and added, "That Aktallian fellow isn't content anymore with assailing our dreams during our short shifts of sleep. He's giving us distracting daydreams too, making it harder to concentrate on Naradawk's portal while we're awake. That's part of why the timetable already moved up, and why it wouldn't surprise me if 'a week' turns out to be optimistic. Make sure your sisters can be gathered up at a moment's notice."

Morningstar nodded and placed the chain around her neck.

"As for the rest," said Abernathy, "Naradawk has been able to bypass the stasis field for a few seconds at a time, but we see no sign that he can bring it down altogether. That should make it very difficult for him and his armies to launch their attack. They'd have to pour out through a narrow bottleneck with a sturdy cork. It would be wise to assume Naradawk has figured out some plan to mitigate our defenses, but his most likely avenue of attack is directly out of the portal itself."

One of the women in military dress stood from the table, her chair scraping the stone floor. "We've already begun preparations, clearing out the woods, building fortifications, digging trenches. The area around your portal will be covered by archers. We intend to make the immediate vicinity a killing ground. I hope you wizards are right about the enemy's likely deployment."

"Understand," said Abernathy, "that in ideal circumstances, all of your preparations will be for nothing. If Aravia is able to master the Crosser's Maze in time, she can seal the portal and prevent even a flea from hopping through it. But if she needs more time, we must do everything in our collective power to buy it for her."

Ernie looked over at Aravia, along with everyone else in the room.

"I am learning as quickly as I can," said Aravia, "but even for me the maze is not something easily mastered."

"Aravia," King Crunard said gently. Ernie tried not to stare. Despite the harrowing implications of this gathering, what most overwhelmed him was the king's presence *in his dining room.*

"Please explain, briefly, for my benefit and for those others present, what the Crosser's Maze is and how you intend to use it to save Charagan."

Ernie bit his own lip to stifle a laugh. Briefly explain the Crosser's Maze?

"Of course, Your Majesty," said Aravia. "The Crosser's Maze is a complex enchanted artifact embedded in my brain. I intend to use it to erase the portal that connects Spira and Volpos, thus making it impossible for Naradawk to escape."

I stand corrected, thought Ernie.

"And can you learn its use well enough in a week?" the king pressed.

"Possibly, Your Majesty," said Aravia. "I would be lying if I said it was a certainty. But my intellect is well suited to the task, and I am applying myself with fervor."

"Thank you, Aravia. The kingdom appreciates your service."

"Yes. Well," said Rosset. His words were clipped, and he graced the room with a thin-lipped smile, as if all of this business with the portal was a distracting sidelight. "If that covers the salient points of your business, I'd like to get on with my questions for Abernathy's servants."

At first Rosset seemed to choose from among them at random, asking for the story of their adventures in Abernathy's service. Tor began, recounting their ill-fated journey to Verdshane and Mrs. Horn's death from a gopher-bug bite. Rosset showed no interest in the details of the battle, but he held up his hand when Tor had described their discovery of the stasis field, and Tor's melee afterward against the Sharshun.

"Did you know, any of you, the importance of the stasis field when you went to inspect it?"

Ernie shook his head along with the others.

Rosset made a noise of disgust. "Abernathy, do I understand rightly that you summoned these people and immediately sent them to the most magically sensitive area in the kingdom without telling them why?" He glanced at King Crunard with an expression that hinted he expected a sign of disapproval from the sovereign, or at least commiseration, but the king was as stoic as a block of granite.

"I did not have time to brief my team as thoroughly as I would have liked," said Abernathy, "but knowing the state of the stasis field was extremely important to us. I'm not certain you understand the constant strain we are under to keep the portal sealed. It was risky for me to have taken even what time I did to send them on their errand."

"So you took the risk to summon them in the first place," said Rosset, "these untried strangers whom you hardly knew, and then you then sent them into deadly danger, to blunder around your carefully constructed magical safeguards."

"Yes. I suppose so," said Abernathy. The old wizard spoke in a quiet voice, even-keeled, not rising to Rosset's insinuations. He looked like a man bracing against a storm.

"As for the Sharshun," said Rosset, "did you, Tor, know what you fought against?"

"Not at the time," said Tor cheerfully, "but Abernathy has since told us that the Sharshun are servants of Naradawk."

"Let me tell you something about the Sharshun," said Rosset. "They are servants, first and foremost, of the Black Circle. They are literally the product of corruption. Whatever foul substance infected King Naloric the Just, that same substance was forced into his most devoted followers. We don't know what it was, or if any more of it exists on Spira, but the Silverswords believe that the corruption comes from something physical. It gives the Sharshun extraordinary resilience and longevity.

"Huh," said Tor. "Good thing then that we killed four of them."

Rosset blinked. "You've…you've killed four Sharshun?"

"Not me personally," said Tor. "I only killed one of them. Kibi here blasted the other three. It would be more if Ernie had killed that other one a few days ago, but he did manage to chop its arm off. Oh, and if you count Lapis as dead, that would make five." He paused. "And I'm forgetting the one that killed himself the first time we visited the Mirrors. That would make half a dozen."

The Silversword stared a moment longer, eyes especially wide, his face twitching slightly as though he struggled to regain his composure. Ernie wanted to cheer. Rosset was a bully, and Ernie always enjoyed seeing bullies being put in their place. But his heart sank as Rosset turned to look at him, as if he sensed (and disapproved of) Ernie's glee.

"What then? I assume you returned to Tal Hae to tell Abernathy what you discovered. Ernest, what errand did he set for you next?"

Ernie forced himself to look Rosset dead in the eye and explained about Dranko's letter from Praska, the one that prompted Abernathy to send them to find out what the Black Circle was digging up in the Mouth of Nahalm. To Ernie's surprise, Rosset nodded approvingly throughout the account, and didn't comment again until Dranko had taken over the narrative to describe his harrowing trip to the "floating island."

"This Sharshun, Lapis, had coordinated with the church of Delioch to excavate a blood gargoyle?" Rosset asked.

"Not the whole church," said Dranko defensively. "Mokad and a few others had infiltrated the church, embezzling funds. They've all gone now, though. Once the invasion started, the Black Circle bastards scarpered off in the night."

"Are you certain of that?" asked Rosset.

Dranko paused. "No, of course not. But thanks to my friend Praska, the church knows about what happened and is on the alert for cultists. I'd say the chances are pretty slim that they're still skulking around. Oh, and Lapis was working for someone she called the Sage, who was definitely not part of the Church of Delioch."

"And what do you know about the Sage?" pressed Rosset.

"The Sage is Parthol Runecarver," said Aravia.

The room went quiet.

Abernathy and Ozella exchanged glances.

"Parthol Runecarver is long dead," said King Crunard slowly. "And history tells us he died a hero."

"Aravia," said Abernathy softly, "are you certain? How do you know?"

"Solomea told me," said Aravia. "Before he died, he asked me if I had a last question for him. It seemed prudent to know more about the person behind the Black Circle's scheming, so I asked him, 'Who is the Sage?' He told me he is Parthol Runecarver."

The man in military dress, who'd been announced as General Largent, glanced at General Anapark next to him and cleared his throat. "Who is Parthol Runecarver?"

Ozella gave the man an incredulous look. "Parthol was an archmage of the previous generation. Probably the most powerful and knowledgeable wizard who ever lived, though you could make a good case for Alander. It was Parthol who agitated for the creation of the Spire in the first place, an organization to fight back against Naloric Skewn. When Naloric was banished to Volpos, it was Parthol who gave him the final shove. And when Naloric broke out a year later, it was Parthol, along with Typier and Alander, who used their magic to kill the bastard. But all three of them died in the attack and for hundreds of years have been counted among the great heroes of the kingdom. At least, General Largent, among those of us who know our history."

Rosset Finch gave a little laugh. "I think Solomea was mistaken, Aravia. Or perhaps the Sage is someone who has taken on Parthol's name in mockery. But let us put that aside for now and continue where—"

"I think we need to take the possibility seriously," said Abernathy. "Aravia, I presume this is the same Solomea who showed you the Silverswords' attack on Ivellios's family?"

"Yes. I recall exactly what he said: 'The Sage is a memory, a remnant of a past age. The Sage is the founder of the Spire. The Sage is Parthol Runecarver.' I have a theory, based on what Solomea told me, that Parthol's plan is to assist with Naradawk's escape, then sit back as Naradawk wars against the kingdom's forces. Parthol hopes the victor of that war will be sufficiently weakened that he can in turn gain control of Charagan for himself."

"If Parthol has been alive all this time," said the king, looking pointedly at Abernathy and Ozella, "could he have kept himself hidden from you?"

"Oh, easily," said Ozella. "We've been a bit preoccupied. He could have built himself a gartine cage somewhere to extend his lifespan." She looked at Abernathy. "I don't see how it changes anything, though. If Parthol decides to spring out of nowhere at the last minute and throw his powers behind the Black Circle, we'll be in the same place as if Naradawk escapes. Which is to say, utterly without hope. And even if we could devise a strategy to counter Parthol's emergence, we certainly don't have time for that now. This is taking too long as it is."

She turned back to Rosset Finch. "Let's get back to your pointless interrogation. Though perhaps it would speed things up if you let Abernathy's agents tell the whole story, and ask your questions at the end."

Rosset gave the old woman a withering look, but after a second's pause he nodded agreement. "Fine." He waved at the assembled members of Horn's Company. "Continue."

It took a couple more hours, but they got through the whole thing, a story punctuated by gasps of astonishment from all those present. The truth about how the Ventifact Colossus had died was known to very few, and even though Ernie kept the tale of his carpet-bound acrobatics as brief as possible, it was the only moment that elicited a spoken reaction. Irichan, high priestess of Corilayna, had remarked, "Truly you are blessed by the goddess of fortune."

When the tale was done, finished by Kibi standing nervously, hands behind his back, recounting their recent trip to the Mirrors with an embarrassingly heroic-sounding account of Ernie's battle with the Sharshun, the room fell silent. Rosset had listened to the final hour with a statue-like rigidity, only an occasional contraction of his jaw muscles betraying any emotion.

Now he flexed his fingers again and rubbed together the thumbs and forefingers of both hands.

"Incredible," he said at last. "Astonishing. Your adventures strain credulity to the breaking point."

"Every word we said was true!" Tor replied hotly. "I don't care what—"

Rosset held up a hand and inclined his head slightly. "I did not say I don't believe you. But I have many questions."

"Best get on with them, then," said Ozella. "Salk's a clever fellow, and Caranch knows some tricky enchantments, but who knows how much longer they can hold down the fort?"

Rosset gave her a little mocking bow, then turned his attention back to Horn's Company. Ernie's feet ached from standing so long.

"There are many things about your account that trouble me," said Rosset. "And it is clear that the Black Circle's designs have progressed to a dangerous degree. Alas that my order has become so thin." He sighed deeply. "Kibilhathur."

"Yes?"

"We have long known that the Sharshun have sought the Eyes of Moirel, though to this day we are not sure why. Now you say there are two of them in the basement of this very house, that they cannot be reliably contained, and that they are capable not only of self-motion, but of embedding themselves into a man's eye sockets."

Ernie couldn't stop himself from glancing at Eddings, who stood at the dining room door, translucent blindfold over his eyes.

"You obviously have some affinity toward them," Rosset said to Kibi. "But have you ever considered that they were created by servants of the Black Circle and could be deceiving you at every turn?"

"They was right 'bout the Ventifact Colossus," said Kibi, "and the purple one knocked out four Sharshun, killed Sagiro Emberleaf, and kept itself outta enemy hands."

Rosset shook his head in a way Ernie found condescending. "All of which led you into a course of action that resulted in the ruin of a major city, along with the completion of a Delfirian ritual and subsequent invasion of our kingdom. An invasion, I might add, that is most inconveniently drawing kingdom soldiers away from Verdshane. And now you have two Eyes here inside Abernathy's sanctuary. Perhaps they find this the most useful place to advance the agenda of their creator."

"Guess that's possible," said Kibi, scratching his chin beneath his beard. "Doubt it, though. They don't feel evil to me, if you know what I'm sayin'."

"I'm certain I don't," said Rosset dryly. "Should you be inclined to use them again, I urge extreme caution—though given how you have arrived at your current situation, I doubt that caution is in your nature." He moved his gaze to Aravia. "Your part in your group's adventures is the strangest, no doubt. I will accept that you were drawn into a city inside a bottle, and there you acquired the Crosser's Maze, which now resides inside your brain. But that is not the part I find dumbfounding." He looked momentarily at the ceiling as if he couldn't believe what he was about to say. "After all was done, and the Crosser's Maze acquired, you saw fit to bring the Sharshun Lapis into the Greenhouse also! You say she's here, right now, resting in a bedroom!"

"That is a misleading description," said Aravia. "She is in a semi-static catatonia, incapable of action. We only brought her because, as you have just been told, we were obliged to promise to bring her to Shreen the Fair once I have finished with the Crosser's Maze."

"And you're certain of that?" asked Rosset, voice dripping with skepticism. "Certain that Lapis is harmless? If I understand you correctly, her mind is currently inside your own, inside the maze, and Solomea did not share her disposition with you. She could be listening. She could be spying, at this very moment, and you cannot assure me otherwise."

"No, but—"

"By your own admission, Solomea led you to believe he had sided with Lapis right up until the moment he decided to give the maze to you instead. But there seems every possibility that they are in league with one another, and are playing a longer game that you do not understand."

Aravia shook her head. "I don't think—"

"And worst of all," said Rosset, his voice rising, "You brought *him* into the Greenhouse as well!" To Ernie's surprise, Rosset pointed at Certain Step. "An agent of a foreign god. A man who by your own admission betrayed you. A man who convinced you to let him join you with an opaque bit of prophecy he could have easily written himself. A man who still may be under the thrall of the Sharshun, witting or no, and who has been privy to all our plans and stratagems!" He paused in his rant to let out a long, slow breath. "If your goal was to turn the Greenhouse into an asset for the Black Circle, you've made an excellent start."

Ernie couldn't take it anymore. After all the hardships, the battles, the suffering, to stand there listening to this man—the man who had tried to kill Ivellios—was unbearable.

"You don't know what you're talking about!" he blurted. All eyes in the room fell upon him, but Ernie was beyond caring. "You weren't there. Abernathy needed us to get the Crosser's Maze, and we had a terrible time getting it, but we got it. If Solomea was truly working with Lapis, he would have given her the maze and we'd all still be in Calabash, brainless, and drooling, with *our* minds trapped inside *her* mind.

"As for Step, he's a good man. If not for him, Dranko would have been killed in Culud. You shouldn't discount Lapis's ability to muddle people's minds. After all, we watched a Sharshun do it to you."

Rosset Finch graced Ernie with a thin smile. "Ernest, you are hardly a person to question my judgment. As we have just heard, you have personally sworn both to return to Kivia to aid goblins and to give Shreen the Fair, priest to a Kivian god of monsters, an extremely powerful magical device. I appreciate that you had difficulties on your quest across a foreign land, but you made some extremely questionable choices along the way."

Ernie found his ire blunted; he had lamented those promises on more than one occasion. Rosset walked around the table until he stood only a yard away. "On the topic of goblins," he said, "would you mind holding up your hand? I would like to examine your mark."

Ernie felt no desire to cooperate but assented anyway. Rosset held his right hand by the wrist and bent to stare at it, bringing his head down until his nose practically grazed Ernie's skin. Was he smelling it? Ernie had examined the little red fist tattoo many times since acquiring it, wondering what it would do, how it would feel, if Irligg used it to summon him back to Kivia. Sometimes he fancied that it itched, but never badly enough to make him suspect it was a signal.

Rosset let the hand drop and nodded, as though satisfied it had given up a secret. But instead of asking more about it, he took a step back and asked, "Have you wondered why Lapis had been sent in the first place to find the Crosser's Maze?"

Ernie glanced down at the red mark, then returned his angry stare to Rosset. "We figured it was to stop us from getting it first."

Rosset picked up a water glass and took a sip. "Or, was it because the Black Circle needs it as part of their effort to free Naradawk? You believe that Aravia has control over it, but Lapis is in it with her! It would be a typical Black Circle ploy to let you take most of the chances, brave most of the danger, allow you to acquire the Crosser's Maze, and then take control of it themselves."

"But she is not in control of it," said Aravia calmly. "I am, and that is not going to change. I admit that you are more knowledgeable about the Black Circle than anyone here, but you do not understand the complexities of the Crosser's Maze. Not like I do."

"And again we come back to that opinion," said Rosset. "You've been its owner for less than a week. How much can you truly know?"

"I know enough," said Aravia. "And if we are talking of judgment, it seems to me that your single-minded focus on the Black Circle has clouded your own, making you see all things through a single-colored lens."

To Ernie's surprise, Rosset's expression softened at that comment, and he gave Aravia a small smile. "I only urge you to be cautious," Rosset said. "I can promise you that the Black Circle is planning something we do not currently anticipate."

He turned back to Ernie. "Ernest, you speak well, and your devotion to your friends is admirable. I confess, I am prepared to believe that I have been misled by the Black Circle regarding the death of Ivellios Forrester. In which case finding him is of paramount importance. Ivellios is the last living descendant of Moirel Stoneshaper, who was Naloric Skewn's greatest wizard. The Black Circle believes him a necessary part in their schemes. Until today I have believed that Moirel's line was eliminated, but now, it seems, we are left with only days to find him. I'm sorry to say that the divinatory methods of the Silverswords are not quick. Do you have any idea where he is?"

"Minok," said Morningstar.

Rosset stared at her. "How do you know?"

"It's complicated," said Morningstar. "Suffice to say, I learned it in a dream."

CHAPTER ELEVEN

O

I vellios listened to the sound of Naul's footsteps recede into the quiet of the Black Circle complex.

Mokad let him sleep on a real cot, albeit in a tiny stone cell with nothing else in it. The wooden door had been fitted with an exterior bolt. They didn't offer him a bedpan or bucket; he had to call for a guard if he needed to visit the privy overnight. "Overnight." He had lost all sense of day and night, but every time they let him have a long sleep, he needed it. He figured four or five days had passed since the Black Circle had abducted him.

It was a lucky break that the head of the cot was pressed up against the far wall of the cell. It meant he could tuck his pilfered fireplace poker in the tiny space between the cot and the wall, without having to move the cot and possibly arouse suspicion by doing so. No one would find the poker unless they searched the room. The fact that it hadn't been moved in two days suggested the cultists weren't bothering.

He had been increasingly cooperative since his previous act of ill-rewarded defiance. Mokad hadn't mentioned it, and Quia and Naul acted as though it had never happened. Yesterday he'd nodded sympathetically, even eagerly, as Mokad had again suggested how satisfying it would be to exact revenge upon the Silverswords. Essik hadn't spoken to him since that very first day—they hadn't been alone a single moment—though she'd given him knowing glances the few times they had passed in the halls. While he still held out hope that she was working on a plan to rescue him, it was taking too long. He needed to rescue himself.

Quietly, he rose from the cot and tiptoed to the door, the stone floor cold against his bare feet. Naul had given him a black shirt and pants to wear, but no shoes. Right outside would be the guard assigned to him, always a different bored-looking cultist standing at attention, holding a knife. Ivellios had toyed with the idea of overpowering the guard and stealing the knife, but he'd held out, hoping to procure a weapon of his own to make escape easier and quieter. Now he had one.

The guard made small noises: coughs, shuffling feet, the occasional quiet hum. But Ivellios strained his ears to hear beyond that one man, listening for the distant echoes and faint chants to subside, indicating the cultists had likely gone to sleep. Once enough time had passed without that background noise, Ivellios retrieved his poker—a stout iron rod almost two feet long—and slid it up his right sleeve.

He didn't have a clear plan—well, not beyond the part where he'd take out the guard. His knowledge of the maze of the corridors was not extensive, having been limited to his trips to and from the testing chamber, the privy, and Mokad's lab. But he just needed to find stairwells leading up until he reached the surface. Or the roof, he admitted; he'd been assuming this whole place was underground, but it was possible he'd been held captive in a large windowless building, maybe an old castle. Either way. He'd never find a way out of this benighted warren by staying in his room like a good little conspirator.

At the door, Ivellios pounded with his fist. "Hey! I need to use the privy!"

There came the sound of the bolt being drawn back, followed by the creak of the door as it swung into the cell. The guard was a tall, thin man with a moustache like a fuzzy caterpillar. His robe was too short, revealing the ragged cuffs of black trousers beneath. Ivellios hadn't seen him before.

"You know where it is, right?" the man asked. "You must know by now."

"It's that way, right?" Ivellios pointed to the left.

"No." The man turned to point down the passage to the right. "It's—"

Ivellios let the poker slide out of his sleeve, gripped the end, and swung hard at the man's temple. The cultist crumpled, sliding awkwardly against the wall by the door, coming to rest on the floor. Ivellios set down the poker, grabbed the man beneath the armpits, and dragged him into the cell. Back in the hall, he reclaimed his poker, slid it once more up his sleeve, then closed the bolt to trap the guard.

Now what? His room was in the middle of a short stone hall with stout wooden doors at either end. The door to the right led to the privy. Beyond that was a bend in the corridor, but he'd never been allowed far enough to see where it led. He'd never been taken in the direction of the door to the left.

He tried that one first, taking a moment to lean and listen at the crack. Somewhere in the far distance he thought he heard a voice, but it wasn't immediately beyond the door. He tried the handle, at the same time noticing a keyhole. Predictably, the door was locked.

Damn.

It'd be nice to have Dranko and his lock-picks at a moment like this, or Aravia with her *lockbuster* spell, but Ivellios had no skill with overcoming locks. Smashing the door down would make far too much noise. Maybe the guard had the key, but as frisking him might wake him, that would be a risk of last resort.

That left the corridor past the privy closet. Once more he listened at the door, then pushed it open, thankful it had no lock. A few feet down was the alcove containing the foul-smelling privy, and beyond that the hall took a left-hand turn. He stopped before the bend, listening intently. Hearing nothing save his own breath and beating heart, he stepped around the corner. Before him was a long hall with eight doors along its length, four on either side, and another door at the far end. It was lit, as was everywhere in this warren, with small enchanted globes affixed to the walls. On the one hand that was lucky, since the cultists had taken his light-rod. On the other hand, he'd be seen immediately by any cultists out walking the corridors.

Ivellios stopped at the first door on the left. No sound came from beyond. But as he reached for the handle, realization struck and he pulled his hand back. Instead he moved quietly from door to door, listening at each. From behind six of the eight came the varied sounds of snoring. These were bedrooms, the hallway of a dormitory. Their proximity to a privy was no accident. As he stood at the last door on the right, the breathy wheeze was interrupted by a brief coughing fit, followed by a stirring of blankets and shuffling footsteps.

Gods damn it!

If someone came out into the hallway there was no place for him to hide. For a heartbeat Ivellios stood paralyzed as surely as if Mokad had ensorcelled him, before he thought to try the door at the end of the hall only steps away. He moved quickly, grasped the door handle, but it was locked! With nothing else to do, he flattened himself against the wall on the same side as the door with the waking cultist, just as that door opened. An elderly man in a black nightshirt staggered out into the hall, immediately turning in the direction of the privy. Ivellios held his breath as the man shuffled away from him and turned the corner at the end. Only when Ivellios heard the door to the privy closet creak open and closed did he peel away from the wall. He tried the door one more time, thinking maybe it had just been stuck, not locked, but it held firm, and he dared not make a racket trying to open it.

Think, Ivellios.

Surely these people had keys that would open the locked door, and possibly other doors beyond. He could try one of the other rooms, one with a snorer, but it would be too dark to see.

Ivellios nipped into the room just vacated; the old cultist had left the door open, allowing light from the hallway to spill through. It was a little cell, not much bigger than his own, though the bed was nicer and there was a desk covered in papers. He spared a quick look at these, but they were filled with lines of meaningless numbers and symbols. The desk's single drawer contained a pile of quills, two bottles of ink, a blotter, and a small package of candies wrapped in wax paper. But no keys.

Ivellios spun slowly in place, eyes straining in the dim light. There weren't many places one could hide a key in here; he looked quickly under the bed but saw nothing. He groped with a sweeping hand but came away with only a handful of gritty dust mixed with crumbs. Had the old man taken his keys with him? That would be just his luck.

He stood, running a hand through his hair, listening for the sound of the privy door opening. Would he hear it from inside the little bedroom? Either way, he'd have to get out of this room, and soon. He turned to leave…and saw the key. Two keys, actually, on a little wooden hoop. He could have kicked himself. They hung on a wall peg just inside the door. As he lifted the ring, he heard the distant creak of the privy door. Ivellios wouldn't have time to use the keys before the man rounded the corner and spotted him, so he strode out to the hall, opened the bedroom door opposite, slipped in, and closed the door behind him.

The sounds of snoring came from a spot directly next to his knees. He willed himself not to move, not to breathe. If this second cultist woke up, Ivellios would have no choice but to kill him with the fireplace poker, as quickly and quietly as he could.

Out in the hall, slippers scraped against the stone floor, and then a door clicked shut. Ivellios allowed an additional minute to pass before leaving the second bedroom and returning to the locked door. The first key fit in the lock but didn't turn. The second key jammed for a second, but Ivellios applied a bit of strength and was rewarded with the clunk of a turning tumbler.

On the far side was another stretch of straight hall, again with eight doors, four on each side. He hurried to the end, unlocked the door there with the same key, and found himself in a small square room with two stairways leading up out of it, one to his right, the other to his left. On the wall directly in front of him was a painted black circle, as tall as himself, unmarked by numbers or lines.

Not having any reason to pick one staircase over the other, and finding it oddly discomfiting to stand in the regard of the annulet on the wall, he went left. The stairs spiraled upward for what felt like a single story, then opened out into a large circular chamber thirty feet across, its stone ceiling twenty feet above his head. Ivellios quickly ducked back into the stairwell, then peered carefully around the corner. No sound, no movement, no moonlighting cultists. The air smelled of chalk dust and ink. Nine small wooden desks were pushed up against the round wall, each heaped with yellow sheets of parchment. The center of the room was home to half a dozen freestanding slateboards on wooden frames, all of them covered in densely scrawled numbers, equations, odd symbols, and a variety of shapes. Between two of the slateboards stood an enormous abacus the size of a bed, its polished red stones pierced by smooth silver bars.

Gods, these people.

Other than the way he came in, there were two additional doors, each in its own little niche breaking up the curve of the wall. He crossed the room to the nearest of these, pausing at the abacus to slide two of the stones from one side of their crossbars to the other. He also stopped at one of the desks, slid out a densely written piece of parchment from the middle of a stack, and stuffed it into a pocket.

The door he chose was locked. No sound came from beyond it, and no light was visible around its edges. The key he'd been using wouldn't turn, but the second key popped the lock open. He pushed the door inward, wincing as it creaked.

Beyond it was a large office, similar to Mokad's though less organized. It was dominated by a round black table in its center, shiny with lacquer, with six stout wooden chairs around it. Before each chair was a small leather notebook, a quill, and a stoppered inkpot. But the centerpiece of the table drew Ivellios's eye—a small, thin book with a dark green leather cover. Its title was written in clear white letters.

Prophecies of the Pivot

Naul had called Ivellios the Pivot several times. Ivellios swiped the book from the table and briefly flipped through the first few pages, taking a few seconds to discover it was largely diagrams and numbers, with occasional lines of text that included plenty of unfamiliar words. But this seemed exactly the sort of thing that Abernathy, or even Aravia, could find useful. He returned to the round room with the desks.

A cultist stood by the abacus, staring at him. Ivellios let the iron poker drop from his sleeve into his hand and had taken two steps forward before he recognized the robed figure as Essik. She took a quick step back and held up her hand.

"What are you doing?" she said, quietly but urgently, before casting a quick glance toward the stairwell.

"Escaping," said Ivellios. "You were taking too long."

She shook her head, a quick, wide-eyed movement. "It's lucky I caught you when I did. I can tell from the fact you're alive that you haven't yet tried going that way." She pointed to the second door, the one Ivellios had been about to try next.

"Why?" he asked. "What's that way?"

"The exit, eventually," said Essik, "but that's also how to get to some of the more sensitive areas of the complex. The doors are trapped, and only a few of the senior clergy know the passwords to deactivate them. If getting you out of here was as easy as sneaking away during the sleep interval, don't you think we would have done that already?"

Ivellios narrowed his eyes. "How do I know you're telling the truth? You're a member of the Black Circle yourself, aren't you? Who are you, exactly, and why would you want to help me?"

She shook her head. "No, I'm not a…. Look, perhaps you'll believe me if I demonstrate. Come here."

Essik walked to the second door, the one she said led to the exit. Ivellios followed her. She took a key ring from her pocket, fitted a key to the lock, and turned. As the door swung open, she kept her hands clear of the threshold. Beyond was a dark open space; the light from the desk room didn't reveal any features or details.

She stepped back behind Ivellios. "Don't go in. Put your iron rod through the doorway, but keep your hand on this side."

Ivellios did as Essik suggested. The end of the poker immediately glowed red, as though he had thrust it into the hottest part of a roaring fire. Smoke poured off the tip. Inside of five heartbeats, the final six inches of the rod had gone from red to white, and the section Ivellios still held had grown uncomfortably hot. He hastily drew back the poker, after which its handle cooled to iron gray.

"That would have been you," Essik said. "And that's only the first safeguard."

Ivellios swore softly. "I suppose I should thank you."

Essik stared at him a moment. "How did you get this far? What happened to the guard outside your room?"

Ivellios held up the poker. "Clocked him on the head and locked him in my cell. Pretty sure I didn't kill him. He may be awake by now."

Essik raised a hand to her face and rubbed the bridge of her nose. "That's going to make things difficult." She glanced down at Ivellios's other hand. "What is that?"

Ivellios held up the book, *Prophecies of the Pivot*. "I found it in that office over there. Seemed important, so I thought I'd take it with me."

"You have to put it back!" said Essik. "That's one of their most important books. They'll realize a copy's gone missing and tear this place apart looking for it."

Ivellios didn't move. "Can't you show me another way out of here?"

Essik shook her head. "There are many more locked doors, magical wards, and bottlenecks watched by armed guards between here and freedom. I am still figuring out how we'll get through them."

Ivellios cursed silently. "What do you suggest?"

"Return to your room," she said. "I'll have to take some chances, cast some spells to muddy the mind of your door guard, but I'm already risking a great deal. I'll think of something. In the meantime, let me keep working on our escape plan. Play along with Mokad. Throw off any suspicion that we're planning to free you. Keep observing everything you can, so you'll have information for the Spire when you get out."

Ivellios sighed and turned toward the office, but Essik whispered after him.

"Wait! I have an idea."

"What?" Ivellios snapped, even knowing he shouldn't be upset with Essik. She'd saved his life, after all. But gods, what a disaster this whole escape was turning out to be.

"I want you to read the book, one page at a time."

"It's gibberish to me," he told her. "What's the point?"

"Just stare at each page for about ten seconds, then move to the next. I'm going to cast a spell upon you while you do."

Ivellios tensed. "Why? What will it do?"

Essik sighed. "It will help you recall what you've seen, later. Just trust me."

Ivellios shook his head but assented. He flipped open the book and examined the first page, an annulet surrounded by odd glyphs. Beside him, he heard Essik begin to chant. The entire book was only a dozen pages, and the process was finished in two minutes.

Essik shook out her fingers. "When you return to your wizards, tell them to cast a spell upon you called *prepared recall.* I'm sure at least one of them will know it. That will allow you to call up perfect images of what you've just seen, which you can describe for them or draw yourself. I imagine it will be vital for them to put a stop to the Black Circle's designs."

Ivellios nodded his understanding.

"Now," said Essik, "let's put the book back, return your stolen keys, and get you back to your cell. I'll accompany you; if any lower-ranked priests come by, I'll say we're on official business."

"Wait," said Ivellios. "If this book is so important, why don't we destroy it? Toss it through that door so it gets burned up."

Essik shook her head. "They have multiple copies, and it would alert them to the fact that someone unauthorized has been here."

They made it back to Ivellios's cell, where the guard was still out cold in his room. Essik hoisted him over her shoulder; the woman was stronger than she looked. "I'll take care of this mess. I'm thinking perhaps Lorren here slipped in the privy and knocked his head during his guard shift. Just don't say anything about it to him or anyone else. Get some rest; Mokad's getting ready to run another major test." She smiled at him. "I have some surprises ready for him, though. I'll tell you about them tomorrow."

CHAPTER TWELVE

Dranko lit a candle and set it down on his bedside table. His window was open to the warm autumn evening, which set the candle to flickering and throwing dancing shadows on the walls.

"We can't leave until tomorrow morning," he said to Morningstar. "His Majesty's wizard, a twitchy little fellow named Keff, can teleport us to Minok, but he's tapped out until tomorrow. Turns out, in addition to teleporting the king from Hae Charagan this morning, he's been casting spells all day to keep our sovereign safe from potential spies and assassins. Usually Crunard would have a big honor guard, but since he was traveling in secret, Keff was responsible for his safety."

Morningstar sat upright in the desk chair, her face a serene white mask in the candle's light. "Do you have a plan for what to do in Minok?"

Dranko sat on the edge of his bed, facing her. "I guess we'll start with your warehouse. With luck it'll have a bunch of cultists lounging around inside, rolling dice and smoking cigars, and we'll find a way to interrogate one of them. Heck, maybe they're using the warehouse for their secret ritual. That would be convenient."

Morningstar gave a close-mouthed laugh. "You said 'we.' Who's going with you? Step?"

Dranko let himself flop backward onto the bed and stared up at the candle flame's shifting shadows on the ceiling. "Yeah, but not just him. Ernie wants to come, and Rosset Finch insisted that he come along too. You know, just in case we were in danger of having too much fun."

"Rosset may be unpleasant," said Morningstar, "but I imagine a Silversword will be good to have on a mission to track the Black Circle. He does probably know more about them than we do."

"I know, I know. Though you know how stuck up and righteous those religious types can be. It's a good bet he won't approve of some of my methods of information gathering."

"Yes." Morningstar sounded amused. "I know how stuck up and righteous religious types can be."

Dranko sat back up to look at her. She was smiling at him, the little smile he'd been able to draw out of her more and more often.

"How's your team?" he asked. "How are they dealing with Sable's death? Have you started training them again?"

"Tomorrow," said Morningstar, growing serious. "I've finished building a new place in the Tapestry for us to gather. Tomorrow morning, when my sisters are asleep and dreaming, I'll continue to ready them." She fingered the pendant Ozella had given her. "Some of them won't be happy to learn we only have a week at most. Others, Scola and Jet for certain, will be glad of the shorter wait."

"What about you?" Dranko asked.

"I wish we had another year. Or better yet, that Aravia figures out the maze tomorrow and seals up the portal for good." She sighed. "I fear Aktallian," she admitted. "And I fear that many of my sisters, the only ones I've truly been close to in my life, are going to die in a place I convinced them to go."

"They could have backed out any time they wanted, right?" asked Dranko. "I'm not a military man, but I'm guessing the best generals don't beat themselves up knowing the men and women under their command might die in battle."

"I imagine the best generals do everything they can to minimize those deaths."

Dranko leaned forward. "I'm sure you will too."

"Will I?" Morningstar stood and paced, reminding Dranko of Ivellios's constant movement. Her white hair swayed and shimmered in the candlelight. "If throwing my sisters to their deaths seems like the best way to defeat Aktallian, I'm going to do it. My avatar made it very clear what my priorities should be. If I have to sacrifice my sisters, or myself, to win the battle, that's what I'm going to do."

"I hope it doesn't come to that." Dranko found himself at a loss for anything glib to say and surprised himself by merely offering, "I'd miss you."

Morningstar studied his face. "You could be in just as much danger as I will be. It's very likely that the Black Circle is taking precautions against being discovered. And what if Rosset is right? If Mokad did something to Praska's mind, can we trust anything she's told us? Her dreams seemed genuine to me, but this whole thing could be a trap specifically set to catch you."

"Yeah, Rosset may have mentioned that possibility six or seven more times after the meeting broke up. But he's still coming with us just in case, so he thinks there's a chance it's all true."

"I'd come with you too," said Morningstar, "but I can't risk my life before I'm done with Aktallian one way or another."

"And here I am, leaving you to go gallivanting around Minok."

"I shouldn't have to leave the Greenhouse," said Morningstar. "It's hard to imagine anywhere safer."

Dranko wouldn't have sworn on it, but he thought he heard a note of worry in her voice. After a half dozen heartbeats he understood. "But that's not actually where you'll be. You'll be in your Tapestry, where there's a murdering bastard on the loose."

Morningstar stared at the wall but didn't answer.

"If I stayed," Dranko continued, "I could be here to channel for you if Aktallian shows up and gets the drop on you. Maybe I—"

"I'll be fine. I'll have my sisters with me." She sounded reassuring, but which of them was she trying to assure?

"Do me a favor," he said. "Kibi is already planning to stay here in case Abernathy shows up needing something. Ask him to keep an eye on you, especially while you're in the Tapestry. If Aktallian manages to injure you before you can wake up, Kibi could apply a bit of quick first aid and then carry you all the way to the church of Delioch by himself."

Morningstar brought a hand to her pale chin. "That's a good thought. I'll ask him. I don't expect to need his help, but you're right. Better to take precautions."

Dranko's memory flashed to the hold of a ship, where he had stood over Morningstar while her guts spilled out from between her fingers, courtesy of Aktallian Dreamborn. "I'd rather be in my shoes than yours. My goal is to avoid trouble. Yours is to make it."

Morningstar stretched her back sideways, and walked to where he sat on the bed. She reached down and took his hands. "You're not very good at avoiding trouble. Promise me you'll do your best, and I promise to do my damnedest to stay alive. Deal?"

Her right hand was calloused from her years of sparring practice. Her left was smooth. Both were warm against the skin of his palms. He looked her in the eyes, black in the little light of the candle, intense, unreadable. Dranko hung suspended in the moment, precarious, overwhelmed with the realization that he had never wanted anything as much as to see Morningstar alive on the other side of her upcoming confrontation.

"Deal."

* * *

"Where are we going to end up?" Dranko asked the little wizard. They stood in the Greenhouse's backyard, watching E.R. quietly crop the grass, his tail flicking at insects. The morning sky was overcast, threatening rain.

Keff, court wizard to King Crunard IV, couldn't have been taller than five foot one, and even standing still he made Dranko think of a marionette being piloted by a drunk puppeteer. He sported a patchy gray beard and a badly receding hairline.

"Our destination in Minok is a small tower on the estate of Baron Savhir. The baron keeps the top story empty by royal decree, for times like this when His Majesty needs me to take agents to the city."

"I don't suppose you know much about Minok's warehouse district?" Dranko asked.

"No." Keff looked affronted at the question. "The few times I have been called on to teleport to Minok, I have remained on the baronial estate. I understand the streets of Minok are a bit uncivilized. It is a city of ruffians and sailors by repute."

"Perfect," said Dranko. "Ruffians and sailors are the best sort of people."

Keff sniffed. "I'm sure you would know."

Ernie and Step emerged from the kitchen door into the yard. Ernie held a large carrot, which he took to E.R. The mule took it gratefully and munched it while Ernie patted his brown flank.

"I'm sorry we never take you anywhere." Ernie wiped some mule slobber on his pants. "But we didn't realize we'd be teleporting all over the place when we bought you."

If E.R. minded in the slightest, he didn't show it. A foot of carrot greens vanished inch by inch into his mashing jaws.

"Come on," Dranko said. "You two ready to go?"

Certain Step swung his pack to his shoulder. "We are. I know that we will find your friend. It is said that hope is ever the herald of success."

"I hope you're right," said Dranko.

Dranko had thought of three reasons to bring Step along on this mission. For one thing, Step was a capable healer, and since Dranko couldn't channel for himself, he enjoyed the idea of a backup medic. For another, there was a decent chance that the Black Circle didn't know much about him. Mokad would recognize Dranko, and at least one Sharshun knew what Ernie looked like. Rosset the Silversword would be a liability in any situation where unobtrusiveness was called for. But Step would be an unknown, and that might come in handy.

The third reason was Step's prophecy. What if the "last of five" didn't refer to those Black Circle towers Aravia talked about, but to something they'd find in Minok? He certainly wasn't going to fulfill any divine destiny hanging out in the Greenhouse keeping Eddings company.

"I am ready to teleport us to Minok," said Keff. "Where is the Silversword?"

Rosset Finch emerged from the kitchen door. He wore a simple blue tabard beneath a darker gray cloak, and plain brown trousers.

"Silver cloak in the laundry today?" Dranko asked.

Rosset gave Dranko an aggrieved look. "Are you an idiot? We're about to search for a man who's been abducted by the Black Circle. The cloak would announce my presence as clearly as hiring a crier." He turned to Keff. "I have a name, you know."

"Yes, yes," said Keff. "And you also have a title. Don't get tetchy with me if I use it. Are you ready for the journey?"

"Almost," said Rosset. "Please be silent, and stand back." The Silversword held out his right hand and concentrated on a copper bracelet cinched around his wrist. Dranko didn't remember the man wearing it yesterday during the meeting. The bracelet was wide and flat, and an inch-long shard of dull golden metal appeared to have been glued against its curve. An odd thing happened as the seconds passed: The shard began to glow, its golden color becoming rich and gleaming, like a polished crescent. At the same time, the copper bracelet faded to a light gray, and Rosset's blue tabard also faded, its color leeched away. Even the grass at Rosset's feet seemed like its green was bleeding off, the blades turning the color of charcoal. In minutes, everything in Rosset's immediate vicinity—his clothes, his face, his hair, and the ground beneath him—had been drained of color.

Everything, that was, except the shard on the bracelet, shining like a golden sunrise.

"Good." Rosset lowered his arm, vibrancy returned to him and his surroundings, and the golden shard stuck to the copper bracelet looked as it did at first glance, like a fragment of cheap tin with fading yellow paint. "The Black Circle has not put up any enchantment to interfere with teleportation into Minok. Keff, you may proceed."

"How do you know that?" Dranko asked. "What's that thingamabob on your wrist?"

Rosset's sour look reminded Dranko of how some of the old priests had glared at him after his more memorable pranks.

"It is a blessing of a sort you should not disparage," Rosset answered in a near whisper, his tone full of an angry reverence. "I am honored to carry a shard of the Watcher's Kiss, the blade with which Uthol Inga struck at the heart of the Adversary, weakening him, allowing the other gods to imprison him before they all fled to Spira. The Watcher's Kiss shattered, but fragments remain. They allow the Silverswords to effect divinations and wards against designs of the Black Circle."

"I'm impressed!" said Dranko. "I mean, something like that you could have hocked for enough money to retire, maybe buy yourself a title, a small keep somewhere. But you still keep it around for emergencies."

Dranko was further impressed that Rosset kept his calm. The man said only, "The Watcher's Kiss is not a topic for jests. Delioch would have been destroyed along with the rest if not for Uthol Inga's sacrifices and subterfuge."

While Keff uttered the words and made the gestures to teleport, and his four would-be passengers kept their hands on his shoulders, Certain Step leaned over and whispered in Dranko's ear, "I see I am not the only one offended by your frivolous treatment of the gods."

"No one can take a joke anymore," Dranko whispered back.

Their surroundings changed. The Greenhouse, its lawn, its mule, and the gray sky above it were replaced by a large round room, hung with green tapestries but otherwise empty. A keening of wind outside accompanied a steady patter of rain on the roof.

"You are now on the property of Baron Savhir and thus are his guests," said Keff pompously. "I am to escort you to the gate of the baron's property, then return to His Majesty at once."

Dranko peered out a narrow window into the rain-streaked gloom of a gray morning. Below him he saw only sodden hills, symmetric gardens, and a few low outbuildings.

"Come along," said Keff. "This way." The king's wizard led them down a spiraling staircase that passed around the edges of four more stories of the tower, and out through a wide door at the bottom. A blast of wind-driven rain struck Dranko in the face.

"Beautiful day for some reconnaissance," he said to Ernie.

Ernie pulled the front of his shirt up over his chin. Step grimaced and held up his hand to little good purpose. Rosset Finch seemed entirely unfazed by the weather.

The four of them followed Keff across a manicured lawn to a gate in the wrought iron fence that surrounded Baron Savhir's estate. A lone guard sat looking miserable beneath a tree that might have offered decent cover from the rain on a less windy day. She jumped to her feet at their approach, seemed to recognize Keff, and unlocked the gate.

"Good luck," said the wizard. "Follow the path, turn right and downhill when it meets the road, and that will take you into Minok." As a seeming afterthought he added, "I hope you find your man."

The guard locked the gate behind them.

"Do you have a plan?" Rosset asked as they hurried down the path. "From the tales of your escapades, I gather you consider yourself an expert in infiltration and scouting."

"I have some ideas," said Dranko, and that was true, though he needed to know more about the city of Minok before he could put the pieces together. "First thing, we need to get out of the rain and into a tavern." He peered through the haze of raindrops. "Looks like we're about a quarter-mile outside the city, which means by the time we get there, we'll all be cold, wet, and in need of a drink."

"A drink?" Rosset sounded disgusted. "Is that how you propose to find the man whom the Black Circle is using to free Naradawk Skewn? By drinking in a tavern?"

"Close, but no," said Dranko. "I propose that *you* drink in the tavern. Get comfortable. Maybe get something to eat. Listen for rumors on the off chance someone lets a secret slip. But I'll need some time to scout around, get the lay of the land, grease some palms, that sort of thing, and I can't see that having any of you along will help the process. Sorry, Ernie." He held up a hand to forestall Ernie's imminent open-mouthed protest. "I'm sure I'll need all of you before this is over, but this is my game." He looked at Rosset, standing tall and resolute, and so all the more pathetic for the rain dripping off the end of his nose. "Unless you can use your sword-bit to divine where Ivellios is being kept?"

"As if I wouldn't have done that already," said Rosset stiffly. "The fragment is just that—only a fragment. There are limits to its use and to my ability to use it."

"Perhaps," said Step quietly, "you could have explained its uses before we set out. What if we discover a better way to apply its power?"

Huh. Step didn't *sound* snarky, and sarcasm didn't seem like an arrow in his quiver. But Rosset bristled nonetheless.

"I will not have my wisdom questioned by a foreigner who worships a supposed sun goddess."

"Oh, now you've done it," said Dranko under his breath. Ernie took a tiny step away from Step, who stopped in his tracks and pointed accusingly at Rosset.

"And I will not have the goddess Kemma questioned by a zealot! Her divine nature is not something a mortal should question."

Dranko thought Step would stop there, but he underestimated the man. "Furthermore," continued Step, his face reddening, "my goddess would not demand the sacrifice of an innocent man, not if there were any other options. Your Uthol Inga moved you to commit murder for expediency. I find your wisdom questionable on many counts."

Rosset had calmed himself during Step's outburst. Rather than escalate, he gave his head a small shake. "I hope all three of you understand that if we find Ivellios Forrester, it is very likely we will need to kill him ourselves."

"No!" said Ernie. "Since the Black Circle kidnapped him, we just need to…to kidnap him back."

"That would be preferable," said Rosset, "but it may not be possible. Without knowing the Black Circle's designs, we must prepare ourselves for any eventuality, including killing Ivellios before the Circle can use him."

Dranko prized himself on being able to read people, but Rosset was a tough nut. Did he truly feel badly about killing in Uthol Inga's name? Or was he a bloodthirsty fanatic who paid only lip service to mercy?

"Come on." Dranko looked up squinting into the rain. "Let's keep moving. You can keep bickering about your gods as you walk, as long as you walk."

Minok came into view slowly, revealed a yard at a time through the curtain of the rain. There were fewer outlying houses and shops, fewer farms than were found at the outskirts of Tal Hae. Minok was not protected by an inland-facing wall, but the countryside gave way to buildings and roads all at once instead of over the course of miles. Many people walked the streets despite the rain, though they hurried by without greetings.

"Ernie," said Dranko, "I think someone without tusks should ask a local where the nearest tavern is."

A few minutes later the four of them sat in the warm and dry commons of

Ichabod's Net, cloaks hung on pegs and mugs of decent ale set before them on the table. Dranko peered over the rim of his mug, taking in the room, looking for any sign they were being given unusual scrutiny. Oh, sure, they drew some stares. Between the swords on Rosset and Ernie's belts, Step's dark tan skin, and Dranko's lovely goblinoid jaw, it would be strange for them not to draw some attention. But no one spent more than a few seconds deciding they were just a group of damp, thirsty men, and Dranko was satisfied they weren't being spied upon by Black Circle agents.

"I thought you were going to scout while we stayed here," said Rosset, after a minute had passed in relative silence.

"That's right," said Dranko. "But I'll work better with a bit of fortification. Some food would be good too." He flagged down a servant and asked for four plates of whatever the cook could provide that early in the day. This turned out to be yesterday's bread and some thin vegetable soup, but the ale was good, and that was what mattered.

"Rosset," Ernie asked as they ate, "why did the leader of the Stormknights get so angry when he found out you worshipped Uthol Inga? Nobody knows much about the Watcher, but he sure didn't seem to like her."

Of all the Traveling Gods, Uthol Inga was the one no one knew anything about. She had no churches or shrines, no open worshippers, just the enigmatic nickname of "the Watcher." She had always been dutifully named along with the other gods when the priests of Delioch spoke their lessons, but any questions about her were met with a shrug and "she remains a mystery to this day," or something similarly meaningless.

Rosset Finch took a long pull on his mug. "The Stormknights have an incorrect view of history. I take it you know the story of the Travelers' escape from the Adversary?"

"Sure," said Dranko. "The gods used to watch over the people of another world altogether, but they were attacked by a being we call the Adversary, a more powerful god that overmatched them. The Adversary killed some of the gods, but a few got together, managed to lock him in a prison, and then hoofed it across the universe to Spira before he could get out. The ones who escaped are the Travelers: Delioch, Ell, Corilayna, Werthis, Brechen, and Uthol Inga."

Rosset laughed. "In the simplest terms, that is correct, but it leaves out a vital detail: how the Travelers imprisoned such a powerful being in the first place."

"Yeah," said Dranko, "the priests were always vague on that point. I think they mentioned that Ell wove a net of darkness around the Adversary's head, so he didn't realize he was being imprisoned, and of course that Delioch healed the other Travelers who were wounded during the escape. Honestly, though, my teachers always glossed over the fact that the Traveling Gods only came to Spira because they were running away."

"Then allow me to educate you," said Rosset. "Uthol Inga is a smith and a goddess of craftsmen. At the same time the gods were preparing a secret prison into which they hoped to force or lure the Adversary, she pretended to betray her fellows and join her enemy as his consort. She forged a golden blade called the Watcher's Kiss and used her position to infuse the blade with a tiny stolen drop of her enemy's blood, so that it would have the power to injure him.

"During the gods' war against the Adversary, at the peak of the battle, when the Adversary's confidence was highest, Uthol Inga stabbed the Adversary in the back with the Watcher's Kiss. She lacked the might to kill him, but he was injured and enraged. Ell used this opportunity to blind him with darkness while Brechen blew him toward the prison with a mighty gale. Corilayna made certain that luck would favor their desperate gambit, and Werthis fought off the hordes of servants who still served the Adversary with fervid devotion. Once the Adversary was ensnared, the half dozen surviving gods gathered their remaining worshipers and fled across creation, finding refuge at last on the distant world of Spira."

Certain Step, with surprising indignation, said, "That does not explain why that man, the Stormknight, hates the name of your goddess. He ought to revere her!"

"Yes, he ought," said Rosset. "But he believes something different. Stormknight doctrine holds that Uthol Inga betrayed the other gods and became the Adversary's lover in earnest, joining him in his assault against her own people. They say that once the battle was hopeless, the Adversary turned on Uthol Inga and betrayed her in turn, and that she smote him with the Watcher's Kiss in self-defense. The Werthans, in their blind ignorance, do not believe that Uthol Inga's betrayal was false.

"When the Travelers arrived on Spira and settled their mortals upon its surface, Werthis directed his worshippers to hunt down and destroy those who venerated Uthol Inga. That is why, to this day, her own worshippers keep themselves hidden and will not pray openly."

"And how," said Dranko, unable to stop himself, "do you know that you're right and the Stormknights are wrong? Seem to me you Utholites would be spouting the same line no matter which way things really went."

The Silversword's lips curled into a sneering smile. "You ask for proof of a god's word? You, who I am told channel the healing power of Delioch, are asking me if my faith is not sufficient?" Rosset held up his mug as if giving a toast, then downed what remained in a single swig. "I know the truth in my heart, and I have faith in the righteous power of my goddess. Your doubts are irrelevant." He set down his empty mug. "Now, are you warmed and watered well enough to do your vaunted reconnaissance?"

Dranko sopped a piece of bread in his soup and popped it into his mouth. "I believe I am." He was also just as happy to get away from Rosset Finch. "You three wait here and try not to get into any trouble. I could be a few hours. They shouldn't hassle you as long as you keep buying, but if you need to leave for some reason, stay close and make yourself easy to find."

He slid back his chair, stood, and stretched. "Ernie, you're in charge." He gave the kid a wink, pulled up the hood of his cloak, and headed out into the rain.

Minok wasn't all that different than Tal Hae, though Keff had been right: It *was* full of ruffians and sailors. Half the city had the feel of Tal Hae's toughest dockside neighborhoods. With no surrounding farmland, most of Minok's commerce and trade was maritime, and its heavily folded and crenelated coastline meant a long, curving series of harbors, wharfs, docks, and quays. The central harbor, called the Teapot for its shape, was nearly the size of its equivalent in Tal Hae, but a dozen smaller harbors were spread up and down the coast, all crowded with boats. Dranko would have lost a bet on the smell, which was even fishier than the air of his home city.

The pace of Minok was not slowed by the rain; from chatting with some dockside haulers on break, Dranko learned that it rained several times a week, most of the year round. It sounded miserable, but the locals had learned not to mind. Rain barrels brimmed on every corner, and outside shops awnings were ubiquitous. Many of the merchants and better-off laborers carried umbrellas.

Dranko kept his hood pulled forward to hide his face. If Mokad suspected he would be here scouting, he might have posted people who knew to watch for a scar-faced goblin-touched man. The rain was a fortunate circumstance; it kept people's heads down and made it more plausible for him to do the same.

As he meandered through the streets, taking in the city's layout, its neighborhoods and plazas and markets, he was reminded of that day a half year earlier when he had channeled for an injured beggar. Time's passage in his memory had been muddled by however long they had lived in Calabash, but he remembered that day as clearly as yesterday: the driving rain, the old man bleeding in an alley, the glorious rush of holy power that had healed the patient and knocked Dranko out cold. And, of course, his landlady Berthel handing him that beautifully printed summons from Abernathy, the harbinger of his new life of nonstop magically charged insanity.

But here, making his way through city streets, head down, engaged in a reconnoiter, Dranko could almost pretend that his life was back to normal, that he was simply a clever con man looking for openings.

He ducked into a roper's shop, where two apprentices sat at a long wooden table stringing nets together with wide bone needles. "Excuse me," he said in a worried voice. "My master, Lord Valen, is expecting a shipment of jute and two hundred barrels of ink at warehouse thirty-seven, and he sent me to meet it. But I've lost my instructions, and this is my first time in Minok. Could you tell me which direction I ought to go?"

Thirty-seven wasn't the warehouse Morningstar had seen in Mokad's dream-ledgers; that had been thirty-one.

One of the boys peered closely at Dranko's face. "You...you goblin-touched?" he asked nervously.

"Yeah," Dranko growled. "So? I'm not going to bite you, and Lord Valen will beat me if I'm late no matter what my teeth look like."

"Don't mind Tory," said the other boy. "Everything makes him nervous. All the warehouses are lined up in order along the water. Numbers go..." He paused, thinking. "South to north, up into the hundreds. Thirty-seven should be that way, over Shallot Bridge."

"On Fishhook Harbor," said Tory. "One of the smaller ones. My pa used to unload mackerel at one in the thirties, can't remember the exact number."

"Two hundred barrels of ink?" asked the first boy. "Seems like a lot, doesn't it?"

"Damn right it does," said Dranko. "Can't imagine what anyone would do with that much. I asked Lord Valen the same thing. Who would want to buy so much ink? He just reminded me it's not my job to ask questions. You haven't heard anything, have you?"

"About someone buying ink? No, sorry."

"Maybe a church?" said Tory. "That's where all the books are, right?"

"Many thanks," said Dranko. Ah well. It was worth a shot. "You've probably saved me a beating." He passed them each a copper chit and slipped back out into the rain.

Hood back over his head, Dranko hurried west and north, weaving through the crowd and past at least seven different fishmongers. By the time he had drawn near to the water, and thus along the wide street fronting the rows of warehouses, their numbers were in the sixties.

The warehouses lined the road like squatting giants, massive boxes of stone, brick, or painted wood. They varied slightly in height and width, but all shared a few salient features: large double doors that opened onto the street, barred windows high up near their roofs, and faded numbers in painted stencil somewhere on their outward-facing walls. Often they were strung together wall-to-wall, no alleys separating them, distinguished from their neighbors only by size, color, and material. A quick walk around to the back of one such grouping confirmed that ships unloaded onto wide piled platforms out in the bay, with ramps leading straight into the warehouses from the water.

Dranko sauntered southward, staying to the east side of the street and occasionally poking his head into shops to hide his true purpose. Some of the warehouses were guarded, never by more than two people, hired muscle looking bored. A few had their doors flung wide while cargo was moved in or out. Flatbed carts were lined up outside warehouse sixty-seven, growing ever more encumbered as workers loaded them up with barrels. Dranko had a clear view through warehouse fifty-eight, as dockhands brought small wooden crates up the water ramp and handed them off to a string of energetic teenagers. The line of kids ended at a covered wagon waiting on the street.

Dranko took advantage of the chaos; he walked right in past the laboring teens and produced a piece of parchment from inside a shirt pocket. He waved the paper vaguely at a woman who seemed to be in charge of directing the unloading.

"What's going on?" he asked, putting some mild agitation into his voice. "Why is this cargo being moved today? My master still has nearly full inventory at the shop! He'll never be able to make room for all of this!"

The woman peered at him, her face curling in distaste, probably at the sight of his tusks, scars, or both. "Who are you?" she asked impatiently.

"Matthias Porter," he snapped back. "Manager for Master Efron's haberdashery. And, again, why is our cloth being unloaded *today*?"

The woman, tall and long-haired, stared at him in confusion. "Cloth? What are you talking about?"

Dranko turned in a circle, waving his arms about. "I mean fabric! Velvet! Fine linen! Etravian wool! Some of these even have silk, though I've told Master Efron it's too damp here to store for long."

The woman frowned, shook her head, and sniffed the air as if assuring herself of something. "I don't know what you're on about, but this here's a shipment of cheese from Lanei."

Dranko frowned back at her and consulted his parchment. "This is warehouse fifty-three, is it not?"

The woman snickered. "You're in the wrong place, Mr. Porter. This is fifty-eight. Now stop wasting my time and that of your master."

Dranko looked offended. "I suggest you have your number re-painted. The eight is quite faded." He turned and stalked out past the line of workers.

It wasn't a given that the warehouses shared common interior features, but Dranko had gotten a good look at fifty-eight. It had a wide second story balcony stacked with boxes and cartwheels, and an open-air office in one corner with a desk, chair, and stained bookshelf. Bright lanterns were set on the floor, well outside the path of foot traffic from door to door.

It did not have any interior doors that would open on to the warehouses on either side, which was a shame. But it did have one very promising feature: broad skylights. An iron ladder climbed from the second-floor balcony to a crisscross of catwalks near the ceiling, and Dranko saw the outlines of shutters. On drier days they'd probably open the skylights to illuminate the warehouse's interior.

Would the Black Circle's warehouse share the same features? It could give him a place to start.

Outside, he stopped to talk to the driver of the covered wagon.

"Excuse me!"

The driver, wrapped in an oiled leather cloak that clearly did not keep away the rain to his satisfaction, peered down from his platform. "Yes?"

"My master ordered me to hire three wagons like this one to bring carpets from warehouse fourteen to his shop tomorrow. But I'm new to Minok and don't know where to go. I'm happy to give you a few coppers for a good suggestion."

"Ah." The man bent low so he wouldn't have to shout over the rain. "You'll need to visit one of the wagoners' guild houses. All the hiring for warehouse transport has to go through them. Surprised your master didn't know that."

"Our shop just opened," Dranko explained. "Is there a guild house near to Fishhook Harbor?"

* * *

Soon enough he stood shaking water from his boots beneath an enormous wooden pavilion, crowded with merchants, guildsmen, and drivers haggling loudly. The wagoners were easily identified by their long brown robes marked with the symbol of a wheel on the front. Some poor attempt had been made to keep the wagons and carts lined up and orderly, but for the most part chaos reigned. At the far end of the pavilion was a long row of stalls, some empty, some occupied by horses and mules being tended by a team of grooms. The smell of the animals fought against the powerful prevailing odor of fish.

Dranko picked his way through the crowds until he found what he sought: a woman at a large desk, quill in her hand, leaning over stacks of papers weighted down with bricks. Dranko joined the end of a line of men and women waiting for her attention, and when his turn came a few minutes later, he bowed low.

"Hiring out or dropping off?" asked the woman.

"Hiring," said Dranko. "My master was very pleased with the driver he used some weeks ago and was hoping to hire him out again. I'm sorry I don't have more details, but he recalled using him at warehouse thirty-one on the ninth day of Sunbake."

The woman flipped through a thick leather-bound notebook. "Can't make you any promises that he's not already hired out," she said, thumbing through her journal. She ran a finger down one page, flipped to the next page, then back again. "You sure you have your facts straight? We didn't send anyone out that day to thirty-one. In fact, we haven't hired out anyone to that warehouse in months." She sat up straight and gave Dranko a sour look. "You sure your master didn't go outside the guild? You know there's lashes and a stiff fine for that."

"Outside the guild!" exclaimed Dranko. "I'll bet that's exactly what he did! Lashes and a fine? The old bastard would deserve it. If I discover that's what he's been up to, I'll report him first thing. In fact, I think I'll go confront that horse-beating devil right now." And before the woman could open her mouth to ask if Dranko still wanted to hire a cart, he stormed off.

Dranko spent another two hours on the streets of Minok, making plans, marking locations, querying its citizens as innocuously as possible. A few of these were alarmed enough by his tusks to spurn him, and Dranko worried about too many people recalling a goblin-touched man scrawled upon by the Scarbearers' mercy. But then, the Black Circle's degree of paranoia and watchfulness were utter unknowns.

Putting himself in Mokad's boots: The archmagi and their allies should have no idea where Ivellios was being kept. Perhaps, secure in an illusion of secrecy, the Black Circle wasn't making any attempts to mask their activities. But Dranko couldn't help but remember all the secrets about him that Mokad knew. It was entirely possible that they marked his location with every step he took.

* * *

Ernie, Step, and Rosset sat at the same table at Ichabod's Net, talking quietly.

"I'm surprised you're still here," said Dranko. "Why hasn't the owner thrown you out?"

Step smiled at him. "I told her we were waiting for a friend, that we enjoyed the warm atmosphere of her establishment, and that otherwise we'd have to wait in the rain."

"Also," said Ernie, "I gave her three silver talons as thanks for letting us take up a table."

"Nice," said Dranko. "Now listen, I have news and a plan."

He told them everything he had seen and learned, speaking as quietly as possible.

"So we can't track down a wagoner who unloaded their supplies," he finished. "But I have another approach in mind. Step, you'll be up first once the sun has gone down. The Black Circle may know to keep a lookout for me, and possibly Ernie, but you should be an unknown. Keep your hood up, since your darker skin might attract attention. All I want you to do is walk casually down Warehouse Row past the one Morningstar saw in Praska's dream-ledgers—thirty-one. See if they've posted guards, or if light is coming out through the windows. Note if it has its doors open. Don't make it obvious you're looking. Oh, and see if there's someplace within earshot across the street where you three could plausibly wait while I'm breaking in. Once you're past it, turn left onto Buoy Street, then left again onto Whalebone Way, and meet the rest of us at a tavern called the Happy Haddock. That's where we'll be waiting."

"What then?" asked Rosset. "And what do you suggest I do?"

"That depends." Dranko pointed at Rosset's wrist. "Can you use your magic bracelet doodad to suss out what the bad guys are up to?" When Rosset opened his mouth to reply, his face reddening, Dranko quickly added, "Sorry, I meant the fragment of the legendary blade that your goddess used to stab the Adversary. 'Doodad' was a poor choice of words."

Rosset glared at him. "The shard I possess allows me to divine whether I am in immediate danger from any arcanism perpetrated by the Black Circle. It can also protect me from a direct application of their magic. But it will not tell us where Ivellios is unless I am practically on top of him already."

"Here's another worry I have," said Dranko. "Does your cozy relationship with the Black Circle types go both ways? Will a Silversword showing up trigger any sort of magic alarms for them?"

Rosset shook his head impatiently. "If so, it would be the first time. The fragment should foil any sort of divinations on their part."

"In that case," said Dranko, "would you mind if I borrowed it?"

"You mean my 'doodad'?" Rosset smiled without humor. "No, you may not. Unless you have secretly been worshipping Uthol Inga, and have spent years in deep meditation, attuning yourself to the fragment's power, reciting the Watcher's Obeisance, standing in the—"

"Fine. Never mind." Dranko sighed. "Ernie, you and Rosset are my backup. After I get Step's report, my most likely next move will be to scale the wall of their warehouse and see if I can get in through a skylight. With any luck I'll find some clue inside that will lead us to Ivellios. But if things go south, I may need you to bust in and rescue me."

"How will we rescue you," asked Ernie, "if you're inside a locked warehouse?"

Dranko grinned. "By smashing the lock and opening the door. Or you can try the harbor-side door; most of the warehouses have thin boardwalks that give you access from the shore."

"And how will we know you'll need rescuing in the first place?" asked Rosset.

"Two ways," said Dranko. "One, we'll set a time after which you'll come in after me if I haven't come out. And two, if I'm in that much danger, I'll be shouting at the top of my lungs."

* * *

The first part of the plan went off flawlessly. While Dranko, Rosset, and Ernie sat nursing drinks at the Happy Haddock, Step went out to scout. He returned a half hour later, damp and patting his hands to his sides.

"The rain is letting up," he said, "but it's cold. Even the winters in Djaw are warmer than this."

"What did you see?" Dranko asked.

"Nothing," said Step. "Warehouse thirty-one doesn't have guards, and no light shines out through its windows. The door appears to be locked and chained shut, though I did not cross the street to look closely. Half a block down, opposite warehouse twenty-eight, is a small clam shack with a few tables beneath an awning. I didn't see any customers, but they had lights strung up." He paused. "What is a clam?"

Dranko gulped down the last of his water—no good being even slightly inebriated on a job like this—and smiled. "Clams are delicious if you get them fresh." He stood. No point in waiting. "I'll head out now. Wait about twenty minutes, then saunter over to the clam shack. If all goes well, I'll meet you there. If not, come rescue me after an hour."

Warehouse Row was dismayingly well lit for the evening; the lamplighters had been by, and one of the tall streetlamps cast its light directly onto thirty-one. But around the side Dranko found shadows aplenty to slip between, and he discovered that a plank walkway clung to the back of the warehouse. The ramp and its platform were empty, and the few ships that bobbed in Fishhook Harbor were dark and silent.

Despite the critical nature of this mission, Dranko couldn't help himself. The habit was too ingrained. He retrieved a small sealed vial from his pack, already containing the parchment scrap upon which was written, "Dranko was here." He chucked the vial out into the harbor as far as it would go. Sure, it would probably just come back and wash up on shore tomorrow, maybe break on a rock, its paper turned to a sodden bit of pulp. But maybe not. One never knew where the tipping point was for notoriety. Of course, bottles notwithstanding, if the efforts of Horn's Company ended up saving the kingdom, he'd sure as hell better get a parade out of it, or maybe a knighthood, along with a fat purse of reward money.

The harbor-facing doors were closed and chained, so Dranko sized up the back wall. This warehouse was brick, and its mortar not smoothly set, so climbing was not especially difficult for someone with Dranko's long practice. Near the top he made use of a narrow windowsill to push himself onto the rooftop.

As Dranko had desperately hoped, skylights had been set into the warehouse roof. There were six in all, large rectangles covered with wooden shutters. None were latched. He slowly lifted one up, just an inch, and put his eye to the gap.

Darkness. Good. One more piece of evidence that the place was empty. He tried not to think about Sharshun snipers with crossbows observing from ground level, watching him with magical darksight, lining up their bolts. His ears strained for any sound of motion below, but the only noises were from outside: the chatter of pedestrians, the chuckle of small waves lapping the shore of Fishhook Harbor, rainwater still dripping from eaves, the beating of his own heart.

Now came the moment of greatest danger. He pulled his light-rod from a pocket and let a tiny slice of light escape through his fingers. It showed high catwalks, exactly as he had hoped. Slowly he opened the shutter wide enough to slip his whole body through, then eased it closed as his feet found the catwalk. It was a row of wooden planks suspended by iron rods, running the width of the warehouse, giving access to the skylight shutters.

Just as in the warehouse he had scouted, an iron ladder was bolted to the wall, leading down into the darkness. Dranko considered throwing away all caution and shining his light all around, but the possibility remained that a watcher at ground level had his eyes on the door, and hadn't yet thought to look up. He tiptoed along the catwalk to the ladder and descended, step by slow, silent step.

He reached a balcony sooner than he expected, fifteen feet wide, warped wooden boards creaking under his feet and a rickety railing to his left. He let some more light seep through his fingers and saw hanging ropes—pulley systems meant to lift goods from the warehouse floor up to the balconies. Of greater interest was a line of casks against the warehouse wall, but these were empty and smelled variously of onions, apples, camphor, and yeast.

The balconies he had seen in warehouse fifty-eight had run the full perimeter of the interior, but here they only clung to the eastern wall. He took a few minutes walking from one end to the other, examining several dozen barrels and boxes. Most were empty and any odors long since wafted away—this was long-term storage for empty containers—but one small barrel did at least corroborate his suspicions. It was lined with oiled paper, but in several places, where the oil had dried or been poorly applied, the paper was stained with black ink.

There were two more balconies beneath the highest, all connected by the ladder, but Dranko decided to skip straight to the ground floor. If the Black Circle kept any incriminating paperwork, or clues to the ongoing use of the warehouse, it wouldn't be up here in mothballs. On the off chance someone lurked on the warehouse floor, someone who hadn't yet seen or heard him mucking around above, Dranko concealed his light completely and slowly descended the ladder in the dark, straining his ears between each rung.

Silence.

When the ladder ran out, he crouched by the wall, waiting to be challenged. Nothing.

Screw it. He fully uncovered his light-rod, shining it around the warehouse, ready to spring back to the ladder if anyone shouted a challenge. He saw stacks of shipping crates, piles of tools, long benches, and—aha!—a small room in the corner, two wooden walls, a wooden roof, and a cheap door. It was still a long shot that the Black Circle had left anything juicy behind, but even a small clue could show him the next step on a path that would lead to Ivellios.

Dranko stayed wary, quieting his instinct to hurry. There still might be traps here, tripwires or some such. He played his light along the floor as he walked, but the weathered stones betrayed nothing suspicious. The door to the little room was locked, but half a minute with his tools, light-rod clenched in his teeth, was all he needed to get inside.

The room was only eight feet on a side and empty save for a desk and a chair. Parchments covered the desk, and the topmost of these showed equations, numbers, and diagrams in an inscrutable jumble. Even with his ear-cuff, Dranko could make no sense of them. A little prickle of warning, an extra sense cultivated on the streets of Tal Hae during his years of sketchy enterprise, told him this was too easy. But paranoia had been a survival trait back then. He told himself, not for the first time, that the Black Circle had no reason to think they had been compromised.

But they know *things. The Black Circle is a cult of forbidden knowledge.*

Dranko dropped the paper. He sniffed his fingers, then rubbed them together. No sign of contact poison. He shuffled through the remaining papers, but all were as impenetrable as the first.

The desk had a single drawer. He pinched his sleeves between his fingers to open it, thus avoiding direct contact with the handle. Inside was a small stack of silver talons and five empty glass vials, but nothing of any value to his mission. Dranko pulled the drawer out further, shone his light to its back panel, but found nothing more.

Wait.

He'd seen this before. The bottom of the drawer's interior was higher than it should have been, the telltale sign of a false bottom. Dranko felt around underneath the drawer and his fingers found a small metal peg. He used the peg to slide the false bottom into a hidden slot at the back of the drawer, revealing—

An empty space. Except that, no, a black circle was drawn onto the true bottom of the drawer, a circle filled with little strings of numbers, crisscrossing lines, and smaller circles inside the large one. As he stared at it in disappointment, the numbers began to glow a faint purple, and the small circles spun. The violet light threw strange shadows onto the walls of the little room, odd whispers rasped in the air around him, and a word appeared scrawled across the diameter of the primary circle. A word he could read.

Melen.

Instinct took over, and before his mind had fully registered that his true name had been magically written on the bottom of the drawer, his body had dived out the door, going into a tuck and roll. Behind him came a sound like a gale filled with shrieking souls, and the little room exploded, shadowy blades of purple fog-light whipping through the air and tearing the flimsy wood to pieces. Dranko picked himself up, sprinted away in a clumsy, stumbling run, and only looked back when he had put a good twenty strides between himself and the trap.

It wasn't a trap.

Wasn't *only* a trap. A bruise-colored mist flowed from the ruins of the room, congealing into something twelve feet tall and vaguely man-shaped. Dranko backpedaled and decided this would be a good time to start screaming for help. Would Ernie and the others hear him? Instead of a word, Dranko opted for a good old-fashioned primal scream of fear, which at the moment was not difficult to produce. The billowing purple cloud-man advanced as Dranko retreated, and with a burst of sound like a gust of cold wind, it whipped a tendril of sparkling violet mist towards his head. Dranko dodged to his left, but not quickly enough, and where the mist brushed his shoulder a slicing pain flared. Blood welled up from several cuts, as though the mist had been filled with small sharp knives.

Maybe this thing couldn't fly. Still screaming, Dranko bolted for the ladder. Behind him was a sound like a gathering storm, a distant wind that had caught up some unfortunate birds. The noise of the creature abruptly increased, and Dranko dropped to the ground. A smoky tentacle snapped above and past him, cutting through a raised wooden workbench and sending crowbars scattering. Dranko felt a pang of annoyance at his vows to Delioch, specifically the one that forbade the use of weapons. Otherwise he could at least hurl a crowbar at the creature. Surely the racket the thing was raising, combined with his own constant screaming, would alert the others.

Dranko regained his feet, put his light-rod in his teeth, and surged up the ladder; the lowest balcony would provide cover if he reached it in time. He desperately wanted to look back but dared not do anything that might slow him down. The wind-gust noise that preceded each of the creature's attacks came at the very moment he gained the landing. Dranko rolled frantically to his right as the wooden slats of the balcony tore away, cracking and splintering beneath the monster's onslaught. He ended the roll on his side, took the light-rod from his mouth, and shined it outward. The long, thick tube of roiling purple smoke that had destroyed the section of balcony had not retracted. Instead, it oozed and pooled around the ladder, engulfing it. Then the creature pulled back its vaporous arm, taking a fifteen-foot section of the ladder with it, tearing it out of the wall with a scream of shearing iron bolts.

Dranko fought down panic. He had survived when Lapis had discovered him atop the floating island, and he had plunged into the sucking desert dust of the Mouth of Nahalm. Of course, he had only come out of that fiasco alive because Morningstar had seen him fall, and his friends had come to rescue him. With the ladder to the skylights gone, that was looking like his best bet this time around too.

Or.

This summoned cloud-man didn't seem to be overly concerned about collateral damage. Dranko regained his feet and dashed down the balcony in the direction of the main warehouse doors. Wood planks shattered behind him as the smoke monster blasted a hole in the floor, and pain lanced his ankle as something sharp— maybe the creature's hidden talons, maybe a fragment of flying timber—gouged his skin. Running with a limp, Dranko reached the end of the balcony and leapt, failing this time to roll, instead sprawling awkwardly on his stomach, his face. In something like a half-crawl, half-stumble, and trying to lurch as randomly as he could manage, he staggered his way to the door, stood, and turned around, readying himself to dodge.

Even as he turned, the wind-shriek sound of the creature's attack filled the air, and from only a dozen feet away its deadly pseudopod lashed out. Dranko tried to avoid it, but his lacerated ankle failed him. Though he twisted and slumped sideways, hoping the creature would shatter the door, the knife-smoke slammed into the left side of his ribcage, slicing through his shirt, his skin, his flesh. Blood sluiced out through his clutching fingers, and he fell. As he struggled to hold on to consciousness, a golden light shone out from somewhere behind him.

Well, he thought, *it was a good run*. But heaven was calling him home.

CHAPTER THIRTEEN

Ysabel Horn cringed as Dranko dived from the balcony, landed badly, and struck his chin on the floor.

"Get up!" she exhorted. "Just stay alive a half-minute more!"

* * *

Kay, the former Keeper, had shown Ysabel how to focus her perceptions on the details of the world, to find Charagan, then Tal Hae, then the Street of Bakers. It had taken what felt like days for her to fully understand Kay's instructions, which at first were full of peculiar phrases like "frame of reference" and "cosmic reflections." In the end, hands on her hips, Ysabel had demanded that the woman speak in plain, sensible fashion.

"Clear your mind of what you don't need, you troublesome old woman." Kay had laughed then, a wonderful laugh, rich and ringing. "You can see anything you want inside the maze, if you can get out of your own way first."

Kay was a good and patient teacher. Ysabel had slid herself around the globe of Spira, traveling in ways her mind found odd and confusing, pushing closer, searching, failing, pulling back. But at last she descended upon Tal Hae like a lowering angel—an old, wrinkled, gray-haired angel—until she hovered outside the Greenhouse.

Pushing her sight into the Greenhouse had been a struggle. The windows and walls blocked her passage as easily as they would have done in life.

"Abernathy, you silly old man," she had scolded out loud. "I'm a friend. There's no need to keep me out." But she had persisted, discovering that she could slowly seep her ghostly presence through the front door, as though it remembered that the living version of herself had once been allowed inside.

A meeting was in progress, and the attendants included some very important people, including the king himself, Crunard IV, sitting at the dining room table! Ysabel spent a few minutes floating about the room, waving her arms in front of people's faces and shouting, but none of the living could see or hear her.

"I told you," said Kay, who hovered nearby. "You're just a bit of spirit in a world of flesh and blood."

"You did say that, yes." Ysabel tried not to be too vexed with the woman. She was trying to help, after all. "Then let's hush up, so we can hear what's going on."

And so Ysabel heard about how Naradawk was going to escape within the week, and she heard that obnoxious Rosset Finch interrogating her friends and calling their judgment into question, and she heard from Morningstar that Ivellios was likely being held in the city of Minok. She had never been there herself, but William had visited once and described it as a busy, smelly city she'd be happier avoiding.

"Well," Ysabel said to Kay when the meeting had adjourned, "Verdshane seems to be the center of attention. At least I died in an important place."

"Good for you, looking at the bright side," said Kay.

"I want to go to Minok," said Ysabel. "Now that I've found Tal Hae, that should be easy enough. Up the road to the forest, then west to the coast." She paused, considering. "But I'd like to stay with Dranko and follow him for a while. Watch him investigate. Maybe the clues he finds will help guide my own search."

"And if you find Ivellios in Minok, what then?" asked Kay. "You cannot communicate with the living on Spira."

"I'll think of something," said Ysabel defiantly. "You said yourself that I'm something new here in the Crosser's Maze. But it won't matter if I don't have anything useful to say."

She lost Dranko and the others after the king's wizard teleported them straight to Minok. It took her some time (and to her frustration she didn't know how *much* time) to move herself across Harkran to the coast. She combed the streets of the city, drifting back and forth above the rooftops, close enough to the ground to make out individual faces. The crowds and her top-down perspective made it difficult, and she considered giving up. But she recalled Morningstar talking about a warehouse, and those were easy enough to find. She flitted up and down Warehouse Row until she recognized that new fellow, the one Horn's Company had brought back from Kivia. She spotted him sauntering along the far side of the street, taking furtive glances at the row of boxy buildings. Eventually he led her back to a tavern where Dranko, Ernie, and Rosset were waiting.

Once more she had tried to get their attention, floating in front of them, wafting through them, trying to knock over their mugs or stir their hair. But while she could observe and hear them well enough, nothing she did called their attention to her.

Dranko had outlined his plan, and Ysabel had followed him to warehouse thirty-one, watched him scale the wall and break in through a skylight. For her it was a simple matter of passing ghost-like through the walls. After poking around on the upper balconies, Dranko had dropped to the floor and gone into the little office tucked in the corner.

Then, disaster. A monster, some horrid thing made of purple smoke, had erupted from a desk drawer and assaulted Dranko. He held it off a short while through a combination of dodging and fleeing, shrieking all the while, no doubt hoping to attract attention. And it had done that! Ysabel had floated out to the street to find Ernie, Step, and Rosset racing to the huge double doors, their handles bound up with chains and a forbidding metal lock. Ernie pulled out a light-rod as he ran, shining it at the looming warehouse. From outside, the noise of Dranko's battle was horrific. An unnatural wind, splintering wood, and of course Dranko's manic shouting, had attracted not only his friends, but a growing handful of passersby. These folk had the good sense to keep a fearful distance, muttering to themselves, wondering aloud what demonic terror was unfolding behind the doors.

Ernie and Rosset had immediately set to smashing at the lock with the hilts of their swords. Ysabel shifted in and out of the warehouse through the street-facing wall, desperate for Dranko to avoid a gruesome death, and urging his friends to hammer faster. The lock bent, deforming under the blows from the sword hilts, but by the gods it was going to be a close thing.

The lock surrendered to the pounding and clattered to the ground, but the door handles were still wrapped in chains. Step unraveled them, even as Dranko lurched and stumbled his way to the door. At the same moment the last length of chain pulled free, the cloud-creature struck Dranko in the side. Ernie and Rosset pulled the doors open to see Dranko lying in a pool of blood only a few feet away.

"No, no, no!" Ysabel cried. "None of that! One of us bleeding to death on the ground was quite enough!"

A dozen paces inside, the billowing monster roiled.

The crowd drew back, many pointing or straining to see. But Rosset Finch stepped forward. In a swift, decisive motion, he drew his sword with his right hand and held up his left in a fist. A copper bracelet encircled his left wrist, and a small golden shard of metal adhered to the bracelet. The fragment blazed outward like a sunrise cresting a hill, and in its light Rosset's face went ashen, all the color drained out of it. But it was not a paleness born of fear; the same happened to his shirt, and his sword, and the side of Ernie's face to Rosset's left.

"Stand back, all of you!" Rosset shouted, before stepping into the warehouse to face down the creature. It whipped up a sudden gust and flung a strand of mist toward the Silversword, but the smoky arm broke against a nimbus of yellow light several feet out from its target. Rosset flinched and stumbled back a step but kept his feet.

The creature charged at him, howling and turbulent, glinting from within as if its swirling body were full of butcher's knives. Its advance was checked by the golden aura, its flailing smoke-limbs repelled, but Rosset was forced to one knee before the onslaught. The corona flickered, wavered, danced like a windblown candle flame. One strand of purple smoke slipped past the golden shield and tore bloody pieces out of Rosset's thigh. He screamed but stayed resolute, struggling to his feet with a little limping hop. The smoke-creature fell back slightly, roiling and pulsing, reminding Ysabel of a snake coiled to strike.

"Uthol Inga!" cried Rosset. He pushed forward, arm with the golden shard upraised, forcing its light against the monster. The creature jittered as if caught in a draft, like fireplace smoke when the flue was opened. Its body grew sparse, breaking apart like a morning mist in a rising wind. Rosset raised his sword and swept it through the thing's remaining shreds of substance, which scattered like dead leaves.

Certain Step had rushed to Dranko's side and pressed wads of bandages onto Dranko's lower torso. "Ernest!" he shouted. "Keep pressure on these! And you!" He pointed to a woman who had come close to gawk. "Take this light and keep it pointed where I tell you." Such was Step's authority that the woman did as she was told without question.

"What happened?" she asked, taking Step's light-rod. "And what in Brechen's name was that thing?"

"I don't know," said Step. "But it's dead now. Keep that light on my pack."

While Ernie leaned into the bandages, already soaking through with blood, Step shrugged out of his pack and produced a smaller satchel of salves and ointments. He popped the lid from a vial of grayish cream, scooped a thick dollop onto his fingers, and smeared it around beneath the bloody cloths.

Dranko's face was sickly pale in the cast-off light from the rod. His eyes were closed, and Ysabel felt sick to watch. The blood oozing out from beneath all the cloths reminded her starkly of her own death, losing too much blood before her friends could save her. A maternal instinct seized her, and she moved to hold his hand even knowing she couldn't actually touch him.

She felt something.

It wasn't tactile. There was no skin-to-skin sensation as when she used to hold William's hand on long walks around their farm. But there was warmth, a flow of energy, a… She didn't have the words to properly describe it. Her hand was impossibly intermingled with his hand. When she lifted her arm, his own hand rose up slightly as though the two were connected by thickening honey.

Dranko's eyes fluttered open, and he stared at her. Was he seeing her? His lips moved slightly but no sound emerged.

"Dranko!" she exhorted. "Hold on! They're going to save you!"

Gods, Ysabel hoped so. Step had directed Ernie to shift the bandages and was sewing up the longest of the gashes in Dranko's side. It was difficult for him, with blood welling up between Step's fingers as he worked, but Ysabel had done enough stitching of her own on injured farmhands to recognize the Kivian's skill. Step worked with a quick, confident precision. He applied a different salve once his stitches were in, then held two fingers to Dranko's neck. "He still may die. He needs more than I can do here."

Ernie looked up at the crowd, some thirty people jostling to see what was going on. "Where is the shrine of Delioch here in Minok?"

"Up the hill past the mason's guild hall," said an older man. "They fixed my son's leg when he got kicked by a mule."

"How far?" asked Ernie.

"Not very," said the man. "Fifteen minutes walking, I'd say."

"That man nearly died keeping a terrible monster at bay." Everyone turned their heads to see Rosset Finch standing in the warehouse doorway, favoring his left leg, blood soaking his right. The golden light had faded, color returned to his face, but he looked haggard, like a man who hadn't slept in days. Nonetheless his eyes carried the intensity of his command. "Carry him. Lift him and hold him as steady and still as you can. Take him to the church of Delioch."

Several strong men and women came forward and surrounded Dranko, reaching down to put their hands beneath him.

"Gently!" cried Certain Step. "Don't jostle him! If the stitches come loose, he could still bleed to death."

As Dranko rose from the ground, Ysabel's hand pulled away from his with a slight feeling of resistance, as if they had become slightly stuck together. His head lolled sideways towards her, and did she imagine that he recognized her? She hovered higher to maintain eye contact with him, but once his bearers started to move, his eyes closed again.

Weariness washed over her as she watched the townsfolk carry Dranko inland and up the hill. As Kay had warned her, keeping focus on the "small picture" drained her mental wherewithal. But she had to make sure Dranko would be all right, so she followed the crowd as they marched. Rosset and Ernie went ahead of them, shouting and clearing out clusters of city-folk curious about the procession, while Certain Step walked at Dranko's side, exhorting the bearers to be careful.

The Deliochan church in Minok was small, surrounded by a low stone wall with a single guarded gate.

"This man is a priest of Delioch himself," Ernie told the guard urgently. "He is dying and needs medical care. Please, let him in." When the guard hesitated, eyeing the mob with unease, Ernie added, "Whatever tithe your church requires, I will pay double. There is no time; let us in!"

The guard looked upon Dranko's scar-pocked face and bloodstained shirt. He opened the gate. Several priests rushed out of the main church building and accompanied Dranko and his bearers inside. Soon he lay on a warm cot with healers hovering, tending to his wounds, changing his soaked bandages, and shooing the others away.

"Do you have a channeler?" Ernie asked.

"Only one," said the nearest healer, "but she left days ago. The high priest ordered her to a village called Verdshane." She looked nettled at the thought. "But you brought your friend here in time; he has lost a great deal of blood, but none of his organs were damaged. He'll be fine."

Ysabel shuddered with relief and rose away from the floor. Floating in the empty vastness of the Crosser's Maze was much easier than sticking close to ground level. But she stopped as she noticed the person in the bed next to Dranko's. He was a tall man, covered neck to feet in a dark gray sheet. His face was pale and skeletal, scarred in several places (though not as severely as Dranko's), with flecks of blood at the corners of his mouth. His breath came in wheezy, uneven rasps.

The man turned his head with what seemed great effort and looked directly at Ysabel.

"Are you an angel?"

Ernie and Rosset both turned and also stared at Ysabel—or, rather, at the place the man was looking.

One of the priests moved to the man's side and held his hand. "Rest, Brother Alic," he said softly.

Ysabel was too tired to float down to the sickly man, who smiled at her before closing his eyes. A priestess came to stand by the priest, turned him aside, and muttered, "He can't have more than another few days. But Alic was a good man; there is certainly a place waiting for him in heaven."

That was the last Ysabel heard; she drifted upward in a dreamy daze until Spira was a huge blue and white globe beneath her. Kay was at her side.

"Interesting," said the former Keeper.

"You were right," said Ysabel wearily. "Watching from up close is exhausting."

"We think it's gravity," said Kay. "We have no true physical form here, but objects of great mass pull on our essence, our sense of self. Many Keepers have speculated on the mechanism, but no one knows for certain." She grinned at Ysabel. "I was right about that, yes, but I was very wrong about your invisibility to the real world. That man in the hospital bed could see you, don't you think?"

"Yes," said Ysabel, "and I think Dranko might have seen me too, if only for a moment. But no one else could."

Kay put a hand to her chin and watched Spira spin. Ysabel looked as well. How odd that Spira was so obviously round when it looked so flat when standing on it. And whereas she always assumed that the heavens spun about the world, she wondered now if the stars were not fixed in place, and the sun too, while Spira turned beneath them.

"The dead speaking to the dying," said Kay.

"Excuse me?"

"I told you I wasn't sure how a drifting departed soul like yourself might interact with the maze," said Kay. "I think of the world we see here as an image in a mirror. Perhaps when people are dying they move closer to its surface, just as you move closer when you stand on the surface of a world. Your fingertips, brushing those of someone reaching out from the brink of death..."

"Goodness!" said Ysabel. "I hope that doesn't mean that the priest is wrong, that Dranko is certainly going to die from his wounds."

"We are sailing in uncharted waters," said Kay.

"Yes. I suppose," said Ysabel. "But even assuming I can use this…whatever you'd like to call it, for me to be of any use, I'll still need to find Ivellios myself. And I'm so tired. Can I sleep?"

"A new question every day!" said Kay, looking pleased. "Can a dead woman sleep in the interstitial emptiness of the Crosser's Maze? Centuries of Keepership, and there are still mysteries left unsolved. Ysabel Horn, why don't you add to the annals of our knowledge. Close your eyes, and we will see what happens."

CHAPTER FOURTEEN

Y ou've got to get out of the house." Tor tugged on Aravia's sleeve.
Aravia sat on the edge of her bed, staring silently at the wall. Her eyes
were their usual gorgeous green color, so she wasn't in the maze, but even
though she'd come out several minutes ago, she hadn't moved, or looked at him,
or done anything but breathe. Her pale face was a portrait drawn in chalk.

"Aravia!"

She ignored him or maybe couldn't hear him. Pewter lay on her lap, eyes closed,
sleeping, or lost with Aravia wherever she was.

"Aravia, please, come back."

This wasn't the first time Aravia had emerged from the Crosser's Maze in a
near-catatonia. The more times she went in to study with King Vhadish, the worse
it grew. The last time it had lasted about ten minutes. This time it was closer to
half an hour.

He jostled her lightly, not wanting to harm her or cause her to fall over, and
though Aravia righted herself, she didn't otherwise react. Pewter's tail flicked. Tor
waved his hand in front of Aravia's eyes for the sixth or seventh time.

Nothing.

Should I kiss her? Would that work?

He felt himself redden at the thought. They had joked about that, as a means
to jar her free of the maze should she stay too long. He'd like to, certainly. Would
she mind? What if she was stuck in this state for hours, or days?

"Not enough people," Aravia whispered. "I'd kill them all."

"Aravia!" Tor kneeled before her and gripped her shoulders. "Are you back?
Are you all right?"

Color returned to her cheeks and she took a deep, eye-fluttering breath. "Tor!

What's the matter?"

"What's the matter? You came out of the maze half an hour ago but haven't moved or spoken in all that time!"

"Oh. I've…I've been thinking, that's all. Thinking about how I can do what I need to."

"What did you mean? That thing you just said?"

Aravia closed her eyes. "It's complicated, Tor. I'm worried about a problem with the maze that I'm not certain how to solve."

Tor couldn't imagine a problem that would stump Aravia for long. He stood and held out his hands. Aravia looked at them, then took them in her own.

"Come on," said Tor. "We're going for a walk."

"A walk? I can't. I need to think, and once I've recovered some of my mental fortitude, I should return to Vhadish. I still have so much to learn."

"You need to get out of the Greenhouse," he told her. "Just for a couple of hours. Move your legs. Breath outside air. You'll recover your mental fortitude just as well on a stroll through Tal Hae. Earlier it looked like it might rain, but the sky is clearing and the air has that perfect autumn coolness."

She stood, letting Tor take her weight and pull her to her feet. Pewter leapt from her lap at the last minute, then jumped back up onto the bed.

"I suppose I could stand to stretch my legs," she said. "But I can't stay out long. Vhadish will be expecting me."

"You'll be a better student after you've moved around some." Tor led her by the hand down the stairs. Pewter stayed behind, which was unusual, but Tor didn't mind. "Wait here," he told her in the living room. He dashed to the kitchen, where a basket sat upon the butcher block.

"Everything set?" he asked Eddings.

"Indeed," said the butler. "Enjoy your outing, Master Tor."

Tor grabbed the basket and returned to collect Aravia. "Come on."

Outside the Street of Bakers was quiet, but the rest of Tal Hae bustled with its usual midday fervor. He led Aravia down the street to its intersection with Queen's Way, looked up and down, and turned north.

"Cawvus used to make me go outside in the middle of particularly long lessons, especially arithmetic. 'You'll be useless until you've got your blood pumping a bit,' he'd say. So I'd go to the sparring ground and swing a sword for a few minutes, sometimes run laps around the yard. Cawvus knew his trade; I was always able to think more clearly after I'd exhausted myself."

Aravia smiled at him—nearly stopping his heart as her smile always did—then hopped lightly over a gap in the street where a cobble had freed itself. "Your tutor was a wise man, and so are you." She turned as they passed Tinker's Row. "Where are we going, exactly?"

"You'll see." Tor stopped at the next intersection, crowded and noisy with produce sellers under tents at all four corners. "It's funny that we've been based in Tal Hae for half a year now, but we've spent so little time exploring the city. We're always off on some quest or another. That way, I think." He led her left, down two blocks that smelled of leather and hot metal, then right, skirting a small plaza where a juggler entertained a small gathering of children.

Tor turned to tell Aravia he could see their destination up ahead, but she had stopped to watch the performer.

"I've never seen a juggler before," she said. "She must have practiced for many years to become so skilled." The woman kept five apples aloft in a steady cascade while she repeatedly asked the children if she should eat one. They shouted "Yes!" delightedly until she relented. The juggler threw three of the apples high into the air, then took a quick bite out of one of the remaining two before resuming the pattern. The children shrieked their approval.

Tor threw a few copper chits into the woman's hat. "Do you want to stay and watch the whole show?"

Aravia watched the juggler intensely. "I have to learn to do something just as complex, in only a few days. Vhadish is teaching me shortcuts, clever techniques, and unusual ways of thinking, but it's all so daunting."

She trailed off, eyes defocusing. Tor grabbed her hand. "Let's keep going. We're nearly there."

Aravia shook off the juggler's spell. "Where is 'there?'"

"The Gods' Green," he told her. "I asked Eddings what he thought was the most beautiful place in Tal Hae, and that's what he said. He made it sound like the perfect place for a picnic."

Eddings had good taste. Gods' Green was idyllic, though it was already trading in its arboreal verdure for autumnal reds and golds. Breezes whispered in the branches, and fall flowers bloomed in well-tended beds.

Tor followed a gray gravel path that snaked through the park. He held Aravia's hand, leading her to a stone bench beside a shimmering pond. Hungry ducks had congregated along the far side where two young girls tossed shreds of lettuce into the water.

Tor set down the basket and unfolded a thin blanket on the grassy strip between the bench and the water. Then he produced a bottle of wine, a long loaf of bread, a paper-wrapped wedge of cheese, and a cluster of plump purple grapes. Would she like them, or was she too distracted by her drive to master the maze? Maybe spending all that time in her own head had taken away her appetite, but she had to eat to keep up her strength, especially given the toll her—

"Tor, this is lovely!" Aravia sat at one edge of the blanket, her legs folded beneath her. She took a long, deep breath. Tor silently offered a prayer of thanks to Brechen, handed Aravia a hunk of bread and a slice of cheese, then looked up at the trees lining the pond.

"It's strange to think how recently we stumbled across that glowing hut in the Tangled Green," he said. "On the one hand, all of our days in Calabash and the Crosser's Maze took almost no time at all, but on the other, it feels like years ago."

Aravia nodded absently and chewed on her bread. Tor looked at her adoringly. She seemed deep in thought, which of course she was. Aravia was always deep in thought, which was one of the things he loved most about her, never mind that she often pondered things far beyond his comprehension.

"Do you ever think about destiny?" she asked at last.

"All the time," said Tor. "It's my destiny to protect you. That's what the goblin shaman said."

"Technically," said Aravia, "Irligg said only that you will protect. He did not name me in his prediction."

"But I know that's what he meant," said Tor.

"You did save me from the black rat."

"Sometimes I wonder though," said Tor, "about all the prophecies we've heard and been a part of. There's all that stuff the Eyes of Moirel said to us, and Irligg's bones, and Certain Step's poem about the 'last of five,' and Morningstar's seer-dreams, and Kibi's dreams about the earth speaking to him, though Kibi still says that there's no such thing as destiny. Do you think everything in all those prophecies will come true? And if it will, does that mean everything we do here, everything we decide, doesn't matter in the end? But what if some of them are contradictory? How would we know? What if—"

He stopped himself, realizing that he was babbling. Aravia was grinning at him, a grin that hovered on the verge of laughter.

"What?"

"I enjoy how you talk and think at the same time."

Tor felt himself blush.

"Finish your thought," she prompted.

Tor tried to reconstruct where he had been, which was difficult with Aravia smiling at him. "Er, I guess what I wonder is, if the gods know in advance what's going to happen to us, does it matter what we do? What choices we make?"

"I'm sure it matters," said Aravia. "What I think is, the gods aren't allowed to meddle, but prophecies and dreams are their way of bending the rules. They are trying to nudge us in certain directions. Morningstar shared her opinions on this with me during our journey across Kivia, and I believe she is correct. There are many possible futures, she said, and the gods see them all at once. Some they like more than others, and so they are doing what they can to make one of their favorites come about."

Tor nodded. "So prophecies aren't about what *will* happen, but what the gods *want* to happen." A troubling thought gripped him. "But what if what *we* want isn't the same as what *they* want?"

"We could derail their plans any time we want," she continued. "I believe we have free will to act as we wish. The gods do not constrain our actions or bring them about. Irligg's bones said, 'You will protect.' But wouldn't you have done that anyway? And they said I will 'unlock,' which is hardly revelatory, as I can open locks magically."

"I think you are my destiny," Tor said, before any part of his mind could warn him about how sappy he sounded. "And you've unlocked my heart."

Oh gods that was the stupidest thing anyone has ever said.

Aravia laughed and blushed. "Tor, you're ridiculous." But she took his hand and stroked it, letting her fingers drift across the gap where his left pinky had been. "The gods gave you bravery, skill, and kindness, but what draws me to you, I think, is how you speak straight from your soul."

Tor peered across the pond, his whole body tingling with happiness. *Of all the gods' gifts to me, Aravia, you are the one I treasure the most.* At least he stopped himself from saying that one out loud!

Somewhere at the southwestern corner of the Gods' Green, where the grassy stretch bordered an inlet of the bay, would be a church of Brechen, god of the sea. Tor had grown up praying to Brechen, never thinking much of it. The gods were an abstraction, a collection of all-powerful beings who seemed content to watch their people thrive or wither, without judgment or preference. Each dabbled in human affairs in small ways—water-walkers and luck-benders and channelers and the like—but for most people, prayer was the only interaction one had with the gods. Had they made him the way he was? Did they pay that close attention?

"You're right about free will," he said, looking down at their clasping hands, delighted and still a tiny bit baffled. He truly was the luckiest man ever born. "I'd protect you even if the goblin bones had told me not to."

"I know you would," she said. "I'm counting on it." She looked as though she'd say more, but instead became quiet, thoughtful, staring at something far away. Tor let go of Aravia's hand and took the opportunity to pour two cups of wine from the basket. He handed one to Aravia, but she didn't seem to notice.

"Aravia?"

She started, looked at him, and took the cup. "I'm sorry. I was thinking about my task. Tor, soon I'm going to Verdshane. Probably tomorrow. I want you to come with me. To be my protector."

"To Verdshane? Why?"

"Vhadish told me that to close the portal, I would need to be physically near to it. Its nature is such that magic cannot work upon it from a distance. I'll need to be able to see it directly. And he said that to learn what I must, I'll need to study the real thing up close, not just the version in the maze."

"Of course I'll come with you," he said, thinking of the stasis field, and the gopher-bugs, and Aktallian Dreamborn. "If anything threatens you, it'll have to go through me."

"That's exactly what I hoped you would say." Aravia's smile melted his heart.

She took a sip of wine, grimaced, and handed it back to him. "I never developed a taste for alcohol. Serpicore forbade me anything that might dull my mind, and this would be a poor time for me to start. I still have so many problems to solve."

"When you came out of the maze this morning, you said, 'Not enough people. I'd kill them all.' Is that one of your problems? What does it mean?"

Aravia shook her head, no doubt thinking he'd have no hope of understanding. She was probably right, but then she surprised him by answering.

"In order to use the Crosser's Maze, I have to focus its power using the arcane potential of other people. Willing people. But most people aren't wizards and don't have much arcane potential."

"And what about the killing part?"

"If I draw too much upon a person's potential, I can burn out their life energy. I don't know yet how much power I'll need to seal up the portal, but if my need is great enough, I may end up killing the people helping me."

Tor thought about that. "Who exactly will you be drawing from?"

"The soldiers, most likely," she said. "Vhadish believes that my foci will need to be close to my physical body."

"You can draw on my arcane potential," Tor said, "but I'm no wizard. It won't be very much."

"It's possible," said Aravia, "that the combined energy I can focus from every single volunteer available won't be enough. One of Vhadish's most important lessons is how to maximize what I can draw, but it's an extremely difficult skill to master."

Tor brightened. "You should draw on the archmagi's potential. Surely each of them has as much as a thousand of us normal folk put together."

"I'm sure they do," said Aravia, "but they'll be keeping the portal shut until the last possible moment."

"Well, yes," said Tor, "but when the time comes for you to seal it up for good, won't that *be* the last possible moment?"

Aravia nodded. "Yes, I suppose that's true. But they won't be anywhere near Verdshane. The five of them will be in their protected towers, spread all around Charagan."

"Oh. True. Never mind." Tor shook his head. As if he could think of something Aravia hadn't already considered. He raised his wine cup to his lips but stopped short, another thought bubbling up. "But you just said that to do magic on the portal, you have to be close to it. Somehow the archmagi are managing to cast their spells on it from a distance. How can that be?"

Aravia looked at him sharply. Tor felt a fool. He should stop pestering her with—

"You're right," she said. "How *can* that be? They shouldn't be able to…"

She trailed off, brows furrowed in concentration. Tor watched her expectantly, knowing to give her the silence she needed to think.

"It's too late to ask the archmagi about it," she said slowly. "They made it clear at the end of the meeting that they couldn't spare themselves any more from their own task. But when I return to the Crosser's Maze, maybe it's worth taking a peek at what the archmagi are up to, and how exactly they're keeping the portal closed."

She leaned over Tor's legs, raised her chin, and gave him a long kiss that he wished could last forever. When she straightened up, all of his breath went with her. How odd, that the sensations of exhilaration and peace could become so mixed together. Being with Aravia sped his heart but calmed his mind in a way he had never experienced.

"I should get back to the Greenhouse," she said with a sigh. "I need to speak again to Vhadish." But she didn't get up right away. She turned her body and leaned back against him, snuggling into his chest. Warmth and bliss suffused him.

"Soon," she said softly. "I should go back to the Greenhouse. Soon."

CHAPTER FIFTEEN

Kibi sat cross-legged on the stone floor of the Greenhouse basement, an Eye of Moirel in each hand. He didn't know what else to do.

Dranko, Ernie, and Step were off hunting for Ivellios. Tor and Aravia were out on a picnic. Morningstar was meditating, preparing to meet with her dream warriors. Kibi had promised to sit by her side in case Aktallian found her and injured her, but that wouldn't be for another hour. In the meantime, Kibi was on his own, wondering what to do with himself.

When the time is right and the world is wrong, only those in refuge will be spared. That's what the Mirror had said. And *the wizard's house will serve.* Did it mean Abernathy's tower? Or the Greenhouse?

The unmaking of the world.

The Eyes had warned about that too. It felt like a storm was coming, but only Kibi noticed the stirring of the wind. The others were all so caught up worrying about Naradawk, but this business with the Eyes felt like something else entirely. Or maybe he was overthinking.

Overthinking. Gods, but this whole business was confusing. Abernathy had made it seem straightforward the night he'd summoned the bunch of them, but things had become so complicated since then, and now the wizards couldn't give them any extra help.

Kibi closed his eyes, but he could still see the gems, colored sparks glinting in his mind, green and purple. That was an odd thing: With his eyes open they were both clear diamonds with little specks of blackness in their centers, but through his lids, he saw them as colored.

"Tell me if I got this straight," he said to the Eyes. "There's seven a' you all told. I know Sagiro took the red one, and the Sharshun that Ernie fought has got the orange one. I've got you two: purple and green. There's a fifth one in a place called Het Branoi that we think might be someplace in Kivia. That leaves two more we don't know about, but maybe the Sharshun have already found 'em. How'm I doin' so far?"

The Eyes said nothing.

"I'll just assume you bein' silent means I'm on the right track. Anyhow, it turns out that we only need three of you to do whatever it is you're meant to do. 'Travel nowhere,' I guess, which Aravia figures means take us to Volpos when the two worlds are overlappin'. Still don't know why we'd want to do that, but maybe the Sharshun are gonna use theirs as part a' Naradawk's escape plan, and we'll need three of our own Eyes to stop 'em. Am I close? Wonderful. I'll keep goin' then.

"You've gone and warned us that the Sharshun want to unmake the world. We know Abernathy thinks Naradawk could destroy everythin' if he gets loose. So maybe it's all connected up after all."

The Eyes offered no opinion.

"But," said Kibi, pressing on, "now there's that bit about refuge and how only those inside it will be spared. So let's say the world gets destroyed, but we're safe inside the refuge. What then? World's still destroyed, ain't it? Can't see as that's a good conclusion to all a' this business."

He glared down at the Eyes. "And what about 'time is right, world is wrong'? What the hell does that mean? Just tell me what's goin' on, you blasted rocks!"

The Eyes of Moirel sat cold and quiet in his hands.

"Tell you what," Kibi told them. "I'm not gonna put you back in your sludge pot. Not even gonna close your trunk or lock the closet. I'll just set you down where you can jump out and stick yourselves into any eye sockets you want, in case you change your mind and want to let us know what it is you think's gonna happen."

He placed the gems down gently in the bottom of the trunk, leaving the closet door open as promised, and backed away toward the center of the basement. A part of him worried that the Eyes would take up his suggestion, fly up out of the chest, and use his own sockets to finally impart some clarifying wisdom. Another part welcomed the possibility. After all, Eddings hadn't lost his sight, and a bit of disfiguration would be worth it for a better sense of how exactly the Sharshun were threatening the world with destruction.

Around him, the rest of the basement was empty, quiet. Kibi had been down here (as far as he knew) more than any other member of the company, and, enchanted gemstones notwithstanding, he enjoyed its cool, calm solitude. The floor was packed earth but the walls were good unbroken fieldstone.

He'd never tried talking to the walls; maybe they'd have something useful to say. He walked slowly across the room and pressed his left hand—the one slowly turning to stone itself—against the wall.

"I don't suppose you can tell me if this is the place of refuge?"

The wall didn't answer immediately, but something was odd about the stone, almost as if he could sense it thinking. And it was slightly warm, which was the opposite of his expectation. He kept his hand pressed up against the wall.

It is, Kibilhathur.

"Refuge from what?" Kibi asked, startled. "What will it mean for the Sharshun to unmake the world?"

Minutes crept past, but Kibi again felt not as though the stone had gone quiet, but rather was considering how to answer.

We do not know. Abernathy and Caranch built this place to protect you from change, but we do not understand the nature of that change.

"Caranch!" Kibi recalled what Solomea had told him. "My grandfather was here?"

This time it was harder for Kibi to remain patient.

No, and yes, the wall said eventually. *Caranch and Spira have been becoming more like each other for a long time. He returns to the source, fading into past and future. We are his last great work.*

The rock fell silent. Kibi waited for it to speak again, but it had finished having its say. A quarter of an hour must have passed before he overcame his reluctance and peeled his hand from the wall. But the stone spoke once more, as only his hesitant fingertips remained in contact.

You are where the ends of the circle meet. Abernathy will need you to tell him how things turned out. You have been right all along, Kibilhathur. You make your own destiny.

* * *

Upstairs, Kibi found Eddings wiping down the dining room table with a damp rag.

"Good afternoon, Kibilhathur," said the butler cheerfully. "I trust all is well."

"Well enough," said Kibi, though he suspected Eddings could tell he didn't mean it. He felt a pang of guilt, those things he said to the Eyes of Moirel. He'd practically invited them to leap back into Eddings' face and take over his voice.

"Is there anything I can do for you?" the butler asked.

Kibi chose a chair that wouldn't get in Eddings' way and sat down heavily. "Don't suppose you can tell me why rocks can't tell me nothin' in a plain way?"

Eddings chuckled. "I'm afraid that I cannot. Even having *been* the way."

The butler's ability to take things in stride was astonishing. Abernathy must have had some reason for hiring him, but it was strange how little Horn's Company knew about their reliable servant.

"If you don't mind my askin', how exactly did you come to get hired by Abernathy? Is there a guild for house workers here in Tal Hae? Did you serve some noble family 'fore you came here?"

Eddings didn't answer right away, just kept scrubbing a stubborn corner of the table where General Largent had slopped some sauce. Maybe it was a sore subject for some reason. Kibi was about to tell Eddings to never mind about it when the butler looked up at him.

"I hadn't been a butler before this assignment," he said. "It was all extremely unexpected. I was—" Eddings paused, frowning. "My family were farmers two days' walk north of Tal Hae. We grew all sorts of vegetables—carrots, cabbages, celery, peas, tomatoes, many others—and our hens' eggs were the pride of the local market. We were extremely fortunate over the years; even during dry seasons or when carrot flies swarmed, our yields were high and our income generous as farmers went. Truly, Pikon smiled upon us.

"But I chafed at the farmer's life. I was fascinated by the bustle and energy of Tal Hae, which I saw a few times a year when my parents needed supplies the peddlers and smaller towns didn't offer. They'd send me to buy cook pots or spices or whatever it was they needed. I knew I wanted to live here, find a city trade, be surrounded by all the energy of Tal Hae. The farm was slow and quiet and bored me to tears."

Kibi found that surprising. Eddings himself was slow and quiet.

"So what happened?" Kibi asked. "Did you make a go of it?"

Eddings draped his rag over his shoulder and sat down opposite Kibi. "No. Not at first. I lacked the spine, I'm sorry to say. I stayed at the farm helping my parents, giving them the impression that I'd be happy to inherit when they passed on. My mother died when I was in my early twenties, from rheumy lungs. Father said she'd had the condition for years and was lucky to have lasted as long as she did. Father keeled over out in a field on my thirty-fifth birthday, hale as a horse until the moment his heart stopped beating."

"Sorry to hear it," mumbled Kibi.

"Don't be," said Eddings. "They both lived good lives, doing what they enjoyed. My greatest regret is that I did not do right by their legacy. After my father's death, I went through the motions of farming, but my skills were average at best, and the farm was soon beset by misfortune. Two seasons in a row the fields flooded, and some predator, a coyote I suspect, chewed through the fence around the coop and killed all the hens. Eventually I sold the farm for a pittance and came into Tal Hae to see if I could better my prospects."

Eddings took his rag back in hand and rubbed a spot he must have missed, though the table looked perfectly clean.

"It went poorly for me," the butler said, though with more resignation than rancor. "Though the vigor of Tal Hae, the excitement, was what I had always imagined, I was far too old to take up a new trade. I knew a little carpentry, and how to sew, and had a pocketful of other minor skills, but nothing I could parlay into a living. I survived on odd jobs for a few years, and rented a tiny room down by the water that abutted a bait house and smelled terrible. I resented it, though it was the only place with a roof I could afford…until the fishery that owned the bait house did well enough that they bought my building and kicked out the tenants."

Eddings shook his head as he recalled the memories. "It was a low point, for certain. I took to sleeping in doorways and alleyways. I even stooped to begging, though it wounded what little pride remained to me. On the day that fortune smiled upon me, I was asleep on a bench in Gods' Green, wrapped in a threadbare blanket, my most prized possession. It had been a cold night. A girl shook me awake. I thought at first I was being told off for my choice of bed, but the girl simply said, 'Are you Mr. Brown?' I must have made some noise of affirmation because she then said, 'If you go to the Greenhouse on the Street of Bakers, a man there needs your help.'"

"Who was she?" asked Kibi.

"I don't know. A messenger from the gods, maybe? I've come to think so these past several months. As unlikely as her offer seemed, I had no other prospects, and perhaps the man who needed my help might need it badly enough to offer some food in exchange for it. I walked to the Greenhouse and found its door unlocked, its rooms unoccupied. It appeared recently renovated; I smelled fresh paint, and the furniture was in perfect condition, newly polished. The interior was arranged as a mansion rather than a bakery, which I thought was strange. I called out, but no one answered. A joke, I thought. Someone was playing a cruel joke on a homeless man.

"But I wandered upstairs and found the open door to the room with the crystal ball. A small note beside it said, 'Ask for Abernathy.' I did so. Abernathy's face soon appeared in the globe, which was the most shocking thing I had ever seen in my life. I had never beheld anything magical before. Abernathy asked if I was Conrad Brown. I said I was.

"'I wish to hire you,' Abernathy said.

"'For what?' I asked.

"'I want you to be the butler for this household,' he said.

"'I have no skills as a butler,' I told him. 'I wouldn't know where to begin.'

"'That doesn't matter,' he said. 'Just make it up. Pretend. You'll be fine.'"

"Conrad Brown?" asked Kibi. "That's your real name?"

"Yes," said Eddings, "but that didn't sound to me like a butler's name, so I made up one that sounded more the part." He looked sheepishly down at the table. "I'd prefer you continue to call me Eddings. I've come to like it more than my old name."

"Fine with me," said Kibi. "But I find it hard to believe you'd never been a butler. You're so good at it."

"It's kind of you to say so," said Eddings. "I've done my best to do all the things I imagined a faithful servant might do for the lords and ladies of a fancy house. I'm...I'm afraid I misled young Ernest on that first day. He asked me if I'd been a butler a long time, and I said I had. At the time I told myself that, yes, I had technically been working for Abernathy for several months, even though the house heretofore had no occupants. I spent that time cleaning the place, stocking the kitchen, testing the limits of the Icebox, tending the grounds, that sort of thing. I learned from Abernathy that I should expect you on the first night of spring. He taught me your names. I was extremely nervous when you first arrived, though I tried not to show it."

Kibi laughed. Eddings returned a wan smile. "You sure had me convinced," Kibi said. "I figured you'd been butlerin' your whole life. You speak fancy, almost like Aravia, not like a farmer's son. You practice that too?"

"A little," said Eddings, "though I was lucky that my parents taught me to read and encouraged me to devour books anytime I had the chance. The churches of Brechen, Corilayna, and Werthis all allow visitors to read in their libraries, and I availed myself of their hospitality whenever I could. Also there's a small curio shop on Bantam Way that from time to time acquires story books, and I often bought them when my meager financial means allowed it."

"You do sound properly book-learned," said Kibi. "But sorry, didn't mean to interrupt."

"It's no worry. There's not much more to tell, really. Abernathy would summon me to the secret room from time to time, to remind me of small things or prepare me for what was to come. Occasionally he'd visit himself, outlined in blue light, casting spells on various parts of the house. He spent quite a lot of time in the basement, I recall. On some occasions I thought I heard him talking to someone down there, though I never saw any visitors. He made sure I knew how important the house keys were, and how the enchanted painting worked that disguises the room with the crystal ball, and that the walls were ensorcelled to prevent anyone from seeing what went on inside the backyard. That sort of thing. Apart from being hired by a great wizard in the first place, the most alarming thing he said to me was that I should expect that unusual things might happen, things that would shock or horrify an ordinary man. But he also told me that all would be well, no matter what befell me. Take everything in stride, he said. But while you may wander about enjoying the life of the city, be sure to return to the Greenhouse every day if possible."

"Guess he weren't wrong," said Kibi.

"No." Eddings adjusted the translucent fabric over his eyes. "I asked him then, why me? I was no one special. I had no special training. I had never seen any magic or met a wizard. 'I cannot tell you that,' Abernathy said. 'You'll just have to trust me.'"

"Heh." Kibi glanced toward the door leading to the living room. "If it makes you feel any better, Abernathy won't tell us, either. He knows somethin', sure as sure, but he keeps his secrets locked up tight."

Eddings pushed back his chair and stood. "I hope I didn't bore you with my life's story. I hadn't intended to let it all spill out like that." He got that sheepish look again. "Would you mind terribly if I asked you to keep it to yourself? I enjoy my role here and would not wish the others to think less of me."

"I'm sure they wouldn't even if they knew it all," said Kibi. "It ain't as though any of us had glorious lives before Abernathy summoned us, 'cept maybe Tor. But I'll keep your secrets if you want."

"Thank you, Kibilhathur. Now, if you'll excuse me, it's time for me to see to Lapis."

Ugh. Right. Kibi hadn't been up to visit Lapis since they'd set her down in Mrs. Horn's room the day they'd come back from Kivia.

"Does she need anythin'?" he asked. "Food and drink and whatnot?" He felt ashamed for not having wondered that sooner.

"Oddly, no," said Eddings. "Aravia told me she likely would. I don't pretend to understand it, of course, but she told me that while Lapis's mind is in the Crosser's Maze, her body would probably need the same tending as any other unconscious patient. But that doesn't seem to be the case. I can't force her to eat and drink regardless, but she shows no signs of malnutrition or dehydration. It's only been six days, but I would presume that if her body was suffering, we would notice. Thankfully, I've not needed to use the bedpan."

"I'd like to go see her," said Kibi. "Mind if I join you?"

Lapis was laid out on her back, wearing black pants and shirt. Eddings had removed her boots and set them neatly by the door. Her dark blue face was calm and neutral, her breath slow and even. An unpleasantly greasy smell hovered around Lapis's head. Her eyes were closed.

Kibi didn't want to think about her and what they'd have to do. Shreen's promise still held him. It didn't bother him unless he focused his thought on it, but when he did, a cold, clammy feeling came over him, as though he were covered in a nasty, sticky film. If the archmagi were right and things were coming to a head in a week, it wouldn't be long before they'd have to return to Shreen the Fair and hand this woman over.

What would happen if they ignored it? Kibi could imagine living with the unpleasantness of his promise to Shreen's goddess, but Morningstar would be miserable. She felt it all the time, she said, and it must be a hundred times worse for her. No, they'd have to go back and hand over the maze to that horrid fellow, and hand over Lapis too. She was a villain through and through—he remembered her stabbing Certain Step—and she would deserve whatever happened to her, but Kibi still cringed to think about what Shreen's revenge would be like.

Eddings touched her forehead with the back of his hand, then gently washed her face, as though she were just another thing in the room that needed tending.

"Seeing to an unconscious blue-skinned woman who doesn't need to eat or drink," said Eddings, "is the sort of thing I imagine Abernathy meant when he told me to expect this job to be unusual."

The butler spent another few minutes dusting Lapis's room. After he had left, Kibi stayed a few minutes more, staring down at her sleeping form. Her mind, as

Kibi understood it, was trapped in the Crosser's Maze, which was in Aravia's head. It hurt to think about it. And the Silversword, Rosset Finch, had said the Sharshun were infected with some evil substance. Could they be cured of it?

Kibi supposed not. It was certainly unlikely that they'd want to be cured. He sighed and moved to the door—and heard a sound behind him. Had Lapis stirred? He turned quickly. She lay flat on the bed, arms still straight at her sides, eyes still closed, breath still steady.

Her mouth was turned up into a cruel smile.

Kibi held his breath and stared. Was she about to leap up from the bed? Had she been listening all that time Eddings was there? Maybe Rosset Finch had been right, and Lapis had engineered events to gain access to the Greenhouse.

She didn't move. Her smile didn't so much as twitch, and the more Kibi stared, the more it looked like a dead person's rictus, gleeful and horrid. Beyond that change in her expression, she seemed as lifeless as before.

He should at least tell Aravia when she came back from her picnic with Tor. Slowly he backed out of the room and kept his eyes on her until the door was shut.

CHAPTER SIXTEEN

A knock on the door woke Ivellios from dreams of his parents. He sat up quickly, alarmed. The last few times he had already been awake when Naul came for him, and being caught unawares set his heart to pounding and started up a swift ache in his temples.

Ivellios waited for Naul to let himself in; the knock was a courtesy. And the door did open, but this time it was not Naul framed by the light of the hallway, but Essik.

"We have a few minutes before Naul comes to get you," she whispered. "May I come in?"

He took a step back, which she seemed to interpret as a yes. She followed him in and quickly closed the door. Light flared as Essik produced a familiar-looking metal rod.

"Did you deal with the guard I disabled?" Ivellios asked her.

She nodded. "He remembers leaving your door yesterday to go relieve himself, slipping on some wet stone in the privy closet, and knocking his head against the wall. Fortunately, when he came to and hurried back to his post, you were still in your room. No harm done, unless you count the nausea and dizziness he's likely to experience over the next few weeks."

"Great. And what happened to today's guard?"

"I *am* the guard," she said. "I've been working for days to arrange that."

"And how's the plan coming along for getting me out of here?" he asked.

"I'm working as fast as I can," she said. "But it's a tricky thing, planning your escape while not arousing suspicion."

"Then why are you here now?"

"I wanted to warn you about what's coming next," she said. "Naul and Mokad are ready to move you to the next stage of tests. Remember I told you I was working on a surprise for them?" She held up a small flask filled with a clear liquid. "It's this. We can sabotage their efforts, slow them down. Even if I can't rescue you, we can disrupt Mokad's finely calibrated rituals and equations. Don't misunderstand me. I will still do everything I can to free you. But our highest priority should be preventing my colleagues from freeing Naradawk."

Ivellios nodded at that. "I'm with you. How can we do that?"

"Today Naul is going to take you to a new, larger test chamber. It's meant to simulate the final ritual with more accuracy. I won't lie to you; they expect that the spells they're going to cast upon you will be extremely painful."

"Thanks for the warning."

Essik handed him the flask. "Drink this. It will cause your arcane potential to fluctuate for the next few hours, which will throw off some of Mokad's calculations. As a side effect, it will dull the pain you are going to suffer."

"I hope you understand I have to ask this," said Ivellios, "but why are you helping me and sabotaging your own people?"

"Because they aren't my own people," she said.

Before he could question her further about that, she stiffened and glanced at the door.

"Drink it now," she whispered.

He hesitated. What if this were a trick? A way to get him to drink something they needed him to. But that didn't make sense. He was still playing along with Mokad, so they simply could have asked him to drink. Or forced him magically if he refused.

Footsteps sounded faintly from the hall outside.

"Hurry," said Essik.

Ivellios gulped down the liquid in one go. It tasted like watery syrup.

Essik pocketed the empty flask. "Watch everything. Anything you can remember could be useful to the Spire after we escape."

She slipped out the door without another word. Soon came more footsteps, louder ones that stopped directly outside the door.

"He's awake," came Essik's voice. "I've been listening to him move around for a few minutes."

"Good." That was Naul. The knock came as usual, followed a second later by the door opening.

"Good morning, Naul," Ivellios said congenially. "Let me guess. Another day of bizarre rituals and boring math coming up?"

Naul's smile was spare. "Something like that. You may find today's tests more taxing even than the last set, but I'm sure you'll be up for it." He glanced down at the golden bracelet on Ivellios's arm.

"How come you make me keep this on?" Ivellios asked.

"Stability," said Naul. "Mokad says it simplifies things. Without that bracelet, you'd experience an increasing tendency toward intra-dimensional shifting. Our experiments would be constantly interrupted. It is a blessing of the Circle that you brought it with you."

Ivellios cringed, sifting through the wreckage of his memories. "You mean I'd bounce back and forth between here and Volpos."

"Exactly. But thanks to your bracelet, we've been able to accelerate our timeline. To give our rituals a welcome jolt." Naul allowed himself a small chuckle, as if he'd made a private joke.

"Why is that funny?"

"Intellectual humor," said Naul. "We have been able to quicken the rate at which the alignment gains speed. It's…oh, never mind. Just follow me."

Ivellios's bedroom was on a narrow hall one story below the room in which he had been captured. Naul used a small key to unlock the door to the left and led Ivellios down a dark and narrow flight of stone steps. As they walked, Ivellios tried to remove the bracelet—not that he had any desire to stand again before Naradawk, but he couldn't pass up having the option to screw up Mokad's plans.

But Mokad must have thought of that, because the snug-fitting bracelet, which he could typically slide off and on, didn't budge. It didn't even wiggle. The bastards must have used their sorcery to cut off that possible avenue of sabotage.

They turned left at the bottom of the stairs. The new corridor was cold and poorly lit; the only magical light globe was at the far end. An unfamiliar chemical smell made Ivellios's eyes water.

The corridor ended at a small open room with a tall, wide door opposite. Naul put a hand on his shoulder.

"When you go in, do not step on or over any lines painted on the floor. Step around them and move between them. You'll be safest if you just follow me. You'll be instructed where to stand, when to move. It will be similar to last time, though somewhat more…intense."

"Will it hurt?" asked Ivellios.

"Yes. Some. Nothing a man of your mettle cannot abide."

Naul opened the door. Beyond was a much larger room than the previous one: a round, stone chamber forty feet across with a high, flat ceiling. Like every room he'd been in since his arrival, it had no windows.

Not for the first time, Ivellios wondered if any of his friends were searching for him, trying to rescue him. It seemed likely, but how would they have any idea where to look? Aravia had once said that location magic was difficult even for advanced wizards, and surely the Black Circle was shielding this place with all manner of counter-magic.

This room being circular, there was a single continuous wall interrupted only by the door through which he and Naul entered. A dozen cultists stood scattered, engaged in a variety of mysterious activities: measuring streaks of paint on the floor, chanting softly and moving their hands through quick contortions, turning slow circles in place, or writing upon a huge curved slate that took up a full third of the wall's arc. Mokad was among them, pacing just behind four robed figures who chalked lines of numbers and symbols on the slate. He barked at one like a disapproving schoolteacher.

"Jounce! For the application of Arvigan's theorem, we have moved on to the fourth derivative. Jolt is no longer operative."

The cultist erased a row of numbers and letters with a rag and stared, his other hand on his chin.

The floor and remaining walls of the room were scrawled over with a crazy quilt of shapes, diagrams, and symbols. Its largest feature was familiar: two enormous black annulets painted on the floor by the wall's back curve, barely touching, looking like the number "8."

Naul cleared his throat. "The Pivot is here."

Mokad lingered on the crowded slate, then turned slowly toward the door. "You're early. But there's no reason Ivellios can't observe for a few minutes while we finish our calculations. Bring him to the fulcrum point."

Naul turned to Ivellios. "I will go first. Walk with one hand on my shoulder, tread as closely in my footsteps as possible, and do not step on or across any of the lines."

"Yeah, I sure wouldn't want to mess up your plan to free your all-powerful revenge-obsessed monster," Ivellios muttered.

"You wouldn't," said Naul curtly, "but you could damage yourself severely. My warnings are for your benefit."

Naul walked a slow, weaving path through a maze of painted markings on the ground. Ivellios did as he was bid, keeping a grip on Naul and studying his feet. They arrived at the spot where the two large circles met.

"Stand there and do not move," said Naul.

Ivellios adopted a comically shocked expression. "But then I'll be standing on some of your precious paint!"

Naul exhaled and seemed to spend an effort not to roll his eyes. "That is where you are meant to stand. You may turn in place for now but remain in that spot. Later we will give you more specific instructions."

Ivellios crossed his arms and looked around as Naul walked to confer with Mokad by the slate. A few cultists shot him brief glances but for the most part they ignored him, intent as they were on their inscrutable tasks. Mokad nodded his head as the one he had admonished wrote out a new equation. Quia was here as well, serving as a foreman might at a building site, wending her way around the room, giving instructions or making small corrections.

The door opened once more, and Essik came in carrying an earthenware pot brimming with what looked like sugar.

"I have the crystal arcanum," she said.

"Put it down by the door," said Quia, a bit sharply, as though Essik's arrival was an annoyance.

Mokad again turned, and he gave Essik a long stare that made Ivellios uncomfortable. Did Mokad suspect his acolyte of conspiring against him? Essik returned his gaze as if waiting for a sign of approval. Ivellios looked back and forth between them as surreptitiously as possible.

After a few tense seconds, Mokad moved his gaze to the pot. "Have you brought exactly as much as I asked for?"

"One-twentieth part of a firlot," said Essik.

"Set it down, please."

Essik placed the pot of crystals by the door with great care, as if Mokad were judging her caution. Then she stood, gave a small bow, and left. All of the other cultists, even the ones at the slate, now stared at Mokad as if waiting for a signal.

"You all understand the purpose of today's test," he told them. This assumption was greeted with nods all around. "Our previous trials have proven that Ivellios here is the true Pivot and will serve his purpose when the time comes. And as Abac here will tell you—" He indicated the man he had chided earlier, the one whom Ivellios had assumed was named Jounce. "That time is approaching more rapidly every hour."

For some reason this was met with polite laughter from about half of them.

"Judging by our progress, we should be ready to begin in half an hour. Quia, you and Pelon apply the arcanum. The rest of you should silently recite the prayer of coalescence while reviewing your roles."

Ivellios considered his state of mind and the state of his extremities. Nothing felt numb, and his mind had not been clouded. If Essik's concoction was going to dull his pain—not to mention wreak havoc on Mokad's experiment—he'd expect to feel *something* by now. But he felt exactly the same.

Quia threaded a path through the patterns on the ground and picked up the clay pot. While the other cultists stood about, arms at their sides, mouthing silent syllables, Quia and Pelon moved about the chamber with the pot, picking out pinches and sprinkling the sugar-like crystals onto the ground. Ivellios soon noticed a pattern. They deposited the crystal arcanum inside every closed geometric shape drawn on the floor: mostly circles, but also triangles, rectangles, and more complex multisided forms. There were dozens of these shapes, and the two cultists were obviously careful not to tread upon the paint, so the process dragged on. Ivellios amused himself with thoughts of sabotage: smashing the slate, smearing the paint, body-checking cultists so they stumbled across the floor, and beating Mokad to a pulp.

Certainly a part of him argued that he should be doing all of that regardless. Yes, perhaps they would knock him out, keep him paralyzed, even kill him and use his corpse as Naul had said. But it would set them back, cost them days that Abernathy might need to use the Crosser's Maze. Plus, he might have the added satisfaction of actually landing a punch to that scarred, greasy face before they subdued him.

He shook himself out of it. If nothing else, better to lead them on—let them think he was cooperating, and then screw up their big ritual when it counted. And that was assuming he was still there for the main event; with luck he and Essik would be long gone, and with information that could help the archmagi dig these roaches out and blast them into history.

In the meantime, he should be observing everything, since he had no idea what might be important. Not that he had a hope of memorizing the hundreds of lines of letters and numbers, but he could at least remember the general layout of the room.

His inspection was interrupted as the door flew open. For a brief second he expected to see the rest of Horn's Company come to rescue him, but it was only another cultist.

"Mokad!"

"This is a poor time to interrupt," Mokad snapped at the new arrival.

The man frantically waved him over. Mokad sighed and hurriedly navigated his way through the painted maze to the door, at which point the newcomer turned his back and whispered urgently. Ivellios strained to hear and thought he caught the word "warehouse" before Mokad hustled the man out of the room.

Uncomfortable minutes passed. Some of the cultists, including Quia and Pelon, continued their preparations while others watched the door with open curiosity. When Mokad returned, he was alone. A smile twitched on his lips, but his eyes showed concern.

"Good news?" Ivellios called from his place at the back of the room.

Mokad crossed to the slate. "Nothing that's any business of yours." To the room at large he spoke more loudly. "I would like to begin. Is there anyone who feels they are not ready?"

A small balding man raised a hand. "I'd like an extra check on my variant of the Argivan." The man stepped aside and crouched a bit, so others could see his section of the slate. Mokad and a few others nearby spent a quiet minute staring at the board.

"The multiplier for initial jolt in the calculation of Volpos's final position should be one-sixth, not one-fourth," said one of the women.

The man looked mortified. "Of course." He made his correction, muttering apologies.

"Anyone else?" asked Mokad.

His question was met with expectant silence. Staring at Ivellios, he added, "Once more, remember the purpose of this test." He paused, then added, "If this goes as I expect, it should be the last test we need before the day of convergence. Ivellios, you have my apologies." He spoke a quick spell and twiddled his fingers, and Ivellios's body went rigid from the neck down. "I will release you in a little less than an hour, at which time I will ask you to turn in place and face directly toward that rhombus on the wall." He pointed to a section of wall festooned with diagrams.

Ivellios rolled his eyes, glad that his face was left unparalyzed. "The what?"

"The diamond," said Mokad. "The smaller diamond next to the equ—next to the large H. In the meantime, please stay quiet, and remember that any acts of rebellion or sabotage will only serve to increase your own suffering.

"Quia, please start us off."

The tall woman executed a quick but complex series of arm movements, then rattled off a long string of numbers. Ivellios waited for the pain to come, wondering how effective Essik's potion would be. And if it was going to throw off the Black Circle's ritual, when would that become obvious?

Other cultists chanted and waved, sometimes in unison, sometimes in jarring discordance. Mokad stood in one of the several smaller annulets on the floor, close to the curving wall. Ivellios could see him if he turned his head to the left, but his paralysis meant he couldn't keep an eye on the whole room.

Little by little, the black painted lines glowed a mottled, coruscating purple, reminding Ivellios of bruises on flesh. When the shapes upon the ground picked up the shimmer, their crystals sparked, and as they did, a wave of needle pricks jabbed his skin from feet to scalp.

At some signal that Ivellios could not discern, seven of the cultists moved to stand in front of the circles dusted with crystals. Several more read out loud from the slate, reciting equations over and over. The prickling all over Ivellios's skin increased, growing from a nettling discomfort to a painful stinging.

On the ground, one of the little heaps of crystal flared blue and bright before emitting a little pop and a curl of smoke. Ivellios glanced at Mokad to see if the man had noticed or would react, but the scar-faced man remained unperturbed, chanting words that were drowned in the din of the room.

As the minutes passed and Ivellios's legs protested, the sounds of the cultists' voices were joined by a deep, throbbing hum. It rattled his chest as much as sounded in his ears. Soon after, he felt the first sensation beyond the jabs of invisible needles. It started in his stomach, and he winced in recognition.

It was the pull of Volpos.

The bracelet from Ernie's statue warmed his wrist. His guts rebelled, turbulently, but the pain was less than the previous time, in the mountains of Kivia. Did he have Essik's potion to thank? And that was not the only difference. Before today, whenever Ivellios had felt the terrible pull in his innards, he could have identified a single direction of its force. Now it pulled at him in two directions, opposite from each other, as if two ropes had been tied about his middle and opposing sides battled for his body in a tug-of-war.

Another pile of the crystal arcanum gave a rasp like a wicker basket full of snakes, then popped into a cloud of smoke the color of mulberries. Mokad looked sharply at Quia; both appeared concerned.

Uh oh. Something going wrong? Ivellios resisted the urge to say anything out loud, lest Mokad come to suspect the sabotage.

The rank-and-file cultists continued to chant, to trace patterns in the air, but they all sneaked confused or worried glances at Mokad. The two-sided pulling continued to strain against Ivellios's abdomen, but the pain grew no greater. The bracelet was hotter now though not enough to burn his arm.

Mokad stopped chanting. "Continue the ritual!" he barked. Then, to Ivellios: "I'm going to count to five. On five, pivot to face the rhombus." With a wave and a mumble he freed Ivellios from his paralysis.

"One…two…three…four…five!"

Ivellios did as he was bidden; things were going wrong without him needing to lift a finger. The rhombus glowed a deep, nauseating purple as if it were a cutout in the wall with a corrupted sun shining behind it. The pulling stopped but immediately reversed itself, becoming a pressure against his chest and back.

Mokad shouted a nonsense word, at which every cultist in the room began to recite numbers in unison. The two large circles on the floor, at whose joining Ivellios stood, flared the same sickening mauve as the rhombus. Invisible hands squashed Ivellios, front and back, an implacable squeezing he thought would crush the breath out of him.

All of the remaining piles of crystals erupted at once, each consumed in a flash and puffing out a cough of blueish smoke. The squeezing stopped. The chanting stopped.

"What went wrong?" asked Abac, looking at Mokad with a furrowed brow.

"I don't know," said Mokad curtly. "But the test was not a total loss. You all did well. I will study the texts and figure out why the aether became unbalanced." He walked over to Ivellios, stepping blithely across the painted mathematical tapestry on the floor.

"I did exactly what you asked." Ivellios twisted his torso slowly right and left. No cracked ribs.

"I'm impressed you stayed conscious," said Mokad. "I had expected that the forces the ritual would impart upon your body would have taken a harsher toll."

Belatedly Ivellios realized he should have made more of a show of discomfort, but it was too late now. "I've been in plenty of scrapes over the years. You learn to deal with pain in my line of work."

"I'm sure you do." Mokad smiled at him. "I am pleased. Pleased that you are going to share in our revenge against the murderous Silverswords and the Spire. Pleased that you are willing to do your part in rescuing Naradawk. He is not the monster you fear; his favor is as generous as his wrath is terrible. I do not lie when I predict great rewards for you, in return for your service. When the time comes, I will urge the emperor to let you exact vengeance against your father's murderers in whatever fashion pleases you."

Ivellios stared about the room, trying to remember as many details as he could while Mokad blathered on. Essik had been right. While she worked out how to bypass the traps and locks and guards, he would absorb as much of this arcane mumbo jumbo as possible.

"You must be tired, Ivellios," said Mokad. "I'll have Essik see you back to your room. While you rest, I will try to understand the unexpected energy surges in today's trial. We will need one more test before the day of our victory arrives. Be prepared. We will run the test tomorrow."

Most of the cultists crowded at the far right edge of the slateboard, pointing and discussing its scrawl. Essik waited outside the door. "Make sure he gets plenty of food and rest," Mokad told her.

Ivellios followed her back to his cell. She motioned for him to enter, then slipped in after him and closed the door.

Once more she produced Ivellios's confiscated light-rod, holding it beneath her chin. "What happened?" she whispered.

"Pretty much like you said. The pain was tolerable, despite Mokad thinking it would make me pass out. And something went wrong with his ritual, though I'm not qualified to say exactly what."

"Good." She paused and frowned. "I wanted to warn you. I'm…not certain I'll be escaping with you. If I stay behind, I can buy you more time to get clear of our compound. We're in a coastal city, so your best bet will be to find a ship to take you to Tal Hae. Get those memories of *Prophecies of the Pivot* back to your wizards."

Outside, echoes of footsteps and distant voices. An argument, some shouting.

"Won't they suspect you of having helped me?"

Essik's face was grim. "Perhaps. But what they do to me will be nothing compared to what everyone in Charagan will suffer if Naradawk Skewn breaks free."

CHAPTER SEVENTEEN

T he array of prisms bobbed gently in space like buoys on a rolling ocean. Aravia collected them into her subconscious, letting her mind develop a map of them without any specific awareness of their states. King Vhadish's green oval floated at a distance, playing the part of the portal in the Greatwood.

Aravia collected the energy of the Crosser's Maze and spun it out like silk, threading each pulsing strand through one of the prisms and directing it onward toward the target. Tor had been right; the walk had cleared her mind and refreshed her spirit.

That, or maybe it was all the kissing in the park. I'm surprised your lips didn't stick together.

Pewter!

Honestly, your courtship rituals can be kind of horrifying.

This from a creature who licks his own hindquarters. Now be quiet and let me concentrate.

Pewter stopped commenting, but it wasn't precisely concentration she needed to achieve. In some ways it was actually easier to maintain her channeling of energy while her conscious mind was on other things.

She thought about Tor. There had been quite a bit of kissing, she had to admit. When Tor held her, she was acutely aware of just how strong he was, how muscular. But nonetheless, when she thought about him, what came to mind most strongly was his face, his honest smile, and his guileless sincerity. Speaking one's mind wasn't always a positive trait, but in Tor it was the sweetest thing she had ever known.

Energy flowed, and some deep part of her mind balanced its fluctuations, its ebbs and surges, like a conductor directing a symphony. On the far side of the lenses, the green oval absorbed the reflected energy and slowly brightened.

Vhadish had arranged it to glow in measure with her success.

"You have achieved a stable resting state," came Vhadish's voice, "but the energy is insufficient. It is not enough to let your subconscious do all the work. Your mind is both the army and the general. Draw more energy and keep it evenly divided."

Aravia banished thoughts of Tor from her mind, and Pewter was wise enough not to resume his jibing. Vhadish was right; the energy threads were too weak. She teased a greater concentration of power out of the maze, directed it, shepherded it. Her mastery held. The oval shone brighter until it blazed out like a sun-swaddled emerald.

"Better," said Vhadish. "You'll want more when the time comes, but now you must move to the next stage. Imagine the oval is a hole in the fabric of reality. It will not be enough to direct energy into it. You'll need to use that energy with purpose, to convert it into a new, solid border between Volpos and Spira. This should not be difficult; it is what the Crosser's Maze was created to do. But it does not happen on its own. You, as the Keeper of the Maze, must imagine the reality you wish to invoke."

There existed no analogue, Vhadish had said, no facile metaphor, for the border between two worlds in a Prison Pair. It was a phenomenon unique in the universe.

"You may be tempted to think of it as a wall between two rooms, or a curtain hanging in space, or something similar. Relieve yourself of such thoughts. Volpos and Spira do not, cannot, physically overlap, any more than two boulders could be made to occupy the same space. But in a transdimensional aether-permeated frame of reference, they are in a state of partial overlap at all times. If there is a weak point between the two, someone with enough arcanistic skill could send an object or being from one world to the other, or go themselves. That is how your world's wizards were able to banish Naloric Skewn in the first place."

"Then why," Aravia had asked, "does the Black Circle need to move the worlds closer together, even in a nonphysical reference frame?"

Vhadish had hesitated before replying. "I speculate that if Volpos and Spira can be enticed into a state of complete congruence, the weak spot would become impossible to keep closed. It would become, effectively, an empty space. There would no longer be a portal for your archmagi to maintain. That is why your goal is not to shore up a weakness, as Abernathy and his ilk have been doing these past few centuries. No, your goal is to remake the border so that there *is no weakness.*"

So that was what Aravia would do. She imagined the energy of the maze transforming into a new reality, an unblemished and impermeable sheet where there was now a perforated and failing patch of border. The energy sang through her mind, the universe in harmony with her thoughts.

She was meant for this.

The Crosser's Maze was meant for her.

The green oval began to fade.

In the submerged layers of her mind, subconscious processes balanced and directed the energy threads, lanced them through the prisms, reunited them at a single point like the tip of a sword—or the point of a knitting needle.

Aravia closed her eyes, not needing to see. She was in absolute control, a Goddess of Creation, and sealing Naradawk away in his prison world would be her gift to Spira.

"An acceptable effort."

She opened her eyes again. King Vhadish XXIII floated nearby, nodding and pouting at the same time.

"You have mastered the basics, so I deem there is some hope."

"An acceptable effort? *Some* hope?" Aravia gestured to the place where the oval had been and tried to keep her voice level. "You underestimate me, I think."

"Turn around."

She did.

Almost a quarter of the prisms were gone. Light from the ambient maze coruscated from the drifting flakes of their remains.

"I'm sure you would find it preferable not to kill so many of the volunteers whose arcane potential you will be using."

Aravia nodded, deflated.

"Also, how do you feel now, having sealed my practice rift?"

Tired. When did I become so tired?

"The true border will require both more energy and more finesse," Vhadish said. "And you will need to study it more closely once your physical body is at Verdshane."

"Is it hopeless, then, Your Majesty?"

Vhadish raised his brows at her. "Hopeless? Certainly not. You are a decent pupil with undeniable talent and a knack for manipulating the maze's energy. But I could taste your overconfidence just now."

She said nothing.

"Come," said the king. "Come back to my Tetra for rest and refreshment, and we will discuss some of the trickier aspects of theory."

Vhadish's throne room was as it always was: spacious, gaudy, dominated by His Majesty's overwrought chair. Four marble lions, each as tall as Aravia, sat proudly on squared pedestals at the throne's corners. But this time a small wooden table and two padded chairs waited for them in the center of the tiled floor. A dark burgundy liquid filled two crystal goblets set upon the table.

"Sit with me while we talk." Vhadish sat in the chair closer to the throne, so Aravia took the other.

"This is not wine, obviously," Vhadish said. "But drinking it here will lift the weariness you feel while you stay in the maze. It will not avail you once you resume your physical existence."

"Of course not, Your Majesty. I appreciate your largesse."

Vhadish peered at her. Did he suspect her of sarcasm?

Aravia picked up her goblet and took a sip. It *tasted* like wine, and she did feel as though her body shed some of its torpor. "I have questions, Your Majesty."

Vhadish held out his goblet in a motion that indicated she should continue.

"First, it is clear the Crosser's Maze allows its keeper to wield massive power. If I can focus its energy on a weak point in the fabric of reality, why could I not simply aim it at Naradawk himself and annihilate him? Or use the maze in any number of similar ways to attack my enemies?"

Vhadish swallowed and made a "tut tut" sound. "You haven't been paying attention if you need to ask that. The Crosser's Maze was designed for a single purpose. Its power cannot be harnessed to affect the real universe in direct ways, save for the one I am teaching you."

"Don't you think that's odd?" Aravia asked. "Surely the universe is not constantly unraveling, and holes between worlds cannot be common. Why would someone have created so powerful a thing and then so severely limited its use?"

"You'd have to ask its creator," said Vhadish dryly. "But I would guess it has something to do with the immense capacity for destruction the maze would have if controlled by an unscrupulous or corrupted keeper." His Majesty paused to take another sip of wine. "The Crosser's Maze allows us to see into the real world, but not directly interfere with it. As such it has been a source of great knowledge. The order of the Keepers maintains a library in the city of Kai Kin, though thanks to Solomea's bumbling, it has fallen into severe disrepair this past century. When all of this business with Naradawk is concluded, I suggest you go there and see what you can do."

Before Aravia could ask another question, Vhadish added, "If you're going to suggest using the maze to spy on Naradawk, I have been doing that in your absences. You will not be surprised, I assume, to hear that he spends his time striving against your archmagi and attempting to force passage through the ever-weakening soft spot between Spira and Volpos. Meanwhile his generals prepare his soldiers for the moment of invasion. As such, I suggest you put everything out of your mind save for the task of preventing that invasion."

Aravia bowed her head.

"Did you have any questions more directly related to that subject?" asked Vhadish.

"Yes. You have warned me many times over, Your Majesty, that in order to correct the weakness near Verdshane, I must be physically close to it. But my...my friend, Tor, pointed out to me that the archmagi have been maintaining wards upon that weakness for centuries, and they are not physically near to it. How do they manage it?"

King Vhadish swirled the wine in his glass, setting flecks of claret light to gyrating on the table. "That," he said after a long pause, "is an excellent question. I do not know the answer, though it can be narrowed down to two general possibilities. One, they have developed some heretofore unknown arcanistic principles that allow them to affect a transdimensional border from a distance."

She leaned forward impatiently. She had never seen Vhadish looking so thoughtful.

"And the second?" she prompted.

"The second is that they *are* near to the portal."

"But Abernathy has said from the day we met him that he couldn't leave his tower and that the same is true for the rest of the archmagi. And we know his tower is in Tal Hae."

"That does present a puzzle," said Vhadish, giving her a smile that she took to mean he wanted her to solve it.

"Maybe the inside of his tower is somewhere different than the outside." She spoke out loud but mostly to herself. "But, no, he made a window while we were there, and we could all see Tal Hae right outside." She thought some more. "Your Majesty, I would like to use the maze to examine the area around the portal more closely. Will you come with me? Your experience and savvy may let you see things I might miss."

Good thinking, buttering up His Pompous Majesticness, said Pewter.

Yes, but it's also true. I'm not exactly sure what I'm looking for.

"I would be pleased to accompany you," said Vhadish. "And I believe I understand your line of inquiry."

Good, thought Aravia. *Because I'm not certain that I do.*

With enough practice and experience, Aravia would be able to travel nearly anywhere in the maze in a matter of minutes, but for now she allowed Vhadish to transport her. It was a journey made in two hops: one to the exit from the Inner Maze, and then a second to Spira itself.

The sight stole Aravia's breath. Volpos and Spira, which had been heading toward one another at ever-increasing speed, were now in a state of partial overlap.

"I would estimate a fifteen percent overlay," said Vhadish, sounding like he was guessing at the number of beans in a jar.

"How long do you think I have?" Aravia asked.

"Hmm." Vhadish stared at the drifting planets. "Difficult to guess, as the Black Circle seems to have accessed the fourth derivative of position, albeit with miniscule coefficients. Two days? Perhaps three?"

"Less time than my friends are expecting," said Aravia. "I should teleport to Verdshane today."

"I think you will need to wait until tomorrow," said Vhadish. "When you return to Spira, you will find that our exercises here in the maze have tapped your arcane potential quite severely."

"As soon as possible then," said Aravia. Two days! She still had so much to learn!

"During my tenure as Keeper," said Vhadish, "I had very little interest in a boring little backwater like Charagan. I still don't. You will have to identify Verdshane."

Even through the partially occluding shadow of Volpos, the curve of Spira's globe showed them mostly water, dotted with a few tiny islands. She led Vhadish clockwise from their high vantage point, away from Volpos, and after a time speeding around the world in a high orbit, she recognized the shapes of Charagan. They were such a small part of the world, little green-brown patches of land surrounded by a field of speckled blue-gray. With her encyclopedic knowledge of geography, it was a simple matter to zoom downward to Harkran, then to the Greatwood, with Verdshane nestled in its woody embrace. North of the Greatwood Road, in a wooded ruin, waited the sealed portal that hedged out Naradawk Skewn.

When last Aravia had visited that place, the entire region had been largely abandoned. The woods were home only to uninhabited ruins, and the gopher-bugs had killed or driven off most of Verdshane's tiny population. Only the innkeeper, Minya, had remained in the ravaged little hamlet.

Not so now. Verdshane and its surroundings had become a war encampment.

In the town itself, hundreds of soldiers moved about restlessly, some engaged in light sparring, some polishing armor or sharpening swords, others eating or resting. The Shadow Chaser was the hub of all the activity, with soldiers and runners going in and out in a steady stream.

The building housing the portal and the stasis field had already sat in a clearing, but now that clearing was nearly twice its previous size. Dozens of workers dug trenches or set sharpened stakes in the open space, while others hammered platforms and ladders into the trees at the clearing's edge.

"Your countrymen are wise," Vhadish observed. "Should the portal fail, it will do so incrementally, and because it is arcanistically inverse, those with no arcane skill will be able to pass through first. I imagine that is to Naradawk's liking; he will prefer to send in expendable assets first, and that any arcanists who oppose him spend their energy on his foot soldiers."

But Aravia found herself thinking not of Naradawk's strategy, or the defenses her own countrymen worked to erect, but of the risk she would ask every soldier present to take.

The risk that she would kill some of them. Or all of them.

There had been a time not long ago when she would have shrugged at the possibility. Not that she would have been reckless, but that awareness of others' sacrifices would have stopped there—at simply awareness.

But now she thought of Tor. She pictured his face, imagined his voice. *I know you have to stop Naradawk, but you still should do everything in your power to keep innocent people alive.* In the months she had known him, Tor had chipped away at her prioritization of expedience, replacing it with a sense of compassion.

Aravia shook herself loose from introspection and drifted through the walls of the white marble edifice housing the portal. In the building's center, concentric hemispherical cages made of the time-slowing metal Abernathy had called gartine converged on the blue glow of the archmagi's stasis field. The gopher-bugs were gone; the field must have flickered at least once since their arrival, loosing the monsters into the world. The body was also missing, perhaps discovered and given a proper burial by someone sent to scout.

To her ordinary senses, the building was otherwise empty. If the archmagi were here in secret, working their magic to seal the portal, they were well concealed. But in the Crosser's Maze she had extraordinary senses as well.

In her early days with Horn's Company, Aravia had cast a spell of detection on the Kivian Arch at Seablade Point, and the scope of its enchantment had blasted her off her feet. Now, using the maze to sense for arcane disturbance, she experienced something jarringly similar. The portal itself, the hole and the "door" created and maintained by the archmagi, were as aetherically charged as anything she had ever seen. The gartine ribs glittered, inherently magical, but the portal itself blinded her mind. Around it, the stasis field was nearly as potent, though the aether within it was quiescent.

None of that surprised her. She quested about the rest of the building but found no trace of the archmagi working their rituals. Vhadish floated beside her, looking bored.

"It wouldn't have to be right here," Aravia said. "You yourself told me I only needed to be within a few hundred yards."

She floated up and through the building's ceiling.

What are we looking for? Pewter sounded tired.

Anything out of the ordinary, I suppose.

Aravia halted her rise a hundred feet above the portal. Below her in the expanded clearing, two soldiers worked at bricking up the door—in actuality a gap filled in with an illusion of a door—to the portal building.

In the material world, Aravia would have to cast *aura sense* to detect ongoing arcane effects, but in the maze she merely needed to concentrate. Slowly she turned in place while Vhadish looked on with eyes showing mild amusement.

The sky was a glowering gray, the air cool but humid. The grass of the clearing was rucked with muddy trenches, scored with sharpened saplings, and everywhere trampled into clumpy dirt. Around and above, the trees of the Greatwood rose high and green, standing sentinels surrounding what would soon become the most fraught acreage on the planet.

Below her, and several hundred feet to the east, the air shimmered faintly, a circle of the mildest turbulence. She moved herself towards it, skirting the tops of the trees, focusing her attention.

At her approach, the shimmer resolved into something like a translucent window the size of a barn door, angled at a perfect perpendicular to the archmagi's portal below. A fall leaf caught in an updraft swooped into the window and vanished.

Aravia drifted closer until she hovered directly beside it. It reminded her sharply of the Kivian Arch, inasmuch as there seemed to be nothing behind it, but if she looked *into* it she saw blurry shapes and pulsing lights on the far side of a befogged opening.

"I don't know what's in there," said Vhadish, preempting her question. "It could be part of the Black Circle's machinations to free Naradawk. Proceed carefully."

Aravia tried to focus her perception on the far side of the opening, but even using the maze, her sight was foiled.

We're not going in there, are we? Pewter asked nervously.

I need to know what's happening.

She extended her arm, allowing her fingertips to brush the shimmer. They met no resistance, registered no sensation beyond the cool breeze over the forest. In ideal circumstances Aravia would proceed with more caution, but she had time constraints. She plunged her body through.

"The fifth seal is weakening," Abernathy snapped. "Ozella, you should have the softest region for the next twelve minutes or so. Divert one-third of your energy to the fifth—no, split that. One-sixth to the fifth and one-sixth to the ninth. Salk, how are you holding up?"

Aravia blinked in the pulsing, multicolored lights of a small room. At its center, the five elderly archmagi sat in wooden chairs set around a large and complex three-dimensional pattern in the air. It appeared to Aravia's maze-sight to be made of concentrated aether, and it pulsed, streaked, and winked while she watched.

"I'm fine," said Salk. "The pressure is on Fylnia's third quadrant right now. No, the second. I think."

"Which is it?" Ozella said peevishly.

"Damn," said Salk. "It's getting so hard to concentrate."

"It's Aktallian," said Abernathy. "He's working his mischief all the time now. Focus!"

"It's the third," Fylnia gasped. "No question."

"It could be a feint!" warned Grawly. "Two months ago they tried an attack similar to this, and the pressure was a distraction. We dropped the seals for almost half a second!"

"Not this time, I think," said Abernathy. "It has the feel of a true attack. Salk, invoke *iron wards* around Fylnia's third in thirty seconds. That should hold the sixth through tenth seals for an hour or more. Grawly, be prepared to cast *Alander's variance* in case you're right. Otherwise, reinforce the *iron wards*."

Aravia stared, fascinated. Here Tor's question was answered: The archmagi had constructed a tiny pocket dimension with an opening facing downward onto the portal and hardly more than a stone's toss in distance. The air in the room glowed a faint purple, which Aravia found disturbing for no reason she could explain. The walls were lined with silver metal bars, spaced every few feet, enclosing the entire space like a prison cage. The bars sang like a set of struck tuning forks.

Gartine. They work in a room enmeshed by gartine, the metal that slows the passage of time.

Aravia had often wondered how the archmagi had been able to live for centuries. Now she had her answer to that riddle too. Here, in a space hardly half the size of the Greenhouse living room, the ancient wizards spent most of their lives tending to this complex piece of wizardry. The pattern must represent the arcane locks upon Naradawk's prison door, locks that would soon be smashed apart no matter the effort the archmagi might expend.

Aravia turned to look back through the aperture; the building, trees, soldiers, and fortifications had vanished. The view out of the pocket dimension showed only what she presumed was the portal itself, an ovoid multicolored shape that mirrored the one in the archmagi's room. Glittering motes of aether hovered around it like moths circling a campfire.

"Ozella," came Salk's voice from behind Aravia, "Watch the second seal. Looks like they might be up to something."

"I see it. You just focus on those *iron wards*."

Aravia took a deep breath and closed her eyes. Her mind was tired, and she was eager to return to Tor. To Abernathy and the others she whispered, "Buy me as much time you you can. I promise to do my best."

CHAPTER EIGHTEEN

Thank you all for coming. Ell will be pleased."

Morningstar delivered her ritual greeting somberly and wasted little time after that. She arranged her eight sisters in an outward-facing circle. The three who held no weapons stood shoulder to shoulder. The remaining five were near one another but spaced to allow each room to swing. Scola held her oversized hammer, Amber her two long knives. Gyre wielded a cudgel, Belle a sword, and Obsidia a long, polished spear.

"Your progress has been so great," said Morningstar, "that you've made it extremely difficult for me to devise challenges. This one is meant to test several of your skills at once, to stress your concentration."

Most of them simply stared back at her. Gone was the levity she had worked so hard to infuse into the group. Aktallian had hacked it away as cleanly as Sable's head.

"Tell us," said Jet, her young voice steady. "Whatever it is, we can handle it."

"We'll see," said Morningstar. She concentrated and manifested five hundred black stone triangles, each flat and the size of her hand. They appeared spaced in a hemisphere above and around the circled sisters, fifty yards off, frozen in the air. "When the test begins, those stones will move toward you at varying speeds."

"And we need to knock them away?" asked Scola.

"That is one choice," said Morningstar. "I will leave it to you how best to protect yourselves."

"We can just make a dome, can't we?" asked Belle.

"Yes." Morningstar smiled at her. "And I will try to remove it. Also, there is more to the test." She manifested a dozen round wooden shield-sized boards along the distant walls of the training yard. "I want at least a hundred of the stones to wind up embedded in those targets."

"What happens if we get hit by the stones?" Gyre's voice, like her face, was entirely devoid of emotion. Morningstar was silently thankful she was here at all; she and Sable had been extremely close, but Gyre had no time to heal or even come to proper terms with her grief. After this was over, they would all mourn.

And maybe I'll be mourning for them all. Or they for me.

"If any of them touch you, consider yourself knocked out. Lie down on the ground if that happens until the test is over."

"What else?" asked Previa. "That still sounds too easy."

Ah, Previa. Doing her best to restore normalcy.

Morningstar walked around the circle of her sisters, making eye contact with each. Most looked back at her with unreadable expressions. Jet looked nervous but defiant. Amber did not meet her gaze, looking instead at one of the targets.

"Three more things," Morningstar told them. "One, you may not break your circle." She manifested a ring of black bricks on the ground, five long strides across. "Two, I will manifest a light as bright as the noonday sun which you are not allowed to dim." Some grumbling at that. "And, three, I am going to remove all of the air from the yard."

As she expected, this announcement was met with open mouths and a few small gasps of incredulity.

"Ell's Shadow!" Scola looked horrified. "What do you mean, 'remove all the air?'"

"Exactly that," said Morningstar. "But you will have two ways around that problem. One is to figure out a way to make yourself some new air, in a manner that lets you breathe. The other…you know I've been telling you all along that you can define the reality of the dreamscape. With enough mental discipline, you can convince yourself of this plain truth: You're dreaming, and you don't need air."

Nervous nods. Looks of puzzlement. Belle stared at Morningstar as though she'd lost her mind.

"So now you know the rules. We will begin."

"But—" Scola began, but Morningstar held up a quieting hand and manifested an oversized sun high in the sky. While her sisters winced or (as Morningstar noticed with dismay) still flinched away, she did as she had warned, reimagining the training yard without a single breath of air.

The sisters gasped. Obsidia's eyes bulged in a panic, one hand coming to her throat. Gyre and Starbrook conspicuously held their breaths. Scola's mouth opened and closed like that of a fish flopping on a beach.

Jet was slowest to react, but her solution was ingenious. A round glass globe like an upside-down fishbowl appeared around her head. Within its confines she breathed in and out, a patch of fog appearing, then shrinking, then growing on the inside of the bowl. She must have manifested a pocket of air around her head and then a sealed helmet to keep the air from drifting away.

Morningstar moved the triangle-stones inward, varying their speeds, with the fastest half-dozen of them traveling quickly enough to strike the sisters in only a few seconds. Belle and Gyre swatted at the closest stones with their swords. Scola swept a swath through them with her hammer, mouth opened as though bellowing as she did so, but no sound came from her lips. For that matter, the sisters' weapons made no noise as they contacted the triangle stones. Scola looked about in confusion, seeming to babble silently. That was interesting. Morningstar hadn't intended it, but removing the air had also eliminated all sound from the yard.

Starbrook, Obsidia, Gyre, and Belle copied Jet's trick, encasing their own heads in clear, round helmets. Scola closed her mouth, her face turning red as she began to hold her breath.

Amber and Previa seemed to ignore the lack of air, showing no signs of panic or breath-holding but also not maintaining air globes. Amber hadn't lifted her knives, but the stones approaching her vanished several at a time. Previa was lifting the fallen stones with her mind and flicking them toward the distant targets with perfect precision.

Morningstar accelerated the stones, but her sisters had mastered themselves. Only Starbrook and Gyre squinted in the light, and all had solved the air problem to their satisfaction. The black triangles flew away, vanished, or were knocked aside as fast as Morningstar brought them inward. She tried moving them faster but at least one of the sisters—Jet, she guessed—was contesting her will, slowing down their approach.

Morningstar did manage to slip one stone through to thud into Belle's shoulder—but the sister did not lie down. She shot a quick grin at Morningstar before knocking away two approaching stones. As Morningstar considered how to rebuke her without her voice, the ground buckled beneath her, and she fell onto her back. While she was distracted, her sisters obliterated or flung away the remaining stones. Along the walls, well over a hundred of her triangles jutted from the wooden targets.

Previa reached down to help Morningstar to her feet. With a thought Morningstar restored the air and took a deep breath herself to let the others know.

"Well done," she said to her students.

"You were right," said Previa. "There's no need to breathe in the Tapestry."

Morningstar looked at Amber. "I presume you were able to act on the same conclusion?"

Amber nodded, silently. Did Morningstar imagine it, or were Amber's eyes watering as though on the brink of tears?

"And you?" Morningstar turned to Scola, who still panted.

"I've always been able to…hold my breath a…long time," said Scola, smiling while she huffed. "And those head-bowls…looked distracting."

"And you." Morningstar shook her head at Belle, who was smirking. "You knew the rules. You cheated the test."

"I've been telling you all along that you can define the reality of the dreamscape." Belle's imitation of Morningstar's voice was a high-pitched caricature, but it did capture her inflections. Jet and Obsidia giggled. "I decided to define reality as one where I could ignore that particular rule," Belle said.

Faced with the choice of scolding her sister for violating the spirit of the exercise or applauding her ingenuity and cheek, Morningstar went with the latter. "That was very clever and the kind of thinking we'll all need to engage in if we're to bring down Aktallian."

Most of the sisters smiled and nodded. Obsidia patted Belle on the back. Morningstar dared to hope she could restore morale after all, until Jet spoke up.

"Do you still think we can beat him? I mean, after what happened to Sable?"

"Yes," Morningstar said immediately, knowing even a small pause would make everything afterward sound like dissembling. "I meant what I said before. Aktallian is not all-powerful. The fact that we're all standing here, alive, is a testament to that. If you doubt, think of this. I am stronger than any of you here in the Tapestry, but together you are routinely able to overcome my challenges, or best me in combat. Together we can do to Aktallian what all of you do to me."

Morningstar glanced down at the green gem given her by Ozella. Every few minutes she returned a bit of her awareness to her physical body, to make sure it wasn't flashing its warning to her. "I have more news. We have less time than expected to prepare. The wizards now say a week at most, maybe less. And it's possible, if things go terribly wrong, that we'll need to muster with only two hours' notice."

Her eight sisters stared back at her.

"How will you contact us if it's the middle of the night when we're both awake?" Starbrook looked pointedly at Obsidia. "The others are in Tal Hae, and you can warn them in person."

"You'll just have to arrange it so that one of you is asleep at all times," said Morningstar. "Make up some reason one of you has to sleep during the night."

"But we can't sleep for twelve hours every day," said Starbrook.

Morningstar grimaced in frustration. "We'll have to trust to luck that Aktallian won't attack when you're both awake. Try at least to minimize the amount of time that is."

The others stood, watching her, shifting their feet, looking anxious, expectant, even grim. It would hardly be worth trying to recapture the hopeful camaraderie they had lost; there wasn't time, and she might be better off sharpening an edge on the new emotions Sable's death had birthed.

"You're right to be nervous," she told them. "But Aktallian should be even more worried. He made a mistake with Sable. He made this personal for all of us. If saving the kingdom isn't incentive enough, I want to make him pay for what he did to her."

Some of the sisters nodded at that. A tear escaped the corner of Gyre's eye. But Amber stared back at her, eyes flinty and cold. She spoke for the first time.

"How is this personal for you?" She obviously struggled to keep her voice even. "You hardly knew her. I brought her here because I trusted Previa. You trained her, used her, and now she's dead."

Morningstar didn't rise to the bait. "I didn't know her as well as the rest of you, true. But we trained together for months. I learned to trust her. To *like* her. She didn't abandon us. She returned my trust."

"And look where it got her," said Amber.

"Yes. She did what she thought was best to serve our cause, to serve Ell and the kingdom of Charagan. She took a terrible risk for the greater good and paid for it. Her death was tragic, and by the Goddess I am going to make sure it wasn't in vain."

She kept speaking before Amber could interrupt. "Listen to me. You know what I am. The White Anathema. I was born this way, made this way. Growing up in the church, I was an outcast. A pariah. I had no friends. My sisters—*your* sisters—returned my few overtures toward friendship with scorn and derision—not because of anything I did or said but because of my appearance. They turned their backs, said I wasn't meant to be an Ellish priestess, whispered insults behind my back and loud enough for me to hear them. For years I endured it, armored myself with faith and service to Ell. I had resigned myself to the reality that none of that would ever change."

Morningstar paused to collect herself, forcing herself to look her sisters in the eye. Some looked back at her. Scola and Gyre looked at the ground. Amber seemed to be staring at a place behind her.

"Then it did change," she said, more quietly. "Ell chose me, made me a Dreamwalker, instructed me to find sisters like you to help safeguard the people of our kingdom. I didn't choose this. I didn't want it. Leader, teacher, warlord— those titles should never have come to me, any more than White Anathema. But they did. I found you. You came to me, trusted me, learned from me, have followed me in spite of your doubts. I cannot explain how much that has meant to me. Call it friendship or not, but I have been closer to you than to any sisters of Ell in my life. Whatever that means to you, to me it has been everything. So when I say that the death of Sable was a personal affront, a blow to my soul, I mean every word of it."

Morningstar allowed a few seconds of silence for her words to sink in.

"All right. Enough about me. It's time for full sun."

Her sisters groaned. "Full sun" was an exercise she inflicted on them every few sessions. High on Morningstar's list of worries was how they would react if Aktallian made the environment extremely bright. During their initial encounter, that had been his first aggression toward her: to try blinding her with an illuminated ring.

"On your backs, eyes open."

To inure her team to that kind of attack, she made them endure something similar herself. Once they lay on the hard-packed dirt of the training yard, she increased the brightness of the sun until it seemed it could wash away the shadows.

"Keep your eyes open as long as you can. Remember what I've said. If they feel dry, if you feel like you have to blink, remember that they're not physical eyeballs. They cannot become dry. You cannot go blind. Endure as much as you can for as long as you can. Accept it. When we face Aktallian, we will have robbed him of his most obvious weapon."

Amber had complained about this from the start. "We are already risking blasphemy with you," she had said. "To walk beneath the sun is heretical. If you're concerned about Aktallian blinding us, couldn't you build up our tolerance with anything as bright? Why not use the moon?"

It was a good question, but it had a good answer.

"Because Aktallian knows what we are. When the time comes, he won't inflict you with a brightly glowing moon. He will try to break you with the sun. It won't merely be your sight he targets, but your morale. He will use heresy as a weapon. So I am not merely training your eyes, but also your mind, and your faith. There is nothing blasphemous about preparing yourself according to Ell's wishes. I will help disabuse you of the notion that the sun here in the Tapestry is real. I want you to arrive at a place where a manifested sun troubles you no more than a candle or hearth fire. Or the moon."

Amber had seemed mollified, and now she lay down with the rest, eyes open, staring upward into a sun-whitened sky. Previa was the only one who could keep her eyes open for long with no sign of discomfort. The others had progressed to varying degrees. Jet blinked rapidly from time to time but otherwise endured the exercise gracefully. Scola kept her eyes open wide, as though challenging the sun to burn them out, but every so often she had to retreat, shutting her eyelids tight and squeezing out tears. The elderly Starbrook was able to keep her eyes steadily open half-lidded. Belle, Gyre, and Obsidia closed their eyes more often than the others, but even they had made great progress since Morningstar had started the routine during her long traverse of Kivia.

She made them lie there for half an hour, more or less, before replacing the sun with a pale, cloud-shrouded moon. Jet leapt to her feet while Starbrook struggled just to gain a sitting position. Most of them rubbed their eyes or covered them with their hands.

"I know it's not easy," Morningstar said. "I remember my first day, after Rhiavonne gave me permission to go about under the *real* sun. It was awful, and terrifying, and felt like the worst sort of blasphemy. But Ell's mind is not for us to know. We have to walk where she commands that we walk. We will meet again tomorrow unless Abernathy gives me the signal to attack."

"Have you found Aktallian then?" asked Scola.

"No. That is my next task. But I don't think it will take long. Sable was able to find him, after all, and I have advantages she lacked. I have met Aktallian, in the Tapestry and out of it. Even now, if I concentrate, I can sense a warping of the dreamscape, feel his malice humming through its threads. I once thought I would have to spy out the dreams of the archmagi and trace Aktallian from there, but he has made things easier for me." She smiled reassuringly. "For now, get some rest. Keep your minds sharp and have faith in Ell."

One by one they vanished from the yard until, as always, only Morningstar and Previa remained. Morningstar manifested two cushions and they sat facing one another.

"How are you feeling?" Previa asked.

"Nervous. Dranko went with Ernie, Step, and that Silversword to look for Ivellios. That was yesterday morning, and we have no way of knowing if they've found him, or stumbled into a trap, or are wandering around Minok at loose ends. Aravia still spends most of her waking hours in the Crosser's Maze trying to figure out how it works. Kibi is worried about the Eyes of Moirel and some danger the Sharshun might pose that's different from this business with the portal. And here we are, with no way to know if we're truly ready. I feel like I'm trapped in a whirlwind, praying that when it flings me away I land on something soft."

Previa laughed. "A wise woman once told me, 'Ell's mind is not for us to know.'"

"I wish I knew Amber's mind," Morningstar said. "She didn't look me in the eye once today, except for when she was challenging my feelings about Sable's murder."

"She has been unusually quiet in the temple," Previa said. "I think she's been avoiding me. But remember, she was very close to Sable. The three of them—those two and Gyre—had been good friends for a very long time. Sable was an orphan, did you know that? She was brought to the temple when she was five. Amber isn't much older than Sable was, but in her own way she was like a parent to her. It's not surprising that Amber is angry. But she still comes here and trains. She hasn't abandoned you."

"No. None of them have." Morningstar manifested a small metal triangle, white on one side, black on the other, and twirled it in her fingers. "Part of me dreads what's coming, but a greater part of me just wants it over with." She put a hand on Previa's shoulder. "Get some real sleep and pray to Ell for our success."

* * *

Late morning sun slanted in through the thin gaps left by Morningstar's black curtains. She lay in bed, looking up at the ceiling and letting her mind run through scenario after scenario with Aktallian. How would he fight? Did he occupy a single place inside the Tapestry from which he launched his attacks on the archmagi? Or did he move from place to place, specifically to avoid being found and assaulted? How often was he there? Could Morningstar avoid Sable's fate when she went to find him?

So many questions, and no good answers. At times like this she was used to meditating, praying for guidance, seeking her calm center. But she knew from experience that doing so now would only invite the creeping revulsion of her oath to Shreen the Fair. It lurked behind every moment of silence, like a beast made of rancid oil. Goddess, but that was another reason to hope this all would end quickly. Once the Crosser's Maze and Lapis had been handed over to Shreen, she would be free of that awful oath.

"You awake? Everythin' all right in the dream place with your sisters?" Kibi must have heard her stirring in bed. She sat up and saw him sitting in her desk chair, stretching his arms back across his shoulders.

"Yes, thank you," she said. "There was no danger, but I appreciate your willingness to watch over me."

Kibi stood. "I'll leave you to get dressed. Thought I smelled eggs cookin'. See you downstairs." He left, closing her door quietly behind him.

Morningstar took her time washing and dressing, desiring to be alone a few minutes longer with her thoughts, but eventually the lure of breakfast proved irresistible. Eddings had prepared a bowl of scrambled eggs, slabs of buttered toast, and cuts of fresh salmon, much of which looked to have been eaten already. Kibi ate alone at the far end of the table while the sounds of Eddings washing up drifted in from the kitchen.

Kibi looked up and motioned with his fork. "Tor left enough for the rest of us, if barely."

Morningstar took the chair next to him. "Any word from Dranko and Ernie?"

"Nope. Not a peep, accordin' to Eddings. But they've only been gone a day, and I hear Minok's not much smaller than Tal Hae. Could take 'em some time to dig out those cultists from whatever hole they're hidin' in. And even if they find 'em, I ain't sure how we'd find out about it. Not unless Rosset Finch has some teleportin' trick up his sleeve."

Morningstar heaped her plate. Goddess, but she was hungry. Kibi, as was his way, allowed her to eat in companionable silence.

"How have you been?" she asked when she had finished her meal. "When you're not standing guard over me, I mean. Have you found a way to keep busy?"

Kibi sighed. "Not really, no. Figure it ain't safe to go off by myself in case the Sharshun are keepin' an eye out. I check on Lapis every few hours. She's got a mean-lookin' smile on her face, but otherwise hasn't showed any signs of wakin' up. And I talked to the walls in the basement."

As if that were just something people did. "Oh? What did they say?"

"Apparently the Greenhouse is a sanctuary, or least aways the basement is. I can't get a straight answer 'bout anythin', but I got a feelin' the Sharshun are up to somethin' with the Eyes a' Moirel. All that unmakin' the world business. I'm hopin' they've just been talkin' 'bout Naradawk gettin' loose, but if they're not…well, we got troubles enough, so I suppose there's not much point in worryin' about it."

He took a long drink from a water cup. "Is it strange that I miss the cider we had at the Sands a' Time in Calabash?"

Morningstar laughed. "It's true. We only served the best." Restlessness crept into her bones. Sparring, she thought, would do her good. "Have you seen Tor this morning?"

"Nope. Probably in Aravia's room if you want to talk with 'im."

Morningstar raised her brows. "Maybe I shouldn't interrupt them."

Kibi blushed. "I figured she was in the maze, but if not, well, that ain't none of my business."

Needing to move, and not wanting to interrupt Tor and Aravia no matter what they were up to, Morningstar went out to the backyard and ran laps around it, dodging Emergency Rations as he cropped the grass. When she came back inside a half-hour later, Aravia and Tor were in the living room, bulging packs by their feet.

"Where are you going?" she asked.

"Verdshane," said Tor, who was rearranging his pack to fit more of Aravia's books. "Aravia needs to get close to the portal in order to figure out how to close it."

"I know most of what I need to already," Aravia clarified. "But Vhadish says there are certain things about the portal I can learn only by studying it more directly. Also, I'll need to be close at hand to actually erase it."

"Do you want me to come?" Morningstar asked, knowing she shouldn't. "To protect you?"

Aravia gave her a warm, grateful smile, and Morningstar was struck by how different a person Aravia had become, from that cold, arrogant wizardess Abernathy had summoned.

"I appreciate the offer, but Tor will be able to protect me, and I don't think we should risk you in a possible war zone. Your role is as important as mine, and with everyone else except Kibi gone, it will be good to have one more person here in case Abernathy contacts us and needs something."

"Not to mention havin' an extra set of eyes on Lapis," said Kibi, glancing at the ceiling.

An unexpected lump formed in Morningstar's throat. "I assume, then, that you won't be coming back here until—"

"Until she's succeeded," said Tor. He held Aravia's hand unselfconsciously. "Then we'll come back to celebrate. I'll bet Duke Nigel will want to hold a parade!"

"Yes," said Aravia. "I don't anticipate leaving Verdshane until I have prevented Naradawk's escape or have specifically failed to do so. Tor's optimism notwithstanding, there is a chance this will be the last time we see one another."

"I got faith in the two a' you," said Kibi, who looked at Morningstar as he spoke. "My ma always used to say to my pa, it's the womenfolk who end up cleanin' up all the messes in life. Thank the gods we got you to clean up this mess with Naradawk."

Morningstar thought of Previa, Scola, and the rest of her sisters. "It certainly is a mess," she said. "Aravia, Tor, good luck. Come back safely."

The two finished packing and went to the backyard, so Aravia could teleport them. Eddings hurried out at the last minute with a small package of pastries.

"To help keep your strength up," he said, handing the wrapping to Tor. "Good luck to the both of you."

Half a minute later, the two of them were gone. Emergency Rations spared a brief glance at the spot where Aravia and Tor had stood, then returned his attention to the grass.

"Strange to think," said Kibi, "how fast everythin' is happenin' all of a sudden. When Abernathy first explained what he needed us for, it all seemed so far away. Now we got the end of the world starin' us right in the face."

* * *

Morningstar kept herself busy through the morning and early afternoon helping Eddings in the kitchen, scrubbing pots and chopping vegetables. The butler remained so blessedly calm.

"An imminent invasion by this Naradawk Skewn fellow is no reason not to keep the butcher block clean," he said.

"I suppose not," she replied.

As evening approached, the sun lancing in straight through the westward-facing windows, someone knocked at the door. Eddings insisted on answering it, but Morningstar retrieved her mace and stood ready just in case. A skinny teenaged girl stood outside; she handed Eddings a black envelope.

"For Morningstar of Ell." She scampered away before Eddings could give her a copper chit.

Morningstar frowned and tore open the envelope. The letter inside was short.

Sister Morningstar,

You are summoned to the office of Prelate Milanwy one hour after sunset this evening. Please be prompt.

Sister Arthan

She spat out a profanity, crumpled the letter in her hand, and threw it to the floor. Previa had warned her this might happen. The investigation of Sable's murder had determined that an intruder broke into the temple and attacked Sable during the afternoon while most of the sisters slept. No motive was evident. But some in the temple were convinced that a greater conspiracy was afoot, and it seemed possible—likely, in light of the letter—that Amber, Gyre, or Belle had offered up hints as to the true cause. They still might not have given up Morningstar's specific role in the affair, but—

"Bad news, I take it?" said Eddings, looking down at the wadded parchment.

"Probably. I'll know how bad in an hour."

Might it be wiser to ignore the summons? She had permission to serve Abernathy from the High Priestess Rhiavonne, and the dream-training of her sisters was mandated by an avatar of the Goddess. When it came down to it, she could avoid any direct church punishment by the simple expedient of not inviting them into the Greenhouse.

But no. They would pester her, send more letters, and grow ever more suspicious that she was culpable in an intentional murder. Whatever changes Morningstar's life had suffered, she was still a faithful priestess. She would go to Prelate Milanwy, answer what questions she could, and stonewall where speaking would risk violating the Injunction. It would be awkward and uncomfortable, and they might choose to punish her, but she would endure it.

If she left immediately, she would arrive in plenty of time, but that would make it obvious that she had walked across town before the sun had set, and she had no desire to rub her sisters' noses in her unholy dispensation. Morningstar forced herself to wait, the slow minutes a torment in which worries over her summons warred with the deep-bone chill of her promise to Shreen the Fair. Eddings prepared a dinner of lamb chops out of the Icebox, along with some roasted carrots and potatoes he cooked himself. She ate in silence, which Kibi didn't seem to mind, though she caught him giving her concerned looks a few times.

When the last glint of sunlight flared and died, Morningstar strode out into the night. The temple of Ell, set back from the parks of Gods' Green, was already in deep black shadow when she arrived. A sister she didn't recognize stood by the front door and looked down at her feet at Morningstar's approach.

"Good sunset to you, sister," Morningstar said politely.

"I'm to send you up to the Prelate's office right away," said the sister, still not looking at her. "Take the stairs on your right to the third floor, then all the way to the end of the hall."

You cannot even make eye contact with the White Anathema?

"Thank you, sister."

The young woman opened the door for her, then closed it behind her without another word. The temple's interior was pure darkness, but Morningstar's darksight had never left her, no matter how many months she had spent wandering the world in daylight. The staircase, cold and narrow, spiraled upward, its outer wall etched with a series of tactile murals depicting the flight of the Travelers. First there was Ell weaving a net of darkness around the head of the Adversary, and then the enemy stumbling into a prison of black iron bars. Some of the murals showed the other gods: Werthis doing battle with a demonic minion; Delioch healing a wound in Brechen's side; Corilayna scattering coins, all of which had come up heads. The last panel at the top of the stairs depicted Ell once more, a black silhouette, hovering above the lands of Charagan, upon whose blessed ground stood a crowd of mortals she had rescued.

At the end of the hall Morningstar found Sister Corinne, the priestess who had insulted her on her first visit to the Tal Hae temple. Corinne smiled coldly but said nothing, knocking on a black door etched with an inverted triangle.

"Send her in," came an old woman's voice.

"Is this Prelate Milanwy's office?" Morningstar asked Corinne as politely as she could manage.

"Yes. But the prelate is away visiting the temple at Tal Killip."

Morningstar frowned. "But I was summoned little more than an hour ago to see Prelate Milanwy."

Corinne gave a shrug and pushed open the door. Morningstar pressed her lips together, took a deep breath through her nose, and walked inside.

The room looked much like the prelate's office in the temple at Port Kymer. Dark, austere, cold stone and stained wood, some shelves with scrolls, a simple desk. A black triangular carpet covered the center of the floor. Six black stone statuettes watched Morningstar from a little shelf to her left as she entered; these were the six Evangelists of Ell, sisters who had shepherded Ell's followers in the earliest days following the gods' arrival on Spira. They were depicted as warriors, holding weapons and shields, armored in coats of black chain. Who they had fought was not known (or at least not taught) in the temples, but it was generally understood that without them, Ell's earliest disciples would have perished.

An elderly Ellish priestess stood behind the desk. She stared hard at Morningstar, frowning, as though trying to pierce an illusion. Her short-cropped hair was black as night, but her wrinkled face and spotted hands betrayed her advanced age.

"I thought I had been summoned by Prelate Milanwy," Morningstar said, "but then I was told she was not here. May I ask who you are?"

The woman's frown thinned to a nearly lipless line. "Of course you don't know. Morningstar of Ell, I am Rhiavonne of Ell, your high priestess." Her voice was clear and powerful, not that of an old woman.

Morningstar bowed, still standing just inside the door. "Forgive me, Your Grace, for not recognizing you." She took a step into the room, but Rhiavonne held up a hand.

"Stop."

Morningstar stopped.

"Come no closer." Rhiavonne moved from behind the desk and took two careful steps toward her. Her face contorted, nose wrinkling, as though catching a whiff of something rank. "Merciful Goddess, it's worse than I imagined," she said softly. "Here before me at last stands the White Anathema. I have had news of you through the years and wondered what sin was committed before Ell that brought you into our sisterhood. Now that I behold you in person, I see it must have been something truly terrible. Your corruption is grotesque. It rolls off you like a fever."

Morningstar stiffened. "Your Grace, I assure you I am as Ell made me."

"No." Rhiavonne took a small step back. "Do you think I cannot tell what you are? I am the mortal matriarch of our sisterhood, and as such Ell has bestowed certain blessings upon me. You cannot fool me, White Anathema."

Oh, Goddess, no.

"Your Grace, I think I know why you believe that. Recall, please, that you ordered me to work with the archmage Abernathy. In the course of that service, I was—" She closed her eyes and brought her hand to her forehead. "I was obliged to be part of a promise to a foreign goddess who opposes Ell."

Rhiavonne's eyes grew wide. "Do you speak of Dralla, mother of monsters?"

She knew? Morningstar gave a small nod. "Please believe me. It sickens me more than it does you. I wish every day there had been a different path forward."

"A different path forward?" Rhiavonne sounded incredulous. "You must have had a choice, Morningstar. You always have a choice. What obligation could you possibly have had that would necessitate..." She waved at Morningstar as though flapping away the odors from a midden. "You should have rejected anything, *anything*, that would put your soul in thrall to Dralla. But it seems you put expedience before devotion, and now you are even more an insult to our Goddess."

Morningstar's body trembled with indignation. She could so easily recall the pressure of Shreen's dark magic, crushing her head into the foul dirt of his shrine. That the matriarch of her order should twist a knife into her wound like this...

"Your Grace," she said coldly, quiveringly, "That was an act of sacrifice, not blasphemy. We needed information without which we would not currently have our one best chance to save Charagan. Agreeing to the demands of the Drallan was the only way. Are you aware of what's about to happen near Verdshane?"

Rhiavonne steepled her fingers. "I am aware, yes, that the archmagi claim without proof that something calamitous may soon occur in the Greatwood. They invited me to a mid-afternoon meeting, knowing full well neither I nor any prelate—in fact, no sister but you—could attend. I am aware that a regiment of Duke Nigel's finest soldiers is taking up position in the area. Are you telling me that your defilement is related to all of that?"

"Yes, Your Grace. In order to prevent calamity, Abernathy sent us to find a thing called the Crosser's Maze, which my friend Aravia is going to use to prevent Naradawk Skewn from escaping his prison."

"Naradawk Skewn? Do you mean Naloric Skewn, the Monstrous?"

"Naradawk is his son. He—"

"And the Drallan would only give you the Crosser's Maze if you incurred some unholy debt to him?"

"No, Your Grace. But the Drallan knew where it was."

"Ah. And you had no other way of finding it? You had exhausted every other avenue?"

Morningstar didn't answer immediately. The string of events and decisions would require a long explanation. But while she considered how to respond, Rhiavonne shook her head.

"Morningstar, I did not have myself teleported from Kallor to hear the details of your misadventures. No. I want you to tell me about Sister Sable of Ell."

The high priestess crossed her arms and stared at Morningstar with undisguised disgust.

Morningstar fought against the urge to let loose the full truth like a mouthful of dragon fire. She was the chosen of Ell! The Child of Light and the Daughter of Dreams, mentored by an Ellish angel and handpicked to lead her sisters against Aktallian Dreamborn. *I am your savior,* she wanted to scream. *I am repaying two decades of abuse with personal sacrifice you cannot imagine, and I will not stand here accused, not even by you.* Morningstar balled her fists so hard her nails scored her palms. Goddess, she wanted so badly to lash out, even the sickness of Shreen's oath was swallowed up by her righteous anger.

But…no. Deep beneath the turbulence of her emotions, she understood, or thought she did, why things had come to this pass. Rhiavonne was the high priestess, and if Ell had wanted her to be included in Morningstar's journey, it would have been so. But for Rhiavonne to know of Ell's interference would unravel the Injunction. The avatar had made it plain that no matter what else was at stake, Morningstar had to conduct her mission in secret. The Injunction must remain inviolate.

"I know that Sable was murdered," Morningstar said, meeting Rhiavonne's disapproving gaze. "I know she was much beloved in the temple here. Her death is a tragedy."

"Did you know her personally?"

"Yes."

"And were you responsible for her death?"

The bluntness of the question took Morningstar by surprise. She considered it for a moment before answering. "No."

"Do you know who was? Who killed her?"

Tread carefully, Morningstar.

"Yes. A man named Aktallian."

"And why did Aktallian wish to kill Sable?"

"Because Sable opposed him. Aktallian is trying to sabotage the archmagi's efforts in the Greatwood."

Rhiavonne ran her fingers idly along the edge of the desk. "And was Sable opposing him at your behest?"

Morningstar didn't answer.

The high priestess turned her head swiftly as though a startling thought had come to her. "Morningstar, has someone commanded you to keep secrets from me, someone whom you regard as a higher moral authority than the mortal leader of the Ellish religion?"

Ah. There it was. The choice had been put to her at last, starkly, inescapably. She would have to either lie directly to her high priestess or violate her oath to the avatar and to Ell.

As choices went, it was galling but easy. She kept her face and voice neutral as she answered, "No, Your Grace."

Morningstar recalled her conversation with Dranko about which of their gods had piled on the most indignities. Surely this moment would give her the upper hand in that ignoble contest.

Rhiavonne exhaled loudly. "I knew the White Anathema was living here in Tal Hae. I thought, mistakenly, that allowing you to serve as Abernathy's lackey would remove you as a source of trouble. It seemed a tidy solution. But instead you have used your proximity to sow the seeds of blasphemy and to gather a cadre of sisters by coercion or compulsion to aid you.

"I was summoned from Kallor because of Sable, and because of the stink of rumor that you are fomenting a conspiracy inside these hallowed walls. And here I find you, practically an albino, infected with a foreign goddess's corruption and involved in the most horrific crime inside an Ellish temple that has occurred in my lifetime."

She paused for breath. Morningstar had lost all desire to defend herself. Rhiavonne would see what she wished.

"I have questioned the sisters here," said the high priestess. "The sisters in your circle are protecting you. Previa is involved, I am sure. Amber as well. I have suspicions about the others. Who are they?"

Morningstar said nothing, so Rhiavonne forged ahead.

"I interrogated Previa only an hour ago. I asked her why she was holding back information. She refused to tell me, even when threatened with excision."

"You excised Previa?" Morningstar could not stop the question from escaping her lips.

"No," said Rhiavonne, her mouth quirking into something approaching a smile. "But that moment is close. Confess the details of your conspiracy, and that punishment would become much less likely, especially if it comes out that you forced their involvement with threats or extortion."

Morningstar gave a bitter laugh. "Threats? Extortion? You are giving me a good lesson, Your Grace. You threaten my sisters and hope to pry loose a confession through extortion. But I can tell you no more than they could. I will not tell you what I am doing, except that I feel it vital to the safekeeping of Charagan and perhaps all of Spira. Likewise I cannot tell you why I will not tell you these things even if you command me with the full weight of your position behind you. But if it pleases you, Your Grace, I will swear to you right now, by Ell's holy darkness, that Sable died fighting the same enemy that I am fighting and that I will continue that fight no matter what."

Rhiavonne walked around to Morningstar's left and picked up one of the little stone statues. "This is Aurelia. She was said to be a brilliant strategist. The others are Belshad, Moondark, Onyx, Elta—"

"And Evenstar," said Morningstar. "I am familiar with the Evangelists."

Rhiavonne leaned forward. "Did they inspire you? Did you daydream as a child of being a great Ellish hero? I imagine a sister who looked as you do would have prayed to Ell that she had been marked for some special glory."

"Of course I did," said Morningstar wearily. "As a child. But as I grew, I decided it must have been a punishment instead, though for what sin I couldn't guess. I learned to keep to myself and serve Ell as quietly as possible."

Rhiavonne pulled a piece of rolled-up parchment from her robe. "We know from our Dreamseers that Ell can see the future. I think she was punishing you for crimes you had yet to commit. I was willing to give you a chance, Morningstar. I wanted to see you in person. And what I have discovered, I am sorry to say, is corruption, conspiracy, and murder. Maybe Ell set you as a test, one that I failed by not acting before now. But I have done my best to correct it."

She held up the scroll. "This is a writ of excision, and I now choose to make it official. Morningstar of Ell, you are excised from the Ellish faith, along with Amber of Ell and Previa of Ell. The three of you are stripped of your appellations, are disallowed from the grounds of any Ellish temple, and are no longer considered clergy within the Ellish hierarchy. For your own dignity I will allow you to wear your Ellish robes back to your wizard's residence, but thereafter you are enjoined from wearing them in public."

Morningstar absorbed the words and expected to feel despair, and she did, but only on behalf of her sisters. Regarding her own excision, a sense of calm filled her, more akin to relief than rejection. "I have learned over the years," she said, "that my connection to the goddess does not depend on the temple, but rather that I maintain it despite how I am perceived. Thank you, Your Grace, for clarifying that reality in such stark terms. You drive me from the church, but you can never drive Ell from me. My relationship with her will continue, and I will save all of you, even at the cost of my own life. Good sunset to you, Your Grace."

Morningstar turned her back on the high priestess and walked out.

CHAPTER NINETEEN

D own on the ground! Hands on the floor!"
Tor complied immediately as Aravia had warned him this was likely to happen, and as always she was exactly right.

"We're associates of Generals Anapark and Largent," Aravia said loudly, even as she knelt on the floor beside him and placed her palms flat to the wooden boards. "Have they arrived?"

There was a great commotion in the common room of the Shadow Chaser, one that had obviously been going on before they arrived, but it changed markedly in tenor as soldiers noticed them and scrambled for weapons. A cluster of unarmed people in uniform backed quickly away. Ten heartbeats after their appearance, Tor and Aravia were the focus of at least a half-dozen crossbows.

"We're friends!" Tor shouted. "This is Aravia Telmir, who's working for Abernathy!"

A short, stout woman with gray hair tied back stepped into their view, though she stayed back so as not to be endangered by the crossbows herself.

"And who are you?" she asked.

"Tor Bladebearer. I'm Aravia's...bodyguard. Please don't hurt her. She's on your side. Our side. She's going to stop the invasion!"

The woman crossed her arms. "And what is your explanation for appearing here, of all places?"

"I apologize for that," said Aravia, craning her neck to look at the older woman while she talked. "I can teleport more easily to places I can recall clearly, and during my last visit, this room in the Shadow Chaser was the spot I remembered best."

The rest of the commons had gone completely quiet.

"And how do you know General Largent and General Anapark?"

"They were at the meeting in Tal Hae, as I was," said Aravia. "My understanding was that a wizard in the king's employ teleported them to Minok two days ago, and thus they should either have arrived recently or will be here soon. Either of them can vouch for us."

"The generals are not immediately available," said the woman.

"What about Dalesandro, the head of the Stormknights?" asked Tor. "He was there too."

A man standing at the woman's side bent to whisper something in her ear. She nodded, and the man hurried out the door.

"Please continue to stay where you are, and do not move," said the woman. "Maybe you're friendly, and maybe this is some magic trick of the enemy." She peered more closely at Aravia. "Why is your pack moving?"

"Because my cat, Pewter, is inside," said Aravia calmly.

"You keep a cat in your pack?"

"Only when I believe he would be in danger otherwise." She motioned with her head to indicate the closest soldier with a crossbow.

Tor glanced at Aravia, knowing she lamented every second lost to her work. "This won't take too long, will it?" he asked. "Aravia needs as much time as she can get. You don't understand how important she is! If you don't allow her to—"

"You'll wait there for as long as we tell you to," snapped the woman. "One of you is a wizard, so keep quiet and don't move your hands. I'm not going to take chances with you."

"Oh, I'm not a wizard." Tor tried not to laugh at how ridiculous an idea that was. "I'm not smart enough to be a—"

"I said keep quiet!" The woman looked around the room where dozens of people gawked. "If you're holding a crossbow aimed at these people, shoot them if they do anything unusual or start muttering nonsense. If you're not holding a crossbow, get back to—"

"Tor?" Another woman's voice interrupted the soldier. "Aravia? Captain Vall, what in the gods' names are you doin'?"

Tor risked a glance upward. Minya, owner and proprietor of the Shadow Chaser, walked toward them holding a large tray heaped with rolls. She shoved the tray into the hands of a surprised nearby soldier, then, heedless of the crossbows, stomped to where Tor and Aravia lay on their stomachs.

"Minya!" Tor exclaimed. "I knew you'd land on your feet!"

"Captain Vall," said Minya sternly, "these two are friends of mine, and I'll thank you not to keep 'em on the ground like a pair a' dogs."

Vall blinked. "You know these people, Minya?"

"This is Tor and Aravia, who saved my life back in the spring. Fought off a half-dozen a' those whaddyacallem, skellari. If not for them and their friends, there wouldn't be no Shadow Chaser for you soldierin' types to commandeer. You let 'em up and give 'em something to eat, or I swear I'll kick the lot a' you out, and you can use the outhouse for a headquarters."

The Minya Tor had last seen was pale and emaciated from days spent trapped in a cellar, but even after the gopher-bugs had ripped through Verdshane, she'd been defiant and determined to stay in business. Now she stood tall and confident, her voice clear and strong to match her attitude.

Captain Vall looked back and forth a few times between Minya and the two prisoners before running a hand over her forehead. "Aravia, tell me again why you're here?"

"Certainly, Captain. It is my intention to use wizardry to close the portal in the woods before Naradawk Skewn can use it to launch an invasion. To do that, I will need to be close to the portal, so that I might study it."

"If it makes you feel better," said Tor, "you could put a guard on us until Largent, Anapark, or Dalesandro arrives and assures you we're on your side."

Captain Vall closed her eyes for a second or two. "And your name is Tor?"

"Yes, Captain."

"If you relinquish your weapon and agree to an armed escort, I agree to those terms."

Tor paused.

"It's all right," said Aravia. "The soldiers are our allies, and they'll have weapons too."

Tor nodded.

"Now that's settled," said Minya, "put those crossbows away. Tor, you can leave your sword in the kitchen; I'll keep an eye on it. In the meantime, get yourselves a roll or two while they're still fresh."

She didn't have to tell him twice! Tor and Aravia helped themselves at the food table while Vall again admonished her soldiers to stop gawking. Aravia let Pewter loose and dropped a few bits of chicken on the floor for him to eat. Tor was still chewing on his third roll when a trio of soldiers—two women and a man— approached. All wore full leather hauberks and carried swords on their belts.

"We've been assigned to be your escort while in the environs of Verdshane," said the shorter of the two women. "I'm Laurel, and these are Melody and Richter. We're to, uh, see to your safety." She leaned closer and in a softer voice said, "The captain can be a hard-ass, but if Minya thinks you're okay, that's good enough for me. She's the best part of this whole operation."

"Nice to meet you," said Tor. "I'm Tor, and this is Aravia."

"I'd like to get started," said Aravia. She hastily downed a cup of water. "I want to inspect the portal building."

The soldiers were content to follow them outside, where the little hamlet was as unexpectedly bustling as the inside of the Shadow Chaser. A small squad of soldiers wearing the king's blue and silver unloaded arrows, bolts, and shields from a large, open wagon while others sat on makeshift benches carved from tree trunks. Some talked animatedly or sparred in the road. A runner, with mud to the tops of his boots, jogged out of the woods from the north and handed a scroll to a frowning sergeant. Beyond the road, tents had been set up in every available space among the trees, and everywhere was chatter and motion.

Tor remembered the last time they journeyed from the Shadow Chaser into the woods. Mrs. Horn had just been killed by gopher-bugs, and the group had nearly disbanded. With some pride, Tor recalled how he and Aravia had convinced the others to stick together, to see their errand done. None of them had any idea what was in front of them, with giant turtles and Sharshun and cities in bottles and all the rest, and it was odd to imagine that it was all coming to an end soon.

Compared to Verdshane, the woods were quiet. Someone had chopped a wide trail through the forest, so they made much better time than before, and there were even puncheons laid across the muddiest patches. Aravia reached out to take his hand as they crossed one of these and didn't let go afterward. Tor glanced back at their trio of guards, but if they noticed, they pretended not to.

Soon enough the ruins of a long-dead city rose up out of the forest shadows, crumbling walls and weathered foundations fighting against moss and tree, vine and shrub. The cleared path bent slightly from time to time to skirt pieces of old buildings, though in one spot someone had smashed through an ancient wall to keep the way straight.

"I'm worried," Aravia said, stepping over a branch that had fallen onto the path. "I'm not used to being worried, but I am."

"I don't think you'll have to worry," said Tor. "Remember—"

"I know what you're going to say," said Aravia. "Remember that you'll protect me. I know you will, and I'm more grateful than I can say."

"That's *not* what I was going to say." Tor squeezed her hand. "I was going to tell you to remember that you're one of the smartest people alive, and you're being taught by one of the smartest people who ever *was* alive. You'll figure this out, I know it."

Aravia laughed. "I wish I could bottle your confidence and drink it. I acknowledge my intellect, but the Crosser's Maze is, well, it's unlike anything I've ever tried to understand. You're an outstanding swordsman. Ivellios has seen any number of fighters, and he's said plenty of times you're one of the best he's ever witnessed. But that doesn't mean you could defeat a Ventifact Colossus in a duel. It's possible that the Crosser's Maze is like that. I worry that I'll hit a wall, metaphorically speaking. That I'll come to a place where I'd need weeks or months or years more to learn what I need to know."

"But King Vhadish thinks you have a chance, right?" Tor tensed his arm to steady Aravia as she skirted an unbridged mud puddle. "The way you describe him, he doesn't seem the type to get your hopes up."

"True," said Aravia. She stopped, turned around, pulled his head down by the expedient of his shirt collar, and kissed him for a delightful dozen heartbeats. "I love your optimism," she whispered, their faces still close after their lips parted. "Along with all the rest of you." She pulled back, straightened, looked past Tor's shoulder, and blushed. He turned to see the three soldiers watching them with grins.

* * *

The big stone building that housed the portal and the stasis field still stood in the center of a clearing, but the place could hardly be called "clear" anymore. Trenches scored the ground in concentric rectangles around the building, while hundreds of sharpened stakes had been jammed into the dirt at angles pointing inward. Dozens of soldiers threaded their way through the trench maze, hammering in more stakes.

The five of them had stopped at the edge of the clearing. Aravia frowned at the building for a few seconds before turning to Tor.

"I might be close enough already," she said. "I'm going to go into the maze and look at the portal. Give me two hours, and then shake me loose if I haven't returned."

Aravia took both of his hands and twined their fingers together. Her hands were so much smoother than his, all covered in callouses. She rubbed her pinky over the spot where his wasn't.

"It's unlikely anything will happen while I'm gone. The archmagi think we still have at least a few days before the wards break. Also, I'll know ahead of time. I think we all will. From the study I've already done inside the maze, I'd say that when the archmagi's locks begin to fail, the physical side effects will be difficult to ignore."

Aravia used their connected hands to pull herself to her tiptoes and kissed him one more time. "Keep me safe."

"Always."

She sat down beside the path, heedless of the wet, fallen leaves, and closed her eyes. Tor fidgeted for a second, his shoulders twitching from the absence of his sword.

"I'd feel better if I had a weapon," he said casually. "I'm supposed to be protecting Aravia. I don't suppose I could, uh, borrow one of yours? You'd still outnumber me two to one."

The three soldiers glanced at one another.

"I don't think we should," said Laurel. "Captain Vall specifically ordered you disarmed."

"Did she order you not to give me a replacement?"

Laurel opened her mouth but said nothing.

"The captain didn't order us not to do lots of things," said Melody. "Stand on our heads. Kill you on the spot. Sing a song. Doesn't mean we're going to do them."

"Fine," said Tor, "But if anything comes along that threatens Aravia, I expect you to pitch in defending her."

"Understood," said Laurel.

"Gah!" Aravia opened her eyes and leaned to one side, almost toppling over.

Tor crouched by her side and placed a steadying arm around her shoulders. "What happened? Are you all right? You haven't even been gone a minute!"

"Yes," Aravia gasped. "I just wasn't...the portal...Vhadish warned me, but..."

"Deep breaths," said Tor.

Aravia put a hand to her temple. "The aetheric resonance of the portal is intense, even from this distance. When I look at it inside the maze, it's blinding. It washes out my sense of everything for hundreds of yards around."

"What does that mean?" asked Laurel. "What is she talking about?"

Aravia looked up at her. "Ordinarily, from inside the Crosser's Maze I can observe the real world, or at least an accurate reflection of it. From our house in

Tal Hae, I was able to see detail of this entire area without difficulty. But now that my physical body is this close to the portal, I can't see anything in the maze, in the same way one cannot see one's surroundings if a bright lantern is held up to one's nose."

Richter frowned. "I still don't get it."

"It doesn't matter," said Aravia. "I can still study the portal; I just need to be prepared for its resonance. I'm going back in."

Once again she closed her eyes. For a few seconds her lips twitched, and her eyes squeezed tight, before her face softened into the relaxed expression typical of her excursions into the maze. Her eyes opened, revealing pools of star-sprinkled black.

Melody looked down at Aravia, then up at Tor. "I don't suppose you can explain what she's doing?"

"Using a magical object to figure out how to seal up the portal for good." He pointed out into the clearing and all the preparations being made to welcome the enemy forces. "If she succeeds, all of this will be unnecessary."

"They tell us an army is just going to appear," said Laurel. "Most likely in or around that building. It's why we're making this whole place into a killing zone."

"The trenches are full of little spiky things," said Richter. "Caltrops, I think they're called. That's why we have boards across them now for our own troops. And we're building archer platforms in the trees all around the edge of the clearing. If a regiment of enemy soldiers comes out of the building, they'll be subject to withering fire from every direction while navigating booby-trapped ditches and avoiding a forest of sharp stakes."

"General Anapark wanted to flood the whole place," said Melody. "Divert part of the river and turn the ground around the building to mud soup. But we don't have the time or manpower for that kind of project. It's too bad the Stormknights are mostly off fighting on Lanei, though I'm told we can expect a small detachment."

"It's impressive," said Tor, not taking his eyes from Aravia.

"Even if your friend fails, we'll be ready," said Richter.

"Unless they outnumber us by too much," said Laurel. "We have around nine hundred soldiers stationed here, and we're hoping for another couple hundred in the next day or two from Minok. But nobody seems to know how large an army we might have to fight. If it's ten thousand, even our tactical advantages won't mean much."

Tor glanced up at the building housing the portal and the stasis field. "But where would they fit?" he mused out loud. "If they all have to fit through one small door, you can pick them off indefinitely as they emerge. And ten thousand soldiers wouldn't fit in there. They'd more than fill up the entire clearing from end to end."

"Who knows?" said Richter. "Anyhow, we've already bricked up the only entrance to the building, so any soldiers who appear inside of it will first have to break through the walls."

"You sealed the building?" Tor peered across the clearing at the white edifice with its high central dome. From experience he knew the single doorway—masked by an illusion of a stone panel with a bear's head—was on the far side. "Are you sure that was a good idea? Naradawk has been able to get a few people and monsters through the portal already. There could be something nasty in there right now, trying to get out."

Laurel chuckled. "General Largent thought of that. He figured that if something did slip through the portal, better it be trapped in there rather than free to sneak around causing trouble."

"Like the skellari," said Melody. "Little flying rodents with huge teeth. A swarm came out of that building the same day the first soldiers arrived. Killed three people before they got wise and started pairing up. Glad I wasn't there for that part."

"There were more gopher-bugs?" asked Tor. "That's what we called them. Gopher-bugs. They killed a friend of mine, Ysabel Horn, the nicest old lady you could ever hope to meet. I wished I'd been able to save her."

They all fell silent for a few minutes after that. Tor kept his eyes on Aravia. How was she doing, *what* was she doing, in the Crosser's Maze? She sometimes tried explaining the process of learning to use the maze, the mental and magical techniques she intended to use to seal up the portal between Spira and Volpos, and he always listened attentively, but seldom did he understand the details. He didn't feel badly about that; he imagined that few people in the kingdom could follow along when she talked about the maze.

"How long is she going to sit there?" asked Melody after Aravia had been in the maze for about half an hour.

"Hard to say," said Tor. "Sometimes she's only in the maze for a few minutes, and other times it can be hours."

"In the maze?" asked Richter.

"Oh, right. It's, uh, hard to explain. That magic object I said she's using? She sends her mind into it, and that lets her study the portal."

"Oh," said Richter faintly.

"You don't know the half of how weird it is. I've actually been inside it too and have no desire to go back."

It turned out that the answer to Melody's question was "another hour or so," during which time a young soldier arrived out of breath from the direction of Verdshane. "General Anapark just arrived from Minok," he puffed between catch-up breaths. "She says that Tor and Aravia are to be given full run of the area and don't need an escort. This is for Aravia from General Anapark." He glanced down at her before handing Tor a tied-up scroll. "It gives her permission to conscript anyone wearing the king's colors, for anything she needs. As for you three—" He turned to Melody, Richter, and Laurel. "I've got some bad news. Anapark arrived with three wagons of supplies, so you've been conscripted for food prep."

"Not potatoes?" said Richter dejectedly.

"Lots of potatoes," said the soldier. "And they all need peeling. Oh, and Tor, I was told to return this to you." He handed over Tor's sword.

Laurel turned to Tor with a sigh. "It was a pleasure meeting you both. Please tell Aravia when she wakes up that we wish her all success with her magic spell. We've all trained for combat, but most of us hope not to see any."

"Agreed," said Tor.

The four soldiers headed back toward the town, leaving Tor and Aravia alone, unless one counted the dozens of others who still toiled in the clearing, making it as deadly as possible.

When Aravia did wake up, she stood too quickly and had to lean on Tor to avoid falling over.

"Any luck?" Tor asked.

"Some," said Aravia. "I can see the portal with more clarity when my physical body is closer to it. From here I was able to discern some details that will help when the time comes. But I need to get right up close, inside the building."

"Oh," said Tor. "Richter said they bricked up the doorway."

Aravia looked peeved. "That's right. I saw them doing that when I scouted the area with the maze yesterday. It's unlikely, but if the emperor has managed to translate anything new from Volpos in the past day, it will be trapped inside."

"That's what I said! And there have already been more gopher-bugs that got loose before they bricked it up. If they've tried again, the whole inside of that building could be swarming with them."

"Damn," muttered Aravia. She stared across the clearing at the building as though she could bore holes through it and see inside.

"I don't suppose you have a spell that lets you see through walls?" Tor asked.

"No." Aravia paused. "I wish we had Kibi here, but I'd have to teleport twice to retrieve him, and there'd be a risk that he's not at the Greenhouse. It's been hours since we left, and if he's gone out for a walk, it could take us too long to track him down. Also, there is a spell Vhadish taught me to use when I'm right up close, and if I've teleported twice, I will lack the stamina to cast it."

"But without Kibi, you'll have to teleport in anyhow, right?" Tor asked.

She pondered again. "That would work, but even one *teleport* would leave me more drained than I'd like to be."

"Then we'll have to knock the new wall down," said Tor. "That shouldn't be a problem. We have hundreds of soldiers here who have already been chopping down trees to widen the clearing. I'll bet we can have a battering ram ready in no time."

Aravia nodded. "And we'll want a couple dozen of those soldiers ready with weapons in case the building is filled with skellari." She waved to get the attention of a nearby soldier, who jogged over.

"Yes?" She sounded annoyed at the interruption.

Aravia handed her the scroll; she read it and immediately snapped to attention. "How may I assist, Aravia?"

"I'll need a small battering ram constructed," she said, "capable of knocking down the wall you recently built across the opening into that building. I apologize for undoing your work, but I need to get inside. I would also like thirty soldiers on hand, a few to help with the ram, and all of them ready to fight whatever hostile people or creatures might be inside. Ideally those would be men and women who have already fought the skellari without panicking, and who are uninjured."

"Yes, ma'am," the soldier said.

"I would like this done immediately. Finished within the hour if possible. I begrudge every second lost. Oh, and please advise General Anapark of what I'm about to do."

The soldier handed Aravia back the scroll and dashed off toward Verdshane. Aravia took Tor's hand and gave it a tug.

"Let's take a closer look at the wall."

* * *

"I'm going to go in first." There was never any doubt in Tor's mind about that. Maybe there were gopher-bugs, or maybe someone like Aktallian Dreamborn (dead or dying of thirst, with any luck), or maybe nothing at all, but the whole reason Abernathy had summoned Tor was to be the first person to go into unknown danger.

Aravia held his hand while behind them a half-dozen soldiers hammered chained handles into the makeshift ram. Tor, to his delight, noticed that she found his hand whenever possible, as though the contact of their fingers could make up for years of trying not to feel anything.

"I'm sure I couldn't stop you," Aravia said, "though I want you to promise not to do anything rash. We'll have thirty soldiers out here waiting, so if you go in and find clouds of gopher-bugs or a half-dozen red-armored warriors, come back out and let our numbers make the difference."

The new section of wall did not sit flush with the rest, which made sense, since the doorway was an opening masked by an opaque illusion of stone. To seal it up properly, the builders wouldn't have been able to see what they were doing. The added width was built of chiseled fieldstone blocks dug up from the surrounding woods and mortared into place. Tor held his ear up, thinking that if a hundred gopher-bugs waited on the far side he might hear them buzzing around, but all he heard was silence.

Six soldiers came up with the ram, a hastily cut length of tree trunk a foot in diameter. There hadn't been time to build a proper harness for it, so the soldiers would have to swing it free.

"I helped build that wall," grumbled a large, bearded soldier. "Figures I'd end up here to knock it down."

Half the thirty had crossbows, but Aravia warned them that if they faced gopher-bugs, those would be useless.

"We know," said a short, blond-haired solder. She patted the hilt of her sword. "Everyone here's been briefed on what to do if one of them critters lands on you. Partner up, keep an eye on your buddy, and prepare to pluck and squash."

Tor drew his own sword. "If there's something else inside, and I don't think I can kill it myself, I'll try drawing it out. Everyone be ready."

The soldiers with the ram stepped up. One of them, a reedy woman with a shock of unruly black hair, seemed to be in charge. "On three," she barked. "One! Two! Three!"

The log smashed into the wall with a crack, sending a few bits of mortar flying, but the stones held steady.

"Good wall, that," said the bearded soldier.

"Again!" shouted the leader. "One! Two! Three!"

Six soldiers drove the log into the wall a second time. More chunks of mortar came loose, and a large crack appeared in the centermost stone.

"Keep going," exhorted the leader. "One swing every third count." She continued her cadence while the rammers struck again and again. It took over a dozen swings, but at last the entire center of the wall gave way. Some of the stones fell outward onto the dirt, while others tumbled inward and vanished behind the illusionary wall. The insubstantial carving of the bear's head looked out stoically at chest height.

"Anything in there, it knows we're comin' in after it," muttered the blond-haired soldier.

"Remember," said Tor, "if I start shouting for backup, you need to close your eyes in order to pass through the illusion." He looked at Aravia for confirmation, and she nodded. "You'll all see me go in," Tor added, "in case you're not convinced that's not really a stone wall."

"I don't need to remind you," said Aravia, "not to touch the stasis field. Just like last time." She stepped closer so that the toes of their boots practically touched. "The most likely case is that there's nothing new inside, but good luck all the same. I love you, Tor. Don't get killed." She stood on tiptoe, face upturned, and he gave her a parting kiss.

Then he stepped high over a pile of rubble, closing his eyes as he did so, and moved through the illusionary wall.

Inside, all was as he remembered.

The walls were polished white marble, clean and shiny, and light came from somewhere in the room, though it had no obvious source. Tor chalked it up to the mysteries of enchantment, took a second step, and listened.

Nothing. In front of him was a long empty stretch of marble floor, and beyond that the outermost of the concentric hemispherical cages that bounded the glowing blue sphere at their center. The only sound, except for the occasional cough or muttered utterance from the soldiers outside, was the faint tuning-fork ring coming from the metal ribs of the hemispheres. From this distance he couldn't see anything trapped in the field or any creatures, living or dead, on the floor.

He glanced upward, scanning for gopher-bugs, but the place was empty, which was a relief, though also a bit of a disappointment as there was nothing in here to fight. Still, he ought to be thorough. The blue field was partially masked by all the metal bars, and he moved closer to inspect it more carefully.

As he reached the first of the cages, a few things happened, all of them more or less simultaneously.

One, he caught a brief glimpse of movement above his head.

Two, something like a rubbery arm wrapped itself around his neck, chin, and mouth, filling his nose with a reptilian scent.

Three, and quite likely related to the first two, he recalled that the center of the building's ceiling was domed, and that he hadn't been able to see the near-side curve of its interior from the area near the doorway. He should have kept looking up!

By the time he had registered all of these things, Tor was being hoisted off his feet and up into the air. Craning his neck against the tension of the rubbery arm, he looked up to see that, no, it wasn't an arm at all, but a tentacle, gray and snake-like, dangling from a cow-sized purple blob clinging to the inside of the dome. Many more tentacles hung from its body, and some of these wrapped themselves around Tor's legs and waist.

The monster hauled Tor up in jerks, a few feet at a time, and the underside of the blob roiled and rippled until a glistening beak protruded, shiny red, sharp, and the size of a large dog. Tor had kept a grip on his sword, but his arms were pinned by a tentacle, so that was no good, and at the rate he was rising, the thing would bite his head off in about half a minute, maybe less, and by the gods what a disgusting creature it was! The purple sack of flesh smelled like a rotten lizard, and the squishing of its body sounded like boots being pulled out from sucking mud.

Up. Pause. Up. Tor tried to shout for help, but the tentacle across his face muffled his cries, and of course no one could see his plight through the opaque illusion that filled the doorway, and while eventually they might wonder what was taking him so long and come in after him, by that time he might be torn up by the monster's beak and swallowed into its bulk. How sad Aravia would be if he died up here after all that preparation!

Pause. Up. Pause. Only a few seconds remained until the creature would be close enough to bite his head, and Tor redoubled his efforts to squirm free, or at least work his right arm loose, but the grip of the tentacles was like iron bands wrapped snug against him. It was horribly frustrating, reminding Tor of when Hodge's spell had paralyzed everyone in the company except for Kibi. But Kibi wasn't here, and couldn't reach him even if he were, and—oh!

Up. Pause. Kick! Using every ounce of strength he could force out of his abdominal muscles, Tor flipped himself upside down, the tentacle around his waist serving as a fulcrum, the tentacles around his legs going slack. His left boot smashed into the beak, bending it sideways and provoking something like a hissing squawk. All of the monster's tentacles quivered and lost some of their taut strength; the one around his mouth slipped down to his neck, and (even better) Tor was able to free his sword arm.

"Help!" he shouted. "I'm up in the dome!" Even as he shouted, he let his body swivel back to upright, hoping the beast wouldn't simply drop him thirty feet to the floor. The creature shuddered, the beak realigned itself towards Tor's head, and its tentacles tightened, but this time Tor's sword arm was free. It yanked him upward one more time, and he slashed his blade across its undulating purple mass.

It looked soft and yielding, but its hide turned out to be more like boiled leather. Without serious leverage, Tor only managed to score its body with a shallow cut that didn't even provoke a reaction. It lifted him one last time and the beak snapped downward; Tor tilted his neck frantically and the thing bit painfully into the top of his left shoulder, shaking him back and forth as blood welled up and poured down his arm. He bellowed wordlessly in pain, but kept his wits, bringing the pommel of his sword to his waist, blade pointed upward. Even as the thing chewed on his shoulder, Tor thrust the blade upward into the seam between body and beak.

Thick green blood poured out and splattered his face, so he held his breath and closed his eyes and shoved the blade as hard as he could. The beak let go and the tentacles all went slack, causing Tor to plummet, and opening his eyes only filled them with monster goop, so he flailed blindly until his left hand found a dangling tentacle, but he couldn't grip it properly, not with his little finger missing, but instead of smacking into the marble floor he felt a tentacle seize his thigh, flipping him upside down, and *that* cracked his head into the floor, though not with the same force as the fall would have done. Dazed, Tor still managed to wipe the blood out of his eyes and bend his body in time to see more tentacles descending and enwrapping him, the thing's blood spattering downward like a gory rain from the wound Tor had made. His body rose again, but he reached out and gripped the metal bars of the outermost cage, hooking his elbow around one of them. For an awful moment his body stretched as the monster pulled at him.

Thrum, thwack!

That sounded like a crossbow bolt!

Tor twisted his body around and discovered that several soldiers had arrived, looking upward with expressions of horror and disgust.

Thwack! Another bolt struck the purple blob, and another, and another, as more soldiers stepped in and joined the attack. The tentacles released Tor in order to deal with the new threat; four of them plucked up soldiers and whipped them around, smashing them into each other, the walls, the metal bars. The room echoed with their panicked shouts.

More reinforcements arrived, and soon another half-dozen soldiers were aiming upward, peppering the body with bolts. The ones that struck tended to sink in about half of their length, and though the wounds bled, it didn't seem the monster was particularly injured by them. But it must have been bothered, as it brought the four seized soldiers close to its body, shielding itself.

"Hold your shots!" the tall woman shouted, but Tor knew something had to be done, as the monster brought one of the soldiers to its beak and bit into his leg. A scream of pain rang out.

"Sergeant, what do we do?" one of the soldiers pleaded. "It's going to eat 'em!"

Tor looked up, and another idea sprang to his thoughts. He sheathed his sword, wiped his bloody hand on the one dry patch of his trousers, climbed up the gentle curve of the metal cage, and for a second balanced precariously on one of its thin, rounded bars. When a flailing tentacle came close enough, he launched himself from the cage and grabbed hold of it.

Hand over hand, he began to climb.

"What's he doing?" a man's voice sounded from below.

"Saving your fellows, it would appear," said a woman's voice. Aravia's voice. Tor glanced down just long enough for them to exchange smiles before continuing his upward journey, happy that Master Elgus had made him climb ropes every day as part of his training back at his father's castle.

"Often a duel will be decided by who tires first," Master Elgus had said. "Keep your arms and shoulders strong, and you can outlast even a superior fighter." The old man would be pleased to know his methods were paying off, even if in a somewhat unconventional manner.

The purple blob monster, perhaps realizing the danger Tor posed (and how did it see, anyhow? It had no eyes!), tried to dislodge him by flailing him around, but he was too high up for it to knock him against anything. When he was within striking distance, Tor twined his left arm around the tentacle, allowing him to hold on tightly even with his missing finger, then drew his sword with his right hand

and stabbed upward. Again and again he plunged his blade into the heaving jelly-like mass of its body, its goopy blood spewing out, soaking his hair and clothes. The monster tried smashing the other bound soldiers against him, but he held on and continued to strike, and one of his thrusts went right into its beak with a horrid scraping sound, at which all of its tentacles stretched taut and quivered as if the thing had been struck by lightning. The soldiers in its clutches were flung away, their cries ending in thumps as they landed far below.

With a loud sucking sound, the monster peeled away from the underside of the dome. Realizing he was about to drop thirty feet, Tor released his sword and desperately climbed up the side of the purple blob, using his own inflicted puncture wounds for hand-holds. Even as the last of its sticky underside detached itself, Tor scrambled to what loosely could be called its back and clung on as it fell.

Splat! Tor's bones jarred and his teeth rattled, but the squishy thing absorbed enough of the fall that Tor felt merely bruised upon landing. His head still sang from its knock against the floor, and his shoulder burned from where the monster had savaged it, but he was alive!

While the surviving soldiers stood around goggling, Aravia pushed her way forward until she stood before him, and he couldn't help but feel self-conscious that he was covered head to foot in green blood and oozy slime.

"Gods," Aravia said, shaking her head. "You look…" She trailed off and gestured to his dripping clothes, blood-smeared face, and the revolting purple mound of flesh he currently used as a cushion.

Tor winced. "Disgusting?"

Aravia grinned at him, her eyes shining. "Beautiful."

CHAPTER TWENTY

A man in black shirt and pants slipped around the back of the warehouse, deftly dodging pools of light, treading quietly in soft leather shoes. Clouds covered the moon, and the few small ships in the little harbor had darkened their lanterns for the night. The boards on their piles did not creak beneath the man's feet.

With practiced stealth he unlocked the chain of the harbor-side door and unwound it without even the tiniest clink of metal. A shadow within a shadow, he moved swiftly inside and closed the door quietly behind him.

His eyes quickly adjusted to the darkness. In one corner lay the fragmented remains of a small office, bits of wood and paper scattered amidst scorch marks and smears of ash. The man stepped his way slowly through the wreckage, nudging debris aside with his shoes and occasionally stooping to sift his hands through it. Half a desk lay end-side down, jagged splinters pointing upward, its drawers fallen out or blown apart. He spent a half-minute examining the blasted desk but removing nothing, then walked away from the corner and made a methodical sweep of the rest of the warehouse floor. Near the door he bent and examined a number of dark stains on the floor, going so far as to touch one with a finger and then dab his fingertip to his tongue. He spent a few seconds ruminating, perhaps tasting, then produced a small glass vial and a chisel from a pocket. He scraped up flakes of blood from the floor and tipped them from the chisel blade into the vial, which he deftly stoppered before returning everything to his pockets.

Frowning, the man looked up at the balconies, then back to the floor where the long metal ladder lay flat, torn away from the wall. By lifting the far end and walking slowly forward, he was able to tip the ladder slowly upward, then over, so that it leaned against the wall in approximately its original position. The half-desk, dragged over to the foot of the ladder, served as a brace. He scrambled up to the first balcony and walked its length, stepping or leaping over several gaps in its wooden planks where something had smashed through it from below. Thoroughly he searched each balcony level, and then the trapdoor at the top, going so far as to poke his head out into the night sky. Breeze ruffled his hair.

Seemingly satisfied, he returned to the floor of the warehouse and quietly exited through the harbor-side door, rewrapping the chains and locking the building. For a few moments he stood as still as a lamppost, gazing out upon the black water, listening to the tiny noises of creaking boats drifting across its surface. Somewhere in the distance a gale of laughter escaped a dockside tavern, then quieted at the sound of a door slamming shut. The man turned, skirted the warehouse on its little clinging boardwalk, and returned to the street.

He continued to move like a shadow, slipping from darkness to darkness, always finding spots without sightlines, crevices and alcoves and doorways where he could melt into obscurity. But once he'd put six or seven blocks between himself and the warehouse, his demeanor changed completely. The man shed his shadow-semblance and walked boldly, nodding to passersby, stopping to buy a scarf from a vendor open late, and ducking into a boisterous tavern to purchase and leisurely consume a mug of ale. (Though he did take pains to sit with his back to a wall and leave himself a clear view of the door.)

His drink finished, he left a few extra coins for the serving boy and returned to the late night streets of Minok. For nearly an hour he meandered in a path that seemed designed to appear aimless, often taking unexpected side streets that looped back to places he had been. Finally, having entered a poor section of town with battered buildings crammed closely together, the man slipped into a lightless alley. Halfway down he stopped and faced the left-hand wall, a blank stretch of stained, crumbling brick.

After casting quick glances to both ends of the alley, he drew a small pendant— a little black circle on a metal chain—out from beneath his shirt and touched it to the wall. A simple door appeared. He unlocked this with a small key and went inside. Behind him, the door vanished when it swung shut.

The building was abandoned. Its front door and ground-floor windows were boarded up, and its inside matched the exterior. Once it might have been a shop, but its counter was cracked, its shelves moldy and mostly fallen to the floor. Piles of refuse lay heaped in corners.

The man moved to a door behind the counter, opened it, and stepped into a large square closet. He pushed at one end of a wooden wallboard, indistinguishable from all the others, and the other end flipped up to reveal a small lever. Pulling the lever caused adjacent sections of wall and floor to slide back, revealing a wide staircase descending into darkness.

He traced quick circles in the air, at which a dim light filled the staircase. Down he went, and the light dimmed and darkened behind him as he stepped. At the bottom, some twenty feet below street level, the staircase opened into a corridor branching left and right. He went left.

* * *

Ysabel Horn grinned as she watched the man go, though she was too tired to continue following his path. Feeling as though her mind had been stretched thin as cheesecloth, she let the natural ebb of the Crosser's Maze return her to the empty space high above Spira.

But she muttered to herself as she drifted away.

"Caught you, you sneaky Black Circle roach. I caught you."

CHAPTER TWENTY-ONE

In one of Master Serpicore's lessons on optics, he had explained to Aravia the emergence of a technology called "spectacles."

"It's a shame their use is not more widely spread," Serpicore had said. "With spectacles, a person with poor eyesight would see the entire world come into focus, from blurry to sharp, in an instant. And they will probably not have realized such an improvement was possible."

That was what it was like to observe the portal in the Crosser's Maze while at the same time standing next to it—or as close as she could come while avoiding the stasis field. Aravia had assumed she'd been observing its details, its arcane composition, its ebbs and flows of energy, its warping effect on its surroundings. But she'd been badly mistaken.

Pewter was not with her in the maze; she had left him to guard her body, in the unlikely event Emperor Naradawk managed to slip another unpleasant surprise past the wards. Tor had gone back to the Shadow Chaser to have his wounds tended.

The portal between Spira and Volpos had been a near-perfect oval in her previous examinations, but observed up close its edge was ragged and irregular, as though roughly torn from the fabric of reality. On the Spira side it was just under nine feet tall and about five feet wide; on the Volpos side she sensed it was much larger, which provoked an obvious question. What would happen if Naradawk attempted to translate something small enough to fit through on his end, but too big to squeeze through the Spira-side aperture? Nothing good, she guessed, but that was Naradawk's problem, not hers. Aravia's job was to remove the portal entirely and replace it with a patch of solid, unblemished reality.

She was confident from her trials with Vhadish that she could draw and direct sufficient power into it. But that wouldn't be enough, just as heating a forge hot enough did not guarantee a well-crafted sword. Unthreading and re-weaving a new piece of the universe would require skill, finesse, and a deep knowledge of how the cosmos was put together.

So Aravia observed. Aravia studied. Aravia absorbed. The Crosser's Maze accelerated the pace of her learning, which was already formidable. Not for the first time she was struck by the notion that the maze had been constructed *specifically for her*, that it locked into and meshed with her mind, expanding her intellect and powers of understanding. The Crosser's Maze was a machine the size of the universe, and she was its central cog.

Of course, Solomea had told her that the original point of the maze was to repair weak spots in the fabric of reality, so it stood to reason that it would feel this way while she used it for that exact purpose. When she cast *Aravia's Lockbuster* to pop open a locked door, it felt perfect, like the world had aligned precisely to her arcane will, became subjugated to it. When she had mastered the Crosser's Maze, fixing the rift between Spira and Volpos would feel the same way.

One of the trickier aspects would be working around the archmagi's seal—essentially a magical barrier that prevented anyone from pushing through the portal. Well, *prevented* was obviously too strong a word. "Made extremely difficult" would be more accurate, given the skellari and the tentacled blob monster. Aktallian Dreamborn had been a special case; Naradawk and his agents on Spira—agents who included Parthol Runecarver, if Solomea was to be believed—had gone to great lengths to squeeze Aktallian across. As the portal now stood, with all five archmagi maintaining its arcanistically inverse locks, no one as powerful as Aktallian could get through it.

More relevant to Aravia was that the arcane emanations from the barrier interfered mildly with her perceptions of the weak spot itself. Vhadish had shown her some tricks for mitigating that, but she needed more instruction from him. She added to her mental tally of questions she had for him, groaning a bit inside at the thought of his condescending tone and aura of subtle impatience.

A sharp stinging in her arm startled her out of the maze. She emerged into the real world to find that Pewter had sunk his claws into her skin.

Boss? Everything all right in there? You were in there for hours without even a twitch!

I was?

Yeah. And I have some news about Tor.

A horrific stench assailed her; she clamped a hand to her nose and mouth.

They couldn't fit that blob monster out the door, said Pewter, *so they hauled it into a corner. It smells like a snake carcass full of maggots even from across the room.*

I'm sorry you had to suffer it. Let's talk more outside. Is Tor well? Has he recovered?

Four soldiers, armed with swords and clad in leather hauberks, stood nearby, kerchiefs drawn across their faces.

"Any problems?" one of them asked as Aravia stood.

"None. I assume you were sent to guard me in Tor's absence?"

"Yes, ma'am," said the soldier. He was a tall man with broad shoulders, reminding her a little of an older version of Tor. "I, uh…" He glanced down at Pewter with a skeptical expression. "I was told to give a report to your cat when we arrived, which I have done."

"Yes. Thank you."

They emerged into a cool orange dusk, and the crisp scents of an autumn woodland replaced the rotting stink of the monster corpse. Around them soldiers still toiled in the clearing, cutting trenches, planting stakes, and constructing platforms in the distant trees.

So, Pewter, what's the report?

Tor's fine. But it was a close call.

What? He seemed well after the battle, if a bit bruised.

Well, you know Tor. He always puts on a brave face. But that blob thing that chewed on his shoulder turned out to be venomous too. By the time they got him back to the Shadow Chaser, he could barely stand up and his whole left arm was gray. Bits of it were falling off. Fortunately they have a Deliochan channeler from Minok stationed there, and General Anapark decided that Tor was someone worth channeling for. So the good news is Tor's back to normal, but the bad news is that the healer probably won't be able to channel again before this is all over, one way or another.

At the Shadow Chaser, Aravia found Tor in the field behind the inn, where a medical pavilion creaked in the breeze on its poles. Lanterns had been hung from the supports ahead of the sunset. Tor, his face scrubbed and wearing a fresh change of clothes, stood chatting animatedly with General Anapark beside an empty cot inside the tent.

"Aravia!" He rushed over to her and picked her up, hugging her and twirling her around. "You're safe."

"Unlike you, I wasn't in any danger," she said, smiling up at him. "Pewter tells me you had a scare."

"Yeah. That tentacled thing had a poisonous bite. They had a channeler fix me up, though. That's her over there, sleeping."

"I need to go back into the maze," she told him. "I have more questions for King Vhadish, and a few more training exercises in which I want to improve. But if those answers are satisfactory, and my skill sufficiently honed, I may be ready to seal the portal tomorrow or the day after. General, is this a good spot? Tor can stay here and guard me."

"Of course." Men and women in Deliochan robes bustled about, preparing more cots, folding blankets, making inventories, and staging medical supplies. Though Aravia hoped to make all this preparation unnecessary, it was only sensible for them to plan for the worst. A few of the adherents cast glances in their direction, probably curious about the man whom the general had decided was worth their single shot of channeling.

"General, there's something extremely important I need to speak with you about before I go in."

"Yes, Aravia?"

"When the time comes for me to seal the portal, I will need to draw small amounts of energy from your soldiers. That's how the Crosser's Maze works."

Anapark frowned. "Is that dangerous?"

Aravia considered lying—this was non-negotiable, and she didn't want to give Anapark any reason to protest. A year ago she'd have lied without flinching.

"There is some risk, yes." She spared a brief look at Tor; he watched her with a big smile on his face. "But it is small, and I will do my best to mitigate it. Here's the important part: The energy has to be freely given. I cannot simply take it from them."

"So what are you asking, specifically?" asked Anapark.

"I would like you to spread the word to all of your soldiers. Sometime in the next few days, perhaps as soon as tomorrow, they will feel…" She trailed off, surprised at herself that she didn't know how to continue. "They will feel something internal, a pull, a kind of request. I'm not explaining this well, I'm sorry. The truth is, I don't know exactly what it will feel like. Perhaps a tugging, a feeling like something is trying to drain them. What's important is that, when they feel it, whatever it is they feel, they need to assent to it. Allow it. Let their energy go, so I can use it."

Anapark's frown deepened.

"If it helps," said Aravia, "tell them that by letting me use some of their energy, they greatly reduce the chance that they will die at the hands of Naradawk and his forces."

Anapark looked unconvinced but nodded nonetheless. "I'll send word out as an order. That will make it less likely that anyone will refuse. But again I have to ask: What is the risk I'm asking my men and women to take? What is the danger?"

Aravia sighed. "If I have trouble maintaining control of my work inside the maze, I could drain too much energy from any individual person. I might knock them unconscious or even kill them by accident."

"Is that likely?"

"No. I've been working very hard on perfecting my technique. My hope is that none of your soldiers will feel more than a slight fatigue."

Anapark looked skyward as though imploring the gods for guidance. "I'll trust that you know what you're doing. Now, please, is there anything more you need from me? I have a dozen tasks I need to take care of before sunset."

"Yes. One more thing. As someone may have told you, I ordered that the portal building be reopened. I needed to get inside and will be going back tomorrow. In the meantime, someone should be guarding the building at all times, posted just inside the door. It's unlikely Naradawk will push anything new through, but in case he does, we don't want to be taken by surprise."

"Understood. Anything else?"

"No. But please make sure my warning gets to as many of your soldiers as possible."

The general nodded, turned, and departed.

Tor waited until he was gone before leaning in and speaking in a near-whisper. "I'll be honest, I thought I was going to die. That poison hurt worse than when that Sharshun cut off my finger, and two of the soldiers who came to my rescue died of it. Well, they both died, though for one of them it wasn't clear if it was from the poison or blood loss. I should be thankful its poison was only from its bite and not its blood, or I'd be dead ten times over."

Tor was always so carefree and confident; it troubled Aravia to see such a concerned expression on his face.

"You can't die," she told him. "You're my protector, remember?"

Tor smiled at her, but then he looked over her shoulder in the direction of the portal building, and the worry came back.

"The gopher-bugs and the blob monster have been awfully dangerous," he said. "What if Naradawk can send through an army of creatures like that? I know the soldiers here have experience with them, but what if thousands of gopher-bugs come spilling out?"

"I don't think it will come to that," Aravia told him. "I only need a few more hours with Vhadish, a few more hours up close with the portal, and perhaps an hour to figure out the optimal location for my physical self. After that I will start closing the portal. I think there's a good chance I can permanently divide Spira and Volpos before Naradawk can create a serious breach—perhaps as soon as tomorrow evening."

"Oh. Good!" Tor's smile returned, so full of optimism and confidence, it filled Aravia's own heart with joy. "You haven't eaten anything recently. If you're about to go back into the maze for a while, let me get you some dinner first. Minya and her army of cooks have made a fantastic chicken and dumpling soup. Be right back!"

Tor dashed around to the front of the Shadow Chaser, leaving Aravia to stare after him. What had she done to deserve the good fortune of his love and loyalty? She muttered a prayer to Corilayna.

For the record, said Pewter, *I knew he was in love with you long before you noticed.*

Yes, you're very smart. Now hush.

She used the few minutes of Tor's absence to perform some calculations in her head, puzzling out the optimum location to sit while closing down the portal. Too close, and the emanations from the archmagi's wards, not to mention the arcane aura of the portal itself, would interfere with the work. Too far, and she'd lose the up-close detail so vital to the maze's use. By the time Tor returned—with two platters in one hand, two cups in the other, and two bowls balanced on his forearm—she had arrived at a figure somewhere between four hundred and four hundred fifty feet. Which...hm. That was about the same distance as the pocket dimension in which the archmagi maintained the wards. Probably not a coincidence.

"Soup, bread, pastries, and an orange," said Tor, juggling a bit to get everything set down on the cot. He had brought a small extra plate, heaped with bits of shredded chicken, which he placed gently on the ground.

You're going to keep him, right? Even after we're done with all this?

Yes, I think I will.

Tor stirred Aravia's soup bowl before handing it to her. "Got to keep your strength up if you're going to save the world soon!" She hadn't eaten since breakfast, and the smell of the soup made her stomach rumble with anticipation. For once she ate with as much haste and gusto as Tor.

"General Anapark says they expect another three hundred soldiers tomorrow from Minok," Tor said with his mouth full. "Last-minute volunteers. She thinks that more are on their way from Tal Hae, but they're still several days away."

Aravia drained her water cup in a single pull; gods, but she'd been thirsty. Tor handed her a second, which she finished just as quickly, and only afterward did she realize Tor had given her his own.

"Thank you, Tor. And you're right. I'll need all of my strength, all of my arcane reserves, to do this properly."

For the next few minutes they ate their dinners in silence. Every moment Tor wasn't actively chewing his food, he grinned at her so widely, it was as though this was the happiest moment of his life. She smiled back at him and wished she could stretch out the moment.

"It's time," she said, taking his hands in her own. "I need to consult with Vhadish. I expect to be in the maze for several hours. Give me a shake if I haven't come out by midnight. Will you be able to stay awake? You've had a rough day."

He squeezed her hands. "No trouble at all. Channeling does wonders for one's constitution. I could stand here guarding you until the sun comes up."

"You won't need to. I need a good night's sleep tonight." She gave him a devilish grin. "Which is a shame."

Tor blushed to the tips of his ears, which made Aravia laugh.

"Keep an eye on Pewter too. He's going to come with me."

Ready, Pewter?

Always, boss.

"Stay safe, Tor Bladebearer."

* * *

Vhadish had altered the protections of his Tetra so that Aravia, as Keeper of the Maze, could appear directly in his throne room. Usually she found him seated on his elaborate bejeweled seat, his chin in hand as though contemplating the secrets of the universe, or sipping wine from a chalice as gaudy and glittering as his chair.

This time, the only part of King Vhadish XXIII upon his throne was his head.

His arms and legs, blackened as if by flame and crudely bent to form a rough circle, floated above the high back of the chair. Vhadish's torso was not in evidence.

The furniture floated more haphazardly. Tables, chairs, a bookcase, wine pitcher, goblets, and four statues of lions formed a swirling debris cloud up near the ceiling—or what would be the ceiling given the orientation of the throne. But the gravity, usually supplied by Vhadish, was absent.

"I redecorated."

Aravia spun in place. Ten yards away, Lapis floated serenely, wrapped in snaking black tendrils of coherent smoke that wound sinuously around her indigo body. Her arms hung down at her sides, palms outward, crooked slightly at the elbows, giving the impression of pious meditation.

Her eyes were black fields pinpricked by tiny stars. But when Aravia looked into those eyes, she understood that this was not the reflected expanse of the Crosser's Maze that she herself (according to Tor and Pewter) would sometimes display. No, the space behind Lapis's sockets was something else entirely. Something foreign.

Madness.

In Lapis's eyes, Aravia saw madness. More than that, she *felt* madness, as if it were an invisible creature reaching out from the inside of Lapis's head.

Boss! How did she get here?

"Hello, Lapis," Aravia said to buy time. She certainly wanted to know the answer to Pewter's question, but it wasn't the important one. "What do you want?"

"I have traveled," said Lapis dreamily. "Solomea left me alone, died and passed on. To the other side, he would have said, but that's *not* the other side. That's only a different part of *this* side. The other side is…" She trailed off with a tiny giggle that Aravia found profoundly disturbing.

She killed Vhadish. She's dangerous! We have to get out of here!

No, Pewter. I can't simply leave her here. If she's strong enough to kill Vhadish, she could at the very least distract me while I'm using the maze.

"Solomea cast me out, but I was never alone." Lapis smiled beatifically. "He is in my skin. My blood. My bones." She pushed her neck out slightly and whispered conspiratorially, "My *molecules*. Do you know what those are? Tiny little bits that make up everything. Even you, Aravia. When you die, all of those little pieces will simply float away."

Can you get rid of her? You're the Keeper of the Maze!

Maybe. I don't know.

"You can't hear him," said Lapis. "He's singing, all the time, singing, and my blood hears it. That's how I found him. I found his door, and put my ear to it, and listened to him sing. He's very sad, but very patient."

Who is she talking about? Naradawk? Pewter asked.

She must be. That bit about blood and bones—remember that Rosset told us Sharshun are infected by the same substance that turned Naradawk into a monster.

"He sent me back," said Lapis, her voice imbued with more urgency but less insanity. "I whispered to him through the door, told him all about you, Aravia. He's trapped, but he can see the winding path to his escape. He sent me back to take this place from you. It will save him a great deal of time."

"You can't," said Aravia. "I am the Keeper of the Maze. I could banish you with a thought. Everything in the Crosser's Maze is my reality. How do you intend to stop me?"

That's not true, is it? asked Pewter.

I believe I could exert enough power to destroy her, but I'm trying to think of the way to do it that will minimize my expenditure of arcane energy. As Tor recently reminded me, I will need all of my strength to unmake the portal.

"How will I stop you?" Lapis sounded downright serious now, all traces of her dreamlike state vanished. "Easily, I imagine. Yes, you are the Keeper, but the Keeper only controls the reality of the maze. Which I am no longer a part of. Not anymore. Not entirely."

Lapis did something with her hands, a finger twitch maybe, not so complex as spell-casting, but the smoky black curls wreathing her body flashed out, uncoiling in a heartbeat and twining around Aravia's torso. Aravia felt a moment of relief; she could effectively teleport at will inside the maze, and the smoke didn't press her or constrict her in any way. Lapis didn't seem to understand how a Keeper commanded the reality of the maze. But when Aravia chose to blink away, intending to reappear a few feet to her left, nothing happened.

Boss?

Quiet. She's learned some trick—

"Yes. I have."

What? Aravia, can she hear us talking?

"I hear everything," said Lapis. "And I know how badly you need to conserve your energy." She twitched her fingers again, and a noise like rising wind whispered all around Aravia, the black energy writhing, hissing, roiling. The chill of weakness prickled over Aravia's skin like a sudden onset of fever.

"I took King Vhadish's energy," said Lapis, drifting closer. "When I had enough, I used it to tear off his limbs and then his head. With *your* energy, I imagine I could shatter his entire pyramid. He will be very happy with me. When he finally breaks free of his prison, oh, how my blood will sing in symphony with his."

Aravia tried to move, to retreat, but she was stuck in place, unable even to lift her arms. She struggled to master herself, to make use of the potent aether of the maze, shatter Lapis's magic, but Lapis had cut her off, somehow severed her access not only to the maze, but to her own arcane reserves. Aravia doubted she could even retreat to her physical body in Verdshane.

Lapis hovered so close now that Aravia could have reached out to touch her, had she been able to move. With each passing second, more of her precious arcane potential drained away.

Think. Stop struggling and simply think. Vhadish was not the Keeper. You are.

Lapis had encased Aravia in something like a shell, cutting her off from the rest of the maze. If she could crack it, create even a hairline fracture in its energy field, she could tap into the maze and tear Lapis apart. But Lapis was denying her not only the maze's power, but her own as well. If only there were another—

Oh, gods. Pewter.

Her mind balked at the thought. She couldn't. *Couldn't.*

But it was the only way. Pewter was there with her; she could use his meager arcane potential to force the crack she needed. She didn't know what it would do to him. And she dare not even warn him since Lapis was listening in on their telepathic speech. Of course, it was entirely possible that Lapis, who knew Pewter was present in her mind, had already anticipated the possibility. Part of Aravia even hoped this was true, that she wouldn't be able to resort to a measure that might kill her beloved cat.

Have to do it now, before I'm so drained it doesn't matter.

She reached inward to Pewter and, to both her relief and dismay, found that she could tap his arcane potential. *I'm sorry, Pewter.* She drew power and vitality out of her cat and used it, knife-like, to cut a slice through Lapis's shell. It worked, easily; Lapis must have failed to even consider the possibility.

Aravia! Pewter wailed in her mind, and the pain in his voice nearly shattered her right there and then. *What are you doing?*

The wreaths of black mist shifted, as if Lapis detected Aravia's maneuver and moved to thwart it, but it was too late. Aravia reached with her mind through the gap in the shell, gathered arcane energy from the maze beyond, and did what was quickest and easiest: flung it straight at Lapis's chest.

Lapis flew backward, and the rings of black smoke broke apart and vanished. Her body smashed into the far wall of Vhadish's throne room with such force that the entire chamber rattled. Aravia expected her to die on impact, but Lapis peeled herself away from the wall and floated back toward her. She appeared uninjured.

Pewter? Are you still there?

Her cat did not answer. She fought down a wave of fear, of desperate worry, and she longed to return to those days when she could easily put all emotion to the side. She needed to concentrate and had no time for anger or grief.

Lapis approached, her bands of dark energy already reforming. Her star-field eyes were a corrupted distortion of the Crosser's Maze, black pits of madness that required an effort of will not to flinch away from. She must have contacted Naradawk in the maze, drawn on his malign and mysterious power.

But here, Aravia had a source of power of her own. She was the Keeper of the Maze, with its vastness of aether to command. Its reality should bend to her will, and she willed Lapis be dissolved, scattered, annihilated.

Lapis merely smiled back at her and giggled once more. "You still don't understand," she said softly. "I am *in* the maze, but I am not *of* the maze. Not anymore." Lapis flexed the pinky of her left hand and new swirls of black energy raced out toward Aravia. But this time Aravia was ready, teleporting herself several yards upward. The attack found no purchase and hissed away to nothing.

Fueled by her desperation, she flung her power out using a quick, potent variant of *arcanokinesis*, peppering Lapis with crushing blasts of aetheric force. They warped the space inside Vhadish's Tetra, buckled and bent its iron walls. Lapis dodged the first, deflected the second using her own magic, but the next five slammed into her, three to her torso, one to her shoulder, and the last directly to her face.

Lapis's body jerked and spun beneath the onslaught, her protections insufficient to blunt Aravia's wrath. When her gyrations stopped, her body floated at a mostly upside-down angle relative to Aravia, and her left arm hung loose and nearly detached. If she noticed, it didn't bother her. Lapis giggled a third time, and from her ragged shoulder socket something like a brown rubber tentacle emerged, its egress popping her entire arm free. It floated gently away.

Aravia blasted Lapis again, this time launching a roaring ball of flame. Here in the maze she was not beholden to memorized spell formulae. She ought to be invincible, and whatever power Lapis had borrowed or stolen from Naradawk, Aravia would better it. She'd deal with the repercussions of her drained reservoir later.

The flames engulfed Lapis, and Aravia heard, finally, a shriek from her enemy. But at the same moment something smashed painfully into her back, sending her spinning toward Lapis. As her body tumbled heel-over-shoulder from the impact, she saw that one of Vhadish's marble lions had struck her, no doubt propelled by Lapis's own sorcery.

Aravia steadied herself, halted her rotations, in time to see Lapis emerge from the flames, burned but still moving, directly in front of her.

"Fine," Lapis said, her voice cracking in a scorched throat. "But he's still getting out, Aravia. I'll simply have to go the long way."

Lapis dove towards her, and Aravia gathered aether to block the assault, but she didn't have time. Lapis's face moved directly at hers, those mad eyes seeming to grow to encompass Aravia's entire field of vision. She experienced a bizarre sensation, as though Lapis were diving into her own head, and she shuddered from a powerful wave of nausea.

And Lapis was gone.

Aravia couldn't see her, couldn't sense her. With a moment to breathe, to think, she cast out her awareness to its farthest extent, but Lapis had fled the Crosser's Maze altogether.

But Lapis was not the Keeper. That shouldn't be possible.

Pewter?

Silence.

Pewter, please, are you still with me?

Silence.

Exhausted, Aravia floated, taking in the sight of Vhadish's wrecked throne room. The black circle of his severed limbs stared at her like a disapproving eye. There would be no more exercises under His Majesty's tutelage, no more questions answered. And Pewter…gods, Pewter.

A sob burst from deep in her throat. Her spirit felt broken, but she fought against encroaching despair. The portal still needed closing, and she was the only person who could do it. It would take more time, and her success would be less likely, but she had no choice.

Aravia prayed for her cat. And she prayed that the archmagi could hold out long enough.

CHAPTER TWENTY-TWO

Morningstar walked through the door of the Greenhouse and was greeted by the comforting smell of wood smoke. In the living room she found Kibi sitting by the hearth with his feet up, sipping a cup of tea.

"Back already?" Kibi asked. "What did they want at your temple?"

Morningstar stood, staring into the fire. Its flickering light didn't bother her in the slightest. She forced herself not to blink, an act of petty defiance that nonetheless felt satisfying.

"I was excised," she said softly.

"What does that mean?"

"It means I was kicked out of the temple by the High Priestess Rhiavonne."

Kibi lurched forward as if struck, slopping some tea onto the floor. "What? Dear gods, why? Not for walkin' around outside? I thought your high priestess specifically let you do that!"

"No. It's complicated. Some things have happened with the sisters I've been training in secret. I'm sorry I haven't told you about it, Kibi. The short version is one of my sisters was murdered by Aktallian, and Rhiavonne blames me for it. She can sense the stink of my oath to Shreen the Fair and blames me for that too. She feels threatened by the White Anathema. So she excised me from the church."

Kibi said nothing for a few seconds before exclaiming, "Gods, Morningstar, that's awful. I'm so sorry."

"That's not the worst part," said Morningstar. "Two of my sisters were excised as well. Previa and Amber. They trusted me. They know they're risking their lives for me, and this is where I've led them."

Kibi scratched his beard. "Does that mean you can't keep trainin' 'em? Can you still get into your dream Tapestry?"

"I haven't tried," said Morningstar, "but I'd be shocked if I couldn't. I am still loyal to Ell, and I am training my sisters for her, not for Rhiavonne or anyone else. Oddly enough, I'm not as upset as I probably should be. The temple never accepted me, so why should it bother me that they've made it official? The temple, the hierarchy, the buildings and prayers, they're all things that are supposed to bring us closer to Ell, but for me it has always been the opposite, an institution that tried to separate me from the goddess. Now that obstacle is gone."

"Can you still visit your sisters?"

"Not at the temple, no. I'm forbidden from stepping foot on any Ellish temple grounds. But in the Tapestry I am still free. The Dreamscape is my temple now."

"Morningstar, would you like some tea?" Eddings appeared at her elbow, a steaming cup in his hand.

"That would be lovely, thank you." She took the cup and sipped, savoring its warmth. "I wonder how Dranko and Ernie are faring in Minok."

"Couldn't you find out?" asked Kibi. "Have a chat with 'em while they're dreamin'?"

"Maybe, but it could take all night," she told him. "With my sisters, I know to look in the temples, and it helps that very few others dream during the daytime. In Minok, the whole city will be asleep at night, and I don't know specifically where Dranko and Ernie are. I'd have the same problem with Tor and Aravia in Verdshane; there are hundreds of soldiers there, and they'll all be dreaming at once."

"Ah well," said Kibi, "just figured I'd ask. But I reckon Dranko and Ernie can take care of themselves."

"They've been in Minok for two days," said Morningstar. She sipped her tea and sighed. "Our hopes are all so thin. Can Dranko and Ernie find Ivellios? Can Aravia figure out how to use the Crosser's Maze? Can my sisters and I defeat Aktallian before he infects the archmagi to the point they can no longer keep Naradawk out?"

"And the Eyes a' Moirel," said Kibi. "I'm seein' 'em all the time now, no matter if my eyes are closed or open, like they're waitin' around for somethin'."

Morningstar laughed, though there was no humor in the situation. "Maybe they'll do something useful. They do seem to be on our side, in their own weird fashion."

"I suppose," said Kibi.

For a few minutes they drank their tea in silence. The fire burned low, and neither Morningstar nor Kibi seemed inclined to tend it, but Eddings came in again from the dining room and prodded the burning hearth logs with a poker.

"How does your training with your sisters progress?" the butler asked.

Morningstar hesitated, seeing no need to burden the man with the news of her excision. "Well enough," she said, fingering the green gem necklace Ozella had given her. "I should have four or five more days to prepare them. Whether or not we will be ready to stop Aktallian, I have no way of knowing."

"Should you be training them now, then?" Eddings asked.

"No. They're all awake by now. We train for two or three hours every morning, just after they've gone to bed. Then I let them rest. The mind works best after a good day's sleep, and I want my team sharp when the moment of truth arrives."

"Very good," said Eddings. "May I take your cups? Would either of you like more tea?"

"No thank you," Morningstar said, and Kibi shook his head.

Eddings nodded. "If you need anything else, I'll be in the—"

Someone knocked at the front door. All three turned their heads.

"Pretty late for a visitor," said Kibi.

"I'll see who that is," said Eddings.

A moment later his voice came from the foyer. "Morningstar, you have guests. Shall I let them in?"

Morningstar stood and walked to the door. Previa and Amber stood on the doorstep, shivering. Amber had her toes right up against the sill, a puzzled expression on her face.

"Of course! Come in!" Morningstar said, and immediately Amber stumbled into the foyer.

Previa followed on her heels and threw her arms around Morningstar the moment she was inside. "Goddess, Morningstar, I'm sorry," she whispered as Morningstar awkwardly returned the hug. "I'm so sorry."

Morningstar stepped back. Previa looked as though she held back tears.

"You're sorry? I'm the one who should be sorry," said Morningstar. "I drew you into this, and—"

"We knew the risks," said Previa. "You never deceived us about what was at stake. Goddess, but the church doesn't deserve you."

Amber had walked into the living room without saying a word. Morningstar turned her head to see Eddings approach her while she stood by the fire.

"She's devastated," said Previa quietly, "as I'm sure you can imagine. Rhiavonne arrived two days ago; she'd gotten wind of Sable's murder. I've told you how difficult it's become to hide our activities from the other sisters. There have been many rumors swirling, as I'm sure you can imagine."

"But Amber never told Rhiavonne any of the details?" Morningstar asked.

"No. When Rhiavonne interrogated her, she refused to divulge a single thing. It made the high priestess extremely angry, and she threatened Amber with excision. Even knowing the punishment, Amber stayed loyal to you."

"That doesn't mean she doesn't also resent me," said Morningstar.

Previa cast her eyes to the floor. "No."

"You must have endured similar treatment from Rhiavonne," Morningstar said.

Previa took her hand and looked into her eyes. "I did, and I'd do the same a hundred times over. I have faith in you, Morningstar. We all do."

Morningstar swallowed the rising lump in her throat, and shook her head. "Thank you, Previa." Feeling at a loss for words, she turned back toward the living room. "Would you like Eddings to get you some tea? Or something to eat?"

"Some lunch would be nice," said Previa. "We haven't eaten since an early breakfast at six bells."

The two moved to the living room, where Amber now stood facing the fire, her back to them. She turned at their approach.

"Amber, I—" Morningstar began, but Amber held up her hand.

"Morningstar, you don't need to say anything. I took a chance on you, and what happened, happened. I'm angry. Angry at you, at Rhiavonne, at Ell herself, but I'll get over it. Maybe after all of this is done, we can petition for reinstatement. But for now, like you said, let's make sure Sable didn't die for nothing. Let's focus on knocking Aktallian's head off."

Morningstar breathed deeply. "I thought—"

"I know what you thought," said Amber. "You thought I sold you out to Rhiavonne. Goddess, I'd be lying if I said I hadn't considered it. You can thank Previa here that I didn't. She and I have known each other a long time, and I didn't want to let her down."

"I don't want to let her down either," said Morningstar with a small laugh that Amber did not return.

"Did I hear you would like some food?" asked Eddings, appearing with a fresh cup of tea, which he handed to Amber.

Morningstar was about to ask Previa what she and Amber would like to eat when all present were startled by a shout from Kibi coming from upstairs. "Morningstar!" This was followed by pounding footsteps and the hurried thumping of Kibi's boots on the stairs. Something must have seriously alarmed him; Kibi was not the sort of person who ran around indoors.

He appeared at the entrance to the foyer. "Morningstar! Lapis isn't in her room."

"What?"

"Who's Lapis?" asked Amber, but Morningstar was already running for the stairs.

Inside Mrs. Horn's old room, where Lapis had been comatose, the air was cold. The window shutters slowly creaked and banged in the breeze.

"Figured I'd check on her while you was talkin' with your sisters," said Kibi. "Came in to find the bed empty and the window open. Guess she must a' woken up and jumped out."

Morningstar hurried to the open window and looked out. The wind scraped a few dry leaves across the cobbles of the Street of Bakers, but otherwise all was still and quiet.

"Aravia told us she couldn't wake up," Morningstar said, her heart beating faster. "How…" She trailed off, the reality settling on her. If Lapis was gone, how would they fulfill Shreen's oath to bring him her head? Did this mean she would never be free of her promise? That she'd be forced to live with the sickening taint of Dralla for the rest of her life?

Kibi set his hand on her shoulder. "I know what you're thinkin', but one thing at a time, right? We gotta deal with Naradawk first. And I'll bet if we come back with just the Crosser's Maze for Shreen, he'll be willin' to count our oath settled."

Morningstar wasn't so sure of that. Shreen the Fair didn't seem like the sort of person who would do her any favors.

"When was the last time you saw her?" she asked.

"A few hours ago, I'd guess," said Kibi.

"Damn it." There wouldn't be any point wasting time and energy searching the city for her; she might have fled its bounds already.

"Is everything all right?" Previa had arrived and stood in the doorway.

Morningstar turned from the window, closed her eyes, and drew a deep, shuddering breath. "I don't know. But it doesn't affect you and Amber." She looked around the room, thinking. "Previa, you and Amber can have my room.

I've put up curtains so it will stay dark when the sun rises. I've found it a good place to pray. I can sleep here."

"Sleep?" asked Previa. "But it's—oh. Right."

Morningstar gestured to the open door into the hallway. "You can go where you'd like until sunrise, but my bedroom is the darkest room in the Greenhouse. Well, except the basement, but I'd stay out of there if I were you. Eddings will get you anything you need, at least until he goes to bed. And speaking of bed, I know you're unlikely to sleep anytime soon, but among my many blasphemies is a more commonplace sleeping cycle."

"It's not blasphemy anymore," said Previa. "The Ellish church doesn't recognize you, so its rules no longer apply to you."

For the briefest instant, Previa's statement hit Morningstar like a blow to the stomach. But Previa's warm smile soothed the shock, and Morningstar understood the humor behind the remark.

"In the morning we will train again," she said, "and after that, I think it's time I discover where in the Tapestry Aktallian Dreamborn is hiding. Our time is soon, Previa. I can feel it."

* * *

Morningstar lay in bed, her mind at war with itself. She needed sleep, but the events of the day spun her thoughts in circles. Rhiavonne and Lapis vied for her unwilling attention, and when she tried to find her rock of inner peace, she instead heard the cracking whisper of Shreen the Fair. She shifted her thoughts to Dranko, hoping he was having success in Minok, and it was with his scarred, betusked face foremost in her mind that she finally fell asleep.

Morningstar floats above a vast domed city, so large that it makes Djaw seem a quaint village by comparison. Looking down through its curved translucent roof, she sees that its miles of paved streets are lined with huge marble buildings that resemble nothing so much as oversized mausoleums. They vary in size and shape, their carvings bizarre and wondrous, depicting not only humans and humanoid figures, but odd creatures of a thousand kinds.

Scattered among the buildings and roads, occupying every remaining inch of ground, are graveyards teeming with tombstones, monuments, and statuary. This is a city of the dead, a sprawling necropolis, and not a soul stirs beneath its dome.

The outer wall, a bulwark of clean gray marble, is marked by what seem to be an infinite number of polished iron gates, and away from each gate a road runs, straight and forever. The necropolis is a wheel with a million spokes that blur into one another. From her high vantage point, Morningstar sees groups of indistinct beings slowly moving along the roads, some in grand procession, others in spare, solemn bunches. All move toward the city, but each fades away slowly as it reaches the wall with its metal gates.

On one road, not far from its gate, stand Aravia, Kibi, and Dranko. Morningstar descends, following the curve of the dome until she stands beside them.

"It's locked," Dranko says, gesturing to one of the massive doors. "I've tried my lockpicks, but I might as well have jammed my dagger into the keyhole and prayed."

"It's locked," Aravia says in agreement. "I've tried my spells, but I might as well have asked politely for the door to open on its own."

"It's locked," Kibi says. "I've tried my fists, but I might as well have battered a mountainside."

Pewter, who had been perched in his customary spot on the back of Aravia's shoulder, jumps down and approaches the gate. A large key, glowing green, dangles in the cat's mouth. It emits a noise like a wind chime in the hands of a child.

Morningstar woke in a rush, disoriented and feeling as though her dream had been interrupted. The continuing emerald light of Pewter's key, shining into her eyes even now that she was awake, only added to her confusion. The wind chime sound persisted as well, its source close by. The dream of the necropolis had been a Seer Dream, of that she had no doubt, but never before had the sensory details persisted into her waking state.

She glanced down, and a chill shot through her. It wasn't the key from the dream. Ozella's necklace was pulsing, shining into her eyes from where it lay upon her chest. The glassy clinking came out of the emerald stone, an alarm bell warning of the end of the world.

Then you'll have about two hours, Ozella had said.

Morningstar fought down her fear and organized her thoughts. She had to find Aktallian, then collect her sisters, and launch their attack. Three things, in order, and she should start now; no time left to plan, prepare, or panic. Outside her window were the wan light and long shadows of sunrise.

She dropped back into sleep, her consciousness appearing in the glade where she once trained with her avatar and later instructed her sisters in the ways of the Tapestry. This was where Aktallian had made his error, treading on her holy ground, corrupting it, leaving Sable's head for her to find. When she focused on the Tapestry, she perceived his presence, distantly, as though she were a spider sensing the vibrations of a fly trapped on the far side of her web.

Not that he was trapped; in fact, he may have set up a web of his own. But if she quieted her mind, concentrated, focused, she could track him, trace him, find him out in the Tapestry's patchwork quilt of dreams.

The geography of abandoned dreams was haphazard; sometimes it vaguely matched the waking locations of the dreamers, and other times it seemed entirely random. Someone with Morningstar's training could pass quickly through dozens, hundreds of dreams, following their loose fabric of connections. The boundaries between dreams were hazy, pliant things, like curtains of ribbon or blocks of dense fog. It was impossible to see clearly from one dream into the next, but there was little risk of stumbling into danger. The dream-spaces of the Tapestry might vary in size, shape, color, objects, and the physical rules of their reality, but they all shared one thing in common: they were uninhabited. The dreamers had woken, leaving them empty.

Aktallian might be operating out of someone else's abandoned dream, but it was more likely he had established his own home in the Tapestry, just as Morningstar had done with her glade and her training yard. He might have created defenses, set traps for her, but she had little time left for scouting. With luck, Aktallian would have underestimated his need to protect himself, given how easily he had nearly killed her both times they'd met. She could still hear the sickening hiss of metal as his sword skewered her that first time in the Tapestry, a killing blow but for Dranko's channeling. And again on the rooftop in Sand's Edge, when he'd opened up her stomach with an effortless swing—Dranko had healed her then too. But Dranko wasn't here, not in the Tapestry, not in the Greenhouse. If Aktallian's blade found her a third time, she wouldn't survive it.

Silently she cursed the archmagi for being so wrong about the time they had left. Dream-spaces flew past her, fields and chapels and bedrooms and lakes and kitchens. Some were small and cramped, while others stretched for acres. An unusual number were labyrinthine; being lost in a maze-like environment was a common sort of dream.

Through them all she traced her quarry like a bloodhound on a scent. She sensed his presence nearing, felt his malice and contempt and...something else. Morningstar slowed, stopping in a stretch of dark woods, its trees seeming to watch her with human faces shaped into their bark. Aktallian wasn't far, perhaps only a dozen dreams away, but she felt... she didn't know what. Pulses like waves of greasy energy sent ripples out into the Tapestry. She wanted to turn away from it as she would from a rancid wind, but it wasn't harmful, merely unpleasant. Most likely it was related to whatever mischief he worked to harass the archmagi.

Morningstar allowed herself a smile, as it also served to pinpoint his location. Five dreams away, she found him. She hovered at the edge of a small field of shriveled cornstalks, staring at its border with another dream-space, the one where she was certain Aktallian waited.

Now came a moment of decision.

She could go through, look at Aktallian's home in the Tapestry, glean its size, its layout, its dangers. Information would be vital to the upcoming confrontation, and this was her chance to get it. She could be sly, surreptitious, possibly avoid Aktallian's notice.

But was the importance of foreknowledge greater than the element of surprise? If she passed through now into Aktallian's space, she risked alerting him to the danger she posed. As it was, she could return, gather her sisters, and spring upon Aktallian unawares.

She had no time to spend on the decision. Her choice was surprise. She had, after all, been training her sisters to improvise, and the worst-case scenario was one where Aktallian had time to prepare himself—or to flee. To save time, she woke herself for a second, then returned to the Tapestry directly in her sparring yard.

Her timing could not have been more fortunate. Outside it was an hour past sunrise, and so all nine of her sisters awaited her. They stood in a close circle talking quietly, and when they saw Morningstar appear, they moved as one to surround her.

"Thank you all for coming," she said.

"Ell will be pleased." Her sisters surprised her by finishing her mantra in unison.

"Previa told us. I can't believe that Rhiavonne is such a bi—" Scola paused, glancing at the shocked faces of Jet and Obsidia. "Well, she is! Excision is supposed to be only for the most heinous of crimes and heresies." She smiled wanly at Morningstar. "I can't say I'm shocked she kicked *you* out, but Previa and Amber too? That's horrible."

Morningstar took no offense. On the contrary, it gladdened her to see Scola so righteously on the side of her sisters. "The avatar warned me this road would be difficult," she said.

"And you warned us," Obsidia said. "We're still with you, Morningstar. The

High Priestess is not infallible. She was wrong to excise you three. We all know it."

"And I'm sure they'll let you back in once we've saved the kingdom," said Jet, bouncing on her toes.

Morningstar shook her head. "If Ell wants our involvement kept secret, I don't know that will change simply because our efforts are finished."

"It doesn't matter if they do or not," said old Starbrook, her twinkling eyes reminding Morningstar of Mrs. Horn. "Morningstar is blessed by Ell. What else matters?"

For a long moment after that, none spoke. Morningstar felt the seconds ticking past, but she wanted to hold on to this moment as long as she could.

"What challenges do you have for us today?" asked Jet.

Morningstar looked at her sadly. She was so young, so eager, but Morningstar was about to throw her into the teeth of the beast with all the rest. *Please, Ell, spare her at least. Though if we could all survive what's coming, that would be ideal.*

"Today's test is the final one," she said, and all the sisters tensed and stared. "We have no time left. The archmagi are at their breaking point, and if we don't stop Aktallian now, the portal will open and Naradawk will invade."

"Have you found him?" asked Amber. "Found Aktallian?"

"Yes. And I will lead you to him." She paused. She ought to give them a final inspirational speech, something to fire their spirits ahead of a clash that could bring death to them all, but what came to her instead was practical advice. "Remember, work as a team. I want my disruptors to concentrate on the battlefield, the landscape, and oppose anything Aktallian might do to give himself an advantage. The rest of you focus on Aktallian himself. Disable him, but try your best to let me land the killing blow. Otherwise, though we might save today, he could return tomorrow to terrorize our dreams."

Scola swished her hammer in the air. "Then let's not waste any more time chatting."

Morningstar led her sisters through the Tapestry, knowing now the arrow-straight path that would bring them to Aktallian the soonest. The others couldn't move as quickly; she fretted on two or three occasions when she needed to stop and wait while the slowest of them caught up from several dreams behind. *Two hours.* It was difficult to gauge time in the Tapestry.

She paused when they reached the dream of the face-trees. The pulses emanating from Aktallian's dream still rippled outward. She could tell from the troubled expressions of her sisters that they felt it too.

"Ignore it as best you can," she told them. "We are very close now. We'll stop in the corn field and regroup one last time."

Seconds later they stood in a circle among the withered stalks, close to one of its boundaries. "Aktallian is there." She pointed into the hazy gloom where this abandoned dream blended into the perilous unknown. "He is likely to try blinding us, but other than that I have no idea what to expect. He may be immediately beyond the border or some long distance away. He may have already made his surroundings dangerous to interlopers. Keep an open mind, and don't waste the element of surprise if we get it—which means you should resist the urge to let out any battle cries." She looked each of her sisters in the eye in turn. "And thank you. Thank you for your trust, your faith, and your hard work. It's been my honor to train you, and even if we fail, a place waits for all of us in Ell's heaven."

"If we fail," said Scola, "heaven is going to become extremely crowded. So let's not."

She manifested her enormous hammer. Amber caused a long knife to appear in each hand. Gyre already readied her wooden cudgel, and Belle her iron-tipped spear. Previa squeezed her hands into fists. Obsidia released a long, drawn-out breath. Jet, as always, bounced lightly up and down on the balls of her feet. All of them wore armor, some of metal plates, others in hardened brigandines or chain-link tunics. Morningstar herself wore a black shirt of mail rings, and on her left arm was a black triangle shield. She was armored just as in that long-ago dream when the avatar of Ell had first named her a Dreamwalker.

"Let's go, Morningstar," Jet said. "We're as ready as we'll ever be."

"Then may Ell give us her blessing," said Morningstar.

What happened to the sister who wanted nothing more than a simple life of solitude and prayer?

"Follow me."

She plunged through the border of the dream, and her sisters followed.

* * *

Circles.

Morningstar had hoped to quickly scan the dream-space, locate Aktallian, and lead the attack, but instead she hovered, staring, dumbfounded. Around her, floating at different angles, her sisters wore expressions of bewilderment.

There was no ground here, no floor, and no gravity. That didn't trouble her;

they had spent two full days of training exploring the ramifications of unusual or absent gravity in any possible direction. But...

Circles. Black circles, like massive versions of the one on the Black Circle pendant Dranko had stolen and worn.

There were at least ten, each twenty feet across at least and two feet thick, black stone rings cut with intricate glowing runes. They rotated slowly, spinning at odd angles to one another, as though some great stone machine with a dozen wheels had flown apart in mid-air. Some spun so close to their neighbors that they seemed more like gears meshing together, while others hung in relative isolation.

Arm-thick strands of purple energy threaded their way through the interiors of the stone rings, bending in many different directions so as to join in a chaotic web. The ropes of energy pulsed in concert, growing bright and dim together, and with each flare of their sickly purple glow, a wave of unease rolled past Morningstar like an ocean swell.

She couldn't see Aktallian, but he could easily be hidden among the circles, which blocked lines of sight in many directions. Conscious of how she and her sisters clustered together, vulnerable to a single attack, Morningstar spoke quietly, "Spread out in pairs. Check every direction. If one of you sees Aktallian, alert the rest."

Her team drifted apart, naturally forming pairs with one warrior and one disruptor each: Scola with Starbrook, Jet with Obsidia, and Belle with Gyre. Amber, skilled enough to serve as either, gripped her knives and stayed near Previa. Morningstar flew alone, swiveling her head around as she moved, heart thumping, feeling those unsettling pulses pass through her body like shivers of disgust. She avoided crossing through the centers of the black rings, and hoped her sisters would have the sense to do the same.

The silence was unnerving. For all of their massive weight, the stone circles spun noiselessly, and the pulsing energy neither crackled nor hummed. If she closed her eyes there would be no indication at all that she didn't float in an empty world, save for the nausea that sloshed in her stomach each time one of the waves moved through her.

She stopped for a moment, more closely observing the pattern of the rings and the beams of energy. Where were the spots most completely hidden by the turning stone wheels? She identified one such place where five different black circles combined to block a large wedge of space, and she cautiously drifted sideways until she could see what lay beyond. At the corners of her vision she saw that

Amber and Previa, as well as Scola and Starbrook, had the same idea.

Morningstar's breath caught in her throat; beyond the cluster of occluding stone rings, Aktallian Dreamborn sat cross-legged in the air. He wore the same blood-red armor as when she had last seen him, bull-rushed by Tor from the top of Arrowshot Tower in Sand's Edge. His expression was impossible to discern, obscured by distance and her side-on, slightly backwards perspective.

Fixed in space a few yards in front of him, a smaller black circle hung motionless, dark as night and made of shining iron. The many strands of purple energy stretched and warped to converge at the center of that metal eye, combining into a writhing cable, thick as a hundred-year tree trunk, that spilled out of the ring's far side and into…nothing. It appeared to vanish in midair as though it poured itself through a hole into another world.

Aktallian didn't seem to have noticed her, or any of her sisters, slowly converging now from different directions. Morningstar held her breath, not daring to believe that fortune would allow them such a tactical windfall. Closer, closer, all nine of them advanced on trajectories out of Aktallian's line of sight—assuming he even had his eyes open.

Was this a trap? Was that only an illusion, with the real Aktallian behind them or elsewhere altogether? Maybe this elaborate Black Circle construction was afflicting the archmagi by some automated process.

No. She sensed him, his malign presence, and he was exactly where he seemed, hovering peacefully like a monk reflecting on the grace of the Travelers.

"Hello, Morningstar." Aktallian's voice sounded in her head. The man himself hadn't moved, hadn't opened his mouth.

Damn. Those two words snapped her out of her caution.

"Now!" she screamed, but even as the words left her lips, Aktallian's body flared bright like the sun, a fierce yellow light that drowned the rings, the energy strands, and her sisters in its radiance. The Ellish priestesses flinched—but only slightly. The sun-flare faded a little, revealing that Aktallian no longer sat behind the iron ring, but stood atop it, his armored body aglow with the solar glare he surely expected to blind her team.

Heavy chains—a favorite of Jet and Previa—snaked out of the air beside him, wrapping his arms and legs. Scola, Amber, Obsidia, and Belle moved in quickly, weapons out. Aktallian struggled for a second before sighing. "Well, fine. We'll do it your way."

Everything went black.

Morningstar thought for a second she must have been transported to a different dream, one that was lightless and empty. Otherwise her darksight—

"Morningstar!" That sounded like Jet's voice, young and worried.

"My darksight!" shouted Scola. "I can't see!"

"What is—" Gyre's voice came from Morningstar's left, but her voice was cut off by a sickening *thwack*.

"Morningstar!" Belle's voice was frantic. "I think—aaaaaugh!" Her scream was horrifying, as though something was shaking her to pieces.

Goddess, no. Darkness was ever the staunch ally of Ellish priestesses, and Morningstar's darksight had never failed her. Now she was blind, helpless, while Aktallian assaulted her sisters. Furious, Morningstar focused on light, manifesting a shining moon to fight Aktallian's impenetrable blackness. For a heartbeat the two realities strove against one another, before Morningstar's moonlight dominated and washed the dream-space in a bright blue-white glow.

Gyre's body drifted, blood streaming from the stump of her neck. Her head floated a short distance away, spinning its own circling trail of blood. But as terrible as that was, Belle's fate was worse. Aktallian must have thrown her into the center of the nearest stone ring, for it was there that her remains slowly spread, broken into dozens of pieces that drifted apart, losing their human shape. Each bloody piece glowed a virulent mauve as a rope of energy ran through the remains of Belle's torso.

Aktallian himself stood beside the lifeless body of Gyre, his long black sword reflecting the pulsing radiance from all around. The chains still floated where Aktallian had been, coiled in empty man-sized loops. Aktallian must have teleported directly out of them. Morningstar's despair deepened; she and her sisters had never managed to teleport in the Tapestry, even after months of trying. Her avatar had told her it was possible, and Aktallian had mastered it. He looked at Morningstar across the dream-space and gave her an amused smile.

"If you wanted your sisters dead," he said, "I'm sure you could have found an easier way than bringing them here to me."

Scola screamed her rage as she flew towards Aktallian, and more chains enwrapped him. Morningstar hung back, using her mental strength to lock him in place; if Aktallian could freely teleport, it would be impossible to defeat him. His smile faded, and he struggled to break the chains, finally bursting them in time to raise his blade to deflect Scola's hammer.

Obsidia and Amber, dodging energy strings, swooped in to press the attack.

They formed a rough three-dimensional bracket around Aktallian, becoming bespattered by the drifting remains of their sisters. The four of them whirled and spun in a violent dance. Amber's knives flashed in the moonlight, Obsidia was a dervish with her spear, and Scola swung her hammer hard enough to smash through a stone wall. Aktallian was the stronger fighter, dodging and twisting and letting his armor absorb some of the sisters' strikes, but he was both outnumbered and harried by Starbrook, Jet, and Previa. Chains snaked out of nowhere to tangle his arms and constrict his neck. He twirled and lunged, graceful as a dancer, but a swing that might have hacked Amber in half was thwarted as his sword vanished mid-strike. Aktallian snarled and re-manifested the blade, barely bringing it to bear in time to block a thrust from Obsidia's spear.

Morningstar sensed Aktallian trying to teleport, but her focus was stronger. She imagined that his armor was melted, molten, burning, but as she did so the moonlight dimmed to half its strength. Aktallian reformed his armor almost before Morningstar had begun, and she was forced to return her concentration to the moon. She would have to move in herself eventually, to strike the blow that would kill him, but for the moment she focused on what she had to while her sisters did battle.

Unable to teleport, Aktallian flew, moving the four-way battle and reducing the Ellish sisters' ability to gang up. As often as possible he cut close to one of the stone circles or barely avoided an energy beam, as though trying to scrape the sisters away on obstacles. It was an effective tactic, as it forced his assailants to disengage or swerve to avoid collisions. Meanwhile, Previa, Starbrook, and Jet trailed the melee, flying in twisting loops while disrupting Aktallian as best they could.

With a resounding *thunk*, Aktallian slammed hard into a section of stone wall that popped into existence. Obsidia drove forward to impale him with her spear, but at the last instant Aktallian melted through the wall, appearing on the far side as Obsidia thrust her weapon into the stone. Scola and Amber skirted the wall and continued to give chase until Aktallian halted in an instant, flipped upside down, and to the obvious surprise of the sisters, went on the offensive. He cut a bloody gash in Scola's leg, the sword shearing through her armor and tearing a cry from her lips, then rotated backward and kicked Obsidia's spear from her hands. Amber's knives skidded off Aktallian's greaves, throwing out sparks, and then she cursed as her weapons vanished from her hands.

A black iron cocoon sprang up around Aktallian, giving the attacking sisters time to fall back and regroup. Obsidia reformed her spear, and Amber her knives. But Aktallian was not incapacitated for long; veins of bright cracks formed in the shell, and then it exploded outward in a deadly shower of sharp fragments. Most of them clanged off the sisters' armor, but one embedded itself in Amber's calf.

In that moment when the sisters flinched away from the spray of iron, Aktallian flew backward and to his left, turned to Starbrook, and gave a little jerk of his head. Starbrook flew as if thrown—directly into the center of one of the stone rings.

"No!" Jet cried, but there was nothing any of them could do. Starbrook came to an unnatural halt, her body transfixed by the streaming energy. Morningstar tried to fling her dying sister away, but her body was stuck.

In seconds, Starbrook's old body was shivered to pieces.

"Eventually only you and I will be left, Morningstar," Aktallian called out. "And you knew it would be that way. Did you tell your sisters that before you came here? Did they know? Did they know you were sacrificing them?"

Rage and grief, both sharpened by guilt, bloomed in Morningstar's heart. She wanted desperately to swoop in, join the attack. The twin necessities of maintaining light and preventing Aktallian's teleportation occupied all of her mind, but she couldn't hover nearby while Aktallian tore her team apart. She brightened the moon so that it shone like an unhindered noon sun, then dove for Aktallian, even as he returned his attention to Scola, Amber, and Obsidia. His body became taut, his limbs extended—Previa and Jet were still at work—and Scola swung her hammer hard into the side of his head. A red helmet appeared in time to bear some of the blow, but still his head snapped sideways, blood pooling at his lips and nostrils. Amber followed with knife strikes to the exposed joint of his right knee. More blood fountained out. Morningstar flew in, her weapon raised, but Aktallian spun and sped away from her, flinging the attacking sisters from him with a burst of telekinetic energy. A shock of hot force struck Morningstar like a furnace blast, halting her advance and shoving her backward. Despite his injuries, Aktallian still fought with mastery. He flicked his eyes toward Obsidia and Amber, and the two of them flew, twirling out of control, toward the closest of the black rings. Morningstar found her equilibrium and exerted her own force, diverting her sisters away from certain death. Amber's body bounced from the outer rim of the circle while Obsidia cleared it with a yard to spare.

But the effort of saving her sisters overburdened her. The moon dimmed from a blazing white circle to a wan, gray thing no brighter than a cloud-hidden crescent.

Aktallian became a flitting shadow, hard to see, and still Morningstar's darksight was foiled. Worse, her lock on his teleporting began to slip. Cursing, she remained where Aktallian had flung her, restored light to the dream, and clamped down again upon Aktallian.

The battle continued to spin wildly around the dream-space, which was big enough to contain the dozen enormous rings, but not much bigger. Aktallian darted this way and that like a swallow at dusk, pursued by Amber, Scola, and Obsidia, sometimes fighting in flying retreat, sometimes swinging around to strike with his gleaming black sword, always moving with an unearthly fluidity and grace.

All the while, Previa and Jet continued to keep the battle in view while navigating the dream's deadly maze of rings and lines. They harried Aktallian mercilessly. His sword and pieces of his armor flickered in and out of existence; blocks of stone and metal sprang up in his path; a bubble of boiling water appeared briefly around his head; unseen forces tugged at his limbs. The air rioted with writhing vines, slowing him down even as he sought to maintain distance. Aktallian was resilient—he shrugged off or countered the flurry of distractions—but Morningstar guessed that without them, he'd have finished off the others already.

Morningstar herself was not altogether helpless, though it burned her inside that she needed to stay removed from the combat. Once, when Aktallian veered sideways and charged toward Previa and Jet, Morningstar manifested a wall of roaring black flames to block him. Aktallian was forced to reverse, which allowed Scola to deliver a bruising swing to his back-plate. But even doing that much caused the opaque darkness to encroach until Morningstar returned her attention to it.

"Morningstar, what are you doing?" Amber's voice, angry and frustrated, carried across the dream. For the first time Morningstar considered how her behavior—hanging back, not attacking—must look to the others. She could shout back an answer, but that would give away tactical information to Aktallian. He might guess that Morningstar alone was thwarting him, but with Amber and Jet also manipulating reality, he couldn't know for certain.

A cold realization fell upon her. If things kept on this way, they would lose. She had let things fly apart, when what she needed was to focus her will. She reached for her rock, that point of stability in seas of confusion, the immovable ground amidst the storm. It was built up from a lifetime of faith in Ell, but also faith in herself. Standing on that rock, she could take away Aktallian's advantages *and* join the fight.

"Just trust me!" she shouted back.

Even that small exchange seemed to have alerted Aktallian. Once more he fought free of his attackers, but this time he sped directly at Morningstar, a red-armored wasp with a deadly black sting. She backed up instinctively but found herself blocked by a wall of glowing red iron. Even as her hair sizzled and her elbows burned, she banished the wall, but it had slowed her down too much. Aktallian was upon her. Her mace met his sword, and the strength of his swing rattled the bones in her arm. The moonlight dimmed ominously...and then brightened again, though that was not of her doing. Previa and Jet must have focused their own efforts on fighting Aktallian's darkness.

Morningstar blocked a swing with her shield, backed up, and took a swipe with her own weapon that scraped along his shoulder plate. Aktallian flipped and spun around her, putting her on the defensive. Obsidia, Scola, and Amber caught up with the battle and joined it, but this time Aktallian didn't flee. With Jet and Previa preoccupied with the moonlight, he was easily able to fight all four of them, twirling and writhing like a serpent with a long metal tooth. His red armor deflected the few blows the sisters landed, but their own armor might as well have been rice paper against his black sword. He cut a gash across Amber's shoulder, another at Obsidia's hip. Morningstar jerked her head back as his sword slashed at her face, drawing a faint red line of pain across the underside of her chin. Undeterred and resolute, she returned a powerful blow with her mace, smashing his wrist and sending his sword flying away. She felt Aktallian try to teleport, but her will was greater, and he stayed put. He scowled and reformed the black blade in his hand, but not before Obsidia had punctured his left greave with her spear. Blood flowed from the wound.

Morningstar had been in a worried turmoil since they had begun their assault, and the deaths of Belle, Gyre, and Starbrook had brought to her a frantic, frenzied grief, but her strength, as always, lay in being the mountain amidst the storm. She planted her feet on that mountain, offering up a prayer to Ell, and time seemed to slow.

"Previa, Jet, disrupt!" she shouted, and she brightened the moon herself, freeing her sisters to do their work. "Keep him close!"

For a moment nothing changed. Aktallian smashed Obsidia's spear into pieces, dodged a slow swing of Scola's hammer, and let Amber's knives slide pointlessly along his breastplate. But Morningstar found now that she could maintain the moon, stop Aktallian from teleporting, *and* fight as the avatar had trained her. She ducked beneath a sword strike and smashed his knee with her mace. He grimaced in pain, twisted away, and began his flying retreat—but was halted only twenty feet away. Previa and Jet had surrounded the five of them with a sphere like a translucent soap bubble, a boundary that warped but did not collapse when met by Aktallian's weight. A hole appeared in it, but it sealed itself up before he could escape. Aktallian slid up and around the bubble's surface, dragging his sword along its yielding interior, but the slice it left healed itself—or, rather, was resealed by Previa and Jet—as fast as it was cut.

Brilliant! Jet and Previa had done exactly as she'd asked, shrinking the scope of the battle, forcing Aktallian to stand and fight, outnumbered four-to-one. His confident, arrogant expression was gone, replaced by an angry snarl. His body spun like a child's top as he threw himself at the Ellish sisters, blade flashing in murderous arcs—but thick vines slithered out from nowhere and tangled him as he spun. He thrashed like a fish in a net, kicking and twisting while eliminating the vines, but new ones appeared even as he withered the old.

Morningstar and her sisters struck, taking full advantage. Aktallian's writhing served to make his unarmored spots harder to strike, but the four of them wore him down, denting his metal plates, finding seams, landing crushing blows. He manifested a helmet, but Morningstar removed it in time for Amber to slash a deep cut across his cheek. Scola smashed his ankle with her hammer so hard, Morningstar heard his bones crunch beneath the red metal banding.

They had him. Morningstar kept her calm even amidst her anger and sorrow, feeling time slow down even further, Aktallian's contortions becoming less frenetic. In a state of near serenity, she sustained the moonlight, locked down Aktallian, and drifted to her squirming, enwrapped enemy. She had to land the killing blow herself. She followed his motions, understanding where and how she would finish him off.

His eyes widened as she approached, but then he smiled once more, a triumphant smile that froze her blood.

Morningstar felt it as it was happening.

Aktallian was waking himself up.

No!

She reached into the dream around him and stopped his escape, struggling to keep him in the Tapestry. Should she let him go? If he truly fled, they would have done their task, halting his machinations against the archmagi, allowing them to keep the portal sealed that much longer. But he might be able to heal himself and return, refreshed. Or perhaps he could resume his attack on Abernathy from a different place in the Tapestry. And even if they expelled Aktallian, what would stop him from murdering them when next they dreamed, as he had done to Sable?

All of these things she considered in an eyeblink, while time seemed to slow nearly to a halt. No, she had to keep him here in the dream and make an end of him.

She had never attempted to forcibly keep someone trapped in the Tapestry, and Aktallian's will was great. She succeeded, but in doing so lost her hold on his ability to teleport. Time snapped back to its ordinary speed—too fast—and Aktallian flung himself, still twined about with vines, into the abdomens of Obsidia and Scola. All three of them vanished from the bubble, leaving a crisscrossed tube of empty vines behind.

"Rrrrrrggggggh!" Amber screamed in frustration. The bubble vanished, and Morningstar looked around the maze of purple beams and stone rings, desperate to see where Aktallian had gone with her sisters.

"There!" Jet pointed, though Morningstar's view was blocked by the bulk of one of the great rune-carved rings. She flew forward at a diagonal until Aktallian again came into view.

He had teleported to where the final thick torrent of purple energy poured into empty space. Obsidia and Scola struggled, wrapped tightly in black iron bands, one held in each of Aktallian's hands. He grinned at Morningstar as she came into his view, and before she could react, he thrust the heads of his captives into the sizzling flow of purple energy. Immediately their bodies went slack, jittering only slightly as the energy raged over and around their heads.

"It didn't have to be this way," Aktallian called, letting go of the sisters. "Even if you'd succeeded, it would have bought you a day or two at most. Naradawk is coming, Morningstar. All you've done is thrown a few extra lives away. Do you wish to discard the rest?"

The bodies of Scola and Obsidia drifted out of the energy stream, and their heads were…gone. Erased. To her left, Jet let out something between a scream and a sob. Amber and Previa floated at her right hand, staring.

The calming rock still stood in Morningstar's mind, but she was not calm. All of her horror, her anger, her guilt, and her sorrow had become a hard, crystal thing inside of her.

"Bind him," she whispered. "All of you. Do whatever you can to hold him in place."

"And you'll fight him by yourself?" asked Amber, her voice bitter.

"Yes. Do it. In Ell's name, do it now."

"I know what you've been doing," said Previa quietly. "How can you fight him while maintaining—?"

"DO IT!" Morningstar had seldom raised her voice during their training, but she screamed at Previa, which shocked her few surviving sisters into action. They fanned out, and immediately chains and vines clutched at Aktallian.

He tried to teleport out. Morningstar stopped him.

He tried to wake up. Morningstar stopped him.

Her focus was shadow-sharp. She had remade her rock; no longer was it a bastion of equanimity and composure, but a focus of her wrath. *You are the haft of the spear*, she had told her sisters. *I am the blade at its end.* She made herself cold and deadly.

As she flew towards him, the light began to fade. For all of her determination, she couldn't retain the moonlight while also stopping Aktallian from escaping, either by teleportation or waking out of the Tapestry.

She didn't care.

As she arrived before him, in the failing blue glow of the moon, she now could see over his shoulder that the thick strand of energy, the output of this hellish machine Aktallian had constructed, discharged not into a void, but through something like a window. Beyond it, in defiance of her understanding of the Tapestry, was a room where five figures sat in chairs around a colorful glowing pattern.

The archmagi.

As the purple beam emptied into that room, its energy dispersed, suffusing the space with a faint violet glow, a whisper of color.

"You can't hold it," Aktallian said, even as he squirmed in his bonds of chain and vine. Previa, Jet, and Amber had anchored them to the iron ring just behind Aktallian, preventing him from flying away. "If you attack me, you'll lose your grip, either on me or on the light. In my darkness, you're helpless, but if you leave now, at least you'll have saved three of your sisters."

She stared down at him, savoring her fury. She could taunt him, or deliver a speech, or simply spew invective in his face, but she had no desire to do anything but end him.

Morningstar lifted her morningstar-mace, and for one sliver of time, the moonlight failed entirely. Aktallian's dream was the darkness of oblivion. But

Morningstar didn't need to fight against the nature of his dream. She funneled her wrath into the head of her weapon, and it blazed like an angry white sun. It wasn't enough to light up the entire dream, or anything more than a dozen yards away, but it didn't have to. Its radiance burned away the darkness around her, illuminating the unflinching faces of her sisters and glinting off of every spike of her mace. In its light she saw Aktallian's last expression of realization and terror before her arm came down and obliterated him.

CHAPTER TWENTY-THREE

Afull day and night had passed since Dranko's brush with death. The Deliochan healers had worked upon him for hours, administering medicines, stitching wounds, and chanting prayers to the god of healing. Rosset's physical injury had been less severe, but yesterday he had spent the day in a sweaty delirium, his life energies drained away by his vigorous use of the shard of the Watcher's Kiss.

Now, on the second morning following Dranko's ill-fated scouting mission, Ernie looked down on his sleeping friend, whose midsection was wrapped tightly in freshly changed bandages. Certain Step sat in a chair nearby, looking as sleepy as Ernie felt. They'd been sleeping on makeshift cots, unwilling to leave Dranko alone during his recovery.

"What do we do now?" Ernie asked Dranko's unconscious body. "The warehouse was empty, except for whatever it was that attacked you. We saw that much before we brought you back here. That was our only lead."

"Surely the Black Circle cannot easily hide a ritual involving the enormous quantities of stone and ink Morningstar observed on their ledgers," Step said. "Someone in Minok will know of it."

"I hope so," said Ernie. He resisted the urge to give Dranko a little shake, maybe wake him up. "But whoever that is, how do we find them? Dranko, I'm not sure how we do this without you."

"Do what?" The elderly patient in the bed next to Dranko stirred and sat up with an effort.

"I'm sorry," said Ernie. "We didn't mean to wake you."

"Wasn't sleeping." The patient, Brother Alic, had been so still and quiet, Ernie would have thought him expired if not for an occasional rasp of breath. A medic had come in the last hour to gently wipe away the blood that tended to seep out of his mouth.

"It's nothing," Ernie said on instinct.

"Oh, you can tell me," said Alic, his voice dry and crackly. "It's not as though I'm going to get up and tell anyone if it's a secret. I'm as good as dead. Some kind of disease in my bones, they tell me. Worst part is, most of my teeth are gone and my gums don't stop bleeding."

"I'm sorry," said Step. "I wish there were something we could do to help."

"Don't be sorry," said Alic. "I've lived a good, long life, and soon I'll be in Delioch's heaven, serving at his side if I'm lucky. So you said something about a what, a ritual?"

"I don't see the harm in telling him," said Step quietly.

Ernie didn't see what help he could be, either, but nodded his agreement. "Some bad people are performing a magic ritual that could cause some trouble," he said, trying to keep it simple. A full explanation would be so long, Alic might well die before he was finished. "We think they're hiding somewhere in Minok, but we don't know where to look."

"Ah," said Alic. He coughed, wheezed, leaned away from them, and spat over the side of his bed. "And it's a big production, if I heard right?"

"We think so," said Ernie. "But truth be told, we know very little about what we're looking for. The bad people have kidnapped a friend of ours. We don't even know if he's still alive. And they could be anywhere in the city, from the harbor to the outskirts. Hells, they might have shipped their supplies here and then hauled them miles outside of Minok. We only have a few days to find them."

"Maybe try some of the nobles' estates on the eastern hill," said Alic. "They're large and secluded, and one of them might be helping with the money."

"Oh," said Ernie. "That's a good thought."

"Or," Alic continued, "there are over a hundred warehouses with lots of space. You could try those."

"Yes, but we already—"

"And of course if equipment was shipped in to the harbor, some dockworker or other might remember it. Perhaps visiting the dockside watering holes could provide you a clue to follow."

"Thank you," said Ernie. "Those are all—"

"Or there's the Thespian Hall. It's a privately owned theater in the Stripes, one of the southern neighborhoods. I'm sure it has a big empty space."

"Those are all excellent ideas," said Ernie quickly. "Step, why don't we go confer with Rosset, share some of Brother Alic's thoughts?"

"Happy to be able to help." Alic coughed a few more times, and by the time his fit had subsided, his eyes were closed and snores rumbled in his throat.

"Come on," said Ernie to Step. "Maybe one of the old man's ideas will pan out."

Rosset Finch, somewhat recovered after a full night's rest, waited on a wooden bench on the church's front lawn. His eyes were closed.

"Is he asleep?" asked Step.

"I don't think so," said Ernie. Rosset was sitting bolt upright, and the chip of the Watcher's Kiss on his bracelet glowed faintly, as though fixed by a gentle sunbeam. In a quieter voice, Ernie added, "Maybe he's using his sword piece to find the Black Circle."

The two stood quietly for another five minutes or so, watching the Silversword. Ernie was beginning to wonder if maybe Rosset *was* asleep when his eyes opened, and the fragment lost its glow.

"Nothing," Rosset said.

"You already told us you couldn't use your magic to locate the Black Circle," said Step. "What were you trying to do?"

"I said I couldn't use the fragment to find Ivellios," Rosset said testily. "Nor will it penetrate Black Circle abjurations unless we are quite close. But the properties of the Watcher's Kiss fragments are not fully catalogued. I thought perhaps I could use it to get a feel, a sense, maybe even a direction. But I sensed nothing. We should find another avenue to locate the Black Circle's operation and save the power of the fragment for when we oppose the cultists directly." He looked pointedly at Ernie. "You wasted an entire day while I convalesced."

Ernie bristled. "After Dranko was attacked, I thought it best not to leave the two of you alone and helpless. Step's no fighter, and as you just said, you want to save the power of your sword-piece. Certainly none of the priests here could do anything if another one of those smoke monsters came to finish you off."

"I doubt you could have, either," said Rosset, though his voice carried no rancor or mockery. "But I appreciate your instinct to safeguard us. Now, having had a day to think, have you thought of anything that could help us find Ivellios?"

"One of the other patients had some ideas," said Ernie. "I say we return to the Happy Haddock and ask some questions."

"What kind of questions?" asked Rosset. "Excuse me, drunken laborer, but have you seen a large collection of cultists performing a vile ritual, probably involving a kidnapped mercenary?"

Ernie was in no mood for sarcasm. "Stop that. Of course not. How about, 'Excuse me, but do you recall offloading an unusual amount of black stone from a ship in the past few months? Or maybe a large cargo of ink barrels?' We have to start somewhere."

Rosset glowered up at him. "Don't you think Dranko already tried that? He was gone for hours."

"He was focused on the warehouse where the cultists' goods ended up," said Ernie. "We don't know if he asked at the docks about who unloaded them or where the people went who took them."

"But we know what they'd say," said Rosset. "They'd tell us the goods were sent to warehouse thirty-one, which we already know. I highly doubt they'd know more than that."

"Fine," said Ernie. "Let's hear your better idea."

Rosset was silent for a moment, his forehead creased, before speaking again. "I would seek an immediate audience with whomever rules Minok. Perhaps they have a wizard in their retinue who knows some relevant divination magic. Failing that, we could try convincing them of the peril the kingdom faces and be given use of a larger force to search the city."

Ernie opened his mouth to protest, but Rosset's idea wasn't terrible. "Then I propose this," he said. "We'll split up and try both. You go find Minok's ruler, and I'll question some dockworkers."

"In other circumstances I would agree with your plan," said Rosset, "but Dranko's misadventure may have alerted the Black Circle that we are close to tracking them down. They are very dangerous, and we are more vulnerable individually. Ernie, my understanding is that you are an excellent swordsman, and that you, Step, are…less so. And my own skills with a blade are not exceptional."

"Fine, said Ernie. "Let's start with your idea, then. Step, I hate to say this, but we still should have someone stay behind with Dranko. Do you mind remaining here?"

Step shrugged. "No. As Rosset just pointed out, I won't be much good if the Black Circle comes looking to finish him off. But I suppose I could at least shout for help if Dranko is asleep."

It didn't take much sleuthing to determine that Minok was ruled by a baroness—the Baroness Tilidia in particular, whose small castle perched on a hill at the eastern border of the city. She had a reputation for being fair but prickly. The baronial estate was surrounded by a tall stone wall, and petitioners presented themselves at the western gate.

Half an hour of uphill trudging brought Ernie and Rosset to their destination, but they found themselves eleventh in line behind a number of merchants, peasants, laborers, and craftsmen waiting to deliver their own petitions for an audience.

"We don't have time for this," said Ernie, "but we can't—"

"Excuse me!" Rosset shouted. Most of the men and women in line turned to look at him. "I will give three silver talons to everyone in line if you allow us to go straight to the head of it."

Ernie felt this was somehow scandalous (and straight out of Dranko's bag of tricks), but after a moment's reflection he decided there was nothing specifically wrong with a voluntary transaction. And it worked; each other person in line was willing to take three silvers in exchange for a slightly longer wait. Rosset counted them out from a large coin purse. They had only to wait a few final minutes outside the gatehouse while the current petitioner was inside.

Soon enough a woman emerged, grumbling.

"Next!" came a call from inside.

Ernie and Rosset walked into a small stone building, built like a miniature tower. An old, harried-looking bureaucrat in a bright yellow vest sat behind a desk. He stroked his droopy moustache and gave them a weary look. Over his shoulder a narrow stairway wound up into the darkness.

"Names?"

"Ernest Roundhill and Rosset Finch."

"Purpose for wanting to see the baroness?"

Ernie paused for a moment. When Rosset didn't jump in with an explanation, the man sighed. "Are you wasting my time, good sirs?"

"No!" said Ernie. "It's… We need to see the baroness about a matter of life and death!"

"Of course you do, good sir." He flipped open a book that rested upon the desk and thumbed through several pages. "Her Ladyship can see you the first Bridgeday of next month, at three bells."

"Did you hear me?" Ernie exclaimed. "Our friend could be killed at any moment!"

The old fellow closed his book. "Young man, you may be surprised to learn that you are not the first, nor the tenth, nor the hundredth person who has tried to gain Her Ladyship's ear by claiming someone's life is in imminent danger."

"But we're telling the truth!" said Ernie. He leaned forward and thought of what Tor would do. Spill the whole truth, was what. He took a breath. "A group of evil cultists is engaged in a ritual that threatens the safety of the entire kingdom. We need the baroness's help to find them and put a stop to them!"

The man smiled. "I'll grant you, that's more original than most. Next time I suggest some interim steps between claiming one man's life is in peril and that the entire kingdom is endangered."

Rosset stepped forward. "Sir, I am a member of the order of Silverswords, an organization devoted to opposing the Black Circle, the cult mentioned by my colleague. By ancient law I demand preference in all matters pertaining to my mandate. As such, we will see the baroness at once!"

The man's smile dropped. "First a claim of exaggerated peril. Then an appeal to outside authority. Please let me save you the trouble and reject your upcoming bribe ahead of time, and also inform you that should you draw steel or attempt to bully me by threat of violence, you will be treated to at least half a year's vacation in Her Ladyship's dungeons. Now, I can see through the window that a dozen or so honest citizens of Minok are waiting patiently to petition for appointments, so if you'll just see yourselves out…"

He opened his book again, lowered his eyes to the desk, and proceeded to ignore them.

"I don't suppose pleas to your better nature would work?" Ernie asked faintly.

"My apologies," said the man without looking up. "I should have included that between the bribes and the bullying. Goodbye."

Ernie turned to go, shoulders slumping, but he had a final thought. A gamble. He should take it. He swiveled around and put his hands on the functionary's desk. "Earlier this week, the baroness sent a large contingent of soldiers to Verdshane on the orders of the king and Duke Nigel of Harkran."

For the first time, the man looked mildly interested.

"The danger we are talking about is the same one those soldiers were dispatched to fight," Ernie continued. "The friend I mentioned is being used by the Black Circle cultists in a ritual that might get all those soldiers killed if we don't stop them. Please. Send word to the baroness. She'll know what I'm talking about. If she doesn't want to see us, we'll leave and never bother you again."

For a few long seconds the old man stared at them. Without speaking, he tore a page from the back of his book, scrawled out a note, and rang a small bell that sat on the corner of his desk. A boy of twelve or so years hurried down the stairs from the tower's upper floor.

"Please deliver this straight to the baroness." The old man handed the boy the paper. "Return immediately with her reply."

"Right away, sir!" The boy scampered off.

The man motioned to the door. "Please, wait outside by the gate. Next!"

* * *

"That was good thinking, Ernest," said Rosset.

They both stared off in the direction the boy had run, down a tree-lined path and over a green hill toward the distant castle.

"We should have figured that out on the way up here," said Ernie. "And it might not work. We have no idea if Baroness Tilidia was involved in any way with the mustering of the local soldiery. That was just a hunch."

"We shall soon find out."

Ernie's eyes fell to Rosset's wrist and the golden chip of the Watcher's Kiss stuck to his copper bracelet. After a few seconds of silence, he asked a question that had been on his mind the past couple of days. "How come you Silverswords haven't been working with the archmagi? You've got your pieces of your famous sword that you said can divine what the Black Circle is up to."

Rosset idly picked up a stone and flicked it through the bars of the gate. "There are two things you ought to know, though one I'd prefer if you kept to yourself. First, though we can detect the foul enchantments of the Black Circle, even our pieces of the Watcher's Kiss cannot penetrate their guarded sanctums and ferret out their innermost secrets. Something massive, like an ongoing magical effect that could divert a *teleport* spell, that I could detect. But the fragments of the Watcher's Kiss are more potent as wards against direct Black Circle attacks."

Ernie thought he felt a raindrop and instinctively held out his palm. The sky was overcast and threatened rain, but it appeared to be holding back for the moment. "What's the other thing?" he asked.

Rosset grimaced as if recalling a foul memory. "The other thing is that there aren't 'you Silverswords.' I'm the last one. Most of our order was wiped out decades ago during our failed attempt to eliminate Moirel Stoneshaper's bloodline. The rest have died more recently in the execution of their duties." He sighed. "There could be one more, an old colleague of mine named Essik, but she was sent away by the Watcher's daughter—that's what we call the high priestess of Uthol Inga—almost a decade ago. The daughter refuses to tell me where she is or what she's doing. In the meantime I have been serving my high priestess, doing as she bids, and I am answerable to no one but her and my goddess. Only recently did she instruct me to travel to the Greenhouse and invoke the Silversword Pact."

He turned abruptly to face Ernie. "I want you to know that I sincerely hope we are able to rescue Ivellios."

Ernie didn't know what to say and didn't trust what he might say if he spoke. Rosset had been more than willing to kill Ivellios and his father. Ernie had seen it with his own eyes. Or mind. Or however one saw things in the Crosser's Maze.

"I know what you're thinking," said Rosset. "And I don't blame you for it. But you don't know the Black Circle the way I do. They're not a typical gang of villains. They represent an existential threat to our world in a way that nothing else does."

"I don't know what that means," said Ernie.

"It means that if the Black Circle succeeds in their designs, everyone on Spira will die."

"You mean Naradawk? We've already been told how dangerous he is."

Rosset again peered through the gate. "Yes, I mean Naradawk, but not *only* him. It's what he's a part of. It's the Black Circle itself. The Circle is knowledge, an understanding of the way the world works at its most fundamental, mathematical level—but twisted, evil. It is arcanism in the service of destruction. Even with the entire leadership of the Utholite church meditating upon the largest pieces of the Watcher's Kiss, we haven't gleaned the source of its power, only its extent. And its extent is bottomless."

"But that's the other side of the chit," said Ernie. "Your side is your own to define, isn't it? If you're driven to murder in the name of your cause, isn't your cause already lost? Wasn't there some other option you could have taken with Ivellios and his father? Kidnapped them, hidden them away, disguised them, something?"

Rosset ran a finger up and down the length of one of the bars. "Ernie, you agreed to give the Crosser's Maze, one of the most potent artifacts known to man, to a horrific follower of an evil goddess. Wasn't there some other option *you* could have taken?"

Frustration quickened Ernie's breath, made him grind his teeth. Why was nothing ever easy? In White Ferry, training with Old Bowlegs and imagining battles against evil, mindless goblins, he had learned to think in clear terms of good and evil. Why couldn't reality be as simple? "You asked me that back at the Greenhouse," he said, not caring he sounded surly, "even knowing you did something equally difficult, faced with the same sort of dilemma."

"It was my duty to challenge you," said Rosset. "I had to know where the Black Circle and its agents might have influenced you. But in the end, I was satisfied. I think you made the right choice in Djaw, faced with the consequences as you were. Just as I do not regret our decision to end the line of Moirel by killing Ivellios and his father. Sometimes, Ernie, the stakes are so high, we must do distasteful things. Terrible things. Only a coward acts as if his choices have no consequences outside of his own personal morality."

Ernie was spared having to think of a reply. The boy from the tower crested the hill and walked toward them, accompanied by two tall men in what Ernie assumed was the livery of Baroness Tilidia, bright yellow tabards with a green fish insignia. Both wore chain shirts beneath their tabards and had swords on their belts.

"I wonder if they're here to shoo us away?" Ernie muttered.

"Ernest Roundhill and Rosset Finch?" asked the taller of the guards, staring down at them through the bars.

"Yes, that's us," said Ernie.

"The baroness will see you immediately. Give Rollie here your weapons; he'll keep them in the gatehouse until you return."

"Is there no opportunity for us to keep them?" asked Rosset. "We may be attacked by the very enemy the baroness wants to talk to us about."

"Sorry, sir," said the guard. "But you'll be accompanied by an armed guard at all times. No need to worry."

Ernie handed Pyknite to the boy. "Take good care of this. It means a lot to me."

"Don't worry, sir. I'll keep it safe."

* * *

To Ernie's surprise and satisfaction, Baroness Tilidia not only believed their story, but was efficient and helpful once the particulars had been explained. While conceding they were faced with a needle-and-haystack problem, the baroness nonetheless dispatched fifteen of her already depleted personal guard, as well as a dozen members of the serving staff, to aid in the search for Ivellios.

Rosset suggested that the searchers stay grouped by the half dozen and that each group include a guardsman. A lone individual who stumbled into a Black Circle hive might be captured or killed without a chance to report back. Recalling Brother Alic's advice, Ernie suggested they start with some of the closer noble estates and then move on to the Thespian Hall. The baroness agreed that her people would report back to the church of Delioch with any news.

Satisfied they had made some small progress, Ernie reminded Rosset they should still pursue other avenues of inquiry, specifically the Happy Haddock tavern. Rosset greeted the idea with a shrug but didn't object.

"As I said, I doubt a room full of drunken dock hands will recall anything relevant about deliveries made months ago. But I'm at a loss for better ideas. Lead on, Ernest."

It was an hour after noon by the time they arrived, and the tavern was filling with laborers and their attendant smells of sweat and brine. Ernie stood in the doorway, scanning the commons for an empty table, and was shouldered aside by a huge man with anchor tattoos on his bulging forearms.

"Bad place to stand, friend," said a smaller man right behind the first. "In or out?"

"In," said Ernie, but the man had already moved past him. To Rosset, he said, "Let's just go to the bar and order something to drink."

The Happy Haddock was loud, its atmosphere boisterous, and its patrons hungrily slurping bowls of soup and chewing hunks of bread. Ernie and Rosset threaded their way to the bar in back, Ernie thinking hard about how best to approach the task at hand. Just sit down beside a stranger having lunch and start asking questions? Would they get kicked out for doing that? There were already thirty people here at least; where even to begin?

Dranko would know what to do. Though abrasive by nature, he had a knack for getting people talking. He turned to Rosset, but the Silversword just shrugged, as if to say, "this is your game, not mine."

Maybe if he sat down with food and drink, someone would come and sit with him by chance. His thoughts flashed back to Perri, the barmaid in Seablade Point who, as Ernie had frequently reflected since, had almost certainly been flirting with him shamelessly. A pang of guilt struck him; what had happened to her? The Delfirian army had seized the entire region at the end of the peninsula, so what had they done with the people of Seablade Point? Killed them? Enslaved them? Driven them off, or conscripted them, or sent them back through the arch to Kivia?

He was right to feel guilty. Horn's Company had been responsible for the arch opening…or at least they could have stopped it and chose not to.

"What'll it be?" The bartender was a tall, lanky woman with a scarred face and short black hair.

"What do folks normally have to drink this time of day?" Ernie asked to buy time.

She gave him a sidelong glance, as if suspicious of such a simple—or simpleminded—question. "Round lunchtime, in this chilly weather, I mostly serve tea. Folks don't want to get back to work tipsy. A few order what we call gullygrape; that's watered-down wine, or spruced-up water, depending on your point of view."

"How much for two cups of tea and two plates of stew with bread?"

"Twenty-five chits would do."

Ernie nodded. "We'll take it, thanks." He turned to watch the crowd and again tried to imagine what Dranko would do. "Rosset, you were quick to pay off those folks ahead of us in line at the baroness's castle. How much money do you have?"

Rosset leaned in and spoke softly. "I have enough. The Silverswords were well off. Coin makes everything easier."

"Do you have enough to buy food and drink for everyone here? Say, ten silver talons?"

"Yes, but why?"

"I think I know what Dranko would do."

He turned back to the bar and thumped his flat hand against it several times, hard.

"Hey!" shouted the bartender. "What do you think you're doing?"

"Getting everyone's attention. Sorry!" He banged a few more times, then turned to find that as he hoped (and feared), the patrons of the Happy Haddock had quieted and were staring at him. They were a rough-looking lot, muscled laborers with scars, stubble, and scowls. They no doubt wondered why this young man they'd never seen before was interrupting their lunch.

"Excuse me!" he shouted.

"Who're you?" someone shouted from the back.

"My name is Ernest Roundhill, and this is my colleague Rosset Finch. We'd like to pay for lunch and drinks for everyone in the tavern, if you don't mind."

A stunned silence was followed by murmurs and a few chuckles.

"Why you want to spend all that on us?" This was asked by a broad-faced woman not more than three yards away. She sat at a table with four others, all looking skeptical.

"Because I also want to ask you some questions about some shipments that came in a few months back, and I figured I'd have more luck if I bribed you all first. It seemed more polite."

Ernie gave the room a big smile, hoping to show them that he was serious but not sinister. Several of the patrons laughed, though some still glowered.

"You a spy or somethin'?" a large man asked from the middle of the room. His face was mostly hidden beneath a fiery red beard, the size and approximate shape of a large beehive, woven through with a dozen or more silver rings. "A smuggler?"

"No. My motives are not criminal. But a good man, a friend of mine, has been kidnapped by criminals. Our only lead is that the people who have him received some unusual shipments here in Minok. I was hoping one of you might remember something, anything about them." A few more of the patrons nodded. Encouraged, Ernie added, "If you don't trust me or don't want to talk, we're still happy to pay for your food and drink."

"You spring for everyone's gullygrape," a man shouted from the middle of the room, "and I'll tell you every damn thing I've loaded and unloaded since last autumn."

That did the trick. The room erupted into babbling, some of the patrons raising mugs and toasting their new benefactors, others flagging down servants to order extra food and drink now that it was free. Ernie thumped the bar again, then waved his arms until the commons once again quieted.

"I could walk around and ask you each individually, but I don't want to take up too much of your time or mine. My friend is probably in trouble right this minute. So if you don't mind, I'll just ask you all at once, and if you know something, you can come tell me. The shipment I'm talking about was of large quantities of black stone blocks from Sentinel and an unusual number of ink barrels. If that rings any bells, I'd love to hear about it."

"Black stone, you say?" called a short, stout woman with curly brown hair. Ernie hadn't meant that the whole room should listen to every lead, but this would do. "I remember that well enough. The sailors grumbled about it the whole time we were carryin' the crates off the ship. Guess it were so heavy it slowed their vessel, made 'em miss a stop in Port Kymer, where they'd hoped to pick up more cargo to trade. 'Bout three months ago that was, but that were the hardest day on the docks I've had in a year or more. Must've been hundreds of stone bricks in them crates. Only knew the color 'cause one of 'em slipped and cracked open."

"Do you remember anything about the people collecting it?" asked Ernie.

The woman scratched her chin. "Now that you bring it up, yeah. It were high summer, and a hot day for Minok, but the fellahs takin' possession was wearin' all black, long pants, long sleeves on the shirts. Musta been sweatin' like pigs, those poor blokes."

"That's them!" said Ernie. "Do you remember where you unloaded?"

"Hm. One of the warehouses off a' Fishhook Harbor, I think. Don't remember which."

"We knew that already," whispered Rosset.

"Did you notice where the people in black went after all the stone had been brought ashore?" asked Ernie.

"Why'd I know that?" said the woman. "We brought 'em into the warehouse straight off the ship, and that lasted most of the day. The owners made sure we knew we'd catch it if we cracked up their bricks. Thought one fellah was gonna drop dead from a busted heart when we dropped that box. But when we was done, we went straight to the harbormaster to get our pay. Which, sorry to say, weren't anything more than what we'd get for five hours carryin' peacock feathers."

A few additional men and women had come into the Happy Haddock since Ernie had offered to treat everyone, but these were quickly informed and then hushed up.

"Well, thanks anyway," said Ernie, while Rosset shook his head. "Anyone else? Anyone else here work on lugging that stone? Or an unusual quantity of ink barrels?"

Some of the diners muttered quietly, but no one else spoke up.

"This is exactly what I thought we'd get out of this," said Rosset quietly. "And now we're ten talons lighter."

"You're right." Ernie leaned closer and whispered into Rosset's ear, "How much money do you have altogether?"

"On my person? Why? Do you have a plan to spend more of it?"

"Yes. How much?"

"I don't see how—"

"Listen," said Ernie, his whisper harsh, "if we don't find Ivellios and the Black Circle succeeds, what good will any of your money be? How. Much?"

"Two hundred talons and eight gold crescents."

"Good enough. Hand me a crescent."

"What?"

"Just do it."

Rosset stared at him, then pulled a gold coin from his money pouch and placed it into Ernie's palm.

While some in the crowd still watched them with apparent curiosity, most of them were returning their attention to their food and drink. Ernie turned and spoke to the barkeep. "Last time, I promise." He banged again on the bar until the Haddock was quiet.

"Now what?" cried the red-haired man with the beehive beard. "You gonna pay for our dinners later if we tell you who shipped a cargo full of pig bladders?"

A laugh rippled through the room.

"No," said Ernie loudly, "But we are prepared to offer a great deal more money to anyone who can help us." He held up the gold coin. "The criminals I mentioned, the ones who have our friend, we think that they've set up a base of operations somewhere in Minok. It would be someplace large, where they'd be using all that black stone. You seem like good men and women, willing to help with a good cause. We'll give one gold crescent to anyone who can get us information that leads us to them."

That set off another round of excited talk among the laborers. A gold crescent was probably several months' pay for harbor strong-arms.

"But it's dangerous!" Ernie shouted over the din. The crowd became quiet again. "I won't lie to you. The people I'm talking about are willing to kill to stay hidden. If you want to help us, go in pairs at least, and don't try to fight them. If you find out where they are or have any clues that could help, come meet us at the church of Delioch a block from the mason's guild hall."

The huge man with the anchor tattoos shouted back. "I'll take some risk for a gold crescent, and I'll wager I'm not the only one. Ain't no walk on the beach, haulin' freight and workin' pulleys all day. But how'll we know we've found the right people? And how long do we got?"

"Should I tell them?" Ernie whispered to Rosset.

"You've gone this far. I think you must," Rosset answered.

"We know that time is short. Today or tomorrow would be best. The enemy is called the Black Circle. That is their symbol. They are likely wearing black clothing and will probably be using the black stone in their rituals."

"Rituals?" asked the brown-haired woman. "Like sorcery?"

"Something like that," said Ernie. "Like I said, if you locate them, don't try to stop them yourselves. Come tell us at the church of Delioch."

"And what's your name again?" asked the woman.

"I am Ernest Roundhill."

"Well, Ernest Roundhill, I don't know that I'm willing to skip out on a day's pay and risk my skin for you, but if you're that committed, and since you're payin' for everyone either way, I'll raise my mug at least. To Ernest Roundhill!"

"Ernest Roundhill!" the crowd said in ragged near-unison.

* * *

"You have a natural charisma," said Rosset as they returned up the hill. "I'd have thought a room full of rough folk like that would have shouted you down or mocked you from the start, free drinks or not. But you speak like a thespian, and honesty practically oozes from your pores. It's a rare gift."

Ernie didn't reply right away, partly because he didn't know what to say and partly because he didn't know what a "thespian" was. It hadn't been long since the Spire meeting where he'd decided he loathed Rosset Finch, but it also seemed impolite to ignore that kind of compliment.

"Thanks," he said eventually. "Though I'm not certain we'll get any takers or that any of them will find anything."

Rosset made a grunting noise that sounded like agreement. "We did our best with so little time to act. We have our small fragments of hope. Perhaps the baroness's people will find something, or your dock workers. Maybe Dranko will regain consciousness and be able to tell us about something he found in the warehouse before the attack." He slowed his walk, then stopped. "And I will keep trying with the shard of the Watcher's Kiss. I may get lucky if I'm close enough. Ernie, you should go back to Dranko. One of us should be there in case someone has a discovery to report or if Dranko wakes up. And we should inform Certain Step of our progress. I will wander the city a bit, meditating in different places on the shard."

"Didn't you say it was too dangerous for us to split up?"

"I'll be careful," said Rosset. "None of our options now are good ones."

* * *

Everyone was asleep when Ernie returned.

Certain Step napped in his chair, head tilted back, a bead of drool hanging on his lip. Brother Alic lay corpse-like on his bed, his little finger twitching slightly every few seconds. Dranko slept soundly, chest rising and falling beneath a fresh sheet, his face peaceful.

A priest, his arms full of linens, came into the room a few minutes after Ernie. He set them down on a small table in the corner, then noticed Ernie standing at Dranko's side.

"He's doing very well," the priest said. "Though I have to ask…" He looked down at Dranko, head tilted, opening and closing his mouth as though he was searching for a polite way to continue. "It looks as though he has spent an unusual amount of time undergoing Scarbearer discipline. And he has goblin blood in him, obviously. Is he truly in good standing with the church?"

The priest himself must have been a very well-behaved man throughout his own life as the scars on his face and hands were few and faint. Ernie smiled, though he was unsure how much this man might know about Mokad and his accomplices.

"There was some difficulty at the Tal Hae church earlier in the year," Ernie said. "Perhaps you heard about it?"

"Oh!" The priest's eyes widened. "Yes, though I know very little about the particulars. Something about some of the priests betraying the Deliochan faith and fleeing when they were found out?"

"That's the gist of it," said Ernie. "Dranko grew up in the Tal Hae church, and most of his scars were given him by one of those betrayers. He's really a good man. He's a channeler himself, in fact."

"And a fast healer as well," said the priest. "Tomorrow he should be able to move around if he takes care to move slowly and not exert himself. His wounds were quite serious, but by good fortune none of them struck his heart or a major artery." He paused again and grimaced. "Do you know what attacked him? We cannot agree on whether his injuries were inflicted by repeated knife slashes or a wild beast of some kind."

"The second one," said Ernie, though he'd only gotten a fleeting glance at the shadow-thing in the warehouse. "A monster."

"Oh dear," said the priest. "Is it still on the loose, do you know?"

"No, it's not. My other companion, Rosset, was able to kill it."

"Oh. Good." The priest blinked a few times. "Might I bring you and your sleeping friend here some food and water? I believe there is some roast chicken and vegetables remaining from our lunch repast."

"That would be wonderful," said Ernie. "Has Dranko here woken up at all? I'll bet he's hungrier than any of us."

"He has not, though don't be worried. The medicines we use to heal his wounds more rapidly also keep him sleeping. He could wake up in the next few hours, so I'll bring some extra food in case he does."

The priest departed, leaving Ernie to watch his sleeping companions and fret about their chances of finding Ivellios. Despite their meager successes with the baroness and the Happy Haddock, their best hope was that Dranko had discovered a clue before almost dying in that warehouse. Otherwise, what hope was there, really? Rosset might get lucky with his shard. Or maybe Ivellios would free himself from the clutches of the Black Circle. Maybe he already had! He could be hiding somewhere in Minok, keeping his head down in case the cultists were searching for him.

Yes, that would be nice, but they couldn't act on the assumption. If the Black Circle had the means to yank him out of a long-distance *teleport*, certainly they'd be able to prevent him from escaping afterward.

The Deliochan priest returned with three plates of food: chicken with gravy, hunks of brown bread, muffins with bits of apple baked into them, and a pitcher of water along with several tin cups. Ernie held a drumstick under Dranko's nose for a few seconds, but his friend didn't stir.

Certain Step let out something like a snort in his sleep. His head tilted to the side and the pitch of his breathing changed, but he didn't wake up. Ernie looked back and forth between him and Dranko, wishing one of them would wake up, but he was effectively alone.

He missed Tor and his endless optimism. He missed Kibi and his even-keeled philosophy. He even missed Morningstar and Aravia. What were they all up to right now? Were they all still alive? After so many months of Horn's Company traveling together, their recent separation had him feeling adrift and helpless. He didn't feel like he knew Step very well, beyond his piety and associated quick temper whenever the gods weren't being given enough respect. And Rosset Finch, while perhaps not quite as awful a person as Ernie had first thought, was hardly comforting as a companion.

Step did wake up a few minutes later. Ernie told him all about his day's activities while the two ate their lunches. After that the hours crept past largely in silence, their time measured by the shadows cast through the window crawling across the floor, then up the far wall. Sometime in the late evening Rosset returned, dejected and exhausted.

"I have failed," he said. "I have seen no sign of either Ivellios or any nest of Black Circle cultists. Has anyone been to visit? Or have you needed to defend yourself from assailants?"

"No to both," said Ernie. "But the priest says Dranko is healing well. There's some food for you, though it's gone cold."

Rosset slumped into a chair; the Deliochan priests had thoughtfully brought in extras, though it made the room quite crowded. "The more I consider it, the more I deem it unlikely that the Black Circle is performing their foul rites in Minok. Yes, they had supplies delivered here, but they could have transported them anywhere after that."

Ernie nodded in doleful agreement. He glanced at Dranko.

"Dranko, wake up. I need your help."

"I am awake." Dranko still lay with his eyes closed. His voice sounded even drier and rougher than normal. "The sound of Rosset's lovely voice must have done it."

"Oh, thank the gods," said Ernie. "How are you feeling? Are you hungry? There's some cold food and water."

"Like crap, and hells yes," said Dranko, "but more thirsty than hungry. Water? What about beer?"

Ernie opened his mouth to explain that the priest recommended only water to drink until he was more recovered, but Rosset spoke first.

"Dranko, what did you find in the warehouse?"

"Some kind of tornado with swords in it." Dranko opened his eyes, then narrowed them in confusion. "Which I must have escaped from, somehow. I thought it had killed me."

"Rosset saved you," said Ernie. "He killed it with the piece of the Watcher's blade."

Dranko pulled himself to a sitting position, back to the wall behind him. The movement made him wince and clutch at his bandaged ribs. "Well, thanks for that," he said to Rosset. "I was certain I was dead and gone to heaven."

Rosset waved off Dranko's gratitude. "What else? Did you discover any clues as to where the Black Circle is keeping Ivellios?"

"No. And it's worse than that. They knew I'd look for them. They knew I'd look for them *in that warehouse*. That slashy whirlwind was a trap set *specifically for me*. Hells, I'm starting to wonder if this whole thing has been a set-up, all the way back to Mokad's notes that Praska saw. Ivellios could be on the other side of the kingdom for all we know."

Rosset stood and turned to the window. "Throughout the Silverswords' long striving against the Black Circle, we have suffered more defeats than victories. The

Watcher's Kiss fragments have protected us from direct assaults, but an enemy who knows so much, can predict so much, can manipulate events with such ease…even what I thought was our greatest victory turned out to be a lie, a trick of the Black Circle's agents who were one step ahead of us even then." He rubbed his forehead with his palm. "And I am so tired. I have used the fragment more than I should have and am drained down to my core. Even if I knew at this very moment exactly where the Black Circle was conducting their ritual, I couldn't do a thing about it. I need sleep. I need to think. I need to—"

"I know where they are," said Brother Alic.

Ernie jerked his head around, as did Rosset and Dranko. Certain Step, who had been resting with his eyes closed, sat bolt upright.

Brother Alic was sitting up as well. He still resembled a living cadaver, pale spotted skin stretched across his cheeks and around his jaw, rheumy eyes, brittle and thinning hair. When he looked straight at Ernie, his expression one of grim determination, there was something slightly unnatural in the way his neck moved.

"Go to the northeast section of town," said Alic. His voice sounded strained, more so than when he had spoken earlier, and a bit slurred, as though he wasn't fully in control of his tongue. "There's a long alley off of Bootblack Street between an abandoned brick building and a nasty little pawn shop. In that alley is a door on your left, hidden by magic. Inside, go to a closet behind the counter and…oh, fiddlesticks, I'm losing him." His chin slumped down to his chest, and his whole torso tilted toward Dranko. Dranko reached out to stop him from toppling to the floor, grimacing at his own sudden movement.

"What in the gods' names—" Rosset began, but Brother Alic jerked himself back upright with startling strength.

"There is a lever behind a secret panel," said Alic. "It opens a stairwell down to where those Black Circle villains are up to their shenanigans."

Ernie shook his head as if to clear away a dream. "Shenanigans?" he said weakly.

Alic smiled and winked. "Stay positive, Ernest." Having said that much, his body toppled the other way, away from Dranko, twisting and pulling his sheets after him. He landed with a muffled thud on the floor.

* * *

Ysabel Horn, as exhausted as she had ever been in her life or after it, turned to Kayrimpa-Tem-Sonolaf, who grinned back at her.

"Not bad for a little dead thing," said Kay.

"Not bad at all," said Mrs. Horn. "Now the rest is up to them." Far below, the blue globe of Spira and the brown globe of Volpos continued to merge into one another. "Kay, I'd like to get back to William now. He's sure to be getting anxious."

"Then I will take you to him." Kay spun about, sending her green dress flaring. "And I thank you, Ysabel Horn, for showing me something I have never seen and didn't think was possible." She took Ysabel's hand. "Come. You've spent enough time away from the Endless Shore, little ghost. Let us return you to your husband."

CHAPTER TWENTY-FOUR

I vellios lay in his cot, surrounded by darkness and doubts. His fingers and toes no longer felt like they were on fire, which was an improvement over how things were a few hours ago.

Yesterday—or what he might as well call "yesterday," though his sense of time had frayed beyond repair—Essik had knocked three times as promised, giving him a few seconds' warning. Not long after had come Naul's perfunctory knock and a wedge of light shining through his open door.

"Up you get," Naul had said. "It's time for the final test run." They had passed Essik, standing outside his door, but she hadn't met his eyes, let alone offered him any potions that might dull his pain or sabotage the Black Circle's preparations. He hadn't risked looking behind him as Naul had led him away. Mokad might already be harboring suspicions about her.

The test had taken place in the same round chamber as the previous day. More cultists had joined the party, perhaps thirty in all, chanting, waving their arms, reciting their strings of numbers, and generally carrying on like a cabal of evil schoolmasters. Mokad had led the proceedings, meting out orders, threats, corrections, and exhortations to his minions. Ivellios's role had, once again, been to stand on the spot where the two largest black circles touched one another on the floor.

Despite the full house, Essik was absent. That could still prove to be a good thing; if most of the cultists were in here with Mokad, she'd have freer rein to map out their eventual escape.

Preparation took longer this time. More of that crystal stuff, the arcanum, was brought in and carefully apportioned. Teams of cultists moved slowly around the curved slate, checking and re-checking one another's equations for a full hour. To

Ivellios's admittedly untrained eye, the slate was more crowded with letters, numbers, and symbols than the day before.

As before, Ivellios did his best to remember as much of the room and as many details of the ritual as possible. It went on much longer than the earlier test, hours it seemed, and the detail involved was dumbfounding. Say what one might about Mokad and his fellows, but they sure had put a lot of effort into memorization.

Ivellios thought he was getting a handle on things—he imagined that he noticed some patterns in the numbers, and he thought he could draw a reasonable copy of a section of the slate that was mostly shapes—when the pain started. The skin-prickle from the previous test, which had been more an annoyance than something painful, was much harder to bear this time around. It progressed from needle-pokes to wasp-stings, and then to wasp-stings whose venom was pure fire. If not for some magic the Black Circle had worked to keep him standing upright, he would have collapsed in agony.

Worse yet was when the pulling started. Naul had warned him about that specifically on the walk to the testing room. As Volpos and Spira were brought into ever-closer alignment, the strain on the Pivot—him—would only become more intense. Naul had some fancy name for it he couldn't remember exactly, something like "aetheric sympathy," but it felt like the gods fighting over his stomach like the last drumstick on a platter. And just when he thought he'd be pulled in half, the pull became a crush. The gods had decided he wasn't a chicken leg after all, but an orange, and they could get a good fresh cup of juice out of him if they squeezed hard enough.

It was enough to make him wonder how he was going to survive the full ritual the following day if Essik failed to rescue him.

Maybe Mokad had been lying, and he wasn't expected to survive.

Eventually the test ended—successfully, judging by Mokad's optimistic demeanor—and some of the cultists dragged Ivellios back to his cell. He was conscious, but his legs wouldn't move, and the thought of putting any weight on his screaming feet was…well, it was unthinkable.

* * *

That had been a few hours ago, to the best of Ivellios's reckoning. The pain had receded to an unpleasant memory, and now he lay there, asking himself questions he was entirely unqualified to answer. He closed his eyes, thinking he should rest so as to be as alert as possible if and when Essik was ready for them to make their escape, but before he could quiet his mind enough for sleep, another knock sounded at the door. Essik slipped inside and closed the door behind her.

"Are we escaping?" he asked.

"Not yet, but it's much more likely than it was a few hours ago. Let's keep it dark in here; no one should be walking by for an hour or two, but let's not take any extra chances."

The cot creaked as she sat down.

"While you were in the testing room, I was able to disable most of the traps between here and the exit. It wasn't difficult. The traps are there to stop people from getting in, not out. Even better, I was able to get a wax impression of the master key to the complex. As soon as I leave here, I'll make us a key that will get us past the locked doors."

"What about the guards?" Ivellios asked. "And have you found my sword?"

"No, I haven't found your weapon, but you should bring your poker, just in case. I have a plan for the guards."

"Which is?"

"We're going to make our break about an hour before the final ritual tomorrow. All of the cultists, even the ones usually guarding the entrance, will be assisting Mokad's preparations of the Merging Chamber. There will be a narrow window before Mokad sends for you when we can get out unchallenged."

That sounded uncomfortably convenient. "How do you know that? About when Mokad will need me?"

Essik laughed. "Mokad has the timing worked out down to the minute. If you're in the Merging Chamber too early or too late, your presence will throw off some of his precious equations."

"What, just by standing there?"

"Just by standing there. You're the descendant of Moirel Stoneshaper. It's in your blood."

Ivellios rubbed his temples and paced back and forth in the dark. He knew the dimensions of his cell well enough not to walk into the walls.

"How long until they come for me?"

"Just over ten hours," said Essik. "But with luck we'll be gone in nine. In the meantime, I want to tell you about the ritual. If you get out but I don't make it, I think your friends in the Spire will find it useful to know what the Black Circle's plan had been."

"Good," said Ivellios. "And start with this. My friends in the Spire, as you put it, told us that their seal on the portal between Volpos and Spira was breaking down. If I'm understanding what's going on down here, you haven't actually *done* anything yet. You've only been practicing. But if the portal is opening anyway, what exactly is the Black Circle accomplishing here? Mokad told me I'm important because I'm Moirel's great-great-whatever-grandson, but what is the Black Circle using me for?"

"Good questions," said Essik. "The answers, as far I can tell, are straightforward. Naradawk Skewn has been trying to force the Verdshane portal open for a long time, and it's going to happen tomorrow, but even when it does, there's the problem of the Spire's stasis field. Naradawk has been able to knock it down for a second or two at a time, but he can't move an army through that way."

"So tomorrow's song and dance is about getting rid of the stasis field?"

"No, not exactly. The primary purpose of the ritual is to widen the portal itself. Right now the portal is small, not much more than a large doorway, and the stasis field surrounds the whole thing. Once Mokad is finished and the two worlds are brought into alignment, the portal will be miles wide. The stasis field will be immaterial, and Charagan's defenses will be pointless."

"You say that's the primary purpose. Is there a secondary one?"

"Yes. The Black Circle is also speeding up the convergence of Volpos and Spira, and they're going to use you to calibrate the moment they overlap. Have you seen or heard some of the cultists talk about 'jolt' and 'jounce?'"

"I thought Jounce was one of the cultists."

Essik snorted. "No. They're terms to describe how the convergence isn't just speeding up, but that the rate at which it's speeding up is speeding up. The Spire has been keeping the portal closed successfully for centuries. The reason they're failing now is because Naradawk is making his push now, and the emperor needs the portal expanded, as I just said. The Black Circle has been accelerating, jolting, jouncing the process, pushing the two worlds into alignment at an ever-faster rate. Your conjecture that the Black Circle 'hasn't done anything yet' is wrong. They've been down here for almost two years, enacting the rituals that are merging Volpos and Spira. They only need you for the final stage."

Ivellios frowned in the dark. "Morningstar thought we still had three weeks, but I can't have been down here more than one. I hope they've figured out that the schedule's moved up." He took a long, deep breath, and exhaled loudly. "I have one more question."

"Yes?"

"Who are you? How did you get in here? Why are you helping me? And if the Black Circle knows everything, why don't they know you're helping me?"

"That was four questions."

"Fine. It was one set of questions. Will you answer them?"

"Yes," Essik answered, but then she went silent for an uncomfortable interval. Somewhere far off in the Black Circle complex a gong sounded, followed by faint chanting. Ivellios resisted the urge to find Essik's shoulders in the dark and shake them.

"I haven't wanted to tell you." Essik's voice was little more than a whisper. "My order tried to kill your family thirty years ago."

Ivellios felt ice in his chest. "You're a Silversword."

"Yes. Though I hadn't yet joined when your family—"

"When your group murdered my father and tried to kill me," Ivellios finished. He considered what he knew. "You've assumed I was dead. It must have been a shock to discover I wasn't."

"I didn't believe them at first," Essik said. "I read the report from the one survivor from that day, a young man named Rosset Finch. He reported that you and your father, the last direct descendants of Moirel Stoneshaper, had been killed. I thought we had fooled the Black Circle into thinking you were still alive since they've been planning with that assumption. But it turned out that it was we who'd been fooled."

"You certainly were," said Ivellios. "The Silverswords got as far as killing my father, but then I was rescued by Sharshun. The survivor's memories were altered so he thought I'd been killed too. They also changed my memories so I'd forget all about the Sharshun *and* the Silverswords having been there. I've lived my life thinking my parents were murdered by goblins."

"How did you learn the truth?" Essik's voice was full of surprise, though Ivellios couldn't tell if that was because Essik hadn't known herself or because she didn't expect Ivellios himself to know it.

"Long story, and I don't want to talk about it," said Ivellios. "So why aren't you killing me now? You've had several opportunities to correct your mistake."

"What would be the point?" Did Ivellios imagine it, or did Essik sound wistful? "The Silverswords tried to end your line to prevent you from being here at all. Killing you now would serve no useful purpose because they'd still have your body." She paused. "Now that it's come to this late pass, my best hope is to get you out of here entirely. That will be easier if you're alive."

"Glad to hear it." Ivellios's heart beat faster than it should. In the week—had it only been a week?—since learning the truth about his parents, exacting revenge against the Silverswords had never been far from his thoughts. It galled him that now he was relying on one for rescue. "I have to ask. Would you have killed me, like the other Silverswords tried to do? Cut me down in front of my mother, so the Black Circle couldn't use me later?"

"Of course." Essik didn't even pause to consider. "It was two lives measured against millions. Wouldn't you have made the same choice?"

It struck Ivellios then that he *had* made the same choice. The memories from his one convulsive journey to Volpos, when he had confronted Emperor Naradawk in his throne room, were still patchwork, piecemeal. But he knew for certain that he had tried to kill himself, so that Naradawk couldn't use him for exactly the same purpose as Mokad. But that had been his own choice. Self-sacrifice was noble. Sacrificing others without their consent was abhorrent, even if both were to bring about identical outcomes. It wasn't the same!

Was it?

Damn.

"How long have you been working undercover?" Ivellios asked. "And how have you kept the Black Circle from noticing you?"

"I've been part of Naul's team for almost nine years. I'm able to keep my secret because for a full year before that, the Silverswords worked dozens of enchantments on me to prevent the Black Circle from seeing through the ruse. That doesn't mean I'm not in constant danger of discovery. I have to be very careful. That's why your rescue has been taking so long."

"Hm." Ivellios scratched at the week of stubble covering his face. "I assume you have no way to communicate with the other Silverswords while you're here."

"No. That would be far too dangerous. Naul or Mokad or Quia would detect it if I performed any kind of magic that extended beyond the boundary of this place."

"Pity." Ivellios yawned, and then the cot creaked again as Essik stood.

"Get some rest," she said. "Nine hours. Be ready."

Essik slipped quietly from the cell, leaving Ivellios alone in the silent dark. He found his cot and flopped down on his back, thinking about everything Essik had told him, but soon his mind moved on to grumbling about the crappy hand fate had dealt him.

"If Abernathy hadn't summoned me in the first place," he muttered to himself,

"I'd never have crossed the sea or wound up inside the Crosser's Maze. Then the Sharshun's prophecy wouldn't have come true, and maybe I wouldn't be in this mess."

But, no, in that case the prophecy simply might have been different.

Prophecies. He hated the stupid things. They implied that he wasn't in control of his own fate. Of course, here he was in a little cell deep in some Black Circle warren, waiting to be used as the centerpiece for an evil rite that would effectively destroy the kingdom. If he truly was in control of his destiny, he sure in the hells wouldn't be in this predicament right now.

Pondering these imponderables, Ivellios drifted into an uneasy sleep, from which he was woken several hours later by Essik shaking him with unseemly vigor.

"Something's happened," she said.

Ivellios instinctively grasped for his absent sword, swore, and rolled to his feet. "What? Is it time? Are we escaping?"

Essik's face was illuminated by the light from the hallway. Should he be worried that she hadn't closed the door behind her?

"Mokad has suffered a setback," she said. "One of his agents has been targeting the Spire's wizards, weakening them, but it seems they've overcome that, with disastrous results." She smiled at him. "Or promising ones, depending on your point of view. Can you think of anything your allies might have done to assist the archmagi?"

"How could I know that?" he answered. "I've been down here with you." But he did know, or at least he could take a guess. He thought of Morningstar, meeting with her Ellish sisters every night while they crossed the continent of Kivia. She must have stopped what's-his-name, the dream-fighter in the red armor who summoned the turtle. Good for her! But Ivellios didn't quite trust Essik enough to say any of that out loud.

Essik blinked at him. "I suppose it doesn't matter. But I wanted to warn you; they're resetting the testing room, and I'm here to take you there. They need to rewrite their equations, revise their rituals, and they need you to do it. You'll have to endure it; there wasn't time to mix a new potion. I'm sorry."

"I can stand it," said Ivellios, though the reality of more acidic wasp-stings and crushing forces pulverizing him was not exactly what he'd choose to wake up to. "But couldn't we escape right now, while they're all distracted?"

"They're not." Essik glanced over her shoulder at the open door. Shouts and the echoes of running footsteps sounded in the distance. "The opposite, in fact.

Mokad ordered extra guards, in case whatever happened is part of a two-pronged attack."

"Damn." Ivellios's spirits, lifted momentarily at Essik's news, returned to grim pessimism.

"It's still a positive development. The final ritual is going to be delayed by a day, which will give me more time to polish our escape plan, not to mention give me some margin for error when casting the master key."

"What about the extra guards?"

Essik shook her head. "They'll still have to pull them when the time comes for the full ritual. Now, come on, Mokad may start to get suspicious if we wait too long."

Ivellios followed her back to the testing chamber, fretting all the while. Something about Essik's plan seemed too facile, as though she failed to take something obvious into account. He couldn't put his finger on it. Meanwhile, bleary-eyed, black-robed men and women dashed through the corridors and stairwells, heading in the same direction.

The round room, already so familiar to Ivellios, swarmed with cultists like hornets from a fallen hive. They had crammed themselves shoulder to shoulder at the slateboard, pointing and jabbering, erasing and chalking, shouting and arguing. On the ground behind them, several people with robes hiked past their knees chiseled out or painted over many of the equations on the floor.

Mokad looked up from the floor, where he knelt studying the array of circles and lines. His eyes narrowed as he stared, though Ivellios couldn't tell if it was he or Essik who had earned Mokad's obvious displeasure.

"Bring him in!" Mokad shouted to be heard above the din. "Put him at the convergence point! Naul, freeze him once he's in place."

"Come on," said Essik. Despite the chaos in the room, she led Ivellios carefully, making sure they did not step over any of the painted lines or cross the boundaries of the black circles on the floor. Once he stood at the spot where the two largest circles touched, Naul approached and cast a quick spell that paralyzed Ivellios's legs.

"He's ready," Naul called to Mokad. "But it will be hours until we're prepared for a new test."

"I don't care," answered Mokad. "What's a little more suffering before tomorrow?"

"Tomorrow?" That was the woman Quia, turning from her place at the slateboard. "Mokad, the wizards of the Spire have quadrupled the aetheric counterforce in the past two hours. It could be days before—"

"Tomorrow!" Mokad practically screamed. "We have to align our efforts with Naradawk! We will be ready by tomorrow, or all of this will have been for nothing!"

Ivellios smiled. *Well done, Morningstar, assuming this is your doing. I hope an extra day is enough.*

CHAPTER TWENTY-FIVE

"A ravia, wake up."

She swam up through the dark silt of a stifling sleep, breaking free of a nightmare in which she sobbed over Pewter's body. Green-filtered sunlight stung her eyes through the tent flap.

"I brought you breakfast." Tor sat down beside her. "Honeyed oatmeal, buttered bread, and an apple tart, with Minya's compliments."

She rolled over onto her side, facing away from him. Inches from her face, Pewter lay curled in a ball, nestled in the folds of a blanket Tor had set out beside her. Terrified, she placed a hand on his side, but her cat didn't so much as twitch.

"Pewter!" She gently shook his body, at which the cat stretched out one forepaw, yawned, and briefly opened one eye. The ragged gray fur of his flank gently rose and fell. Relief overwhelmed her.

Pewter, please...

She waited a heartbeat to hear his comforting, snarky voice in her head, but there was only silence, the same terrible silence that had endured since she first escaped the Crosser's Maze after encountering Lapis.

Be thankful he's alive, she told herself. *He's still the same cat you grew up with. The same one you rescued as a kitten when the Cotters next door thought he was dead.*

But it wasn't the same. Yesterday he had stayed with her, mostly, and showed his old affection, but the voice and the intelligence were gone.

I still love you, Pewter. I always will. But I wish you would come back.

"I brought some chicken scraps for Pewter too." Tor scraped some bits of meat from the edge of the plate onto Pewter's blanket. The cat didn't stir.

Aravia sat all the way up. "How did you know I was sleeping and not in the maze?"

Tor's face reddened.

"What?"

"It's just…you never snore when you're in the maze."

"So I was snoring just now?"

"Not loudly! And only a little."

"Oh, Tor." She accepted the plate and took a ravenous bite of the bread. Gods, but she was hungry. "Aren't you going to have anything?"

"I ate in the mess tent already while Minya was making your breakfast."

She finished the bread and crammed the fruit tart into her mouth. "I have to get back," she said while she chewed. "I need more time to study the portal. I shouldn't have slept so long."

"Yes, you should have." Tor looked so serious, so unlike how she usually pictured him. "You need your rest. You said so yourself."

He was right, of course. Her confrontation with Lapis had drained her to the dregs, and even a full night's sleep hadn't restored her to the potency she'd need to seal the portal. Yesterday she had alternated between fitful naps and fearful excursions into the Crosser's Maze. The former were plagued by terrible dreams: of failure, of Pewter, of unformed terrors that she couldn't remember upon waking. Her trips into the maze mostly served to frustrate her. She needed more time, more study, more answers from King Vhadish that were never going to come. And always lurking was the specter of Lapis. Where was she? What was she planning? Aravia couldn't begin to guess, since what Lapis had already accomplished shouldn't have been possible.

Pewter twitched in his sleep, his little paws running in place for a moment.

"Has he spoken yet?" Tor asked.

Aravia shook her head. "I…" She swallowed a lump of despair. "I must have burned away our connection, as well as his higher intelligence, when I used his life-force in the maze." Hearing herself say the words brought tears to her eyes.

Pewter, I'm so sorry.

"But he's alive," said Tor, "and he obviously still adores you. He's hardly left your side since…"

"I know." Aravia reached out gently and scratched her cat's side. Pewter began to purr in his sleep. "I know."

She shook the last vestiges of sleep from her head, blinked away her inchoate tears, and stood, her head brushing the top of the tent's peaked interior. "This morning I will need to determine the ideal location to stand while sealing the portal. To do that, I must first spend more time in the maze—perhaps two hours of real time. I need to measure aetheric feedback resonance along overlapping ovoid…" She trailed off at the sight of Tor's blank look. "You have no idea what I'm talking about. I shouldn't babble at you like that."

Tor held her hand, and the feel of his fingers on her skin blunted the sharp edge of her worry. "You're right. I have no idea what any of that meant, beyond that you have to measure some magic stuff inside the maze, but it doesn't bother me a bit. In fact, I find it comforting that you know so much more than me or anyone else. You'll do this, Aravia. You'll succeed. I know it."

Aravia sighed and embraced him, feeling the strength of his arms and the warmth of his affection. "The only reason I know more than anyone else is that Vhadish is dead," she murmured. "He was going to teach me how to take those measurements. Now I'll have to work it out on my own."

On my own. The words made her think again of Pewter, still sleeping on his blanket.

"Wherever you go, I'll be beside you," Tor said, giving her a squeeze. "I will protect, the goblin shaman said, remember? I wouldn't want to make a liar out of him."

* * *

Ivellios felt like he'd been dropped from a tall building. Everything hurt. His shoulders and knees screamed when he moved. His abdomen felt as though a large man had struck it repeatedly with a club. One of his ribs was almost certainly cracked. Even his teeth ached if he closed his jaws too tightly.

Lying in the dark, unsure if he had slept since being dragged back to his cell, Ivellios tried his best to remain perfectly still, but even then a throbbing pain burned in his neck, his hands, his feet. Mokad, Naul, Quia, and the rest had not been gentle during their frantic rejiggering of the ritual test room. They had run through several sets of chants, spells, and revised equations, each one failing in some manner that resulted in horrific pain for Ivellios. In one of those, his torso had been twisted so far around he would have sworn he could look down and see his own arse before passing out. He had come to a few minutes later, gagging over some smelling salts a cultist had shoved under his nose.

"This will go faster if he's alert!" Mokad had shouted. "Quia, get him to his feet, paralyze him, and we'll try again using the Asadar theorem in its third variant. That should balance the reduced acceleration. Back in your positions. We start again in three minutes!"

It had gone on like that for what felt like hours, Ivellios forced to stand immobile while around him the mathematicians rioted. Once he had gone blind for several minutes, his eyes burning as though someone had rubbed hot peppers into them. Near the end, during the part when the squeezing happened, the pressure against both sides of his torso had grown so severe, and with such suddenness, Mokad had screamed for his minions to halt before their sorceries crushed Ivellios to death. That was when he had likely sprung a rib. His nose had been bent sideways as well, though he didn't think it had broken.

The worst of it was, by the time Mokad and his minions had finished, they seemed to have worked out their problems. Mokad had circles under his eyes, and his voice was hoarse from shouting at his fellows, but he was smiling. The cultists had left the room in a cloud of weary back-slapping and mutual congratulations, satisfied with the results of their feverish efforts.

Quia had even given Mokad a little bow. "I'm sorry I doubted you," she said humbly. "Your mastery of integrals is astounding."

Mokad had answered with a weary chuckle. "All those hours when a good little Scarbearer would have been praying to his little healer god, I was studying. Preparing for this moment. Naradawk will be free, I swear it."

* * *

Now it was simply a matter of waiting for Essik, praying to all the gods, Corilayna especially, that luck would favor him during his escape. He strained his ears, listening for the sound of Essik's footsteps in the corridor outside, but in the halls of this Black Circle warren, all had gone quiet.

Ivellios hoped Essik wasn't going to count on his help if they had to fight their way out. Hells, even a light jog might be beyond his ability right now, with his bruised legs and broken rib. She hadn't been there during that last brutal round of testing. She might not realize what a wreck he was.

He stiffened at a sound from outside, but, no, it wasn't a sound, more of a sensation in his innards, a heavy vibration, and it came from somewhere beneath him. Its intensity grew over several seconds, then faded, but it never ceased entirely. After a few more seconds it began another cycle, an increasing rumble that he felt in his bones more than heard with his ears. Gingerly he sat up and put his bare feet to the stone floor. The vibrations made his soles tingle. It reminded him of how Kibi had described being near the Seven Mirrors on Flashing Day.

What did it portend? Was it a good sign or a bad one? Had Mokad's ritual entered a new phase?

"Come on, Essik," he muttered. "Let's hurry things up."

Footsteps pattered outside, but they stayed in the distance, then faded. Over several minutes he heard more and more, as though dozens of cultists moved quickly through the complex. But eventually they ceased, leaving behind only the quiet rumble from below.

The door opened, light slicing in. Essik stood silhouetted in the doorway.

"We have to go now," she hissed. "Can you move? Mokad said you might have been injured during his last round of tests."

"Yeah, I can move, but maybe not very fast." He stood gingerly, wincing at a dozen different pains. "Have you cleared us a path?"

"Yes. As I hoped, the guards have joined Mokad in the merging room, and I believe I've disabled almost all of the traps. But in half an hour he will grow suspicious if I haven't brought you. I want to be far away by then."

Ivellios took three steps to the door, his right leg threatening to buckle beneath him, his cracked rib giving a stinging complaint. "I can make it. You're coming with me?"

"I intend to," said Essik. "But if I need to stay back to buy you time, I will. Now let's go. And stay quiet. I doubt we'll encounter anyone, but we shouldn't take any chances."

Ivellios limped along behind her as they moved silently down the stone hall. His bare feet were purple with bruises. They passed the privy, the rows of dormitories, then ascended to the round room with the giant abacus. Essik opened the fire-trapped door with a silver key and strode through it without bursting into flames. Ivellios followed. They crossed a second circular chamber, smaller and empty, though its walls were painted with hundreds of varying shapes and inscrutable glyphs. Beyond was a wide staircase heading downward. Glowing orbs threw light out of small niches in the walls.

"Why are we going down?" Ivellios whispered. "I thought we were already far underground."

"We have to go down to go up," Essik whispered back. "One of the bottlenecks is trapped to keep out intruders, but we would still set it off, and I couldn't figure out how to disable it."

Each step sent pain lancing up his right leg, but he bit back his complaints and followed his guide. The vibrations grew more intense as they descended the stairwell.

"What *is* that?" Ivellios asked.

"The merging ritual," said Essik curtly. The stairs bottomed out into the side of a long, evenly lit hallway, cold stone like everywhere in this place. Essik paused, looking left and right as though unsure which way to go.

"You're not lost, are you?" Ivellios whispered.

Essik shook her head. "Left. Stay close behind me."

They passed more closed doors and then an open one that Ivellios couldn't help but glance through. The room beyond looked like a smaller, messier version of Mokad's office, papers and books everywhere, and a slate-board crowded with diagrams.

"Come on." Essik tugged at his sleeve. Ivellios had slowed to look in the room, giving his aching body a tiny respite.

"Right. How much longer? When do we start going up?"

"Not long. Do your best to keep up."

Essik moved past the open door, and Ivellios limped along after her. Her pace increased. A half-minute later they came to a three-way junction. Ahead of them the corridor widened, its ceiling higher. Illuminated by the glow of the light-globes, the wide section was heavily scuffed, its floor littered with wood fragments and chips of black stone. The remaining branch was to the left, and that too was wide and seemingly well-traveled.

"We turn here," said Essik. The heavy, pulsing vibrations grew more powerful after they had turned the corner.

"If that's Mokad's big event, why are we getting closer to it?"

"We need to skirt quite close to the merging room," she said over her shoulder. "It's the only way out. The Black Circle didn't build this place with our escape in mind."

The new wide branch ended at a large pair of double doors, ebony wood with black metal bands. Whatever caused the vibrations sounded as though it waited just on the far side.

"You're sure this is the right way? You haven't simply been taking me straight to Mokad all this time?"

In response, Essik shoved open the double doors.

* * *

"This is the spot."

Tor turned a slow circle, peering through the trees. "You're certain?" As soon as the words were out of his mouth, he felt foolish; of course she was certain.

"It makes sense," she said, looking upward toward the canopy. "The archmagi already figured out the optimal distance from the portal. This place is exactly as far."

"Aren't we farther?" Tor recalled a few minutes earlier when Aravia had looked straight up and told him the wizards were directly above, casting their spells to keep Naradawk out as long as they could.

"Imagine a circle with the portal at its center," said Aravia. "Both the wizards' pocket dimension and this pine tree are on that circle. We seem farther away because the portal is near ground level, while the archmagi are high in the air."

Tor ran his hand along the rough bark of the tree. "Does that mean we have to chop this down, so you can sit on the stump?"

Aravia laughed, though it sounded brittle. Most of her humor had left her since Pewter had lost his voice. "No. The measurement doesn't need to be that exact. Though perhaps I will set my back against it when I go into the maze."

Tor frowned. This place, a random patch of forest, wasn't particularly defensible. The pine tree itself would offer some protection, and the surrounding trees might slow down a larger group, but an attack could come from any direction. The closest of the forest ruins was fifty yards to the south.

A cluster of soldiers, Werthan Stormknights recently arrived from Minok, moved about nearby. There were twenty-two of them in all, swords at their belts and clad in chainmail, their over-tunics showing the shield-and-gauntlet emblem of Werthis. General Anapark had assigned them to Tor and Aravia, making it clear they had the most important task of all the collected soldiery. They were scouting the immediate forest, talking quietly about defensive positions and possible lines of attack.

"Are they likely to target you?" he asked. "If some of Naradawk's soldiers get through before you've finished, will they know how important it is to stop you?"

Aravia sighed and tested the springy floor of leaves and needles with her foot. "My hope is that we never see any soldiers. If some do arrive, they should be caught in Anapark's killing zone and never make it this far. But what you suggest is certainly possible. I may be a target, though I would hope the enemy will not know specifically where to look."

A sound like the low peal of thunder rolled through the forest, which was odd because the sky was bright and cloudless. Tor and Aravia exchanged looks; the noise had come from the direction of the clearing. Most of the Stormknights paused and looked that way also.

"Is that bad?" Tor asked.

Aravia glanced eastward toward the portal. "Probably." She stepped closer to him, bringing them toe-to-toe. "Tor, I need to go now. Into the maze. I'm unlikely to come out again until either I've closed the portal or demonstrably failed to do so. It…could be dangerous for me inside. My lessons with Vhadish were cut too short, and my encounter with Lapis has left me weakened. But don't shake me loose. I have to stay in the maze until the very end, whatever that end might bring."

"I understand," he said, his voice quiet. "I'll be here, guarding you. I promise not to leave you."

She looked up at him. "My champion," she murmured, and then her hand was behind his head, pulling it down so she could kiss him, fiercely. Her body trembled, so he wrapped his arms around her, pulling her even more tightly to him, and all thoughts and worries dropped away, everything evaporating save for the circle of their embrace. After a timeless interval their lips parted, her breath hot against his cheek.

"Take care of yourself, Tor," she whispered. "Not just me. And if anything happens to me, if the strain of the maze is too great, promise you'll take care of Pewter."

"Of course I will," he told her. "But that's not going to—"

She cut him off, pressing her finger to his lips. "Just tell me you love me, Tor Bladebearer."

"I love you, Aravia Telmir."

She planted a final kiss on his chin, sat down at the base of the pine tree on the bed of undergrowth, and her eyes became the stars.

* * *

"Good. He's here."

Ivellios stared through the open door, needing only a few heartbeats to go from confused to scared to furious. He wheeled on Essik, who had taken a few steps backward. She quirked her fingers at him, whispered a fast syllable, and all feeling left his arms and legs. He crumpled to the ground.

The truth unspooled itself in his mind. "You're not really a Silversword, are you? This whole thing was a setup from the beginning."

Essik looked confused at the question. "Why are you…I…no. Of course I am…"

"What she means to say," said Mokad, appearing in the door along with two particularly large cultists, "is yes, she is a Silversword, and no, you were never going to escape from us."

Essik nodded uncertainly.

Mokad turned to his goons. "Carry him in. Set him down gently, standing, at the point of convergence."

One of the two burly cultists got his arms beneath Ivellios's armpits, and the other took his legs. Pain knifed through him, especially in his ribcage, as they carried him through the doors.

The previous testing room had been impressively large, but it was a closet compared to this place. It shared the same circular shape but must have been two hundred feet across and four stories high.

The stone floor was a crazy quilt of shapes (mostly circles), lines, words, equations, and patterns, stretching away into a dark blur. Through this mazework of geometry, several dozen Black Circle cultists moved with purpose, some carrying tools, others consulting with one another over strings of letters and numbers. A few moved about with pots of crystal arcanum and sprinkled it into piles inside the closed shapes. As before, the cultists avoided stepping over any of the painted black lines that connected the obsidian annulets. In fact, when Ivellios turned his head and squinted, he saw shimmering curtains above those lines, as if they were hot enough to warp the air that rose from them.

The curved wall lacked a slateboard, but it was scrawled upon in the same manner as the floor. Ivellios recognized many of the same shapes and configurations as in the test rooms, but everything here was writ many times larger. A few circles inscribed upon the walls reached nearly to the ceiling, forty feet above the floor.

But what impressed and terrified Ivellios the most was the pair of translucent spheres on the far side of the room. Thirty feet high at least and separated from each other by a hundred more, they slid slowly along the edge of the round wall toward an inevitable convergence. The spheres were marbled, striated, streaked with wisps and patches in various shades of color. One was mostly blue, with some green, white, and brown. The other was almost uniformly brown with occasional swaths of orange. They brightened and dimmed in time with the rising and falling of the bone-rattling rumble, more forceful here than anywhere previous.

On the floor, where that convergence seemed destined to happen, were two enormous annulets made of obsidian bricks set into the gray stone floor. At the one point these two circles touched, Mokad's servants set Ivellios down. He expected to fall over, but some unseen force kept him upright. He was numb from the neck down. Mokad came to stand before him.

"Ready for your big moment?" Mokad's smarmy smile made him want to puke.

"Go to hell, Mokad."

Mokad took a step back and looked thoughtful. "It's funny you say that," he said. "Given the divinations we cast regarding you and the rest of Abernathy's team, we believe that most of *you* are going to the hells. Perhaps you haven't all been as nice as you pretend?"

Ivellios couldn't tell if Mokad was kidding. "Essik," he said. "She really is a Silversword?"

"Yes." Mokad's smile widened. "She tried to infiltrate our organization almost a decade ago. A foolish notion. We figured her out inside of a week. But we thought it would be useful to cultivate someone who *thought* she was a spy, and that decision has proved most beneficial. The Black Circle's greatest strength has always been foresight."

Ivellios seethed. He had bitten down hard on that hook, and Mokad had reeled him in as neatly as you please.

"Was any of it true?" he asked. "Or has everything both of you have told me been lies?"

"Five minutes!" Quia's voice rang out, sounding above the earthquake rumble of the spheres.

"Very little of it," said Mokad, his tone apologetic. "Oh, there are a few guards watching the ways into the complex, but no one is going to find it, through magical means or otherwise. The idea of traps and locks and such was entirely an invention of Essik's. We didn't want you nursing any notions of escape."

Damn. Damn, damn, damn. "But Essik sabotaged one of your tests! Screwed up your equations and set you back a…"

Mokad was smirking. Smirking! "Just a little charade. The test went exactly as planned, including how it cemented your trust in Essik."

Ivellios shivered with rage at his own gullibility. He didn't want to ask the next question that came to his mind, but as long as Mokad was in the mood to gloat, he had to know.

"Could you have performed your rituals if I was dead?"

Mokad clucked his tongue. "I have always felt that we each have an obligation to keep ourselves alive at any cost, in order that we might serve masters worthier than ourselves. That's one of the many reasons I find the Sharshun so repugnant; they have poison sacs set into the roofs of their mouths, so that they cannot be captured and interrogated. But suicide cuts off every possible avenue of redemption. It's a recourse of cowards." He showed his spit-slick teeth. "Ivellios, let's just say I'm very happy that you've lived long enough to join us for this monumental event."

He turned away, took a step, then looked back. "Oh, and in case you still wondered: I don't expect you to survive to the end of the day. All of what I told you about getting your revenge on the Silverswords was true, except for the part where you get to personally participate. When Naradawk arrives, I'm sure hunting down and slaughtering Utholites will be high on his agenda."

Ivellios had a wild hope then, that Mokad had taken his gloating too far. "Then why should I cooperate with your ritual? Why should I turn left or right, or stare at your stupid shapes, or whatever else you need me to do?"

Mokad raised his eyebrows, chuckled, shook his head, and turned his back on Ivellios.

"You heard Quia!" Mokad shouted, smug triumph in his voice. "Our time has come. May the blessings of the Black Circle fall upon us."

* * *

Something new was affecting the portal; Aravia could see it, could feel it.

As before, being so close physically to the portal made it impossible to discern anything else inside the Crosser's Maze, but that no longer mattered. She drifted closer, examining the ragged glowing oval, the blemish in the fabric of reality that connected Spira and Volpos. It rippled in a way she hadn't seen before, like a sheet hanging in a slight breeze. It wasn't what she'd expect if something were about to come through it. Troublingly, she didn't know what it meant, and she had no time to worry about it.

Aravia circled the portal slowly, observing, measuring, taking in its magical properties using maze-derived senses impossible to describe in mundane terms. Vhadish had hinted at shortcuts, promised to help her refine techniques, but she couldn't dwell on the disappointment of his death.

She missed the presence of Pewter. Some number of seconds flittered away from her as she considered whether she could use the maze's power to restore their connection and his intelligence.

Focus, Aravia!

But it was so difficult. Focus here in the maze came from mental fortitude, and she was still so tired, so drained, from her battle with Lapis. Tor and Pewter vied for the attention of her thoughts, as her mind shied away from the task at hand. The cost of failure was…everything. Tor, Pewter, Horn's Company, the archmagi, her parents back in Sentinel. Gods, her parents! It shamed her that she thought about them so little, but life had moved past them so quickly, and hadn't they been eager to apprentice her to Serpicore?

Focus!

The portal.

She had to eliminate it. Reconstruct reality in its place so to eliminate every last crack and seam between the two worlds. She thought of the exercises with his prisms and ovals that Vhadish had put her through before Lapis had killed him. Even during her most successful trial run, she had burned out eleven prisms. That would be eleven soldiers dead. But better that than hundreds, thousands, and the eventual death of every citizen of Cha—

FOCUS!

With a monumental push of will, Aravia shoved all distraction aside and reached out into the endless expanse of the Crosser's Maze. Finding its power, gathering and organizing it, helped calm her mind. When she thought she had enough, she took a deep breath. The first real test was now before her.

The proximity of the portal washed out her sense of everything else, but she had to thread the maze's arcane energies through the bodies of living people. To do that, she had to *find* those people. King Vhadish had been teaching her ways of locating them, sensing them through the portal's blinding outpouring of power.

"It will be like finding glass beads under water," Vhadish had told her. "They may be effectively invisible, but the water itself knows of them, flows around them. Don't ask your eyes to find them, Aravia. Ask the water."

It was a technique she had not quite mastered, but there was no time left to practice. She cast her awareness out in a slow spiral, feeling for eddies in the wash. Nothing. She saw only the uniform opaque light of energy. Frustration threatened from the edges of her mind; she fought it back. She persisted, focused, *trusted* that she would see, and was rewarded with a slow emergence of dark forms coalescing out of the fog. Most were faint, tenuous, each containing only a bare trace of arcane potential. The kingdom's soldiers were not wizards. A small handful appeared sharper, having some minimum capacity for wizardry, like her mother had. But none of these individually would contribute any meaningful amount of power. It was the collected output of hundreds that would let her seal Naradawk away.

Now came the next test: Would the soldiers follow their orders and willingly allow her to use them as lenses? If too many refused, held back their meager potential, Aravia would not have enough power to seal the portal. And she had no idea what the soldiers would feel. If they interpreted it as an attack, would they withhold themselves on instinct even if they were intellectually willing?

It was too late to wonder. These questions were academic, meaningless.

She passed beams of the maze's energy through three of the soldiers. Tor and the Stormknights would be easiest, they being so close at hand to her physical body, but that was a risk she dared not take, not now. She chose soldiers near to the portal. There was a tense moment of resistance while Aravia waited for them to decide to give their assent. Time passed, only seconds, she hoped, and nothing happened. They balked at her request. Her energy threads passed through them uselessly.

Had they received General Anapark's order? Did they understand what was happening? Perhaps they didn't feel anything, and that was the problem? With some trepidation she increased the intensity of the energy thread.

One of the soldiers glowed in her mind, and the energy passing through her changed its nature, becoming refined, pure. What she needed. Success! She directed it into the portal, where its meager output became engulfed, a rivulet emptying into an ocean. Soon after, the other two soldiers also gave their assent, and she bent those beams as well.

Something inside her, a barrier built up from doubts and worry, broke apart and drifted away, a dark cloud shredded in a fresh wind. She could do this. She *was* doing it. Everything else was a matter of degree, of her applying her intellect, her finesse, her understanding of the maze and knowledge of the portal's nature.

She would save the kingdom. She *knew it.*

* * *

"What is she doing?"

The Stormknight's name was Carius, a warrior who reminded Tor of himself: young and impatient.

"Trying to save you," said Tor.

Another low roar of thunder sounded from the direction of the clearing. Several of the Stormknights looked up nervously.

"This is idiocy," said Carius. "We should be on the Balani fighting the Delfirians. There is no battle here. There are no armies to fight."

"You heard the general," said another of the Stormknights, a middle-aged woman named Mara. She commanded this contingent of holy warriors. "The enemy's coming from another world. They could be here any minute."

"Another world?" Carius didn't hide his skepticism. "It's crap, is what it is. And how is she saving our lives?" He pointed accusingly at Aravia, calmly sitting with her back to the pine tree. "She's just sitting there."

Tor didn't blame him for doubting. He still found the particulars baffling himself, and he'd seen all manner of inexplicable magical things since Abernathy's summons. "If the enemy soldiers do come, it's going to be through a magical doorway. Aravia's trying to get rid of the door."

Carius rolled his eyes. "And how is she doing that? Anapark told us she was a wizard. Shouldn't she be...wizarding?"

"She is! She's in the—she's casting spells. Trust me. She's doing everything she can to prevent any fighting. That's why we're here. Protecting Aravia is the most important thing."

Carius looked down at Aravia. "Yes, that's what Anapark said."

Another crack of thunder, and with it came the strangest thing, a blurry jump in everything Tor could see, as though something had knocked him hard on the side of the head. Every tree, every Stormknight, had briefly doubled and shifted before snapping back into place. The Stormknights must have seen it too; they gestured and muttered to one another.

Minutes later a chain of calls echoed through the woods, followed by movement all around them in the trees, as kingdom soldiers headed in small groups toward the clearing.

"General must've given the order to surround the killing zone," said Carius. Under his breath he added, "If you're right about the invasion, that's where we should be."

"That's enough, Carius," said Mara. "You should be where I tell you to be."

Thunder again blasted the air, louder than before, and with it came the weird doubling of the world. More worrying was a new sound that followed as the thunder receded: a noise like a thousand men shouting in an unfamiliar tongue. It reminded Tor of the shouts of the goblins while Kibi fought in the arena against their champion. The clamor did not rise or swell out of quiet; one second there was only the thunder and a few friendly voices through the trees, and the next it sounded like half a city screaming all at once, all around them. It lasted two, maybe three seconds, before it cut off entirely.

Several of the Stormknights who had sat down leapt back to their feet. Some drew their weapons as though expecting an imminent attack.

Through it all, Aravia never even flinched, the lines of her face set in a look of furious concentration, her star-field eyes open and staring.

You can do this, Aravia. I know you can.

* * *

Ivellios was going to die kicking himself.

No, not even that. He was going to die wishing he could kick himself, but he couldn't because he'd let these brainy bastards paralyze him. Gods, but what a mess he'd made of this whole thing. Throughout his life, from the moment he believed goblins had murdered his parents, he'd been a man of action. Nothing frustrated him more than waiting, than being passive when there was work to do, progress to be made. He had ignored those instincts and let Essik string him along, always rationalizing, always thinking he was being clever by waiting. The whole time they were pacifying him, like distracting a baby with a rattle. How had he been so stupid?

He could vow never to let it happen again, but seeing as he wasn't likely to survive the day, what value was there in a promise like that?

His head moved, and his neck, but that was all. He'd tried shouting at first, to distract the cultists from their carefully calculated rites, but they'd only ignored him. Worse, when their black magic needed him to do something, it yanked him around, faced him in different directions, lifted his arms. Once a force had even hoisted his body slightly into the air, spun him around twice, and set him down again.

It was humiliating. He'd become a ragdoll, a toy for the cultists to play with—or perhaps more accurately, a cog in their evil machine. His place near the wall gave him a full view of the cultists working their magic, chanting their numbers, sprinkling their magic dust. That was the one thing he had tried—spitting as far as he could, hoping to land a gob in one of the dust piles, maybe disrupting some finely tuned measurement of the stuff. But he wasn't close enough, and who was he kidding, really? He'd been reduced to a spectator, a helpless victim, doomed not only to watch the world end, but to cause it as well.

Essik was there, chanting along with the rest. He couldn't make out her expression—she was too far away—but maybe she was planning something. That was his only remaining hope: that she had turned the tables, was playing an even longer game than Mokad, and was planning some sabotage at the last second.

Yeah. And maybe gopher-bugs would fly out of his arse.

The golden bracelet on his arm grew warmer as time passed, while the two translucent spheres inched ever closer. When they touched, he'd be standing at the very spot, and that would be the moment Mokad's ritual would climax, resulting in Naradawk stepping out of his prison world.

The pounding, pulsing vibration from the spheres shivered his body and rattled his teeth. Here in the chamber there was sound as well, an unnatural sound, a low grumble, like a giant with unceasing indigestion. Mokad had all but admitted that Ivellios would die here; maybe that was how. When the spheres converged on him, he'd be shaken to pieces, cracking apart like an old piece of pottery, his bones splintering.

Gods, if only he could make use of his anger, his frustration. That was all he had. Ivellios screamed again, uselessly. Mokad stood near the center of the room, a hundred feet away, reading from a large black book held in one hand, tracing patterns in the air with the other. He didn't turn to look at Ivellios. None of them did. They probably couldn't hear him over the noise from the spheres.

All of the cultists shouted something at once, and a new sensation struck Ivellios, something like a smell, or heat, and he knew it. It was a warm, oily force, a wind blowing off a rancid pool, a corrupted sun shining on his face. He had felt it before, once, when he had been transported to Naradawk's throne room. The same greasy headwind that rolled off of Naradawk was here, pressing lightly against him from the left side.

He turned his head. His despair deepened. That feeling, that vile emanation from Naradawk, was coming out of the brown and orange sphere that, like the other, slowly, slowly came nearer.

* * *

Bright strings of the maze's boundless energy stretched from its bottomless, timeless reaches. Aravia deftly threaded them, passed them through the cores of hundreds of people, the willing soldiers whose scraps of arcane potential added up to a thick torrent of energy. She focused this upon the portal, and it was here she directed the largest share of her concentration. It was not sufficient to reinforce the portal; Vhadish had been precise on that point. Her goal was to erase it, leaving behind not a sutured wound in the substance of reality, but a seamless piece of unbroken creation.

It was working.

So many times Aravia had felt as though the maze had been built exactly for this, exactly for her. Now she was more than simply a cog in a machine. She was the professor instructing a crowd of students, a general commanding her legions, the conductor of an astral symphony. The full force of the universe surged around her, hers to command.

Aravia was a goddess of creation.

From time to time she returned her focus to the soldiers, tuning the streams of energy so that none of them would suffer too greatly. What did they feel? How drained were they? For Anapark's men and women, was she bringing them to their knees in weakness? Would they still be able to fight, should it come to that?

A great majority of them were assenting to her use of them, at least nine out of every ten. It would be enough. The portal was vanishing, and in its place she left pure, unsullied universe. She could stop the invasion before it started. Whatever the soldiers experienced, she was saving them from battle and death.

Solomea had once called the Crosser's Maze a "sovereign knitting needle." The metaphor wasn't perfect, but close. The maze was meant precisely for the purpose to which she put it, and it sang for her, doing her will. She was the Keeper of the Maze, destined for this moment.

Tor would be proud.

The portal itself still rippled slightly, a phenomenon Aravia didn't understand but which also didn't interfere with her work. She continued to ignore it. Some of her energy strings fluctuated mildly, but a semiconscious portion of her mind evened them out. She teased out several new threads and passed them through a handful of soldiers she hadn't yet tapped. All but one acceded to her unspoken request, lending her their arcane potential, strengthening the focused power she used to erase the portal.

That was when the first enemy arrived.

Aravia sensed nothing about the stasis field; it could be flickering, or brought down entirely for all she knew. The enemy must have done *something* about it, as it had managed to do many times already, because three or four beings passed through from Volpos into Spira without being immediately suspended. They wouldn't be wizards; the arcanistically inverse nature of the portal would hedge out arcanists until it was almost completely gone anyway. In all likelihood, a handful of enemy soldiers had arrived in the portal building, soldiers who would find themselves the targets of several hundred crossbows if they stuck their heads out.

Still, their emergence implied she'd best not dawdle. Aravia once more increased the total energy she drew from the maze, distributing it as evenly across what were now over three hundred soldi—

The portal's ripple became a flap, then a bulge, and then, to Aravia's absolute horror, it *expanded*. Much of her progress was undone in an instant, and her mind reeled from the implications. Her energy strings surged and ebbed. Keeping everything balanced became a desperate exercise. She thought of the juggler in Tal Hae and how she might have struggled had the street become the deck of a pitching ship.

By the time she regained her equilibrium and evened out the energy, five of the soldiers had vanished from her skein. She hadn't released them, which meant they had died. She had burned the life right out of them. Five innocent lives gone, the first casualties of the battle to come.

Gods, no.

The portal was no longer the width of a doorway, but more like the size of the Greenhouse kitchen. Soldiers poured through it in greater numbers, several dozen, perhaps more. The stasis field would no longer matter; they could move around it. At least the whole of the portal was still inside the building, and the enemies would still be funneled into the killing zone.

She had to regain control, return to her task, but now it was much more daunting. A small relief: Not all of her work thus far had been in vain. But the scope of her work had increased greatly. She would need to syphon more energy, draw it through more soldiers, and work faster to seal the expanded portal. It would still be possible, but her earlier confidence was shaken. Grim in spirit now, she bent her mind once more to the maze.

* * *

The Stormknights turned toward the sound like a pack of wolves scenting a deer. Crossbows twanged, followed by the clatter of bolts against stone, along with screams of pain. Tor sidestepped slightly to put himself directly between Aravia and the distant noises of combat.

"Our soldiers are shooting the enemy," Mara said calmly.

"Which means there *is* an enemy," said Carius. He looked down at Aravia, who still had not moved or spoken. "She failed. Whatever silent magic she's doing, it didn't work."

Tor looked down upon Aravia's grave face, desperate to know how she fared. "Don't give up on her. Whatever happens out here, without what she's doing in there, it would be worse."

"How do you know?" asked a third Stormknight. About half of them had crowded around Aravia, while the rest looked out anxiously toward the clearing.

"I—"

"We should be fighting," said Carius, pointing in the direction of the clearing. The loudest sound now was shouting, but behind it came the *thwap-zip* of crossbows loosing.

"No!" said Tor, so loudly that all twenty-two Stormknights turned to stare. "We have to stay and protect Aravia. Think of yourselves as her honor guard. She needs to stay safe."

"We'd do a better job of that assisting at the killing zone," said another of the Stormknights. She looked down at Aravia as she spoke. "We'll only be of use here if soldiers escape the perimeter, so it would make more sense to help prevent that from happening in the first place."

"Aravia needs more time," said Tor. "And didn't General Anapark order you to stay here and guard her? You can't disobey her orders."

"That's not technically true." Carius turned to Mara. "Stormknights answer to church authority, and Dalesandro has not officially appointed any commanders to this region. Captain Mara, we may be expected to defer to General Anapark as a courtesy, but that is not a binding obligation."

Tor fought down the urge to punch Carius in the face. If he had to, he'd drag back any Stormknights who tried to abandon Aravia.

"That's enough, soldier," said Mara, the weary tone of her voice suggesting this was not the first time Carius had given her trouble. "I am treating it as an obligation, and so will the rest of you. From the sound of things we may be engaged in combat very soon, so stay alert."

Several of the Stormknights continued to look longingly toward the sound of battle, but none of them left to join it.

* * *

Ivellios winced as another of his ribs cracked with an audible snap, but the pain of it merely blended into an all-encompassing, unfocused agony. Mokad's ritual was in full frenzy, and the forces it exerted on Ivellios's body were varied and violent. His limbs were bent, breath was pulled from his lungs, and once he would have sworn his feet had been squashed into balls the size of apples. Unlike during the early tests, Mokad and his team showed no concern about the lasting effects on his person.

The Merging Chamber had warmed noticeably; sweat beaded on Ivellios's forehead and pooled around the waistline of his pants. The heat-shimmer above the painted lines gave off wispy strings of lurid purple vapor. But if the heat bothered the cultists at all, they didn't show it. They continued to chant, to cast their spells, to read off lines of letters and numbers from the walls and floor. A dozen of the buggers stood around the perimeter of the room ringing bronze handbells in a haphazard rhythm. Every minute or two, one of the piles of crystal arcanum flashed with a puff of colored smoke. More and more of the shapes on the wall lit up with a virulent purple glow, casting the faces of the cultists in sickly violet.

And still, the spheres came closer. Pressure assaulted him from both sides, the squeezing, roiling, pulling at his guts that had plagued him since his very first week with Horn's Company. That was what would probably kill him in the end. When the spheres converged at his body, they'd either squash him flat or tear him in half. Maybe both at once.

A gruesome thought came to him. If he bit his tongue hard enough, would he die of blood loss before the ritual was done? Would one of the cultists notice in time? If they did, could they spare one of their number to tend to him? Probably. Three of Mokad's minions seemed to be serving in support roles, moving unhurriedly, adding crystals to the piles, stopping to study the equations, and casting frequent glances toward Ivellios.

While he contemplated the possibility, all of the cultists abruptly ceased their chanting and turned to face him.

"One!" they shouted in unison. Ivellios rose up several feet from the ground.

"One!" They surprised him by not proceeding to "two." He flew upward another few feet.

"Two! Three! Five! Eight!" With each number, he jerked a bit higher, though the distances grew less as the numbers increased. "Thirteen! Twenty-one! Thirty-four! Fifty-five!" Ivellios settled at a height about two stories up, right across from the centers of the ever-encroaching spheres. When they reached nine hundred eighty-seven, they ceased the count, but the cultist closest to him continued to read increasingly large numbers from a long scroll.

Despite his predicament, his pain, Ivellios began to laugh, feeble though it was. He had survived swords and spears, escaped from goblins, somehow evaded capture or worse at the hands of the Delfirians, survived being swept out the side of a cliff by a river a mile above the ground, escaped from a city in a bottle, and even come out the far side of the Crosser's Maze. But here was where he was going to die, horribly, painfully, and with the fate of the world in the balance.

Killed by math.

CHAPTER TWENTY-SIX

I t was too much.

If the portal had stopped expanding when it was merely the size of a room, or even the building that housed it, she might have maintained control. But now Aravia couldn't even guess its dimensions. A hundred yards? A quarter mile? The stasis field was no longer anything more than a tiny barrier on a wide bridge, easily avoided by those crossing it. Enemy forces were likely arriving outside the killing zone.

Protect me, Tor!

Her certainty in her task had all but vanished. The quantity of energy she required, and the finesse she'd need to avoid snuffing out the lives of her living candles, were far in excess of anything she'd tried to manage while training with Vhadish. She'd have to improvise a new solution, now that the portal was orders of magnitude larger.

Perhaps she could find a way to amplify the power of the refined beam of energy *after* it had passed through her willing soldiers? Vhadish had warned her against it, talked about the dangers of feedback loops, of interference patterns, back-surges of energy, of damaging her own mind with something he called tangential reflections. But he hadn't said it was impossible. Just foolish.

Worse, she'd have to manifest an amplifier while not pausing in her other work. There was a component of momentum to how she used the Crosser's Maze, and if she ceased her current efforts, she'd never be able to restore them. Altering the process in mid-stream, as it were, would make a supremely difficult task even more challenging.

But still not impossible. As she had configured the process, the hundreds of refined beams of arcane energy that coursed out of the soldiers and into the portal met *at* the portal. From that single point, the energy rushed out in all directions, like liquid soaking into and spreading across a thin sheet. She then wielded that energy to unmake the portal, transforming it directly into solid, unbroken reality.

She would need to place her amplifying lens quite close to the portal; far away, and it would have to be unmanageably huge in order to encompass all the incoming threads. But too close, and it would be too small to provide the amplification she needed.

Panic gripped her. While merely contemplating this new solution, she had lost some of the fine balance of energy strings drawn from the maze. She scrambled to equalize the forces, but by the time she regained control, four more soldiers had died, little candles blown out in an instant.

Her heart quailed, and a corner of her mind railed against the feeling. How much easier this would have been had she kept that emotional detachment she harbored for so long. Now she contended with grief atop the absurd difficulties of wielding the maze. As best she could, she pushed her sorrows aside.

A lens. She relegated its design to a walled-off section of her mind while the rest worked out how much more energy her soldier-candles could funnel without being extinguished. She had no time for precise calculations, and she hated guesswork, but her choices had dwindled to nothing. When her guesses were good enough—*please let them be good enough*—she instantiated a wide oval lens a short distance out from the center of the now-enormous portal.

The effect was immediate and promising. The intensified power of the maze poured across the portal's wide expanse, and Aravia went back to work, erasing, mending, sealing. Her confidence returned, surging along with the new currents of power. She refined her new technique on the fly, calibrating flows, offsetting forces, and soon she once again felt like the conductor of a cosmic orchestra. The Crosser's Maze existed for this, for *her*.

A spike of pain. Aravia flinched. Power flared, speared outward like a shaft of sunlight in her eyes. Something was wrong. To her credit, Aravia tempered her reaction, keeping control of the maze's outputs while she sought out the problem.

Damn. As Vhadish had warned, her lens was not perfectly focusing the energy. A tiny amount was being reflected back into the skein of incoming energy threads, disrupting them. Even as she identified the new problem, it escalated. Incoming beams were splintered apart by the reflections from other beams, and in moments there would be a cascade, the entire system shattering. She could try refining the lens, or removing it altogether, reverting to her original plan. Both ideas carried risk.

More spikes, more flares, and beams of energy reflected crazily out in all directions. At the same time, the portal itself rippled madly, like a pond disturbed by a large boulder falling into it. Something powerful, something with a strong arcane aura, crossed the world boundary.

Naradawk? She didn't think so. She'd have expected his passage to shred the entire portal into tatters. But something powerful, more potent than any normal soldier, had passed from Volpos into Spira. Its passage distracted her, worsening the spirals and spiking reflections. Pain lanced through her head, a dozen more of her soldiers died, and in her dread of catastrophic failure, Aravia removed the lens altogether. The system reverted to its previous state, easy for her to control but entirely insufficient for erasing the expanded portal. Enemy soldiers passed through by the dozen, and they could be appearing anywhere, inside the killing zone or out of it.

I can't do it. I need too much energy, and it would kill all my soldiers. If the portal grows much larger, all the energy in the universe won't do any good. Naradawk will escape because of my failure.

No.

There must be a solution.

There must be.

Think!

* * *

Tor's heart crumbled. Carius was right. Aravia had failed.

Fighting raged all around in the woods, Charagan soldiers in their red and gold uniforms striving against men in dull gray armor. Steel rang on steel against a backdrop of shouts, grunts, and screams. Maybe the killing zone had worked, and maybe it hadn't, but either way, dozens of enemy soldiers had escaped from it.

The twenty-two Stormknights arranged themselves in a rough circle with Aravia in the center. Tor himself stood just inside that circle, closer to Aravia than anyone. All swords were out, all heads swiveling.

"Did you see that?" One of the Stormknights pointed north into the trees. "A splash of yellow light, and four men appeared as if from nowhere!"

Tor turned and stared. "Where? Are they coming this way?"

"No. They dashed off to the left."

"We should chase them down!" another of the Stormknights said, frustration in his voice.

"We need to stay here," Tor insisted. "With Aravia."

"Why?" asked Carius. "She didn't stop the invasion. She's not doing anything at all!"

"You don't know that," said Tor, more hotly than he intended. "She could still seal the portal, stem the flow of the enemy, save countless lives."

A particularly horrid scream sounded from not far off, a wet, bubbling cry that cut off abruptly.

"We could be saving lives right now," said Carius. To Mara he implored, "Captain, I know what General Anapark said, but you have to give the order to—"

He was interrupted by a violent thrashing through the trees, heralding the arrival of seven enemy soldiers, broad-shouldered, torsos encased in dark gray metal cuirasses. Each wore a round leather buckler on one arm and carried a long blade that grew wider as it approached its curved tip. Tor wasted a second trying to recall from his lessons with Elgus what those were called. Falchions, maybe?

The twelve Stormknights closest to the enemy pivoted out of their circle, crisply inverting their semicircular formation. Tor was in the wrong half of the ring to join immediately, and hesitant to move farther away from Aravia. The remaining Stormknights reformed a tighter ring.

Naradawk's men were all of a type: pasty white faces, stringy black hair, small noses, and thick, dark eyebrows. They pulled up hastily, seeming to realize how badly they were outnumbered. One in the back turned and ran off eastward while the rest hesitated, glancing at one another, perhaps waiting for a signal.

They didn't need to wait. The Stormknights stepped forward, collapsing their semicircle, and fell upon the enemy with a fury. Their coordination and teamwork were astounding, to say nothing of their footwork and timing. Carius himself was a wonder, chopping down two of the enemy in the first few seconds, with a perfectly executed feint between killing blows. The others worked in pairs, staggering their strikes and protecting each other's flanks. It was a beautiful, deadly dance, and in half a minute all seven of the pale soldiers were dead.

One Stormknight came away with a slight limp, and another suffered a shallow cut across his cheek, but without a word they rejoined the circle around Aravia.

"Amazing!" said Tor.

Beside him, Mara grinned, though she didn't look at him. Her head and eyes never stopped moving, watching the woods, gauging each pocket of chaos.

"We train our whole lives for something like this," she said. "Even in times of peace, our commanders tell us to—unnh."

She staggered, swayed, and leaned against a small tree, bending it. Tor expected to see an arrow sticking out of her, or some enemy creature that had sneaked up behind them, but she quickly righted herself.

"Are you all right?" Before she could answer, Tor saw that all the Stormknights were reacting similarly.

"Something is attempting to enchant me," one of the Stormknights cried. "Like it's trying to suck the life out of me. But if I concentrate, I can block it."

"That's Aravia!" Tor shouted. "Didn't you get General Anapark's order? She needs some of your energy to close the portal."

"What are you talking about?" asked Carius.

"That feeling! Aravia needs a small amount of energy from every soldier here in order to stop the enemy invasion. She's still trying!"

"Bugger that," said another of the Stormknights. "More likely, it's some enemy sorcerer trying to weaken us."

"But…" Tor flailed for an answer. "But it can only work if you let it. If it really were an enemy, wouldn't they just suck out your life and not give you a choice about it? General Anapark gave a direct order for all his men and women to agree to give a bit of their arcane potential if they felt something like…like what you're feeling."

"Arcane potential?" That was a tall, thin Stormknight, three people over from Tor in the circle. "What does that mean?"

"Sorry, I mean your life essence."

"You're saying Aravia wants to drain our lives away?" asked Mara, incredulously.

"No! I mean, yes, but only a little. And every bit matters."

"And what proof do we have that it's Aravia causing that feeling?" asked Carius. "She's not moving. When I was little I saw a wizard performing tricks in Hae Kalkas, making objects move on a table with puffs of smoke. The whole time she was whispering strange words and waving her hands around. Aravia hasn't even twitched since we got here."

Tor looked down again at Aravia, at her placid face, her hastily braided hair, her star-speckled eyes. What was she going through right now? Naradawk's forces rampaging through the Greatwood was not a promising sign; had she succeeded, there would be none at all. But she was alive—her continued request for life-force proved as much. Didn't it? Or had Lapis come back, attacked her while she was distracted? Maybe Lapis was the one trying to drain the Stormknights. Aravia had told Tor that she wouldn't ask for his own life-force unless there was no other choice; wouldn't she have made the same decision about the Stormknights assigned to protect her? But then, they had arrived after she had gone into the maze, and she might not be able to tell precisely where they were.

"Truth is, I have no idea about any of that," he muttered.

"What's that?" asked Mara.

Tor took a last glance down at Aravia. "Listen to me! I swear on Brechen's name, on all the Traveling Gods, that what you feel is Aravia trying to save your lives, save your kingdom. I beg you, let her have your energy. She wouldn't be asking for it unless she was desperate."

Mara gave Tor a long, searching look from her place in the circle. "You love her."

Tor blinked. "I don't see what that has to—"

Mara smiled wanly and shook her head. "Do it," she barked at her soldiers. "Whatever it is that's asking for your energy, let it go. Our forces here are meager, and we'll get swamped if the enemy can field a real army. If Tor's wrong about Aravia, it's probably hopeless anyway."

The Stormknights, all twenty-two of them, rocked slightly on their feet, swaying like saplings in a fresh breeze. Some leaned briefly on their comrades. But all of them recovered quickly.

"How do you feel?" Tor asked Mara.

"Like I have a mild fever," she said. "But I can still fight." She inspected her soldiers for a few long seconds. "We all stay!" She shook her head as if in disbelief. "Protect Aravia at all costs."

Some of the Stormknights grumbled, but more of them offered brisk nods and dug in their heels.

Tor wanted badly to put a hand on Aravia's shoulder, stroke her hair, give her some assurance that he was still here, but he dared not. Who knew what even the mildest distraction might cause?

The fighting all around them grew louder, more intense. In every direction battles raged, warriors slashing, colliding, falling, screaming. Not more than ten yards out from the circle of Stormknights, four men in gray armor ran past in pursuit of a young and weaponless Chargish soldier. The faces of the Stormknights showed how much it pained them not to rush to the man's rescue. Tor himself would have been off like an arrow had Aravia not needed him. Minutes after that, a squad of six gray-clad men, blood dripping from their falchions, stopped short a dozen yards off. They stared at the ring of Stormknights, then quickly moved off in a different direction.

Tor returned his gaze to Aravia constantly. She still hadn't moved, but her face had grown pale, and did he imagine that her breathing was faster? What was it like for her, working her unknowable magic inside the Crosser's Maze with so much at stake?

"Augh!" One of the Stormknights on the far side of the ring cried out, collapsed to his knees, and fell over sideways onto the mat of fallen leaves and needles. Three others also bellowed in agony, hands flying to their temples, swords dropped.

The latter three recovered, but the fourth remained still. The woman beside him bent down and put fingers to his throat. Her face twisted, and in a cracking voice she said, "Sabo is dead."

"How?" shouted Carius. "What killed him?"

The woman turned the body over. "There's no wound."

"It was her!" One of the remaining three pointed at Aravia. "We should never have agreed to her attack upon us. I felt it, broke off my connection to it. Sabo must have held on too long." He turned to Mara. "I've had enough of this. Not only has Tor's wizardess failed, she's as much a danger to us as the enemy. I will not stand here as my countrymen are butchered. Carius is right; we only obey General Anapark as a courtesy. I am done extending that courtesy. Stay here if you wish, but I am going to go do some good."

Tor expected Mara to order the man to stand down, but the leader of the Stormknights merely shook her head. "How many others feel that way?"

Eight hands went up, including Carius's.

"Fine," said Mara. "You eight are released from this assignment. Stay together and remain within fifty yards of our position. There's plenty of fighting to be had without going farther. Every ten minutes return here and report."

She was met with eight crisp salutes. The remaining thirteen Stormknights tightened the circle around Aravia.

"They will still serve a similar purpose," Mara said, before Tor could voice his objection.

The seconds crawled. Out in the forest it was complete bedlam, and compounding the chaos, it began to rain, straight and hard. First it was just noise on the canopy, but soon the drops found the gaps, pouring through in a million little torrents. Sometime later the eight Stormknights returned, except that there were only seven, and one of those bled profusely from a slash to the scalp. Mara gave them a quick nod, and the seven vanished beyond a hazy curtain of rain and shadow.

"Captain!" a soldier cried out. "There!"

A mob moved toward them through the trees from the east, a blobby cluster of dark shapes. Voices chanted softly as they approached, low and gruff, the sound barely cutting through the patter of rain.

"Temen, Vari, Lop, keep your eyes out behind and to the sides. Everyone else, form up."

The Stormknights maneuvered quickly into position.

Twenty yards out, and the mob congealed into individual soldiers, impossible to count through the trees and the rain. Twenty? Thirty? They continued their chant, which sounded like "El Deen," or something similar.

"Stay in formation," said Mara. "If they keep coming, we'll move ten feet to engage, but no more. Remember that Aravia's safety is our priority. If we fight too close, we risk her getting caught in the melee. But if we move out too far, one of them could slip behind our line."

"I'm the last line of defense," Tor said. "I'm going to stay as close to her as I can without jeopardizing her safety."

"Understood."

The mob of soldiers fanned out, their movement not as orderly as the Stormknights, but with obvious purpose. Their chant continued, and now Tor was certain of what they said. "Meledien! Meledien!"

Who or what is Meledien?

As if the world couldn't wait to answer, the front-most cluster of soldiers parted, and a figure stepped forward, wearing blood-red plate armor and wielding a long, glistening black sword.

Aktallian? Here?

But no, this person was shorter, more lithe, and her armor was shaped for a woman's shoulders and waist. She lifted the visor of her helmet and pointed through the circle of Stormknights, directly at Aravia and Tor.

"That's the one," she said. Her voice was clear and sharp above the rain. "Aravia Telmir, the woman sitting at the foot of the tree."

"What is she saying?" Mara hissed in Tor's ear. "What language is that?"

His earcuff! "They're going to target Aravia," Tor shouted. "Don't let them get past you!"

The warrior named Meledien smiled. Oh, right. She could understand him too.

"And you would be Darien Firemount, the protector," she said. "Naradawk told me you were formidable. I expected someone older. No matter. You'll just have to die young."

Sword raised, she came straight at him.

CHAPTER TWENTY-SEVEN

O

Maybe Ivellios had died and gone to the hells, but how would he know? The hells were probably exactly like this.

He looked down upon the mass of cultists, chanting, writhing, some of them nearly dancing among the pulsing bands of purple light. The air smelled of smoke and sulfur, as the heaps of crystal arcanum continued to spark and pop, casting off snaky tendrils of colored vapor.

The chanting itself was all numbers now, endless numbers. The fellow with the scroll stood closest to Ivellios. His parchment was ridiculously long, its finished length piling up around his feet, but still he read his figures, impossibly large. 3...5...4...5...2...9...

You really drew the short straw on this one, didn't you, buddy.

Ivellios would have laughed if not for the pain. He hung suspended between the two translucent spheres, now more than halfway to full overlap. The pulling at his guts from both directions was so powerful, so unrelenting, it was a miracle Ivellios hadn't lost consciousness. Was something about the ritual itself keeping him aware and lucid? And worse than the pain, horrific in a way he could not describe, was the furnace blast of greasy malevolence rolling in waves off of the brownish-orange sphere. Ivellios's whole body recoiled from it, should have been blown in the opposite direction as surely as a leaf caught in a blast of wind, but something kept him locked in place.

He glared at the bracelet on his wrist. That was probably the culprit. Its heat threatened to scorch his skin. He was going to die without having learned its mysteries. How had it gotten onto the finger of a statue of Ernie, buried below his hometown? Had the Black Circle been conspiring for centuries so that he'd be wearing it today? Of course, there were more pressing questions he'd also never see answered, like "After all that business with the Crosser's Maze, why hadn't Aravia used it to rescue him?" and "Had he been a good enough person in life to merit a place in Pikon's heaven? Or bad enough to truly end up in the hells?"

His body was, by now, entirely inside the boundaries of both spheres, pinned in their expanding wedge of overlap. From the inside, the spheres were nearly transparent, giving him a lovely if entirely undesired view of Mokad and his cohort. Essik stood close to her master, waving her arms and droning on with all the rest. Ivellios wanted to hate her, but she was a victim as much as himself. What a worthless cadre of zealots, the Silverswords—created to fight the Black Circle, but ultimately no match for them.

Perhaps better if they had killed me after all, way back when. Then I wouldn't be here, about to die anyway, so that Mokad can free his monster from his prison world.

Prison world! Understanding came to him, even through the miasma of pain. Aravia had told him once that Spira was in truth a giant ball, despite appearances. Being so close to the surfaces of the spheres, Ivellios saw that the lighter-colored streaks resembled clouds. The spheres must be representations of Spira and Volpos, and when they fully overlapped, that's when Naradawk would make his escape. Tangible malice poured out of the brown sphere, and once more his broken memories stirred, memories of that one brief visit he had paid to Naradawk in his exile.

Guess I know which one's Volpos and which is Spira, then.

Ivellios could still turn his head, the only part of him under his own control. The spheres would converge in minutes; how would he die, then? Actually pulled apart? Burned up by the bracelet? Consumed by the pure evil of Naradawk himself? Or maybe he'd simply drop to the ground, whereupon Mokad would walk up and stab him or beat him. *Or bore me to death with his equations.*

He couldn't even maintain that train of morbid speculation; the pain was simply too great. Consciousness threatened to leave him to his inevitable death; he wished it would. The purple glow of the room deepened, the chanting grew ever louder, and the spheres inched closer, bringing the end of the world, starting with his own miserable, wasted life.

For the first, and he presumed last, time since Essik had brought him here, Ivellios closed his eyes and waited to die.

A stinging surge of pain lanced up Ivellios's body, from his foot to his groin, as though his leg had been set on fire. It startled him into alertness; pain wasn't exactly unexpected, but this was of a noticeably different sort, sharper, swifter. He glanced down to make sure his leg wasn't actually burning, and when he looked up again, several of the cultists had turned to face the room's single massive doorway. Mokad himself continued to chant, but a new expression had claimed his face: worried annoyance.

The spheres were not entirely transparent, the room's light was mostly the lurid purple leeching away from the cultists' symbols, and he was over a hundred feet from the door. On the other hand, his body floated high above the floor, and his body was held at the ideal orientation. So it was that he had a good look as the double doors flew open as if kicked, revealing two men.

One was a huge redheaded fellow with an enormous beard studded with metal bits. He held a long plank in one hand.

The second man...Ivellios couldn't make out his features beyond a shorter black beard, but something about him seemed familiar.

The three roaming cultists moved to intercept these newcomers; two were swept aside easily by the bearded man's plank before the third closed and grappled. More cultists turned to look, just as a swarm of people pushed into the room following the first two. Some of these arrivals wore matching yellow uniforms with a green crest. A wave of shouting clashed with the faltering chants of the cultists, some of whom continued on with their parts of the ritual while others broke off to meet their unexpected guests.

A short, balding man charged through one of the curtains of warping air above a glowing purple stripe. Ivellios cringed as the man's body fairly well exploded, showering all those around him with blood. Screams followed, though Ivellios couldn't tell if they came from the mouths of the newcomers, the cultists, or both.

Well, Mokad, at least that's one thing you didn't lie about.

Was this a rescue? If so, who was leading it? At least thirty people—half dressed like laborers, half wearing the official-looking yellow uniforms—had barged in through the open doors, but the attack, or rescue, or whatever was going on, seemed entirely haphazard. The far side of the room was in utter chaos as though a bar brawl had merged with Mokad's mathematical spectacle.

Let's see how this affects your stupid equations.

The red-bearded man picked up a cultist and threw him against the curved wall, smack into a glowing violet triangle. The man screamed, his body frozen against the shape. A heartbeat later his body was torn apart, his remains scattering. A piece of him thunked into the back of another cultist, who stumbled into a tall pile of crystal arcanum, sending the stuff shushing across the stone floor. Purple fire flared up in several places, and then the real chaos unfolded.

Tendrils of violet flame sprouted up from some of the shapes on the floor and whipped around like maddened tentacles. Those struck sizzled into clouds of red vapor. The chanting stopped entirely, the cultists now engrossed in the new activities of battle and survival. Streams of crimson and mud-green smoke floated through the air. Combatants on both sides wrestled with one another, skidding in gore. Two rolled together across one of the glowing lines and exploded upward in an obscene geyser of shredded flesh. Ivellios was no stranger to blood and battlefield chaos, but this was far beyond anything in his experience. Despite the clamor of his pain, he felt sick.

The world lurched, and Ivellios dropped a short distance before some unknown force caught him. Twice more this happened, until the translucent spheres vanished, popping like soap bubbles. He fell the final five feet and landed on his stomach with a jarring thump, his chin cracking against the floor. The impact probably hurt, but he was in far too much pain already for a short fall to add anything significant. No longer paralyzed, he rolled to his back and craned his neck, watching the chaos upside-down.

Two figures emerged from the clouds of smoke, and Ivellios really did laugh this time, though it sent lances of pain through his bruised flesh and broken ribs. Dranko and Ernie hurried to his side.

"You look like the gods wiped their boots on your face," said Dranko.

Ivellios opened his mouth to answer, only to find his voice wouldn't work. Dranko and Ernie bent to pick him up.

Dranko grimaced, clutching his side. "Maybe you should get his legs."

"Just help me get him up," said Ernie. "You're in no condition to lift anyone."

Ivellios blinked in the smoke as his friends struggled to lift his deadweight from the ground. His fractured ribs screamed in protest.

"Stop!"

The three of them turned. Mokad stood not ten yards away, face wild with rage.

"Mokad!" Dranko exclaimed. "You're looking well. But you've got something on your...no, right there on your...no, I mean your left..." Dranko pointed to Mokad's shoulder, on which sat a dripping chunk of gore.

"This is your doing," Mokad said hoarsely.

"I'd say Ernie here had more to do with it than me. I've been laid up the last couple of days."

Behind Mokad, a body soared upward out of the maelstrom, vivid sparks coursing over its clothing and skin. Somewhere further back, it landed with a thump and a clanging handbell.

"You think you've won," said Mokad, panting. The fury on his face twisted itself into a smile. "But you're too late. We've done enough. Naradawk is as good as free."

Ivellios wished he could tell if Mokad was lying.

"One thing at a time," said Dranko. He looked left, then right. "I'd say for now, this counts as my good deed for the day. What do you think, Ernie?"

"I think less gloating, more escaping," said Ernie, and Ivellios was inclined to agree.

"You're not going anywhere," said Mokad, his voice rising. He pointed a finger at the three of them. "Dranko, your days of meddling are over. I don't know how you've survived so long, but this is where it—oof!"

Mokad was knocked to the side as Certain Step barreled into him. Both staggered sideways toward one of the deadly lines on the floor, and for a moment they clung to each another, forced into a dance of desperate cooperation, teetering beside a curtain of certain death.

Step's poem came to Ivellios, one line in particular. *Go with them to certain doom.* Maybe this chamber was the "last of five" where Step's doom awaited? But together Mokad and Step managed to lean away from the heat shimmer and stumble a few steps to safety.

Panting, Mokad pointed a finger at Step and uttered a quick syllable. Step froze in place, after which Mokad shoved him, sending Step crashing to the floor like a toppled statue.

Mokad returned his attention to Ivellios, Dranko, and Ernie. "Now, where was I?"

"You were about to die horribly," said Dranko, gesturing to Mokad's left. Mokad turned as a rope of purple energy whipped out of the smoke and struck him through the waist, neatly separating his top half from the bottom. Mokad's eyes might have widened at the last minute, but Ivellios couldn't be sure. Step was spared by dint of laying prone on the ground.

With Dranko's help, Ivellios was hoisted up onto Ernie's shoulder. Dranko grabbed Step under his armpits.

"This whole place is tearing itself apart," said Ernie. "We've got to get out of here."

"How…" Ivellios finally managed to croak out sounds. "How did you find me?"

"Long story," said Dranko, as Ernie headed toward the distant door. "But the part you won't believe is—"

Ernie lurched sideways and then spun around as a scrambling dockworker clipped his knee. Draped over Ernie's shoulder, Ivellios caught a glimpse of something unusual (even for this place) near the middle of the room: the black-bearded man stood in the center of a huge hemisphere of golden light. The yellow radiance emanated from a chip of metal on his wrist, and everything else inside – which included over a dozen of Ivellios's rescuers – showed not a trace of color.

That man. Who is he? Ivellios could have sworn they had met.

With a sound like a lightning strike, the largest pile of crystal arcanum erupted in a volcano of energy. More tendrils of the sort that had cut down Mokad writhed from the spot, splitting, dividing, threshing the air like scythes.

One of the cultists dove for the dome of light and bounced from its edge, staggering backward and falling into one of the death-curtains with a brief scream. At the same moment, two others, a man and a woman in the yellow uniforms, passed safely through, joining an ever-growing crowd of rescuers. A whip of deadly lightning cracked across the surface of the hemisphere, breaking into a spray of sparks that glittered upward and away. The man with the shard on his wrist flinched but held steady.

Ernie got himself turned back around and ran for the protection of the golden sphere. Behind them the air roared with whipping energy, gouging stone from the walls and floor, separating heads and limbs from cultists, filling the room with a sound like the screams of an army, a smell like an abattoir.

Ivellios and Ernie slid into the golden light, followed by Dranko dragging Step, just before a barrage of purple blasts smote it from a dozen directions. The bearded man fell to his knees, eyes shut tight in concentration or pain, but still the shield held. Everything inside the light, himself included, was bereft of color.

Naul's face appeared at the edge of the dome, his body pressed against it as if he could will himself through to the safety of the sanctuary. But he stayed plastered to the outside, and a few seconds later a torrent of energy swept him away. Ivellios wished he had the strength to wave goodbye.

Ernie set Ivellios down gently on the stone floor, and as he rolled over, one last person dove into the warded space. It was Essik. She curled into a ball at the feet of the bearded man, sobbing.

Ivellios looked up at the man who had saved him, the man who kept the band of surviving rescuers alive while all around the storm of Mokad's screwed up ritual raged and rumbled.

"You." Ivellios's voice was a whisper. No one could have heard it. But recognition had struck him like a thunderbolt.

The man looked down at him, blood pooling at the corners of his eyes and mouth, his face cast in grays.

"Ivellios Forrester, I hope this sets us even," he said.

Ivellios rolled over to his back, closed his own eyes, and let the blackness of exhaustion swallow him up.

* * *

Tor squished his feet down into the damp ground, steadying himself for Meledien's charge, but two Stormknights leapt to intercept her. Tor had already seen several of the Stormknights in action, and these two were no less capable. They maneuvered into a classic bracketing position, each distracting Meledien from the other while timing their slashes, seeking the gaps and joints in her armor.

For a few seconds Meledien hardly seemed to defend herself, twisting and bending just enough so that the strikes of the Stormknights clanked harmlessly from her plates. When her counterattack came, it was a blur of red and black, her footwork impossible to follow. One moment the Stormknights had the obvious upper hand, and the next they lay dying on the ground in expanding pools of blood. Like Aktallian, Meledien was entirely unhindered by her armor.

She straightened, rolled her shoulders, and smiled at Tor. "I hope you're more of a challenge."

Tor took a quick step backward, buying time to look to Aravia. The remaining Stormknights tightened their circle further, establishing a strong defense against Meledien's soldiers.

He turned back to Meledien and raised his sword. "I defeated Aktallian," he told her. "I can do the same to you."

"Aktallian was always the lesser pupil." Even as Meledien spoke, she advanced, sinuous as a cat. Tor watched her hips, not her eyes. That was the key to fighting a savvy opponent, Master Elgus had always told him. "A warrior can fool you with their eyes, but the hips tell a story without lies."

Wait. Had Elgus intended that to be a rhyme? Tor had never noticed that it—

Meledien aimed a slash across Tor's stomach, which he avoided with a small jump back and a downward parry. He followed up with a fast riposte, aimed for a gap in the plates at her hip, but she twisted slightly and took the blow against the bottom of her cuirass. She struck again, snake-quick, and he couldn't return his sword in time to parry. Though he bent backward and sideways, the tip of her sword drew a bloody line across his left arm.

She stepped forward quickly, no doubt intending to finish him off while he was unbalanced, but a Stormknight appeared behind her, blade raised. Tor did his best not to look, to betray his ally, but something, a noise or a shadow, gave the Stormknight away. She leapt sideways as the strike came down, and Tor had to fall over into the mud to avoid the startled Stormknight's lunging strike. Meledien turned, graceful as a dancer, and hacked most of the way through the Stormknight's neck. She allowed her motion to continue all the way back to where Tor lay, and he barely raised his sword in time to block her downward stroke. As he struggled to rise, she kicked him onto his side, but instead of finishing him off she took a step past him, toward Aravia.

In one violent motion, Tor surged to his feet and bull-rushed Meledien, driving her sideways as his feet skidded on the increasingly wet ground. But there was no railing to drive her off of, no eighty-foot plunge to keep her from Aravia. Meledien kept her balance, steadied herself against a tree, and dodged Tor's wild swing as he tried to stand. In the same motion, she turned to her left and thrust out with her black sword, skewering the stomach of a Stormknight whom Tor hadn't even seen approaching.

She drew out the blade, letting the Stormknight fall face forward with a squelching thump.

Tor found his feet and once more raised his sword. Behind him came the grunts and clangs of battle, which meant the Stormknights still fought. Meledien feinted left, moved right, trying to get around Tor to where Aravia (he hoped!) still sat against her tree. Tor interposed himself, flicked the tip of his sword at her face. She batted it aside effortlessly.

"You can't protect her," Meledien said. "Not for long." She tried again to move around him, but this time when he moved to intercept, she bent, turned her shoulder, struck so quickly Tor never even saw the weapon move. Pain leapt up in his hip, and blood poured down his left leg. He stumbled back, but even through the fire of his wound he kept his body between Meledien and Aravia.

You will protect.

Tor blinked back the pain, stood tall, and lifted his sword in a classic vertical guard. She was a more skilled fighter than Aktallian, but they fought the same way, and Tor understood the spinning, dancing nature of their technique. Both tended to spin toward their left shoulder and timed their ducking and swinging in the same fashion. Tor recalled a riposting technique Ivellios had taught him, designed to take advantage of his opponent's movement. He feinted left, and Meledien spun away, leaned, ducked…and Tor's sword caught her up and under the plate at the elbow of her sword arm. Her arm twisted back, blood fountaining out, and her black sword fell to the earth.

He followed up quickly, raining blows down on her while she was unarmed. She deflected some of them with her left arm and shoulder, using her armor as a shield, and dodged others meant for her head. She was still appallingly fast, but Tor had her on the ropes, and if he kept pressing, he was bound to—

"Tor!" Mara's voice carried over the rain and the din of battle. Tor raised his weapon high as if to strike downward, but instead kicked Meledien near the bottom of her breastplate, sending her backward even as a searing agony flared up at his waist. As Meledien stumbled away, Tor turned to see that the outnumbered Stormknights had nearly broken. Any second now, one of Meledien's soldiers was going to break the line and have unimpeded access to Aravia.

Grimacing with pain, Tor turned and ran back, abandoning Meledien for the moment. *I shouldn't have left Aravia like that.* He hurtled into the ranks of the enemy soldiers, knocking them aside, chopping and hacking in a frenzy. Two of the pasty-faced men turned and bolted in the face of his fury; one of these was expertly hamstrung by a Stormknight before he had taken three steps.

Tor leaned away from a swing and returned with a strike that took off an arm at the shoulder. His backswing took another man in the throat, and he returned his weapon in time to block a downward stroke aimed for his head. He kicked his attacker in the stomach and smashed the man's face with the pommel of his sword as he doubled over.

The remaining enemy soldiers backed away; Tor roared at them wordlessly, trying his best to ignore how his left leg trembled. The fabric of his trousers was soaked through, not with rain, but with blood that wouldn't stop bubbling up at his hip.

Nine Stormknights remained, reforming their cordon around Aravia's tree. All of them were breathing hard, chests rising and falling, and at least five were wounded. Mara's off arm hung uselessly at her side. But the piles of corpses lying before them in the mud spoke to their prowess and courage.

Tor met Mara's eyes, which widened suddenly. Tor whipped around to find Meledien running directly for him. She had regained her sword, holding it steady despite the wound at her elbow. Tor raised his own weapon to meet her, and the clash of their steel rang loud in his ears. Three other Stormknights joined him, one slipping sideways to get behind Meledien while the others moved swiftly left and right.

Meledien closed her eyes, smiled, and became a whirlwind. She moved through and around the Stormknights so quickly, with such fluid perfection, Tor hardly dared swing for fear of hitting his allies. Her black sword seemed to be in several places at once, blocking, whirling, cutting through armor, flesh, and bone. Tor felt its sting across the back of his left hand, but he was the luckiest, or the fastest, of the four. Inside of ten seconds the three Stormknights had fallen, one clutching at a gaping stomach wound, another speared through the heart, and the third on her back, lifeless eyes staring upward toward the dripping treetops as blood poured from her opened throat.

Meledien herself panted in the rain, and one of the Stormknights must have gotten through the armor at her knee. Blood trickled out of the joint, and she favored the opposite leg.

"Where were we?" she asked, though she didn't seem interested in an answer. She strode forward, and for several frantic seconds Tor did everything he could to avoid being sliced to ribbons. She was so devastatingly quick, no wasted motion, smooth and strong despite her wounds. Tor parried blow after blow, seeking any opening to counterattack, finding none.

Behind him, where Aravia sat, the sounds of combat had slowed. Tor wanted desperately to turn around, to be certain that the Stormknights still shielded her, but taking his eyes off of Meledien would have been a deadly mistake. She struck again, and he blocked, stepping forward into a clinch. He was taller by half a foot, but she was every bit as strong. His shoulders quivered as they pushed against one another, his hip screaming, his leg threatening to buckle.

Each of them gripped their weapons with both hands, but Meledien unexpectedly released her left. For a heartbeat that gave Tor the greater leverage; he leaned forward, bending her backward, and then—pain, a pain so cold and deadly he nearly passed out. He looked down to see a red metal dagger jammed deep into the side of his gut.

Tor blinked. The world slowly faded towards white. Meledien's smile was almost pitying. "You fought well," she said. "But—"

A crossbow bolt ricocheted from her right pauldron and up to her face, leaving a bloody furrow in her cheek. Meledien screamed and fell back, letting go of the dagger protruding from Tor's side. A half-dozen Stormknights— the ones that had lost faith and left them—charged at her from Tor's left, shouting as they came. Meledien fell back before their onslaught, but Tor didn't watch for long. He stared at the dagger, fighting against the onset of shock. Ivellios had told him once what to do if anyone ever stuck him like that. Leave the dagger in, or take it out? One of those was better, but he couldn't remember which.

A scream from behind him broke his thoughts. He spun, the pain from the dagger nearly dragging him to the ground. Only three Stormknights remained, Mara among them, facing off against the last five of Meledien's soldiers.

I'm going to die. But I will protect Aravia to my last breath.

Once more Tor staggered toward the woman he loved, still seated, unmoving while the storm of battle thundered around her. His legs were numb, but he willed them to carry him forward, and almost as in a dream he blocked two incoming blades, sidestepped another, slashed through a man's ribcage, felt a bite in his shoulder, turned, and sliced most of the way through a thigh. The edges of his vision blurred. He stumbled sideways, found himself leaning against Aravia's tree. He was so very tired.

Movement from the side. Without conscious thought, he pushed himself off the tree as a sword thunked into its bark, wedging itself. Tottering, Tor brought down his sword and cut right through the arm holding the weapon. He hardly felt the impact, barely registered another spatter of blood on his cheek. Once more he let the tree bear his weight.

Heavy breathing to his left. Mara stood, bent forward, hands on her knees. Blood spilled over and leaked through her gashed armor from more wounds than Tor could count. The brutal sounds of combat still rang out from every direction, but at a distance. No one else stood nearby. The last of Meledien's retinue lay dead in a wide ring around Aravia.

Mara looked down at where Meledien's dagger protruded. "Gods, Tor, I'm sorry."

But Tor didn't look at the dagger. He looked at Aravia, her face dotted with mud and blood, her hair a mess, her breathing rapid.

"There's still time," he whispered.

"Tor!"

Mara pointed a trembling finger into the woods.

Meledien walked toward them, slowly, her black sword sucking the light out from the forest around her. She walked with a limp, one of her greaves had been knocked loose, and the left side of her face showed more blood than flesh.

Her smile was still the same.

"You can't fight her," said Mara, looking again at the red knife in Tor's guts. "But Werthis has put me here at your side for a reason." The Stormknight straightened and brought up her blade, but she was nearly as badly wounded as he was himself. Once more Tor pushed himself upright, away from Aravia's tree, just as Meledien closed.

Tor put up his sword, saddened by the weight of it, so much heavier than it should have been, but he deflected Meledien's swing away from his neck, down into his shoulder. There was no pain at all; his body had no room left for more pain, no place to put it. Mara swung, a feeble blow that scraped down along the side of Meledien's breastplate. She smashed Mara's face with her left gauntlet; the Stormknight dropped to the mud.

But as Mara fell, she pulled her sword hard along the ground, smashing the flat against the ankle of Meledien's injured leg. She stumbled, falling into Tor, and for a moment they both leaned entirely against one another for support.

"This is mine," Meledien said. She grabbed the hilt of the red metal dagger still jammed into Tor's side, twisted it, then yanked it free. Tor felt the last of his life sluicing out of him, the shrinking window of his awareness growing bright and befogged.

Leave it in. Ivellios said to leave it in.

With his failing shreds of consciousness, he saw Meledien lean backward as the knife came loose, just the tiniest bit off-balance on her bad leg. He pretended to topple—an easy thing to feign—and with the last of his ebbing strength stabbed upward with the tip of his sword, finding the seam between gorget and helm. His blade slid hard along the side of her neck, blood spraying out; she screamed and fell backward. As Tor swayed, Meledien dropped her sword, clutched at her throat, and staggered away into the forest.

Tor fell sideways into the mud. Beside him, Mara struggled to her feet, her nose a bloody wreck, and moved to give chase.

"No," said Tor, his voice sounding strange, tinny in his own ears. "Please. Stay. Take care of Aravia."

He rolled sideways so that he looked up into Aravia's face, a dirty, blood-splattered vision of perfection. "I'm sorry," he told her. "I wish we...I wish..."

His body felt so light, a sparrow could have carried him off.

"I love you, Aravia. I think I've loved you since that very first day in Abernathy's tower. You were so lovely in that pointy hat."

Tor no longer seemed to have a body. He looked through a slender tunnel, so that Aravia's face was all the world.

"You know what?" His last breath filled his lungs. "Here we are, both with stars in our eyes."

But the tunnel narrowed to a point, light pouring in, and all the stars went out.

CHAPTER TWENTY-EIGHT

O

The portal's expansion ceased, but it was too late.

That didn't stop Aravia from experiencing a wild surge of hope. Erasing the portal while it grew was an exponentially more difficult endeavor than doing so while its size was fixed. Given enough time and enough willing subjects, she could still succeed.

But she had neither of those things. A sundering force pressed upon her from the far side of the portal, the Volpos side. Naradawk was hastening the portal's collapse, overpowering the archmagi's efforts to keep it sealed, and though its arcanistically inverse nature would keep Naradawk out until the very end, that end was rapidly approaching. Minutes, rather than hours, were all that remained.

But even if Aravia had hours, or days, the portal had simply grown too large. The soldiers, her little candles, didn't possess enough arcane potential. She could increase the output from the Crosser's Maze—it supplied more than enough raw power—but she would kill every single one of her volunteers and *still* lack the energy she needed.

She ought to cease her efforts altogether. Funneling energy through the soldiers, drawing down their life-force, was certainly weakening them on the battlefield—to say nothing of the ones she had accidentally killed already. If she broke off now, they'd feel a boost in energy. They'd have a better chance to win the battle on more ordinary terms, and as for Naradawk—well, soon the archmagi wouldn't have to worry about the portal anymore. They would be free to contest him directly. Yes, they had told her they'd be no match for him, but they outnumbered him five to one. Maybe they underestimated their chances?

No, that was a fool's hope. The archmagi had been striving against Naradawk for decades, centuries, and doubtless knew exactly what their chances were. If men and women that powerful, that wise, had decided—

Men and women that powerful.

The archmagi.

Gods, that was the answer.

Yes, it would drain them. Yes, the portal would collapse that much faster, perhaps instantaneously. She would have to work dangerously quickly. But with enough focusing potential at her disposal, what couldn't she do?

There would be terrible risk. She was already weakened, well beyond the limits of safety. Could she control that much focused power? How much would there be? She had taken educated guesses at the arcane might of the archmagi, but she didn't *know,* and all of her training had involved subjects with only trace amounts of potential. And what if the archmagi refused to grant her their power? The old wizards might reasonably decide that an unknown tug against their life-force was an attack from Naradawk, an attempt to weaken them and hasten his escape.

But she had to try. Thanks to Tor's curiosity, she knew that the archmagi were close enough for this to work, barely a hundred feet above her. Finding them was a matter of an instant, five incandescent stars of arcane power. Their pocket dimension opened directly into the air above the trees, and inside the old wizards continued to pour out their own power, working their complex rituals that had kept Naradawk at bay for so long.

Aravia estimated the quantity of energy each of the archmagi could focus, and started out with about half that much, pulling the power of the Crosser's Maze from its infinite depths and passing it through one of the five—she couldn't tell which. This was the moment of truth. Would they understand, or deduce, that it was she and not the enemy?

Nothing. Her energy passed through, unrefined, unaugmented.

Come on! It's me! I need this!

Maybe she had started with Grawly, probably the least trusting of the five. She chose a different wizard and tried again, lancing a thread of power from the maze through the lens of that wizard's life-force.

Again, nothing. The wizards weren't giving their assent.

Please! Have faith!

No. Faith was not the issue. The archmagi were creatures of logic, and the most logical explanation, from their point of view, was that she was Naradawk. But she had no way of communicating, not without levitating up there and telling them, and that would unravel everything she had done. If she moved from that spot, the perfect spot, she would never recover. Not to mention she would never be able to muster the arcane wherewithal to cast *levitation*.

Think!

She did, and the answer came to her. Well, *an* answer. Would it work? The archmagi were brilliant, and her idea was little more than a child's game. Surely one of them would figure it out.

She drew energy through them, all five of them, in a single quick pulse.

A.

She followed with a rapid series of pulses, eighteen of them, spaced apart just enough to be easy to count. Eighteen, signifying the eighteenth letter of the alphabet.

R.

Then a pause, and another single pulse.

A.

Twenty-two pulses, and another pause.

V.

The surge of arcane energy momentarily blinded her, almost knocked her out of the maze with a hammer blow to the mind. First one archmage had given assent, followed quickly by the other four, and the maze energy that emerged after passing through them was like geysers of lava beside drizzles of tepid water. When the energy touched the portal, it sizzled with potential.

Would it be enough to heal a rift in space a half-mile across?

She steadied her mind and set to using her newfound source of energy. The Crosser's Maze sang with power, and her body vibrated in sympathy with it. She created new reality in great swaths, dozens of times more quickly than before.

Still, it was not enough. The portal was too large, and behind it she sensed something immense approaching, something that dwarfed the potency of whatever had slipped through moments earlier.

Naradawk. It must be.

She drew more power from the Crosser's Maze, and the archmagi withstood it. Five times more, twenty times more, a hundred times more than she could safely thread through an ordinary person, and the candles of their life-force didn't even flicker. She healed the rift between Volpos and Spira a dozen yards at a time, power heaving into it like a great cataract crashing into a lake.

And it wasn't enough. How much energy could the archmagi withstand? All of her preparations, her practice, her careful calibrations, assumed people with only minimal arcane potential. There wasn't time to figure anything out. Naradawk's presence acted on the portal like the moon pulling at the sea, bending it, warping its fabric. All of Aravia's instincts tended toward finesse, patience, calculation, but the time for all of that was over.

She reached into the vast stretches of the maze, pulling so deeply for its power she thought her physical body might catch fire. Rather than carefully threading it through the archmagi, she allowed it to course through unabated, like a mighty river ripping through the remains of a dam. It poured across the surface of the portal, covering it from corner to corner, and her mind, incandescent now from its union with the Crosser's Maze, erased the weakness of the universe.

Naradawk arrived, pressing his might against the portal, unhindered now by the archmagi but finding his doorway rapidly fading to nothing. A hot, greasy force beat against the far side of the dwindling threshold, an angry fire seeking to burn down creation. The space between Spira and Volpos grew fulminant with his malice. Heedless, Aravia drew yet more energy out of the maze's infinitely deep well. The entire portal, thousands of feet long, thousands of feet high, was vanishing beneath her focus.

The fabric of creation bulged beneath the terrifying strength of Naradawk Skewn, who must have been making a final desperate push. Aravia let go of the last shreds of caution, allowing the full force of the maze to rush through the bodies of the archmagi. She knew, but did not care, that it was probably damaging her mind, might well be burning the lives out of Abernathy and the rest. She tasted Naradawk's fury as he strove against her, struggling to force a breach before the gap between the worlds disappeared.

The universe bent.

It stretched.

Buckled.

But it *did not break.*

Naradawk's presence moved away, smoldering in its defeat. The boundary between Spira and Volpos was smooth, immaculate, with no sign that a hole between them ever even existed.

A distant part of Aravia's consciousness knew she should stop funneling energy, should leave the maze, but her mind felt shattered, helpless, as the Crosser's Maze heaved and hissed with apocalyptic surges of energy. She had broken the dam and loosed the river, and there was no repairing it. Power coursed up and through the archmagi, through Aravia, in uncontrolled gouts. The maze shuddered, its stars wheeling, its reflection of the universe blurring and blending into a bright miasma. A tiny voice, a butterfly's breath of voice, warned of catastrophe, a cosmic earthquake, a cleansing fire. Her mind was a twig in a tempest, but she was beyond caring, and so very, very tired.

The Crosser's Maze had served its purpose, and so had she.

For a time, she slept in darkness. Shapes moved massively in her dreams, detached mountains of reality gouged away to drift like icebergs, then finding haphazard purchase like abandoned glacial erratics. "Stop," someone told her in her dream, but who was she to put the universe back together? She would be the maze's last owner, the agent of its destruction.

"Stop. Awaken. Quiet the storm, little Keeper."

"I can't." The butterfly's whispered voice was her own. "I'm too tired."

"You must," said the voice. "You are tearing the maze to pieces and wrecking your mind."

"Then the maze will end, and me along with it," Aravia whispered back. "I am already drained beyond recovery. I'm sorry."

"Silly child," said the voice. "All you must do is return to the world. Awaken, and be at peace."

Aravia's last shred of dream was of a coal-skinned woman in a storm-tossed cloud of emerald green fabric, smiling sadly down at her.

* * *

Aravia woke with a snap of her eyes and a juddering breath. She looked out into a forest dripping with recent rain, the patter of drops broken by occasional distant clangs and the moans of dying soldiers. With her body bereft of strength, her head drifted gently back against the tree, leaving her to stare upward into the deep green canopy and piece together what had happened.

She had done it! Used the Crosser's Maze. Stopped Naradawk's escape. Saved Spira from destruction. The cost had been great—to herself, to Pewter, to the archmagi, to the maze itself—but the reward was victory. Victory! After all that had happened since that first day in Abernathy's tower, it seemed beyond reason that it was over.

Could she stand? No, her muscles were too weak, almost to the point of paralysis, but she could at least sit up a little straighter. Aravia shifted her body, looking around her for the first time.

Bodies. Gods, so many bodies, contorted, still. They lay all around her, mannequins in armor, limbs twisted, smeared in blood. A cold realization gripped her, but she forced herself to look downward.

Tor.

He lay on his back at her feet, looking up with unblinking eyes as the rain fell upon his face. A faint smile played on his lips, and that was almost enough to let Aravia deny the truth, but as she struggled to lean forward, a raindrop splashed onto his eye. He didn't so much as twitch.

"You're...you're alive." A hoarse woman's voice sounded from her left, but she couldn't bring herself to turn her head, to look away from Tor's peaceful face. She reached out to clear away a speck of mud from his cheek; his skin felt cold, rubbery, not at all like a person. Not like Tor.

"He—" the voice beside him broke into a wet cough that took a few seconds to subside. "He gave his life to save you. I hope it was worth it."

Gave his life.

"Tor..." It began as a whisper but ended in a sob. Grief rose up and swallowed her triumph, grief and anger and emotions she couldn't name. Aravia threw herself forward, falling onto Tor's damp, lifeless body, her cheek hot and tear-streaked against the chill mask of his face. Her shoulders shook, her body heaved, wrenched and wracked beyond her control. Only when her muscles gave out did she slump to stillness.

"No," she whispered into the hollow of his neck, or perhaps she only thought it to herself. "It can't have been worth it."

CHAPTER TWENTY-NINE

B elow the window, in the spacious backyard of the Greenhouse, a crowd was gathering.

"You know who I should have invited?" Dranko said, looking down. "Berthel, my old landlady. The thought of that old crow rubbing elbows with nobility…"

He trailed off, leaving a crude jest unspoken. He shouldn't be joking, not today, though his every instinct was to lighten Morningstar's mood. She sat in his desk chair staring blankly at the far wall, her eyes still ringed with dark shadows of exhaustion.

"The service was last night," she said, her voice flat and just a little bit wistful. "I met Jet in the Tapestry an hour ago. She told me all about it."

Dranko turned his back on the window, walked to his bed, and sat down facing Morningstar. "What did she say? What was it like?"

"Jet said it was an…emotional ceremony," said Morningstar. "They buried Scola, Gyre, and Belle in the temple graveyard, lined up in a row next to Sable. I wish I could have been there. No report or rumor about either Starbrook or Obsidia has made it back to Tal Hae."

"What was the official word about what happened to them?" Dranko wasn't sure if Morningstar wanted to talk about the details, and he was prepared not to press if she preferred to stay quiet.

"A madman," she said. "Official word is that a madman broke into the temple and—" Her breath caught, but she composed herself quickly. "Jet is terrified. She's had to lie several times to Rhiavonne. Goddess, but it's bad enough the high priestess excised Previa and Amber. If they excise Jet from the temple, I…"

"I'll tell you what you should do," said Dranko. "Visit Rhiavonne's dreams each night, and make it so she's giving a sermon in her underclothes while all her sisters point and laugh." He paused. "And then have her teeth fall out."

"That's not how it works." Morningstar sounded severe, but a smile twitched the edges of her mouth.

"Or just tell her everything, and damn the Injunction," said Dranko. "The gods aren't supposed to interfere, we all get taught that, but they're the ones who broke the Injunction, not you. What's the worst that can happen if you tell her?"

"I don't know," said Morningstar. "But the avatar made me swear on Ell's name to keep her interference as secret as possible and very specifically not to tell the high priestess. I cannot break that oath, even for Previa's sake, and Amber's, and Jet's."

"Or your own?" A righteous anger surged through him on her behalf, an anger he seldom felt for anyone, including himself.

"Or my own."

"Well, I didn't swear any oaths to an avatar," said Dranko. "I should march myself over to your temple, wake up Her Holiness, and—"

"Dranko, don't. Please."

He sighed and turned again to the window. "Oh, I won't. It's just that…dammit, you played as important a role as anyone in saving the kingdom. If Ivellios is right, without you, the Black Circle would have summoned up Naradawk before Aravia could stop him. You've suffered more than any of us. You finally made friends with your sisters, and most of them died. And your reward is that you got kicked out of your own damned temple. It's not fair!"

She gave him a bitter smile. "Which of us signed up for 'fair?'"

Dranko's thoughts went immediately to Tor, who, technically, had suffered the most. If one looked at the wider picture, surely Tor's death would top the list of unfair things. The kid had possessed such boundless energy and optimism, and never had an unkind word for anyone. What Dranko would remember most of all was Tor's perpetual conviction that everything would always turn out for the best.

And yet, he was the one who died. Sure, one could see it as inevitable, given Tor's recklessness, but that didn't make his fate any easier to swallow. A person that good deserved better.

"At least we're having a parade in our honor. That counts as some reward, wouldn't you say?" Morningstar's words jolted him from his gloomy contemplation. He looked up to see that her smile had softened.

Dranko grinned despite himself. "Yeah. That's going to be fantastic. Finally the people of Tal Hae will be pointing and looking at me for a good reason."

"Promise you'll try not to make too much a spectacle of yourself," said Morningstar. "And keep in mind that Aravia is technically the grand marshal."

Dranko gave the briefest of chuckles before they both went silent, the little flickers of mirth snuffed out by mention of Aravia. Since teleporting back to the Greenhouse a week ago, she had hardly left her room, and when she did emerge, she was as emotionless as a corpse. Pewter stayed by her side, but some maze-related accident had stripped away his intelligence, not to mention the telepathic bond the two of them had shared. Aravia hadn't wanted to talk about the details.

Yesterday the surviving members of Horn's Company, gathered again at the Greenhouse, had been paid another visit by an assemblage of noblemen and high-ranking clergy, again including His Majesty King Crunard IV. The bigwigs wanted a full report of everything that had happened, all the activities of Horn's Company leading up to the end of the Battle of Verdshane.

In addition to providing their report, the Company had also heard from others. A priest of Delioch delivered the news that Rosset Finch, having redeemed himself after being so obnoxious during that first meeting, had died the day following the disruption of Mokad's ritual. His physical injuries had been minor, but the spiritual drain from drawing on the power of the Watcher's Kiss fragment had been too much for him. The guy might have been a self-important twit, but Dranko had to give him credit for his sacrifice.

After the priest was done, a Stormknight named Mara, the last person to have seen Tor alive, described his heroics in Aravia's defense with such dramatic and heartfelt oratory, not an eye in the room was dry.

So. They had lost Tor, and Rosset Finch, and Pewter, sort of. Morningstar had lost Scola, Obsidia, Starbrook, Gyre, and Belle, in addition to Sable. Nearly a thousand kingdom soldiers had died, as had about half the rescuers who had followed Ernie into Mokad's hive. Perhaps worst of all, no one knew for certain if the archmagi still lived. Regarding the fate of the old wizards, Aravia simply shrugged her shoulders, unwilling to offer an opinion. While Abernathy wasn't answering his crystal ball, Mister Golem at least gave them a sliver of hope: "Abernathy is unavailable for the foreseeable future," he had said, which was more promising than "Abernathy and the other wizards are stone dead. Now leave me alone."

On the other side of the ledger, they had rid themselves of Mokad, slain Aktallian Dreamborn, and prevented the escape of Naradawk Skewn. Though the cost had been high, Horn's Company had made invaluable contributions to the defense of the kingdom, allowing the archmagi to fulfill their mission of centuries and safeguard Charagan, indeed all of Spira, from the greatest threat ever to beset it.

At least, that's how King Crunard IV had phrased it yesterday, right before awarding them honorary induction into an order of royal agents known as the Spire Guard. Furthermore, each of them would receive a generous royal stipend in perpetuity, so long as they agreed to make themselves available should the crown have need of their services.

And tomorrow, in honor of the new Spire Guard members and the rescue of the kingdom of Charagan, there would be a parade.

For all the emotions surging through Dranko, from elation at their victory, to sorrow over Tor's death, to concern over Morningstar's excision, the one that bubbled most often to the surface was a joyous satisfaction. Forget all of those bottles he had thrown into seas and rivers and lakes; Dranko Blackhope was a famous man by dint of his own heroics. Tomorrow, every citizen of Tal Hae would know his name, his face, as they paraded through the streets of the city. Children would cheer, young women would toss flowers, and men would feel gratitude and envy in equal measure.

Well, maybe a bit more envy than gratitude.

Praska would be amazed and delighted, of course. Dranko didn't want *her* to feel jealous, and in fact he felt a bit guilty that her part in saving the kingdom had been underplayed. After all, had she not followed up on her suspicions of Mokad, Morningstar wouldn't have been able to discover the Black Circle's whereabouts. But Dranko still couldn't wait to see the look on her face when she beheld Horn's Company marching victorious through the city.

He thought of Pietr Tock, the boy who had chipped his tusk with a rock as a child. He thought of his cruel grandfather, who had always blamed him for his parents' deaths, and who had cast him off to be a ward of the Deliochan church while his grandmother's corpse was still warm. He could return to his home village now, triumphant, could shove his fame and fortune in all of their faces.

Or he could stay in Tal Hae, occupy the Greenhouse while eating magical food three times a day, and enjoy the fact that he'd likely never again have to buy himself a drink inside the city's walls. He did, after all, have a memorable face.

A quiet sigh from Morningstar snapped Dranko from his reverie. She hadn't moved from the desk chair, though her eyes were closed, and her face twitched in discomfort.

"What's the matter?" he asked, realizing belatedly how many possible answers there were to that question. Tor was dead. Half a dozen of her sisters were dead. She'd been thrown out of her temple.

She gave her head a little shake as if a fly had landed on her nose, and looked up at him. "It's our oath. The one we made to Shreen. Its weight has been growing heavier this past week. Have you felt it?"

"No, can't say that I have." He frowned. "Though now that you mention it, yeah, when I think about that hunchbacked bastard, the greasy feeling comes back."

Morningstar stood and walked to the window, looking down into the yard with nary a squint. "I feel that discomfort every waking moment. I think now that Aravia used the Crosser's Maze to stop Naradawk, we need to fulfill our end of the bargain. Each day that we don't..." Her mouth twisted, as though finishing the sentence might cause her physical pain.

"But we don't have Lapis's head," Dranko pointed out, "and we don't have any idea where she's gone."

"I know," said Morningstar, "But we still need to return to Shreen, so Aravia can give him the maze."

"How is she going to do that?" Dranko asked. "It's inside her own head. She can't just pull it out and slap a bow on it. Er, can she?"

"I have no idea," said Morningstar. "But it has to be possible. Solomea gave it to her, after all." She paused, frowning. "Shreen will have to make do without the head for now. The day after tomorrow, I think. After we've recovered from the parade. I'll ask Aravia to teleport us back to Djaw. Goddess, but I dread that moment when we face Shreen again."

Dranko stood and joined her at the window. The crowd in the backyard had grown while they talked, nobles and dignitaries and other guests milling about, talking quietly, sometimes taking little sandwiches from Eddings as he navigated the throng with a wide tray.

He wasn't sure how it happened, but he and Morningstar were holding hands, fingers entwined, as they looked down upon the gathering. He glanced over at her face, but she didn't look back. Her mind was somewhere far away. Dranko allowed her that silence, that meditation, soaking in their shared melancholic peace until someone knocked at the door.

"Dranko?" came Ernie's voice from the hall. "It's time. We're starting."

* * *

A half-dozen priests of Brechen, their robes fluttering in a light autumn breeze, lowered Tor's coffin into a hole freshly dug in the Greenhouse back lawn.

There must have been a hundred people standing in respectful observance, mostly dressed in somber hues—blacks, grays, browns. Only the high priestess of Corilayna, Irichan, wore bright clothing, a full-length orange dress and a yellow silk scarf draped around her neck. She plucked a breaded sausage from Eddings's tray as he passed, then leaned in to whisper something in the butler's ear.

Dranko lifted himself onto his toes to get a better look at the assemblage. All of those who had been at the previous meeting were in attendance, including King Crunard IV with a retinue of guards and attendants. His Majesty stood at the end of a line of mourners. The king talked quietly with a tall, red-headed man whose rich tabard featured the symbol of a shining sapphire. There could be no mistaking who that man was, so much did his features resemble those of his son. It was he, Baron Olorayne Firemount of Forquelle, who spoke first once the rest of the crowd had quieted.

"Earlier this year," said the man, "the archmage Abernathy contacted me and bid me not to worry that my son Darien had disappeared. He said that Charagan had need of my son's talents and that he could not foresee the day of his return. I asked Abernathy if Darien's life would be in danger while executing those new duties, and the wizard told me in no uncertain terms that it would be. Still, I held out hope that I would see him again when his errands were finished. Darien was one of the most skilled swordsmen I had ever seen, so I—"

The baron swallowed hard, his breath hitching.

"So I assumed I had not spoken my last words to my eldest son," Olorayne continued, his voice wavering a bit. "I have been furious with the archmagi this past week since receiving the news about Darien. Abernathy stole my son from me and sent him to Brechen's endless shore."

Beside him, a woman in a black gown—the baroness Kitrin, Tor's mother—blotted tears from her cheeks with a handkerchief. Tor's younger brother, Alomayne, stood stoically on the far side of the baroness, staring down at the coffin with something like confusion.

Olorayne took a long, deep breath. "But from what I have been told, Darien died in service to his king and his kingdom, saving it from certain destruction with a sword in his hand. Every one of us owes him a debt of immeasurable gratitude, a debt which we now can only repay by honoring his memory." The baron did not bother hiding the tears that now fell from his own eyes. His hand found that of

Tor's mother beside him. "I tried my best to prepare Darien for the day when I would fade, when he would take my throne and rule Forquelle. Despite his flights of fancy and obsession with swordplay, I think he would have made a fine baron of the isles. Darien was a kind man, a good man, who would have overcome his obstacles and done right by his people. I grieve that he will never have that chance, but I also rejoice that he was able to apply his greatest talent at the time and place where it mattered most. I loved my son, loved Darien, more than I can express. When you attend the parade tomorrow, spare a thought for him, and remember that no one would be celebrating if not for his sacrifice."

The crowd looked expectantly at Tor's father, as if he were pausing in a longer speech, but Dranko sensed he'd said his fill. If the man went on much longer he wouldn't hold himself together. Olorayne turned to his wife and remaining son, and the three embraced before slowly walking back to stand in the mourning line.

Ernie stepped forward to speak next. For an awkward handful of seconds, he stood with his fists tightly bunched, saying nothing. Dranko found himself growing nervous on Ernie's behalf. The boy's face trembled, and his eyes were wet.

"Tor was…" Ernie stopped and glanced at Tor's parents. "I'm sorry, Your Lordship, Your Ladyship. I know his given name was Darien, but I've only known him as Tor, so that's what I'm going to call him. I hope that doesn't offend."

Baron Firemount gave a slight, thin-lipped nod.

"Let me start at the beginning," said Ernie, his voice mostly steady, but with a tiny quaver Dranko doubted most in attendance would notice. "Half a year ago, Abernathy chose a group of us to work for him. None of us knew one another. None of us understood what we were in for. None of us were ready to face the dangers Abernathy put in front of us.

"I was terrified that first day. Truth be told, I'm still terrified. I don't know why Abernathy chose me, and now that he's…missing…I'll probably never find out. But I know why he chose Tor, and Tor knew it too. He told me himself, more than once. 'Ernie,' he said, 'I figured it out. My job is to keep the rest of you alive. To put myself in danger, to go first when we don't know what's ahead of us.' And that's exactly what he did. He put himself in the greatest danger, every time, right up to the end."

Ernie reached up and wiped a tear from his cheek, then gave a loud sniffle. "Tor was my best friend," he said simply. "He made me brave when I was afraid. He listened to my self-doubts without judging me for them. He kept his sense of humor even when things looked grim and hopeless. Tor made me a better swordsman, a better person, and a better friend." He turned to Tor's family, all of whom wept openly. Somewhere along the line Ernie had turned into quite the orator. "I think you were right, Your Lordship. Tor might not have enjoyed it, but he would have made a wonderful baron." Turning back to the crowd, Ernie said, "I'm glad all of this business with Naradawk Skewn and his army is over with because I don't know how Horn's Company could go on without Tor. He wasn't just our best warrior. He was our heart."

Well spoken, thought Dranko. The kid had come a long way since that first night in Abernathy's tower.

A priest of Brechen stood on the far side of Tor's grave, and when it seemed that no one else was going to speak, he opened his mouth to deliver a few last words. But Aravia, who had hardly spoken this past week and who had shown no sign that she wanted to speak at Tor's service, walked forward swiftly. Pewter frisked around her ankles.

"Tor is dead," she said, sounding as though she were about to deliver a schoolroom lecture, "but I may be able to fix that."

CHAPTER THIRTY

Kibi blinked in astonishment. A startled murmur rippled through the assemblage. The baroness of Forquelle gave an audible gasp.

What is she on about?

"As some of you may know," Aravia continued, "I was able to prevent Naradawk's invasion by using a potent magical device called the Crosser's Maze. That device is partially a mental construct, and it currently resides inside my head. The Crosser's Maze has many unusual functions and properties, not all of which I have had time to investigate.

"In our very first week serving Abernathy, one of our company, Ysabel Horn, was killed by skellari in Verdshane. But a man named Solomea, who possessed the Crosser's Maze before me, was able to bring Ysabel out of the heavens, after which she was able to speak with us directly. More recently, Ysabel was able to communicate, posthumously, to some other members of my company, assisting them in the rescue of Ivellios from the clutches of the Black Circle.

"It is my opinion that with study, I should be able to use the Crosser's Maze to restore Tor's soul to his body and return him to the living."

Tor's mother had gone pale, his father red-faced. The priest of Brechen walked slowly to stand before Aravia.

"My child," he said, his voice sympathetic, "Grief is a powerful force, and it is not uncommon for it to bring forth such delusions. But the laws of the gods—"

"Are not immutable, as I have discovered," said Aravia with unnerving calmness. "Also, I personally have been imbued with a divine nature by a Kivian deity and so consider myself to have unique potential when it comes to this sort of endeavor. I have already taken the liberty of enchanting Tor's body, such that it will not decay or be consumed while I conduct further research. Once I have recovered fully from my recent trials and can return to the maze, I will—"

"No!" shouted the Baroness Kitrin. "What you propose would be an abomination, even if it were possible! Have you not been listening? My son died a hero, and now he walks the Endless Shore of Brechen's heaven. I forbid you to practice your necromancy on his body."

Aravia stared, betraying no emotion. "I thought you would be pleased, Your Ladyship. But what I do is not necromancy. I loved your son, and he loved me, and I will not give up as easily as you."

The baroness flushed a hot red, though she spoke no words to match her visible anger. The baron took a step forward, his thunderous expression showing that he battled against an urge to do violence. The sound of the gathering swelled, and here and there Kibi caught phrases like "mad with grief" and "doesn't know what she's saying." One thing was certain in Kibi's mind: Tor would not have wanted his funeral service to go like this. Before he knew what he was doing, Kibi walked up to Aravia and put a hand on her shoulder.

"Come on, Aravia," he said quietly, turning her body toward the Greenhouse back door. "I know you loved the boy. We all loved him, you most've all, but this isn't the time for talkin' 'bout bringin' him back. Let his family mourn the way they ought. Maybe you *can* bring Tor back from the dead, but that ain't what they need to hear right now."

Aravia didn't resist as he led her back into the Greenhouse, the swell of the crowd's chatter rising behind them.

"Perhaps you're right, Kibi," she said, once they stood in the kitchen. "In time they'll grow more appreciative of my efforts, but I suppose I shouldn't burden them with hope that may not come to fruition. In truth, I haven't been able to access the maze since I fixed the hole between Volpos and Spira. But eventually I will return to it. Solomea was able to reach into heaven for Mrs. Horn. Someday I will do the same for Tor."

It frightened Kibi to see Aravia so calm.

She yawned. "I need to rest. My mind is still recovering, but until I can return to the maze, I can do little more than theorize about the particulars of how resurrection will work."

Aravia departed in the direction of the stairs, Pewter scampering after her. Kibi watched her go, frowned, and returned to the funeral service to find the Brechenish priest finishing his final prepared words. Ernie, his eyes red and puffy, approached him with a sad smile.

"Thank you," Ernie told him. "That was horrible, what Aravia did. Tor's family is having a hard enough time, you can tell."

"Ah, don't be too hard on the girl," he said to Ernie. "She was in love with Tor, so it's hittin' her hardest, is all. And who knows how the maze is scramblin' up her brain. I'm sure she'll come 'round eventually."

Ernie paused awkwardly, clearly wanting to say more, so Kibi waited patiently and smiled.

"Do you think she can, though?" Ernie finally asked. "Bring Tor back from the dead?"

Kibi shrugged. "Ain't really for me to say what Aravia can or can't do. But I won't lie and say I'm comfortable with the idea. Dead is dead, or should be, seems to me, and it ain't like Mrs. Horn actually popped back to life."

The Eyes of Moirel, absent this past week, flared brightly in his mind, making Kibi flinch.

"What?" asked Ernie. "Are you all right?"

The day Tor had died and Aravia had saved the world, the Eyes, to Kibi's indescribable relief, had faded from his mind. He'd been able to eat and sleep and talk without the damn things twinkling like impatient stars right through his eyelids. All of that nonsense about the unmaking of the world, and *time is right, world is wrong*, must have been referring to Naradawk, now locked away good and forever, to hear Aravia tell it.

He'd returned to the basement the following morning and found the Eyes on the earthen floor, exactly where he had left them. He'd picked them up, talked to them, but they'd been dead silent. The stone walls of the basement likewise had nothing new to say to him, so Kibi had decided that whatever need he might have had for a "place of refuge" had been made moot by Aravia's success.

But now the eyes were back.

"It's those damn Eyes a' Moirel!" he exclaimed. "After everythin' last week, I thought I was done with 'em and they were done with me, but now I'm seein' 'em again."

Ernie's eyes went wide. "Have they said anything?"

Kibi listened intently for several heartbeats. "Nope. Nothin', though they only just started up. Suppose I should go check on 'em." He forced out a chuckle. "Give me an excuse to get away from all these noble folk millin' 'round our house. You want to come?"

As before, when he closed his eyes, the gems' twinkle changed to purple and green.

"Sure," said Ernie.

The crowd had drifted apart, breaking into little whorls and knots of people. Eddings announced that food and drink would be available in the living and dining rooms, so Kibi and Ernie hurried forward, descending into the basement ahead of the throng.

The Eyes of Moirel sat on the ground, exactly where Kibi had last left them, inches apart from each other, making it seem as though the floor itself peered up at him.

"They shinin' to you?" he asked Ernie.

Ernie squinted downward. "No. I mean, they're diamonds, but they're not glowing or anything."

"Well, here I am again," Kibi told them. "You got something to say all of a sudden?"

He reached out to pick one up, then pulled his hand away. "You stay out a' my eye sockets," he said sternly. "Eddings' too, and Ernie's. Anything you got to say, just say normal like, into my head."

A little snorting laugh burst from Ernie. "Normal like? We sure have come to a strange place, where magic rocks speaking to your mind is normal."

Kibi smiled and this time picked one up. It might have grown a little brighter in his mind, but he wasn't sure. He waited for a few seconds, but the Eye showed no sign of speaking. Kibi picked up the second one and flinched—both became slightly warm in his hands.

"I wish they'd do whatever it is they're gonna do and have it done with," he said. But a minute passed, and then another, without any change in their behavior. He set them down and shook his head.

"Maybe the walls?" Kibi walked to the nearest wall and placed his palm against it. "Whoa!"

"Whoa what?"

"Walls are warm too. You feel it?"

Ernie moved to stand beside him and also put his hand to the wall. "Feels like stone," he said. "But not any warmer than I'd expect."

"Huh." To Kibi the fieldstone felt like one warmed by proximity to a campfire. He reached his mind out to it.

What is happening? Should we be worried?

He kept his palm pressed to the stone for a minute while Ernie looked on in fidgety silence. The murmur of the mourners trickled down from upstairs, but no one came poking into the basement, which was just as well.

"Can you imagine?" Kibi said to Ernie. "If King Crunard came down here and the Eyes jumped into his head?"

"Gods, that would be awful!" said Ernie. Then after a pause, the boy asked, "Anything?"

"Nope. The Eyes and the basement walls both are givin' me a sense of, oh, I dunno, anticipation? Agitation? But whatever it is that's botherin' 'em, they ain't tellin' me about it."

He let his hand drop to his side. "Ernie, maybe you should try it. The Mirror spoke to you, so maybe the Greenhouse will too."

Ernie tentatively returned his hand to the wall and held it there for a minute. "Sorry, Kibi. Nothing. And it doesn't feel warm to me."

"Damn," said Kibi. "Well, it still seems to me that all that 'place a' refuge' stuff was in case Naradawk broke free and we needed a place to hide and regroup, but Aravia went and solved that problem for us." He laughed, a bit forced. "Maybe the Eyes just want to be around for the parade tomorrow."

* * *

The attendants at Tor's funeral had eaten all the food prepared for them (as well as some extra from the pantry), leaving the Greenhouse littered with dirty dishes, wooden cups, bottles, utensils, and napkins. Everyone in the group except Aravia had pitched in to help Eddings clean up afterward. With the Icebox depleted, Eddings made a stew the old-fashioned way. Horn's Company ate their dinner in unusual silence, even Dranko forbearing from his usual off-color humor. Eddings had set out a full dinner service at Tor's usual seat, a kindly gesture that nonetheless left a void in the room.

Kibi listlessly stirred his stew with a spoon and looked around the table, ignoring as best he could the pinpricks of light shining out of the Greenhouse basement. How much longer would Horn's Company all be together? To his surprise, he was saddened by the notion that they'd soon drift away from one another. He'd always preferred the company of an empty room, an empty workshop, and keeping his own counsel. But he'd become so unexpectedly attached to these people, this odd assortment, that the thought of losing their regular company filled him with a melancholy not much different than the loss of Tor.

Kibi smiled across the table at Ernie, who looked up from staring intently downward into his stew bowl. As though Kibi's look had emboldened him, the boy stood abruptly.

"Friends," said Ernie, gazing at Tor's empty chair. "I want to propose a toast. It's been half a year since we agreed to work for Abernathy, and after living who knows how long in that bottle city, it feels a lot longer. None of us are the same people we were back in the spring, given all we've been through. I…"

Ernie paused, tears welling in his eyes. He wiped his cheek with the back of his hand. A sympathetic lump formed in Kibi's throat.

"I miss Tor," he said, gesturing with his wine glass to the empty plate. "I said most of what I wanted to say out in the yard. But I need to add…Tor wouldn't have wanted us to be so maudlin. We beat Naradawk, and every one of us had a hand in it. Morningstar killed Aktallian, so the archmagi could hold out longer. If Dranko hadn't gotten into Mokad's warehouse, we never would have rescued Ivellios and stopped their ritual. Aravia, you figured out the Crosser's Maze and locked Naradawk back in his prison world. Kibi and Ivellios, without you, we'd never have found the Crosser's Maze in the first place. Step, if not for you, Mokad would have killed us, and Dranko would probably have died back in Kivia if you hadn't, uh, stepped in."

Ernie paused to swirl his wine glass.

"Tomorrow is the victory parade, and we're the guests of honor. I'm not saying to forget about Tor. I'm never going to forget him, and I'm sure none of you will either."

Kibi stole a glance at Aravia, who stared blandly at Ernie, as though thinking of something else entirely.

"If Tor were here, and we asked him what he'd say, I'm pretty certain he'd tell us not to forget those who died but to still go out and celebrate properly. So here's to Tor Bladebearer, and Ysabel Horn, and…" He glanced at Morningstar with a look of great concentration. "And Sable, Scola, Obsidia, Starbrook, Gyre, and… and…"

"Belle," said Morningstar quietly.

"Belle," said Ernie. "Here's to the heroes who have to miss the parade." He raised his glass and took a long sip.

"Well spoken, Ernie!" said Dranko loudly. "To fallen friends, and a bright future where we're famous and everyone loves us!"

"To fallen friends," said Morningstar. Kibi repeated the words, lifting his own glass. The others did the same until only Aravia's wine remained on the table. She looked up as if startled, picked up her glass, and raised it absentmindedly. "To friends," she said.

"So," said Dranko, after noisily draining his glass. "After the parade, anyone else have plans? It's not as though we need to find work, now that we're on the royal payroll."

"I should visit my parents," said Ernie. "If no one objects, I'm going to take E.R. with me so he can finally go on a real walk." He sighed. "I'm dreading the fuss they're going to make in White Ferry when they find out the king ordered a parade in our honor."

Dranko reached for a bottle to refill his glass. "How about you, Ivellios?"

Ivellios rolled his eyes but did so with a little smile. "I guess I'll go back to the capital. I can't imagine suffering through a quiet retirement. I'll bet I can parlay my new cachet into a job as a sword instructor. And I feel like I ought to return to my parents' farm, though it's a good bet someone's moved into it in the last twenty-odd years." He tilted his head back and looked at the ceiling. "Abernathy never told us what we should do after we were done, and it's too late to ask him now. But I consider our contract ended. If the king wants to call upon my services as a member of the Spire Guard, I'm sure he can find me."

According to Aravia, it was most likely that Abernathy and the rest of the archmagi were dead, their lives sucked out to fuel whatever Aravia had done to close the portal. There was no way to know for certain since no one could access their sealed stone towers. Aravia had mentioned that the old wizards had occupied a little pocket dimension while maintaining the locks on Naradawk's prison door, but when she had investigated afterward, she found it no longer existed.

Kibi gave a small shake of his head. If anyone deserved a parade in their honor, it was those five ancient men and women who'd spent countless years protecting Charagan in ways no ordinary folk could imagine.

"We must return to Djaw," said Morningstar, and that comment brought everyone up short. "We have to return the Crosser's Maze to Shreen the Fair. The oath we made grows heavier on my soul with each passing hour. I know I feel it more keenly than the rest of you, but I imagine that eventually you will all suffer as much as I do."

"No!" Aravia shouted, an outburst that led to looks of shock from the others, but which deepened the table's silence afterward. "I'm not finished with it," Aravia continued after a second. "I cannot return Tor to life without the maze. Also, we do not have Lapis's head and so cannot fulfill the terms of our bargain regardless."

Morningstar, perhaps unconsciously, gripped the edge of the table so hard her knuckles whitened. "We need to return the maze. Shreen's vile goddess is demanding we hold to our oath. I can feel it in my bones."

"I will not give it up, not yet," Aravia insisted, seeming to regain her unnatural calm. "We promised to return the maze when we were done using it, and we are not. I am not. Once I have returned Tor to the living, we can go back to Djaw."

"That's not true," said Ernie, his voice soft. "I remember exactly what I promised, and I'm sure you do too. I promised we'd give back the maze after we'd used it to prevent Naradawk's escape, which you've done. And I said, 'We will do everything in our power to bring you the head of Lapis.' Right now we don't have the power to do anything to find her. I think Morningstar is right."

For a long, tense moment, everyone looked intently at Aravia. Her face betrayed annoyance, frustration, anger.

"How long can you hold out, Morningstar?" she asked calmly.

Morningstar's face twitched as she obviously bit back a harsh reply. "Not long," she answered, returning Aravia's calm with composure. "And I've been 'holding out' since the day we bargained with that wretched creature. The corruption I endure is severe and has been growing worse every day this past week. Perhaps, being a wizard, you don't appreciate the seriousness of swearing oaths to gods on their own holy grounds?"

Aravia stared across the table at Morningstar, her face unreadable, unnerving. Kibi took a guess as to what most of them were thinking: that Aravia was the only one who could get them back to Djaw, not to mention that she'd have to give up the Crosser's Maze personally. If she decided not to hand over the maze to Shreen, what could Morningstar or any of the rest of them do about it?

"I need to think," said Aravia, pushing back her chair and standing. As Kibi watched her walk out of the dining room, Pewter at her heels, the Eyes of Moirel shone brightly in his mind.

An awkward silence stretched from seconds to minutes, as those who remained scraped stew from the edges of their bowls.

"Hope you like it here in Charagan," Dranko said to Certain Step sitting beside him. "If we can't get Aravia to teleport us, you're stuck here." Kibi noticed that after his glib words, Dranko gave Morningstar a worried look.

"I would stay with you regardless," said Step. "I am still enjoined to go with you to the 'last of five' as my goddess has commanded."

"But we're finished," said Ernie. "All sorts of prophecies we've heard haven't come to pass, but we stopped Naradawk anyway. Maybe we've been to the 'last of five,' and you just didn't realize." He waved his spoon in the air. "Maybe Minok was the last of five cities built by the same old king, and by going there with me and Dranko, you fulfilled the prophecy."

Step looked down and fiddled with his spoon. When he spoke, his voice was quieter. "Kemma's book also said, 'Don't expect to come back alive.'"

"That doesn't mean you were destined to die," said Ernie, "only that it would be dangerous. And it was! You were there, in that Black Circle room. It's a miracle any of us made it out alive."

"There are also Irligg's bones," said Step. "He told me…" Step closed his eyes, unwilling for some reason to speak further.

"Yeah, well," said Dranko, "that goblin chief also told us we'd fail to stop Naradawk and the world would end. To be fair, he also said we'd win and save everyone. If you ask me, Irligg was making stuff up to cover his arse no matter what happened." He grinned at Ernie and motioned to his right hand, the one with the red mark left by the goblin chieftain Irligg. "But if you end up going back to fight in the goblin battle arena, promise you'll take me along to watch."

Eddings came in from the kitchen and began clearing the table of empty bowls.

"How about you, Eddings?" said Dranko, leaning back in his chair. "Want to stay on here as butler? I don't know about the rest of our group, but I intend to keep on living here until someone kicks me out. If you're worried about not getting paid because Abernathy has gone missing, I've got you covered. Our royal stipends are plenty to keep you hired on."

Eddings picked up the bowl in front of Dranko. "Since Abernathy, as you say, is missing but not proved dead, I would be remiss in leaving the Greenhouse unattended. I would be pleased to stay on and continue to serve you in my capacity as butler."

"Fantastic!" Dranko exclaimed. "And let me be the first to say: Eddings, you deserve a raise. What was Abernathy paying you?"

"That is a private matter," said Eddings. "But I will of course be content with whatever recompense you think appropriate for my services."

"How about this?" said Dranko. "Anytime you need money, just ask for it."

"Whatever you think is best," said Eddings. The butler smiled and vanished into the kitchen with his stack of bowls.

"Kibi," said Ernie, "what about the Eyes of Moirel? Are they still, you know…?"

"Yup," said Kibi. "Still lookin' at me funny. But I couldn't begin to guess what they want. Damn things are cryptic even at the best of times. Like you say, Ernie, not every weird proclamation we've heard has ended up comin' true." He closed his eyes, and the gem-lights shifted from white to purple and green. "I'd say 'time is right and world is wrong' is what would a' happened if Aravia hadn't done whatever it is she did with the maze."

"Don't forget about 'traveling nowhere,'" said Ernie.

"Oh, I ain't forgotten," Kibi assured him. "But Aravia figured that meant we'd cross over to Volpos usin' Ivellios's bracelet. Turns out we didn't need that neither."

"Ivellios?" asked Dranko. "Felt any tugging on your guts since leaving Minok?"

Ivellios had the golden band cinched around his wrist. It still unnerved Kibi to see it, the exact duplicate of the one his own mother insisted she'd never remove from her own arm. Fact was, they might have thwarted Naradawk, but there was still a heap of mysteries that hadn't been cleared up.

"Nope," said Ivellios. "Not even a twinge. With Mokad and his cultists gone, I think that danger has passed."

"But you're still wearing your bracelet," Dranko pointed out.

A haunted look came into Ivellios's eyes, reminding Kibi that Ivellios was the only one among them to have stood face to face with Emperor Naradawk.

"Yeah," Ivellios said, sounding more resigned than anything. "Thing still won't budge. Whatever magic Mokad used to stick it there hasn't worn off." He frowned and closed his eyes. "Though even if I could take it off, I'm not sure I would. No point in taking chances."

Morningstar set her napkin down on the table and stood. "I'm going to bed. Like Aravia, I have a great deal to think about."

Kibi's heart ached for her. Where would she go, what would she do, now that the Ellish temple had kicked her out? She could stay here, of course, live in the Greenhouse, but all of this wizard business had left a bigger hole in her life than any of them. Everyone else could return to what they had left behind, but not Morningstar. Kibi was no expert in the Ellish religion, but maybe now that the crisis had been averted, Morningstar's avatar would allow her to explain to her high priestess what she had done. It burned Kibi to think of how unfair her outcome had been.

Of course, if the gods were fair, Tor and Mrs. Horn would still be alive.

Dranko stood abruptly, citing concern for Morningstar and promising to check on her. Ivellios went upstairs soon after, and then Certain Step. Soon only Ernie remained at the table with Kibi, while Eddings stood nearby, hands behind his back.

Ernie pointed his spoon at Kibi. "You still want to visit White Ferry?

Naradawk may be locked up, but who knows what the Sharshun are up to. I wouldn't mind some company on the road, and if I get attacked at night, it would be good to have someone around to shine a light on things."

"Be glad to," said Kibi. "I figured I'd go back to Eggoggin eventually. Wouldn't surprise me to find that folks there assumed I'd died or left for good and were givin' away all my stuff. But I'm in no great hurry now that the crown is payin' me to live well. I'll be more than happy to walk somewhere with my own legs. Teleportin' everywhere still makes me sick to my stomach."

"I thought I'd leave the day after tomorrow, maybe the day after that," said Ernie, grinning. "It depends on how much of a hangover I have after the parade."

"Gotta warn you, though," said Kibi. "I ain't gonna lie to the folks in your town, which means once they hear what I gotta say, they'll think you're an even bigger hero than they do already."

Ernie blushed. "They're going to want to have a separate parade just for me, then. But if they do, you're going to walk right beside me. This is your victory as much as mine."

Kibi's mind flashed to what Mrs. Horn had told them in the Crosser's Maze. *This is a grand tale you're in, and you, Kibilhathur, are its hero.*

Kibi still didn't see it. The victory ought rightly to go to Tor, no question. Among the living, Morningstar and Aravia seemed more the heroes, braving their strange perils and suffering the sacrifice of those closest to them. Ivellios had suffered more than anyone in terms of physical abuse. And without Ernie and Dranko's efforts in Minok, Naradawk would be walking free across Spira right now. Sure, without Kibi, events might not have come to pass the way they did, but his heroics, such as they were, paled before those of his friends.

Ernie bid him and Eddings a good night and left the dining room, whistling.

"I will finish cleaning up, Master Bimson," said Eddings, picking up Ernie's spoon. "I'll see you for breakfast at dawn; the parade starts early, and I'm sure none of you will want to miss it."

Kibi fell asleep with the Eyes of Moirel still shining behind his eyelids, like a cat waiting for him to drift off. Waiting to pounce.

His dream is Spira. *He* is Spira.

The world cries out in pain. Kibi has been shot with an arrow of death, a sharp shadow plunging down from the heavens. Most of the missile has shattered on the impenetrable stone of his being, bits of it landing on his face, his continents, but a fragment worms its way through his strata of flesh, piercing crust and mantle, and lodges in his heart. It burns there like a slick black flame, hot and oily.

MY CHILD. *The world's voice, Kibi's voice.* THIS SPLINTER CANNOT STAY WITHIN ME. BLESS IT WITH ITS LOVER'S KISS, THE WATCHER'S HOUR COME.

Kibi is the world and the world is Kibi, and a golden light blinds him.

Kibi woke sweating, gulping down breaths like a man fighting not to drown. Two lights shone brightly in his vision, one purple, one green, the colors vivid now even with his eyes open. His whole body vibrated, just as when he had his hand pressed to one of the Seven Mirrors.

"What is it?" he gasped. "What's wrong?"

He didn't expect an answer, but an answer came, sounding in his mind like an earthquake.

Refuge. Now.

"Gods protect us." Kibi bounded from bed, body trembling, a thrilling terror rushing through his limbs. Noting in passing that it was still dark outside, the middle of the night most likely, he crashed out the door and down the hall, shouting and banging on every bedroom door he passed.

"Wake up! Get out here, now! Wake up!"

The others stumbled one by one into the hallway.

"Kibi?" Dranko said, passing a hand through his mussed hair. "You having a nightmare?"

"Listen to me!" Kibi's mind raced as fast as it ever had in his life. "Get clothes, your gear, your weapons, anythin' you'd want with you in a pinch. Then get down to the basement."

"The basement?" asked Ivellios. "Kibi, what's going on?"

"Remember I told you the basement walls said it was a refuge? I think now's when we need it. Could be I'm just goin' crazy from the Eyes lookin' at me all the time, but you can mock me later if it's nothin'. Please, get your things and go. Hurry!"

"Is Eddings in trouble?" asked Ernie. "Last time you woke us all up like this, the Eyes had jumped into his sockets!"

Gods, Eddings! Kibi didn't wait to see if his friends heeded his warning, but hurried down the stairs, through the foyer, the living room, the dining room. There was no sign of the butler, who slept in a small bedroom up a small flight of stairs off the kitchen. Kibi ran there and pounded on his door, the colored Eyes of Moirel making it hard to see. Eddings appeared in the doorway, wearing a long nightshirt and a little white sleeping cap. A brown cloth was wrapped around his head, covering his eye sockets.

"Eddings, grab some clothes and anything else you care about. Get to the basement as fast as you're able!"

"What? Why? Is the Greenhouse on fire?"

"No, it's...I can't explain. No time. Just do it. Please."

"Very well, Kibilhathur."

On his way back out through the kitchen, Kibi stopped before the Icebox, an idea springing to his mind. He wrapped his arms around the silver metal cube and lifted it from its table, finding it lighter than he had always imagined.

Back in the living room, Ernie and Step stood by the basement door, arms laden with clothing and gear. Kibi dropped the Icebox. "Make sure this gets down there too. I gotta go get my stuff."

The Eyes were so bright in his vision, he could hardly see his own bedroom door. As much by feel as by sight he grabbed clothes from his chest, then found his pack, still loaded with cooking gear, his bedroll, and other travel oddments.

Had the Greenhouse started to shake, or was that his imagination?

Kibi was last down to the basement. His friends were all in their nightclothes, surrounded by messy jumbles of their hastily grabbed possessions. Aravia had hauled down an armload of books from Abernathy's library, stacking them atop the Icebox next to Pewter.

"I hope this is the greatest prank in history," grumbled Dranko. "If half-naked dancing girls don't pop out of all these closets, I'm going back to bed."

"What is it, Kibi?" asked Morningstar. "What do you think is going to happen? Is the Greenhouse in danger?"

The basement stretched the entire length and width of the Greenhouse's upper floors, but the rest of Horn's Company clustered only a dozen yards from the door. To their left, the two Eyes of Moirel rested on the floor where Kibi had last left them, burning like agitated stars. Abernathy's heatless lights glowed on the walls, lighting up the space, but the radiance of the Eyes washed them out.

Kibi pointed to them, feeling his hand shake. "Any of the rest a' you see the Eyes glowin' bright?"

His friends shook their heads.

"How about the walls? Do you feel 'em shakin'?"

Again, no one did.

"Maybe you just had a nightmare," Ivellios suggested, sounding annoyed. Kibi looked at him to object and found he couldn't see the man's face through the mixed purple and green light that filled his vision.

Kibi shook his head. "No, it's…I dunno. I feel like…" He walked to the Eyes of Moirel, looked down, and closed his own eyes. Green and purple, purple and green, they seemed to quiver on the ground, impatient. He reached down, eyes still closed, and the Eyes leapt into his hands.

Their light went out. All was calm. He opened his eyes to find his friends watching him with evident concern.

"Kibi?" said Ernie. "Please, tell us. What's going on?"

The walls of the basement trembled, and a sound roared down the stairs as though a powerful gust of air blew through the living room.

"Pikon's pancakes!" exclaimed Ernie. "What's happening?" He ran for the stairwell.

"No!" Kibi shouted. "Stop! You gotta stay down here!"

"Why?" asked Ivellios. Everyone lurched slightly from side to side as the room shook. "Kibi, what in the hells is happening?"

He wished he knew! He repeated the question in his mind, directing it to the two diamonds he held in his hands. *What is happening? Why are we here?*

YOU RETURN TO THE SOURCE.

What does that mean?

THE JOURNEY FROM NOW TO THEN IS A JOURNEY FROM NOW TO THEN TO NOW.

A brilliant shaft of light speared down the stairwell, throwing its radiance into the basement like an angry sunbeam.

"Kibi," said Certain Step, his voice trembling. "Your hands."

Purple crystals erupted from his left hand and green ones from his right. They crawled swiftly up his forearms, past his elbows, his shoulders, then up his neck and down his chest until his entire body was cocooned in a bicolored gemstone crust. A voice like a distant avalanche echoed up out of Kibi's crystalline throat.

YOUR ENEMIES UNMAKE THE WORLD, BUT IN REFUGE YOU SHALL NOT BE UNMADE.

The light lancing down from the living room winked out, but the sound of the rushing wind did not abate, and the basement shook violently, as though something outside was trying to twist the house apart. The upstairs windows yammered in their frames, then (from the sound of it) began to shatter one by one. Kibi retained a full awareness of his surroundings, even as the Eyes of Moirel spoke again through his unmoving lips.

OUTSIDE, THE WORLD IS AS IT HAS ALWAYS BEEN— SLAVES, TOIL, FEAR, AND THE ENDLESS DIGGING. THE EMPEROR DRIVES THEM, EVIL BEYOND EVIL, AND YET HIMSELF ONLY A MEANS TO AN END. FEAR HIM, BUT FEAR MORE HIS SUCCESS.

The shaking and rattling and shattering from upstairs became deafening, and it seemed a miracle that the Greenhouse was not flying apart in a shower of beams and bricks, bits of ruined masonry tumbling down the stairwell. Above the din, the wind wailed in an unearthly voice. Around them in the basement, tiny cracks formed in the walls, the ceiling, the floor. Dust showered down. His friends huddled together, looking around, and at him, with expressions ranging from shock to horror to abject terror. Pewter's fur stood on end, making him look enormous.

INSIDE, THE WORLD IS AS IT NEVER WAS—HOPE, STRENGTH, MEMORY, AND THE SAFETY OF FORESIGHT. THE GEOMANCER IMBUED IT, WISE BEYOND WISDOM, AND YET HIMSELF ONLY A MEANS TO AN END. TRUST HIM, BUT TRUST MORE IN YOURSELVES.

All noise ceased. A silence rushed in that seemed, bizarrely, to be louder even than the din of the moments previous. It was a silence that anticipated, a silence straining to be filled. Kibi held his breath, watching his friends look at him in shocked fascination.

The lights on the walls went out. The air vanished from the room, taking every one of Kibi's senses with it. He no longer heard his friends' breathing, or his own, or even the beating of his heart. It was as though reality itself had fled, leaving them hanging in an empty void.

Time passed, perhaps.

Sound emerged.

HE IS FOLLOWING BACK THE PATH OF MOIREL. WE CANNOT PURSUE HIM WITHOUT OUR BROTHER. IF YOU WISH TO TRAVEL NOWHERE, TO UNMAKE THE WORLD, BRING US TO THE HOME OF SEVEN WORDS AND MAKE US THREE.

The basement lights flickered to life, revealing the rest of Horn's Company still bunched together, now sitting on the ground in their nightclothes. Kibi's green and purple covering fled from his skin, boiling away to thinning vapors, leaving him holding two round white diamonds. They no longer shone in his vision.

The walls of the basement were veined with cracks so thick and winding they looked more like a rampant growth of vines. Pebbles and grit dislodged from the ceiling coated the floor and clumped in his friends' hair.

Morningstar was first to her feet. "Kibi, are you injured?"

Kibi held his hands out before him, an Eye of Moirel in each. The stony patch of skin on his left hand had expanded; the entire hand, as well as his arm to just past the wrist, was a curious blending of brown-gray rock and flesh. He twisted the arm, then placed the Eyes on the ground and flexed his fingers. It felt normal, with no pain, stiffness, or discomfort. He poked the pebbly patch of his left wrist with his right forefinger, and found it less pliant than normal skin.

"Guess I'm all right," he said slowly.

"But what just happened?" asked Ernie. "It sounded like a storm outside."

"Or an earthquake," said Eddings.

"Or both at once," said Dranko.

Ivellios stood and walked to the opening where the stairs climbed out of the basement. He peered up into the darkness of the stairwell, then took a light-rod from his pocket and held it up. "What the...?" He walked slowly up the stairs.

"What do you see?" asked Morningstar.

"I'm not certain," came Ivellios's voice. "I don't..."

"Is the Greenhouse a complete wreck?" called Ernie.

Ivellios didn't answer right away. After a moment he came back down, puzzlement on his face. "The stairs end at a low ceiling. It's just dirt. Some roots are poking down through it. There's no door into the living room."

"But light came down from there," said Ernie.

"See for yourself, then," said Ivellios. "But it looks like the Greenhouse basement has been sealed underground."

"How far underground?" asked Morningstar.

"How should I know?" Ivellios answered, sounding both cross and unnerved.

Except for Kibi and Aravia, the others moved in a group to stand at the doorway, staring upward in shocked silence toward where the opening to the living room should be. After a few seconds they turned, one by one, to look at Kibi.

"Kibi, what did all that mean, what you said?" asked Ernie. "All that about 'only a means to an end' and the rest. Did the Sharshun really unmake the world?"

Kibi shook his head and held up his hands, having no idea how to answer.

"Yes," said Aravia.

Alone among the company, she still sat on the floor, Pewter in her lap.

"You know what's goin' on?" Kibi asked. All eyes turned to Aravia.

"Yes, I think so. Consider everything the Eyes of Moirel have told us—I assume that was them speaking just now, using you as a conduit—along with various other bits of information we've gleaned since the spring. I think I have an explanation."

"Which you're going to tell us," prompted Dranko.

"Of course," said Aravia. "My belief is that the Sharshun have contrived to alter history so that Naloric Skewn, the original emperor, was never banished from Spira. The stairwell no longer leads to the Greenhouse because there is no Greenhouse. Aside from the basement, it was never built."

This was met with stunned silence. Ivellios ran a hand through his hair and began to pace. Ernie opened his mouth as though he would protest but closed it again without speaking. Morningstar stared at Aravia in a kind of horrified fascination. Step continued to look up the stairwell in plain confusion.

Kibi couldn't make sense of Aravia's proclamation. "How?" he gasped. "How did they do it?"

"By using three Eyes of Moirel, I presume," said Aravia. "Recall that after we failed to secure the red Eye from Sagiro, the green one warned us of what we would need to do when the world was unmade. Not if. When. You yourself pointed that out. I was skeptical, but it appears the Eye spoke literally."

"But that doesn't...I mean...how can that..." Ivellios waved his hands instead of finishing his thought.

"And you heard what the Eyes said just now," continued Aravia. "'Outside, the world is as it has always been.' The emperor is out there. He never left, was never banished."

"So what do we do now?" asked Morningstar.

"We need three Eyes of Moirel of our own, so we can undo whatever the Sharshun did to cause this change in history." Aravia said it so calmly, she might as well have been proposing they nip out to the market to buy eggs for tomorrow's breakfast.

"Wait," said Dranko. "Wait wait wait. So what about stopping Naradawk? What about Mokad and the Black Circle and Aktallian and Tor and Morningstar's sisters? What about our parade?"

"All of that has become irrelevant." Aravia's demeanor was still so calm she sounded almost pleasant. "It would not surprise me if none of those people ever existed, nor the events surrounding them."

"But we all remember 'em," Kibi objected. "*We* exist! How could any a' that be true?"

"Because we were spared the unmaking of the world. 'Inside, the world is as it never was.' I think we have Caranch to thank for that, assuming he's the geomancer."

"What's a geomancer?" asked Kibi.

"The word means 'earth wizard,'" said Aravia. "I imagine that's what you are, Kibi."

Kibi stared down at his rocky forearm. "I ain't no wizard," he mumbled, but for the first time in his life, he wasn't sure if he believed it.

"Gods damn it, I knew something like this would happen," said Ivellios.

"You did?" Ernie sounded incredulous.

"Well, no, not this exactly, but having to go to that place Aravia talked about. Het something. The Black Circle tower with the monsters that can kill gods. This means we have to go there after all, doesn't it? Aravia?"

"I imagine so," she said. "Het Branoi. We need three Eyes of Moirel and have only two."

"But what did they do?" Certain Step spoke for the first time since the calamity. His face was pale and his hands trembled. "How did the Sharshun rewrite history?"

Everyone looked to Aravia, who closed her eyes before speaking. "Understand that everything I say is speculation. But I guess that the Sharshun used the Eyes of Moirel and the Seven Mirrors to send one or more of their number back to a time before Naloric's banishment. Armed with foreknowledge about his defeat, Naloric was able to adjust his plans sufficiently to win his war against the Spire. King Vhadish implied that time travel was impossible, that it would invite paradoxes the universe would not abide. I believe he was mistaken."

Kibi picked up the Eyes of Moirel from the ground and stared at them. "So you're sayin' we need to go to this Het Branoi place and get a third Eye of Moirel, and then use 'em to go back in time ourselves and stop the Sharshun from doin' whatever they just did?"

"Yes," said Aravia. "That's what I'm saying."

"But if all of history has been erased," said Morningstar, "did the Black Circle ever build Het Branoi?"

Kibi thought hard, recalling what the walls of the basement had told him. "I think they did," he said. "The stone here told me. *'The infinite tower will protect our child.'* I'm guessin' the tower is like this basement, immune to the time thingy, and the child is the third Eye of Moirel."

"I think I was wrong about what 'travel nowhere' means," said Aravia, running her fingers through Pewter's fur. "I assumed it meant moving from Spira to Volpos while the worlds overlapped. But now I think it more likely it means traveling in time rather than from one place to another."

"When the time is right and the world is wrong," said Kibi. "Seems a good description a' where we are now, if everything you say is true."

"And how do we use the Eyes to go back in time?" asked Ivellios, sounding for all the world like he couldn't believe the words coming out of his mouth.

"I don't know," said Aravia. "Not yet. But one thing at a time, I think. First, we must escape this basement.

"And then we must pay a visit to the infinite tower."

ACKNOWLEDGEMENTS

Well, that's three books down and (if I've planned things well) two to go in the *Heroes of Spira* series. The journey only has been possible thanks to the incredible support of my family, friends, and publishing team.

I will always begin my thanks by mentioning my wife, the inestimable Kate Jenkins. The value of her insights and advice has been eclipsed only by that of her unwavering emotional support. As with all good things in my life, these books would not exist without her.

My daughters, Elanor and Kira, still think it's cool that they have a dad who writes books, but they're also old enough that I'm sure they're rolling their eyes while reading this sentence.

Huge thanks go to my editor, Abigail Mieko Vargus, slayer of wayward commas and all-around smarty pants. Her advice and attention to detail have saved me from embarrassing myself more times than I can count.

A veritable host of beta readers helped me understand the dozens of ways in which the book could be improved. Many thanks to Jim Blenko, Joshua Bluestein, Jim Bologna, Michael Chaskes, Christopher Cotton, Karen Escovitz, Darren Frechette, Sara Goodwin, Fiona Heckscher, Bill Kirsner, Cindy Maka, Justin Sonnekalb, and Christopher Wicke.

My cadre of intrepid proofreaders managed to capture dozens of little mistakes that had slipped past everyone else. Leading that team was Alex Hart, whose superhuman attention to detail is such that I consider him to be almost an associate editor. But my other proofers also came through with valuable catches, so thanks to Andy Cancellieri, Jeff Foley, Tom Linkenback, and Kayla Schlenz.

Again I'd like to thank Steven Cooper, Russell Morrissey, and all of my readers at EN World.

And, finally, a huge thank you to my parents, Charlotte and Jake.

ABOUT THE AUTHOR

Dorian Hart graduated from Wesleyan University with a degree in creative writing. This led circuitously to a 20-year career as a video game designer, where he contributed to many award-winning titles including *Thief, System Shock, System Shock 2,* and *BioShock.*

In addition to writing the *Heroes of Spira* series, Dorian is the author of the interactive novella *Choice of the Star Captain,* published by Choice of Games.

Dorian now lives in the Boston area with his fantastic wife and daughters.

THANK YOU
FOR READING

For information about the *Heroes of Spira* series, please visit
http://dorianhart.com/the-heroes-of-spira/

Made in the USA
Middletown, DE
11 April 2021

36854430R00220